INDIGENT EARTH

INDIGENT EARTH

By Scott Overton

No Walls Publishing

SUDBURY, ONTARIO, CANADA

Scott Overton/No Walls Publishing
Sudbury, Ontario, Canada
www.scottoverton.ca

Book Layout © 2017 BookDesignTemplates.com

Indigent Earth/ Scott Overton. -- 1st ed.

ISBN 978-1-7782844-3-4

We would like to acknowledge funding support from the Ontario Arts Council and the Government of Ontario

To the indigenous peoples of the world
who have been displaced and marginalized.
I can't speak your truth; I can only acknowledge it.

Just as a person who is always asserting that he is too good-natured is the very one from whom to expect, on some occasion, the coldest and most unconcerned cruelty, so when any group sees itself as the bearer of civilization this very belief will betray it into behaving barbarously at the first opportunity.
—SIMONE WEIL

Tradition has it that whenever a group of people has tasted the lovely fruits of wealth, security, and prestige, it begins to find it more comfortable to believe in the obvious lie and accept that it alone is entitled to privilege.

—STEVEN BIKO

PART ONE

1

Killian Morningcloud turned twenty-seven on the day the colonists returned to Earth. They'd been gone for five hundred years.

He'd dreamed all his life of that day. In his mind it was a scene of glowing golden clouds and floating crystalline cities descending from the sky accompanied by unearthly music like wind chimes tolled by moonbeams, and peopled with beings so full of knowledge and wisdom that it shone through their skin.

When the event finally came to pass, the spacecraft that landed was noisy and disappointingly small. Its passage through the air left a taste on the tongue like lightning and burnt fur.

There was no music, no majesty.

And Killian wasn't even there to see it.

\# \# \#

As an armload of newly split birch clattered into the rough-planed wood-box beside the stove, Killian's uncle looked up from his chair.

"I thought you'd be climbing to the top of the ridge to look for more spaceships on the way."

Lewis Partridge had a reputation for dry humor and a perfect poker face. Killian froze and looked hard at the man.

"Very funny," he said.

3

"Not joking. There's no mistaking sunlight off metal, and on a day like this, the flash was visible for kilometers up in the sky. Nothing left on Earth can get that high. Has to be the colonies."

Adrenaline flooded Killian's bloodstream like a torrent.

"When? When did you see it?"

"'Bout a half-hour ago."

"*Why didn't you tell me?*" The crack in his voice embarrassed him.

His uncle shrugged powerful shoulders and rubbed his stubbled cheek. "Like I said, I figured you'da seen it. Couldn't miss the noise—like wind through the pines but higher pitched, and ain't no wind today."

"I was chopping wood, thinning that stand of birch and poplar just north of the creek." Killian slammed the last piece of wood into the box and lurched toward the door. His face felt on fire.

The sky was cloudless and the branches still, a perfect morning for mid-February, its silence broken only by the faintest rustle from the distant creek and an occasional tentative chirrup from the most venturesome sparrows. Winter had begun its surrender but wasn't in a hurry to relinquish the scene of its defeat. Dusky needles of towering pines dripped the remains of the night's frost onto scattered patches of dirty white snow beneath them. An aroma of freshly exposed mud and animal droppings made Killian's nostrils flare: the signature of reluctant spring.

He'd have to get clear of the forest cover to really scan the cloudless blue canopy overhead. The ridge would be best, but the vast shoreline of Wanatay Lake was nearer, only a hundred meters away. He jogged down the dirt path, stopped on Resting Rock, and stared westward. The sun rode an azure sky without challenge, and no unusual sights or sounds called for attention.

The community of Borealis was thirty kilometers behind the treeline to the southwest—only something huge could be seen from that distance, and only then if it had chosen to remain airborne. There was nothing visible now, but Killian didn't doubt his uncle's word. His Uncle Lewis would joke but he wouldn't lie; and he knew how much the truth would mean to his nephew on this subject, above all.

Swallowing his disappointment, Killian hurried back to his uncle's rugged cabin beneath its sheltering maples that would soon be tapped for syrup. Lewis straightened from feeding the wood stove and turned a questioning face to his nephew.

"How can you be so calm?" Killian asked, his own heart racing.

"They said they would return in five hundred years. We knew that time was almost up."

"But we couldn't know it would actually happen. In all that time there's been no contact with them at all."

Uncle Lewis tipped his head but said nothing. What did that mean? Did he know something Killian didn't? Surely it could make no difference now.

"I have to go to Borealis. If it was a colony ship, it must have gone there." Killian began to dig through his small pile of belongings by the guest bunk in the corner. He would take the nested set of cookware he'd fashioned from scrap metal, his magnetized needle, his magnifying glass to make fire, as well as a good flint for sunless days. Those were indispensable tools he always carried in the bush. And with them he included his most precious possession, a wide-bladed hunting knife given to him by Lewis himself.

"That's crazy," Lewis said. "You won't get there before nightfall. There's not enough snow left on the trails for the sled and too much for the wagon. Thirty kilometers of winding track and who knows which will be deeper, the snow or the mud?"

"If it is the colonists, you know I need to be there."

"I *don't* know that. I've never understood that. I know that damned school has you brainwashed..."

"The return of the colonists was the reason I went to that school. They didn't brainwash me. They taught me what I needed to know about the time before The Divide so I could be ready."

"They taught you hearsay. Stories passed down for five hundred years. That kind of school was banned by the colonists when they left—you think those dreamers could have preserved any technical information worth a hooker's kiss?" The big man sauntered up behind his nephew and his arms reached out but didn't touch. Killian was his own man, not to be treated like a child.

"How many times have we talked about this?" Killian asked. "This is something I have to do. Where's Aunt Regina?"

"She went out early to see if any fiddleheads were poking up yet. She'll be heartbroken to find you gone."

Killian hung his head and then finished stuffing clothing into his pack. Maybe he should leave the clothes that needed washing—to show his aunt that he would be back.

"The colonists won't take me right away," he said, though he was hoping they would do exactly that.

"You're expecting gods," his uncle growled. "Let me tell you, any people who would abandon their own kind to the trash heap they left of this planet are no gods."

Old arguments rose to Killian's lips, but to give voice to them yet again would only waste time.

In cold silence, uncle and nephew fussed over small details, getting some cooked grouse from the icebox and shriveled carrots from the pantry. There'd be ample water along the route, but Killian didn't want to have to spend time scavenging for what little food the winter-ravaged forest could provide. He accepted his aunt and uncle's largest ground-cloth and tied it to his pack after insisting he didn't want a tent.

When the packing was done, the two men faced each other uncertainly, both trying hard to show nothing in their expressions. Lewis and Regina were like a second set of parents to Killian, in some ways closer than his own. At times they tried a little too hard to persuade him to follow their path and live an outsider's life, away from town. But at least they wanted the best for him, as they saw it.

Lewis cleared his throat. "I know you're a grown man. But you're also being a fool. Stop this, before it's too late."

Anger rose like smoke in Killian's throat, but he bit back its words. He only gave a sharp shrug and turned away.

There was no easy route all the way to Borealis. The first trail he would take meandered like a thirsty vine along the perversely indecisive Wanatay River as it snaked southward toward its eventual end in faraway Jorjin Bay. The prevailing direction of the Borealis path was south too, until it came to a homestead abandoned for nearly a century where someone had determinedly widened the river channel and filled it with rocks to make a shallow crossing. It could be forded most of the year, but that was far from certain when February's snow melt filled waterways to bursting.

If Killian could get across the ford, a second trail rambled almost due west into an area of tumbled granite scored by glaciers and pierced by the hidden shafts of ancient mines. That would be the roughest section of his journey; but when he had completed it, he would be within five hours' walk of the outskirts of Borealis, and the final stretch was well-travelled. Some people on its fringes actually prodded the stingy land into providing subsistence crops, and traders went back and forth from the town core most days of the week.

In the meantime, he faced a lot of hard walking. On the east-west portions of trail the snow was shaded by ranks of evergreens and had stayed firm, though rough and icy. Along the south-facing sections, the white snow crystals had lost their grip on each other and become like grains of dune sand, constantly shifting underfoot and demanding extra effort with each push. The tendons above his heel and along his foot would soon protest.

Where the snow had melted completely, the going was even worse. Twice in the first three hours, he was forced to pull his leg out of his boot before he could free the boot itself from sucking muck. It was second nature for him to tell hard snow from melting snow from sculpted drifts with just a look. But with only a skin of snow covering the ground, even an experienced bush traveler like Killian found it nearly impossible to tell the difference between solid footing and shin-deep sludge—until he'd stepped into it.

Markings etched into the drier flats of mud revealed stories to Killian's discerning eye: the meandering track of a mouse that suddenly became a double line of puncture holes where the creature had frantically hopped to flee from a fox. Even in pursuit, the fox's dainty pads had left much lighter imprints than the double-pointed impressions punched by deer hooves farther along—a lone young doe or buck, judging by the small mound of fingernail-sized droppings.

Chickadees flitted from tree to tree across the open spaces—winter never chased them away—but he also heard the call of a robin and a sharp *caw* from a woodpecker before it drummed a tattoo on a hollow birch. Once, he saw a black bear far down the path, but it quickly shambled into the bush. Just awakened from hibernation, it would be hungry, but not hungry enough to attack a human.

More likely to taste his blood in the coming weeks were the hordes of black flies that came with the arrival of spring; but it was still too early for that, and he was deeply grateful.

His slow travel gave Killian plenty of time to think. It was no surprise that Uncle Lewis still opposed Killian's life's ambition, but the hurt of that opposition remained like a physical wound. To his uncle, and even more to Killian's fiercely opinionated grandfather, the colonists were traitors to their race who'd abandoned the Earth that they'd ruined, and left behind poorer souls to endure the consequences. To Killian, though, they were visionaries who'd chosen to chart a new course for humankind, to escape the bounds of their birth home and reach for the beckoning stars while giving the abused Earth time to heal itself.

Hundreds of thousands of them had climbed the sky on pillars of fire and ventured across merciless space to make homes for themselves near the Moon, on the satellites of Jupiter and Saturn, and on the sparkling red bead known as Mars. He could picture the great migration in his mind, though no record of the exodus had ever been shared with those left behind, and it was many, many generations in the past.

It could never have been possible to take everyone on Earth into space, but that wasn't the colonists' fault.

Before they left, they had created the *Allocations*: ready-made communities with housing and other amenities provided. They had built the Depots, and most of those still functioned perfectly after all the years, providing food and clothing free of charge. Surely that wasn't the behavior of traitors.

And they had promised to return in five hundred years. Some said that was because Earth would have recovered its balance by then. Others insisted that five centuries of progress would enable the voyagers to take the rest of humanity with them to the stars—with no more eager recruit than Killian.

Burning with that hope, he had gone to the secret school for six years to learn everything that was known of colonist ways. He had stayed ready for the day of their return, certain that they would see he was fit to be one of them.

How could he expect someone like Grandfather or Uncle Lewis to understand— men who thought that forging a life from the resources of field and hillside, forest and lake, was all that humankind should desire?

# # #

A blizzard struck before Killian could reach the abandoned homestead.

He'd been too deep in thought to notice the wind pick up or the first flakes that fell, but within minutes he could barely see the tops of the trees on either side of the path; and soon, any objects ten meters ahead were no more than half-imagined shadows. With the snow, the wind charged up the trail with a bite like a wolf.

Hunched over, hood pulled across as much of his face as it would cover, he blinked compulsively to protect his eyes from stabbing snow crystals. Shielding his face with his arm blocked his vision. There was little chance of him losing the path because the forest grew densely on either side, but it wasn't impossible that he might get turned around and unwittingly head northward again. The weather was too fierce to let him use his compass needle. A sliver of steel wire magnetized by the only known magnet in Borealis, from one of the great Depot loudspeakers that made announcements to the populace, the needle had to be patiently dangled from a thread or laid gently on the surface of still water. In this writhing mass of white it would be useless.

He needed shelter. A thick clump of spruce would offer reasonable protection with the ground cloth wrapped around him, but if a deep freeze followed the snow, the chill would reach into his very bones.

He stumbled onward, falling into newly formed drifts, slipping on snow-covered mud, keeping only one eye open at a time to give the other a chance to thaw. He wouldn't be able to keep that up for long.

The homestead couldn't be this far. Had he accidentally passed it during the white-out?

He staggered to a stop, desperately trying to decide whether to turn around or just push his way into the trees. Then a dark shape solidified for a few seconds through the squall. Was that a hint of rust? He remembered that at the homestead there was a sheet-metal wall that had blown over onto a crumbling woodpile to form a kind of lean-to.

Choosing to take the gamble, he turned aside, stumbled on a hidden rock, regained his feet, and lurched toward the shadow. Within another minute he had crawled through a recent drift into a narrow space beneath the rusting overhang and struggled with frozen fingers to untie the ground sheet from his pack. Spreading it out on the snow as best he could, he lay down and pulled the edges over him. The reprieve from the icy wind was wonderful. He breathed into his cupped hands, and it sounded like a sob.

As darkness came, his last thought before drifting into restless sleep was about the space colonists and the vast blackness they'd defied to forge new worlds from steel and dreams. Natural forces like a blizzard would mean nothing to such people. They'd be oblivious to this storm in the comfort of their mighty ships.

He dreamed he stood high in a dawn sky atop a mountain of glass.

# # #

The storm blew itself out by morning, energy expended in one last vigorous tantrum. The sky had already begun to clear when Killian dug his way out of the shelter and stood straight for the first time in fourteen hours. He rocked his head to ease the fierce ache in his neck and shoulders and warmed his hands in his armpits as he looked around in dismay.

Fresh snow blanketed the landscape, but not everywhere—some patches of ground were still nearly bare, while sculpted drifts swept like frozen waves over the trail. His heart sank at the thought of the snowshoes he'd chosen to leave behind. In this transformed world, they would have offered a huge advantage.

He could make some, but finding what he needed under the new snowfall and trying to work with brittle saplings and grasses would take hours. No, he'd take a chance that the rest of the route would be more passable.

First, he had to cross the river.

In the short walk from the homestead to the water's edge, his legs became sheathed with white up to mid-thigh. His body heat made the snow stick stubbornly to the cloth of his pants. He'd been a fool to set off without leather leggings.

Although the river wasn't in full flood, its current had cut a pair of channels between two outcrops of rock near the middle of the shallows. To cross them, he'd have to wade up to his waist through water that was barely above freezing.

A colonist could have floated across on invisible wings.

Ruefully, he took stock of his own equipment in the small travel pack he'd made last year from a cast-off jacket. He was usually proud of its array of bush tools, almost all produced by his own hands. Bush life required implements the Depot did not provide, at least not directly. His coil of rope, twenty paces long, had been braided from strips of faded Depot cloth destined for the recyclers. The knife given to him by Uncle Lewis had been painstakingly ground from a damaged wood chisel, his axe from a second chisel—a heavy stone-cutter's chisel—married to a mallet handle by nails and wire. Fishing tackle and snares he'd made from bent fence-wire and unraveled blanket-thread. The makers of the Depot wouldn't have approved, though, since killing wild creatures was strictly forbidden.

Other contents of his pack had come from the forest around him: a softened strip of birch bark with twin eye-slits, used to prevent snow blindness; a carefully carved bow drill and palm stone for starting fires on a cloudy day; his hunting bow and arrows, blowpipe, and throwing stick.

None of that would help him cross the dark, fast-flowing water.

He paced the river's edge, chewing his lip. The far bank seemed so close, but that was a dangerous illusion. If he tried to wade across, the swift current could sweep his feet from under him and carry him away. And getting his clothing soaking wet in this cold could be fatal.

The solution presented itself as a part of a storm-broken cedar tree lying on the bank just a little upstream, with its bristly top broken off, leaving a long stretch of trunk with few branches. It was almost too heavy, but he managed to drag it to the shore. While he caught his breath, he stripped off his boots, socks, and pants, and fastened them to his pack. The skin of his legs dimpled with cold, and it took all his will to step out into the river.

The first touch forced a hiss through his clenched teeth, but the fiery pain almost instantly gave way to total numbness. At least he wouldn't feel the rocks dig into the soles of his feet. Tugging the log toward the first rock outcrop, he wedged one end between two of the larger boulders. With every muscle straining, he walked his hands up the log to push it into a vertical position and heaved it toward the far islet of gravel.

It worked!

With the current jamming both ends against rock, water immediately flowed over the log, but its rough bark provided enough grip for his bare feet. He hurried across before he had a chance to change his mind.

The second set of rocks was slightly downstream. He just managed to shove the log across the gap, paused only long enough to check its stability, and scurried over it like a squirrel fleeing the shadow of a hawk. The back end of the log broke free with a lurch that almost threw him from his makeshift bridge, but he was able to turn the stumble into a leap and landed upright in the shallows. Gasping for breath, he rushed to shore, swept snow from a nearby stump, and sat clasping his feet with his hands to restore circulation before getting back into his boots. That wasn't going to be enough. The light breeze set his whole body shuddering.

The thought of more delay galled him, but he had no choice—he needed warmth. He scrounged beneath the nearest trees for scraps of still-dry wood and made a fire with birchbark and dead, resin-loaded spruce twigs, using his fire bow; then he sat as close to the flames as he dared, watching the wisps of steam from his jacket. Fortunately, the inner layer of his clothing wasn't too wet. As soon as he felt able, he mixed snow into the coals of his fire and prepared to resume his journey.

He was tired, and he was far short of the distance he'd hoped to travel by then, but he had succeeded in crossing the river and had built a fire in a snowy and sodden forest.

Then he remembered the people he was travelling to meet and their near-magical technology. His pride evaporated like the clouds of his breath.

Wiping his dripping nose with a sleeve, he shrugged into his pack, and set off.

2

Natira knew how to make the noises that would please a man.

Valenti liked to hear her moans and sighs—it was important to his sense of accomplishment; so, she obliged, even if her mind was less engaged in sex than in speculating about the Confederacy's imminent return to Earth. She could rely on the image projector to show him appropriate facial expressions, though the deception made her feel a bit guilty. Anyway, it wouldn't be for much longer.

There—his outline pulsed red to show that he was climaxing, but Natira would have known that from his own noises and movements. Or did his imager unit have a fake orgasm setting, too?

No, his male pride would never admit a failure to perform.

Natira hadn't climaxed for months, but that wasn't all Valenti's fault. When she'd realized that their encounters left her less and less satisfied, she'd deliberately dialed down the responsiveness of her own coitusuit. It still delivered enough vibration and warmth to let her know what he was doing to the holographic surrogate of her body in his own quarters across the city—and she wanted to be able to give the reactions he expected. But its ministrations were subtle enough to let the greater part of her mind concentrate on other things. She never used the full hood either. Some women loved the stimulation of simulated lips pressed against theirs or nibbling at their ears, but the hood made Natira feel confined, and that was a mood-killer on its own.

Orgasms weren't important. What counted was that she had been chosen as the Intended of a man of status and influence and that she made him happy, which made her family happy. He was a good man, intelligent and varied in his interests; their conversations were entertaining, and his circle of acquaintances included some of the most stimulating minds Telluria had to offer. It would be greedy to expect more than that from a consort. That he was too self-centered to be a good lover did not make him unusual among men. Even her limited experience had taught her that.

His breathing had slowed now, and his face in the hologram showed the smile that effortlessly charmed women. He was pleased with himself, and Natira was glad. She would have liked to talk for a while and find out if he knew any more than she did about who had been named to the official delegation to Earth. The gossip network at the Ministry of Justice might be better informed than her own. But Valenti claimed to have urgent business to attend to. She gave him a warm smile and kissed the air before breaking the connection.

As she began to peel off the coitusuit, she briefly considered setting it to pleasure her on its own, but she wasn't that interested. She placed it back in her closet, got dressed, and stepped into the kitchen corner to have the beverage unit make her some tea.

Her tea had barely cooled enough to drink when an incoming call made her leap to her feet. The eminent Basu Hind, newly appointed ambassador to Earth, appeared in front of her. The background of the hologram looked like the lustrous white of the Hall of Authority, and the smile on the face of her friend and mentor was just as bright.

"Relaxing at home?" Hind asked.

"I should spend some time here if only to justify such a luxurious apartment."

"Just quarters befitting a respected scholar and beloved video host, even if you weren't a member of the Celestia

15

family. But I'm glad to see you getting some rest for a change. You'll need it." His expression became more smirk than smile, and her heart beat faster. Although Hind was more than twice her age, the only signs of it were streaks of silver that swept back from his temples through his wavy hair, and very fine creases at the corners of his mouth and eyes. Since those things were easy to remove, he obviously thought they enhanced his aura of wisdom and respectability. He was still very attractive, though it wasn't his mature virility that quickened her pulse.

"What do you mean, I'll need my rest?"

"Since my assignment to Earth may last many months, there is a need to fill my place at the Centre for Earth Studies, as you know. How would you like to be the Interim Director?"

Natira's breath caught. She tried to hide her disappointment.

"That would be a tremendous honor, sir. But I can't believe I'm worthy of it. Surely Dom Vesta is equally qualified and has much longer tenure at the Centre."

"Oh, you're worthy of it—you would make a fine Director, passionate and conscientious." The corner of his mouth turned up again. "But it's not really what you want, is it? All right, I'll stop teasing. I'll need some brilliant assistants during my mission to Earth if I'm to be successful. I'd like you to be one of them."

She strangled her whoop of joy, but her face flushed with a heat Valenti had rarely produced at his most attentive.

Hind gave a loud laugh. "Don't be so restrained. You'll hurt yourself."

"Do you mean it? You're not teasing me now, are you?"

"I wouldn't be that cruel. It's true that you would make an excellent Interim Director, but I know your heart is set on Earth. Frankly, no one else is so thoroughly versed in Earth cultural practices. I'm told that you listen to the observation feed from the support facilities for hours at a time!"

"Just audio . . . in the background while I work. I like to get a sense of the interplay among people as they chatter to each other. The lineups for food and other goods are the perfect place for that."

"But there are thousands of Allocations. You can't listen to them all."

"I pick them at random, mostly. Sometimes I go from feed to feed just to see if anyone's speaking anything but NorthAm. They hardly ever do, and yet Earth once had hundreds of different languages. And it's incredible to think that over five hundred years and thousands of isolated communities, NorthAm hasn't drifted into something completely indecipherable."

"You can thank our ancestors for that. The holographic teaching programs for Earth children are only in NorthAm. Even more significantly, Depot distribution technology requires NorthAm. If the natives get too creative with their patois, or refuse to speak NorthAm, they go hungry."

"All over the planet?"

"Certainly. It's so much more efficient. For the same reason, the types of foods and goods provided by the Depots is the same everywhere. Catering to local whims about flavor and fashion just encourages people to see themselves as different. Difference invites conflict, and conflict is counterproductive."

"So, we're the ones responsible for eliminating those other languages?"

"I won't say they're all gone—people are stubborn—but at least everyone also understands the language of education and progress. As you of all people know, we haven't eliminated all of their silly superstitions and ceremonial practices either; but we've done our best to civilize Earth's people. And make them ready for our return."

In truth, no matter which of the communities Natira had listened to, hoping to witness some of those peculiar behaviors, she never heard anything terribly interesting. The women gossiped about relationships; the men talked about weather or some trivial repair project. What she really hoped to hear were wise leaders building a future for their people, brave warriors bragging about their deeds in battle or conquests in bed; or shamans sharing secrets while they invoked the spirits of animal and ancestor. But those were not the people who were sent to line up at the Depots for food or clothing.

In old literature she'd encountered the term 'noble savage', and she shivered with excitement at the thought of finally meeting some. Such people would not speak much, but their few words would be full of wisdom born from closeness to their Earth mother.

Hind shook his head in amusement. "You'd prefer to go down there dressed as one of them and just mingle, am I right? But you couldn't—even if you darkened your hair and skin: Your height would instantly give you away. And even your enhanced muscles won't be able to cope with Earth gravity on their own at first. I'm afraid we'll be confined to our own compound most of the time and have to wear lift vests everywhere else."

"Would I really be your direct assistant?"

"My Second Assistant. The government insists that my First Assistant be a bureaucrat—there will be a lot of things to organize, of course, so I can't argue with that."

"I don't know what to say."

"*Yes* would be a good start."

"Yes! Of course, yes. You know it's what I've hoped for. I just wasn't sure I would be considered for such an important mission at my age."

"You weren't, but the Ministry of Intercolonial Affairs has been persuaded. We can't have the Earth dwellers thinking we people of the colonies are all old relics. Besides, as much as we've kept them under surveillance all these years, there are bound to be surprises. I need a creative thinker who can come up with quick responses based on a deep understanding of these natives. That's not Dom Vesta; that's you."

She could scarcely breathe. Yet even her jubilation couldn't keep a wisp of doubt from her mind.

Had she been chosen because of her qualifications alone, or could there be another reason?

It was less than a week since she'd discovered a mysterious unaddressed computer archive buried deep within Telluria's central directory, and dutifully reported it to Hind and the Patriarch. Neither man had been able to conceal his surprise, and both had been uncharacteristically evasive. They'd insisted that an archive unlisted in the directories and invisible to searches must contain only archaic dregs of information of no use to anyone; and yet the next time she'd tried to access those files, she'd found them shielded behind an encryption she couldn't penetrate. It wasn't an official restriction—that would show in the data registries— so it seemed that someone wanted the information utterly forgotten.

Could she have been assigned to Hind's team to stop her from digging any further?

No. The Earth mission was too important to be used as a distraction.

"Thank you. I'm so very grateful..."

"No need." He waved a hand. "I'll see that you're included in all communications, and I will arrange for your gear. We depart tomorrow."

Her surprise made him laugh again.

"Yes, the advance scouts have already been onsite for more than twenty-four hours, though without making any contact with the inhabitants. When the official delegations arrive, we'll be the ones to go out and speak to the crowds. And believe me, there already are crowds. Clearly, they haven't forgotten our promise to return."

"So, the scouts have been making sure it's safe?"

"Of course. There hasn't been any large-scale violence on Earth for more than a century, but it's best to be sure. The natives have been entirely peaceful since the scout ships landed. Just eager and restless, so we mustn't keep them waiting too long." He gave her a wink and broke the connection.

As his image disappeared, she allowed herself to feel the thrill of the news—truly believe it. Her lip was beaded with sweat, and her chest fluttered as if she'd just come back from the High-g Sports Complex.

She was glad she hadn't wasted all that adrenaline on mere sex.

3

The CCC's producer bot sent a "go ahead" tone into Natira's cochlear chip to indicate that video and audio feeds were optimal, and to begin the program. For some reason, the cue always gave her the urge to fiddle with the camera lens affixed by a circlet of metal in the middle of her forehead, but she'd learned to resist the impulse.

With the confirmation of her appointment by Hind just hours earlier, and her departure only a day away, she fretted about not using every moment to prepare for the excursion to Earth. But in truth there wasn't much left to be done—the Confederacy's planned return had literally been part of her whole life. She'd taken care of every contingency that could be planned for, only awaiting Hind's official word that she would go along.

The interview segment she was about to record was part of her commitment to Confederacy Central Communications in return for the time away from her regular duties. There was never a question of the CCC turning down her request for a leave endorsed by the famous Basu Hind, but her promise to produce some short documentary segments showcasing real Earth humans and their lives on the harsh planet would keep her bosses happy. As one of the Confederacy's best known *I&I* personalities, her series would be a big draw in the outer colonies, too. "Inform and Influence"—the more, the better.

The assignment was no hardship—she loved her job. The distasteful part was the executive producer's insistence that the story include the elements of Natira's own background that made her qualified to visit Earth, especially her genetic status as a *Tantum*, colloquially know as a *Big One*. Most of her audience probably knew, but she never talked about it—had never been comfortable doing so, even if adults were much more subtle in their exclusion than school-ground bullies.

She pushed aside her discomfort. If the series was going to include such a germinal component of her life, it needed to show where that life had begun.

A shiver went up her spine as she entered the Parturition Institute. Not just because she was a Big One. Almost anyone would find the place disquieting. Though every citizen knew the clinical facts about how they were brought into existence, very few would ever have seen the process. That was why her producer had been so determined to include it. He said it was because Tellurians loved to celebrate their superior technology, but she wondered if it was really only for titillation.

Shrugging off her repugnance, she strode to meet her guide, the Institute's deputy director, Alyss Laster, and thanked the woman profusely for arranging the interview and tour on such short notice. Then, giving a three-count to begin the segment, Natira launched into a technical description of the building and its operations that she'd researched earlier in the day, and turned to her hostess.

"Where should we start?" she asked, for the benefit of the audience. Laster looked confused by the question, since the itinerary had already been arranged by the network.

"Uh, well, are you still sure you want to show your viewers the actual parturition facilities? Most people are more interested in seeing the babies after decanting. They're so cute then."

"They are, but we feel it's important to show the whole process. After all, this is about the return of our people to the planet Earth; and getting our citizens ready for that starts right here."

"Oh, you're absolutely right. Well, then, follow me." Any lingering reservations faded behind a smile of genuine enthusiasm as Laster led the way to the Genetic Computing Department.

Afraid that the explanation would be horribly dry, Natira instead found herself fascinated by all the permutations involved in mixing the DNA of future Tellurian citizens. Although the number of distinct family lines of the original colonists had been large, it was nothing like the variety of the home planet's population; so it was important to ensure that the smaller gene pool didn't promote the rise of autosomal recessive disorders. The mechanism of most genes had already been well understood by the time of the Exodus, so the shift to deliberate breeding had taken firm hold by the fourth generation in space, first with surrogate human mothers, then wholly independent of any biological container. The Institute's supply of basic DNA provided ninety-nine percent of the coding required for a new human being, and the remaining one percent was carefully selected and arranged by computer. Mandatory collection from all citizens provided plenty of raw material, and the robot technicians of the splicing vats had a success rate as close to perfect as five centuries of refinement could make it.

The splicing vats themselves just looked like hundreds of identical plasglas cylinders; but when Laster led Natira into the next room, the shiver in her spine returned.

These cylinders were larger, and their contents were clearly alive.

Why should that affect her? Even as a schoolchild she'd seen pictures of the procedure. Perhaps it was the strangeness of the shapes—she'd forgotten how alien they looked. Still, this was merely a processing plant like dozens she'd seen before, not very different from the manufactories of the Nutrition Department where her favorite meats and cheeses were cultivated. Her voice betrayed no emotion as she described what she saw for her viewers.

Soft music filled the air, and as she opened her mouth to ask about it, she recognized it as a piece remembered from her schooldays. Study music—one of several dozen compositions that inevitably were played while she and her classmates worked quietly at memory exercises or research assignments. If she remembered correctly, this particular piece had been written not long before the Exodus by a man named Mozart.

Could subtle rhythms and soaring melodies stir even the rudimentary occupants of this place?

The first rows of containers looked empty except for a milky yellow-brown fluid and off-white tendrils veined with purplish grey that dangled from their top ends. Only a close look revealed tiny fledgling embryos at their tips, like an afterthought.

A system of overhead pulleys advanced the cylinders through different sections of the room as gestation progressed. Subsequent rows held larger and larger fetuses. About midway down the long enclosure, one of the dangling forms give a brief wriggle that made Natira jump and drew a laugh from Laster.

That would definitely be cut from the video during editing!

"You probably expected our facility to be larger," Laster said. "It was, until this century. But since the outer colonies took over their own population control, we only have to produce citizens for the five Tellurian colonies; so that just means replacing those people lost through death."

"Replacing?"

"Oh, not in the sense of replacing them genetically. Just the numbers, I mean. No, we never make exact copies of previous citizens—the Council of Five decided against that centuries ago."

Natira knew that to be true, but there continued to be rumors that the five leading families nonetheless occasionally commissioned reproductions of some of their most notable ancestors. Even her newest Celestia cousin, only two years old, was already beginning to look suspiciously like a famous Patriarch of two hundred years earlier whose 3D portrait hung in the Palace's Hall of Prime Councilors.

"And are the genetic combinations performed entirely by computer, with no human interference?" she asked.

A frown crossed Laster's face. "You make 'interference' sound like a dirty word. In fact, sometimes interference is necessary when, for instance, Telluria has an extra need for mathematicians to undertake the planning of new industrial planetoids. Or mechanical engineers when the government decides it's time to revamp the fleet. Specialized human skills are still required, you know."

"Of course."

It seemed as if the question had struck a nerve. Maybe as Deputy Director, Laster really didn't know about the copying of former notables, but Natira had it on good authority that there was also a black market that allowed powerful families not only to select for certain traits among the offspring produced, but even to include DNA from the familial bloodline—a serious infraction of the Reproduction Statutes. Word was, they'd follow the child that came from the modified fetus through all of its early life right up to the highest standard level of education at age nineteen. If the child had performed to expectations, they'd adopt the young man or woman into their clan with great fanfare. If not, their interest ended.

The black market was a poorly kept secret, so those not adopted were left wondering if it was because they'd been randomly bred, like the majority, or had been a disappointment to a wealthy patron.

Natira couldn't help but wonder if that was how she'd become a Celestia. Only someone highly placed within the family would know the answer, but would likely never admit it.

Should she pursue the black-market question with Laster?

As she considered it, a suggestion from her producer appeared in the corneop of her left eye.

With an acquiescent tap of a finger at her temple, Natira asked, "When are the fetuses redirected to become *Tantas*?"

"That has to be done from the very beginning, of course. When the genes are mixed. Haven't you noticed the differences among these cylinders coded in green?"

She hadn't. A closer look still showed nothing obvious.

"See? The umbilical cords are slightly thicker, to carry extra nutrient. And over here, you can notice that the developing bones are a bit wider and more opaque. Even a regimen of almost non-stop exercise wouldn't be enough to prepare an ordinary Tellurian for the high gravity of Earth because our bones just aren't dense enough. And using gene therapy on adults to force an increase in density can never equal the results of modification begun before birth. But the fetuses don't vary in actual size until this final stage."

Laster moved along to the last row. All the cylinders there were marked in green.

"Yes, these are all Big Ones. We've managed to shorten the third trimester of fetal growth for most offspring, reducing the whole gestation period to two-hundred and fifty days from the historical two-hundred eighty. But to produce Big Ones, we allow gestation to extend an extra twenty days. Mainly to provide the extra muscle capacity." She smiled and met Natira's gaze more directly than she'd done yet. "Isn't it nice to know that *you* got special treatment?"

Was the woman mocking her? She actually did seem proud, as if Natira were her personal creation.

Ancient literature from the time when women had gestated children within their own bodies often mentioned a special link between offspring and their direct progenitor. Would that have been like this woman's pride in her work?

Natira didn't think it would be a worthwhile trade for the gruesome pain and effort involved.

Well, let the woman be proud. Laster wasn't the one who'd had to spend hours every day of her life in a high-g exercise facility to ensure that these genetically enhanced bones and muscles were kept at optimum capacity. Natira's own efforts would soon be rewarded, but she thought of all the *Tantas* who'd endured that ordeal for their whole lives, yet, for whatever reason, would never be chosen for a mission to Earth.

The next room was where the decanting took place, and Natira checked with the producer bot to make sure it was getting good picture quality—this would be the footage they most wanted. Here, the room lighting was noticeably dimmer and more golden, and the background music softer.

"I don't know if your viewers all realize," Laster was saying, "that babies were once wholly grown within the bodies of women, and finally expelled with great difficulty and pain. Such an event was terribly traumatic for both adult and infant, which is another reason our way is so much better. Look here—this fetus is ready to leave its gestation environment, but there will be nothing about the process to cause it shock or discomfort. You can see the fluid surrounding it slowly draining until the child's nose and mouth are exposed, then deposits of mucus in its respiratory passages are gently sucked away to allow air into the delicate lungs. A combination of chemicals and a mild electrical charge in the fluid stimulate the baby to begin breathing on its own, but it will remain suspended in warm, comforting fluid for most of another day as its body is gradually exposed to air heated to its skin temperature."

Laster's eyes glowed with pleasure. "No trauma. No reason for the child to even awaken until it is fully ready, and then the ambient light is set at a frequency and intensity that's comfortable for little eyes to see the world for the first time." Her voice was pure syrup, but Natira detected no falseness— the woman was sincerely delighted by the scene unfolding before her, though she must have seen it many times before. The technology was impressive—a thoroughly sensible and efficient solution to the continued survival of the race.

Though infants were normally decanted a dozen at a time, the Institute had arranged for this single child to be discharged individually for the sake of the news video.

The chosen subject was even a *Tanta*, but if the Deputy Director expected an expression of gratitude from her interviewer, she was disappointed.

Natira watched as the cylinder, now in a horizontal position and nearly drained of fluid, was mated to a larger container into which the still sleeping child was floated. The remaining liquid drained away while the top half of the new container slowly opened.

There were several other people in the room by that point, young men and women Natira assumed to be assistants, and she expected one of them to take the new baby into his or her arms. Instead, a robotic arm descended from the ceiling, poked padded fingers under the still form, and slowly raised it into the air where various pairs of human eyes and a number of electronic instruments on dangling cables performed a thorough inspection.

Alyss Laster suddenly began to applaud and was quickly joined by the assistants, startling both Natira and the baby. It wriggled at the noise and scrunched up its face, so the clapping halted and the baby settled down again. Natira obligingly leaned closer to enable her camera to get a good close-up.

"Isn't it wonderful?" Laster gushed. "A brand-new life. An entirely new citizen named . . ." she glanced at a projection near the wall that displayed readouts of the infant's vital signs in graph form, "Landra Tellurian! What a lovely name—also chosen by computer, of course."

Despite herself, Natira felt drawn to the little girl who was just beginning to lift her eyelids for a few seconds at a time, readying herself to face her future. Was it because Landra was a Big One? Did Natira somehow see herself in the wrinkly, vulnerable entity lying before her?

At a sudden whim, she asked, "Can I hold her?" The audience would eat it up.

"Oh no. No, no." Laster sounded shocked. "There will come a time when little Landra will be exposed to human contact naturally, in a couple of days. But first we need to monitor her immune system to make sure it's responding properly to the environment before we subject it to all of the . . . *germs* carried by a human adult." Her look of distaste seemed to say that she didn't mentally include herself among the germ-ridden. But Natira was included. Very definitely.

She shrugged. There was a new smell in the air that she identified with the infant, though that didn't necessarily follow. A sensation of warmth and well-being spread through her, probably because of the well-warmed air Laster had described.

But little Landra was already being whisked away by the robot arm to continue this new stage of her existence. Laster explained that the child would be taken to a nursery, then an early edu-centre within a few months, and wouldn't encounter anyone but especially trained personnel until her first public excursion at the age of three.

The network wouldn't get a follow-up visit, then, at least, not by Natira. Within twenty-four hours she would be on Earth.

It was incredible that she'd actually forgotten about that, even for a few moments!

With little more to be seen at the Institute, she went into the show's standard wrap-up, thanking all the necessary executives and offering some special words of appreciation to Alyss Laster. The woman still glowed.

CCC would add some stock footage of a nursery and various school settings later, set to a narration that Natira had already recorded.

As she walked from the building, the recent experience mixed in her mind with the adventure ahead.

She'd just witnessed the beginning of a new life. And in only a few hours she would begin a new life of her own!

4

Killian walked in a daze, drained by hours of trudging through mud and snowdrifts while cold and damp penetrated deep into his being.

Even before his memory of the landmarks confirmed it, a furry harbinger told him he was approaching Borealis. A raccoon rustled through leaf debris at the base of a tree stump that had been sheltered from the fresh snow, nosing for grubs or worms. It was rare to see a raccoon in the daylight—they were mostly night feeders.

His grandmother claimed that her people long ago had 'spirit guides'—wild creatures whose spirit would accompany a person through life. While most of Killian's childhood friends had gushed about eagles and bears, he had quietly decided that his spirit animal was probably a raccoon. A misfit. A mask-wearing, equal-opportunity robber of birds' nests, food caches, and trash heaps, scrounging a living on the fringes of human habitation with precocious cleverness and daring.

For a moment, the animal's small eyes met his. There was no fear in them, only a mischievous curiosity, as if wondering how to con this clumsy giant out of some food. If the creature felt inferior, or envied Killian's tools and coverings, there was no sign. It knew its place and was content. It turned back to its task, blithely stuffing some grubs into its mouth. Killian gave it a nod of respect and continued on his way.

He barely noticed when he passed the first huts—dismal dwellings whose featureless plasticwood walls in faded brown and white blended into the landscape of trees and snowbanks.

A sound finally caught his attention. Like a tree splintered by frost on the bitterest of winter nights, he recognized it as the sharp crack of plasticwood being broken. In warmer weather the stuff was very flexible and hard to cut, so people waited until sub-zero temperatures made it brittle and then snapped the three-by-two-meter sheets into usable pieces. In a settlement the size of Borealis there were always abandoned huts or barracks where sheets could be removed and put to other uses. He saw a stocky man working over a pair of sawhorses while a teenager leaned on the plasticwood panel that protruded a meter or so beyond a sharp edge beneath. They looked up as Killian passed. The teen hoisted his weight onto the end of the sheet, and it parted with a loud report.

Even the most flexible things could be made to break under sufficient stress.

The roof of the family's shack might be the next thing to snap, Killian thought, shaking his head at its badly sagging peak. And the water cistern leaned at a precarious angle, with a dingy streak down its side from a slow leak, like blood oozing from a wound. Were these people too pressed for time to spare some for simple repairs? Or did they just not care? Although they wouldn't be unique in that respect.

Killian would have been grateful for the warmth of a fire, but the stingy trickle of bad-smelling smoke from the shack's stubby chimney proclaimed that it wouldn't be worth his while to ask. Likely they were burning worn clothing or old baskets. They'd probably used up any naturally fallen wood or other allowable fuel by this late in the winter, and it was forbidden to cut live trees. Borealis's shared geoheating service didn't extend this far from the center of town, which was one of many reasons he was mystified that anyone would choose to live in the fringes without taking the ultimate step of making a homestead in the bush, like his aunt and uncle.

It was pointless trying to understand the motivations of others. When the colonists left five hundred years ago, they'd created the Allocations to be a form of community that would meet the needs of all, but there could be no such thing. Even Killian knew that.

A half-hour later, he was pleasantly surprised to see Barton Creek emerge from behind the hut that was home to a good-looking girl named Amantha. Her bedroom window was probably back there. Another time, Killian would have had plenty to say about that, but something more important was on his mind. Though five years younger, Barton had gone to the same unauthorized school as Killian. He would certainly know if a spacecraft had landed in Borealis.

"Nothing's happening, though. It just sits there," Barton reported.

"Where did it land? When?"

"Yesterday morning, an hour after sunrise. It just coasted to a stop on the roof of the Depot and hasn't done anything since then."

"No one came out, not even to go inside the Depot? What's on that roof, anyway—have you ever been up there?"

"Why bother? It's just a roof. But my cousin Wade climbed onto the roof of his hut to get a better view and says nobody's come out of the ship. No flashing lights or strange sounds either. More than a day without nothin' going on." The account had to be true, because only utter boredom would have caused Barton to leave the scene when there was a chance to see colony tech in person.

"You sure it's a colony craft?"

"No way to be sure. It looks like the holos we saw in school. But five hundred years, you know—the promised time is up. That has to mean something. Where you been anyway? You look like shit."

"My uncle's place in the bush. The trail is all mud and snowdrifts, and I'm freezing my ass off. I got to get some drier clothes at my mother's. You heading back to the Depot? I'll meet you there."

The temptation to go straight to the spaceship was fierce; but once there, he'd never pull himself away, and if he spent much longer in sodden clothes, he'd get sick. Then the colonists would never let him near them. He gave Barton a last nod and turned in the direction of his mother's shack. It wasn't far from the Depot—not many of the homes were. He'd heard that the original town layout had been a series of barracks in concentric circles with the Depot at the center. But over the years, about half the barracks had been dismantled and their plasticwood used to build huts for individual families. Even so, few people had moved far away. After all, the Depot was the source of food and goods, manufactured by unknown processes inside the vast building. According to Killian's instructors, nearly everything the Depot produced, edible and inedible, was made from strains of yeast, but he'd doubted that part of their lessons. How would clothes and furnishings come from the powdery stuff his father and uncle used to make beer?

A noise from behind made him turn. Five scruffy dogs trailed him with their pink tongues lolling out. He shook his head at them. He'd eaten the last of his food hours earlier, and though he'd gladly share scraps with one stray dog on its own, feeding them in a pack usually triggered a fight.

As likely to get a kick as a handout from most humans, they kept their distance; but their eyes glinted with unquenchable hope.

Uncle Lewis and Aunt Regina insisted that human beings were only one link in the vast chain of species on Earth, and no more important that any of the others; but Killian knew otherwise. Maybe it wasn't obvious from the listless people in the ramshackle structures around him, but the universe belonged to humankind. The colonists were proof of that. They weren't just the best that humanity had to offer, they were the pinnacle of all living beings.

The packed-dirt pathways around him were completely empty, as if the community had been abandoned. The only sounds were the occasional bird call or the flap of fabric in the breeze. Everyone must be gathered at the Depot, eager to see what would happen. Unless they were hiding.

What was there to fear? The past? Or the future?

Open spaces between the rows of shacks let in enough of the spring sun to have replaced the recent snow with mud churned into ruts by passing feet. Even the paths weren't really deliberate—they were just the only places free of the drooping clotheslines that connected nearly every dwelling. Because clothing from the Depot came in only a few styles and colors, one of the most popular pursuits during the oppressive winter months was to personalize garments with homemade dyes, colorful appliqués, and knit sleeves and collars to replace the Depot's fabric ones. Every manner of alteration had been tried, and the popularity of certain styles came and went year by year. It was one of the few ways people could proclaim their individuality and still align themselves with others. The clotheslines bore brightly varied testimony to the personalities of their owners. A good thing because they were the only touch of color in Borealis.

Killian easily identified his mother's place by a clothesline bearing a tan-colored dress with an appliquéd thunderbird on the front in blue and turquoise. The sight brought a touch of warmth to his chilled bones.

Her shack was the same size as most—six meters on a side—but kept in better condition. There was an actual door with hinges that did not sag and a latch that caught and held. Pulling the door open fanned a handful of carved cedar wind chimes into musical motion. The smell of sweetgrass collapsed time, restoring the days of his childhood as if they were only hours behind him. A cleansing smudge had always been a part of his mother's routine, especially in winter months when hot water for bathing was hard to come by.

A needlepoint hanging in the light of the single window made him smile. Made by his grandmother, it was a portrait of Killian and a young cousin named Suzu, when he was nine or ten and Suzu just a toddler. On a narrow table beneath it, plain ceramic bowls were stacked beside a hardplast pitcher and a pair of woven baskets. Other serving dishes were arranged on various shelves—there were no enclosed cabinets such as Uncle Lewis liked to make—and in the far corner was the drum stove that could be used to heat water for tea and provide extra warmth if someone was willing to walk a few kilometers to fetch dry sticks or, on rare occasions, an armful of peat. It must be burning something now because Killian had already stopped shivering. On a hook above the stove hung the most valuable item in the household: a kettle made of beaten copper that had been handed down through his mother's family for generations.

A gasp came from the curtained-off side of the cabin.

His mother stepped from behind the fabric with a smile as bright as the sunlight that spilled at her feet.

"Killian!"

"Summer," he said with a deferential nod of his head, then a deeper bow as his grandmother appeared. The two women could have been sisters except that his mother's long hair was still lustrous black and the other's uniformly gray. Both had slight builds, wide smiles, and long arms that reached for a hug. He was glad to oblige, though he'd only been gone for a month. Surprisingly, his grandmother's embrace had more strength than his mother's. He thought Summer had lost more weight than the hard winter months usually took from her.

"You've come back early because of the spaceship," she said.

"I couldn't stay away."

"Many people are there now, but nothing is happening. Perhaps they are testing us."

"Testing us? Why?"

"It has been five hundred years," his grandmother said. "They will not be sure that we are the same people they left behind, and we should not expect it of them either."

"You're not afraid, are you? I know they must be even more powerful than before, but they'll still know us as their own kind. Still care for us. Otherwise, why come back?"

The old woman simply shrugged. Summer said, "My mother's friends have lived long and seen much. Old bark is rough, and sometimes bitter." The words brought her a cuff on the arm.

"And shiniest clothes are shared the least," Grandmother replied. "Just because the colonists have everything they need does not mean they will not want more." She wrapped her arms around her simple shift as if someone might try to take it from her.

"Don't be . . . ." To call her silly would not be respectful. " . . . worried. We have nothing they will want. And if they cared enough to make the Allocations and Depots to last us all these years, they can't wish us harm."

She gave another shrug, took the copper kettle from its peg, filled it with water from a large jug, and put it on the stove. Tea was the response to most issues, good and bad, in the lives of these women.

Six chipped mugs were on a nearby shelf to serve three generations—Summer's mother, her two daughters, plus Killian. Another shelf held three mugs for guests. Any other visitors had to bring dishes of their own.

Killian sometimes felt out of place in this mostly female household, but he drew comfort from their rituals. He could have gone to live with his father, and often visited for days at a time if there was a project to work on; but he didn't always get along with the women with whom Jacob chose to share his life. His father's current companion, Novia, was all right, though she often acted as young as Suzu.

Grandfather's home had once offered a warm welcome, but the strong bond he and Killian had enjoyed in earlier times had not survived the clash of two conflicting wills as Killian forged an adult identity of his own. The pain of the estrangement was still fresh as frostbite.

Summer scanned him from head to toe with a disapproving look.

"You look as if something dragged you all the way from Lewis and Regina's."

"The storm left some deep drifts, and the mud was even worse. I'm just going to change my clothes and then go to the Depot."

But as he moved toward the sleeping area, there was a sound that grew in volume like a sudden strong wind. The faces of the women showed they'd heard it before. He rushed to the door.

The oblong silver shape that passed overhead was wider at the front than the back and as it slid downward through the air, he could see no sign of what kept it aloft. Without knowing how high above the ground it flew, he couldn't judge its size either; but its destination wasn't hard to guess. Forgetting about his wet clothes, he broke into a run toward the center of town. Faint cries behind him went unheard.

Something was happening, and he would *not* miss it this time.

Though any event that broke the monotony of Allocation life could draw a crowd, he was shocked by the size of the gathering he found. Maybe a thousand people jostled as close as they could get to the Depot building, as if the entire population of Borealis had abandoned their daily routines to witness this Second Coming.

The northeast end of the Depot, where four of the original barracks had been torn down, was the only large space in the center of town. That was where most of the crowd was concentrated, so Killian was sure the colonists would choose that spot to make their appearance. He worked his way slowly through the press of bodies, helped by his extra size and muscle. Or maybe it was the smell of marsh mud on his clothes.

He looked around for Barton Creek. Maybe he was one of those figures hoping for a better view on the nearby rooftops. They were taking a foolish risk—Borealis roofs could barely hold the weight of the winter snows. The ring of shacks closest to the Depot were especially suspect. By tradition they were occupied by the town's elders; and at some point in the previous century, there had been an attempt to make them more impressive by adding fancy roofs of red clay tiles.

Although most of the tiles remained in place, the wooden pegs that held them often rotted and they were known to fall off without warning.

As he reached the edge of the main crowd, he heard his name. An arm waved above the heads. He pushed gently toward it.

"Elder Quarry," he said with real pleasure as he finally drew near to her. The onlookers had reserved a space near the front for the leaders of the community, and Momoko Quarry was the current head of the elders. Killian gave a deep bow and raised her offered hand to his forehead. It was a gesture that signified affection as well as respect. He didn't know why the woman had always given him special attention—they weren't related, as far as he knew—but it pleased him.

She struck an impressive figure, her skin dark as river mud and her hair like milkweed cotton atop a tall frame that she always wrapped in hand-made fabric, never Depot clothes. Killian's eyes darted around, but saw no sign of his grandfather, her predecessor, and he was glad to turn his gaze back to her. Her poise and calm took away some of his own nervousness. Even citizens of the sky would have to respect a woman like this.

"I am glad that you're here, as a well-educated representative of our young adults," she said. Then the right side of her mouth crinkled. "Although I would have thought you might dress differently for the occasion."

Jaw sinking in dismay, he began a stammered apology, but just then a roar went up from the crowd. Every face turned toward the Depot roof.

Five human figures stood near the edge looking down at the audience. The three in the middle were dressed in loose-fitting clothing that fluttered very slightly in the breeze, all of a gleaming white that was like lightning at midnight in the midst of drab Borealis. The two people at either end wore form-fitting bodysuits of a slate grey that caught light in strange silver ripples. Those two had wide bands on their wrists that looked like some kind of metal, but no one held anything in their hands.

No weapons, Killian thought, *a good sign.*

Or would he simply not recognize one if he saw it?

The man in the middle stood a little ahead of the rest. Their leader, obviously. His skin was the coppery shade of Killian's own, in stark contrast to his full head of white hair. An elder, then. And more than his skin and hair reminded Killian of Momoko Quarry—they shared a commanding attractiveness. It was hard to stop looking at him, but Killian pulled his eyes away and noticed for the first time that one of the five, the figure on the leader's immediate left, was a woman.

Though her clothing was no more feminine than that of the men, the shape beneath it definitely was. With pale skin and waist-length blond hair almost as light as her garments, he might have taken her for an elder too, except everything about her radiated health and youth. A circlet of something shiny around her head held a small oval or octagonal shape just above the bridge of her nose. Not quite as still as the men—perhaps she was restless with excitement, a feeling he shared. He felt an urge to see her up close, out of curiosity.

Then suddenly she was looking straight at him, taking in his mud-spattered clothing. Their eyes met.

In that gaze he was transformed from a man into an insect, and he shrank away from it in dismay.

What a fool he'd been to think that he could ever become one such as these: People so far above his own as to be nearly a different species. Their kind had risen while his continued to sink. He wasn't even worthy to be standing in their presence.

He searched for a way to run and hide.

5

The giant azure orb of Earth had hung amidst the obsidian vault of space all of Natira's life, but that hadn't prepared her for its magnificence up close. As the inter-system shuttle encountered the planet's atmosphere, she realized that she wasn't breathing and made a conscious effort to draw in air. To faint at that moment would be disastrous. Even with Basu Hind as her mentor and friend, she could give no sign that she wasn't up to this task.

So many times, the view of Telluria Prime while returning from one of the four other Tellurian colonies had given her a swell of pride that her race had forged something so beautiful out of the stygian void. But this . . . this was a moment of transcendence. As she looked down upon the home planet of their species, she could no longer see it just as a mass of rock and water and miscellaneous biological material. For the first time, she could make sense of a concept she had encountered in her research: the primitive belief that the whole Earth was one living entity. A mother, because mothers were the source of life. From the edge of space, it was impossible to look upon those expanses of life-giving liquid, soil, vegetation, cloud, ice, and not see all of it as a vital, inter-connected whole.

All her life she'd heard about the ruined Earth that her ancestors had escaped—had deliberately left behind, not only for their own sake, but to allow the planet to heal from the ravages inflicted by humankind. She'd always wondered how the Exodus of hundreds of thousands of beings could make any real difference when *billions* had remained. Yet, through the passage of centuries, her people had watched from above, and their plan had not changed. And now her own generation had grown up knowing that the return to the home world would occur within their lifetime.

That was why the *Tantas* had been bred—why Natira and a select number of her contemporaries had been genetically altered to equip them with stronger bones and muscles.

Such abnormality had been distressing enough in early school when other children had called her "fat one" and worse; but in her teen years it had been devastating to feel like a cow beside more slim and graceful classmates, helplessly enduring the boys' barely hidden smiles at her expanding chest and hips. More and more she'd avoided social gatherings of any kind. There were private clubs for Big Ones, but she could never bring herself to join one. Instead, her studies were her refuge, and her academic achievements her vindication.

It wasn't enough to be genetically designed to survive conditions on Earth—she'd worked to make sure that her credentials would earn her a place among the returning host. As her list of accolades grew, Basu Hind had taken her as a protégé. There had never been any question that he would lead the Earth mission. Though not a *Tantum* himself, he had undergone substantial DNA modification over the years to prepare him, and he would have the best technological support that Telluria could offer.

As if Hind's patronage hadn't brought her enough attention, her reclusive youth was irrevocably ended by a shocking development when she turned twenty. At her entrée into adult society, she had been claimed by the Celestia clan—the leading family of Telluria, and therefore all the colonies. No longer Natira Tellurian, among thousands given that generic surname at birth, she became Natira Celestia, *de facto* member of the ruling class, with full entitlements!

A recommendation from Hind had prompted Confederacy Central Communications to give her a chance as a video presenter; and within five years, she'd become one of their most recognized hosts.

Yet, even her sudden gain in social status from the infotainment limelight hadn't prepared her for the next shock: the romantic attentions of Valenti Oliver and an eventual inter-family commitment contract with one of the most promising young men of the Helios family operations. That he would be attracted to a Big One, let alone choose her as his Intended, still surpassed her understanding. It was that, more than anything else, that made her suspect that, as an embryo, she had been secretly encoded with Celestia familial genes.

Valenti hadn't been pleased to learn that she would be going to Earth for an extended stay; but to his credit, he hadn't tried to change her mind either. After all, her ambition had never been a secret. Given the smallest opportunity, she'd bend anyone's ear with her speculations about the planet of their origin. Rolled eyes and yawns had taught her some restraint, but it was hard.

The swelling Earth drew her attention again, its horizon spreading outward and upward like the rim of a gigantic bowl. The mosaic landscape didn't look ruined to her eyes. Maybe it truly had regenerated itself over five hundred years. Only minutes from landing, there was still no sign of a settlement. Dark land below—an emerald patchwork threaded with brown and grey—displayed holes of deep navy that faded to silver in the distance.

Lakes, she realized. Hundreds . . . thousands of them, most of which would make even the Great Central Reservoir on Telluria Secundus look like a pond. Suddenly, it came to her that the expanse of blue she'd been seeing along the horizon to her right was not one of the oceans, as she'd thought, but something Hind had called a *Great* Lake—a body with the surface area of a small moon, yet filled with fresh water. She shuddered in amazement. The Halo shield that enclosed the Tellurian colonies like a vast bubble held many millions of liters of water, but here were quantities far greater just strewn profligately over the countryside. In the open air. Unused and unneeded by anyone.

That single revelation more than any other brought home the mind-boggling culture shift ahead of her.

In contrast, her first sight of an Earth settlement was a severe disappointment.

She'd known that there were no longer any megacities such as those in ancient accounts, but the Allocation of Borealis was little more than a wart on the face of the forest. Without navigational assistance from the NEO station in orbit they would never have found such an insignificant blot. As the shuttle eased lower, she saw living quarters that looked like square healing pads leaned against each other, as if slapped over raised wounds. The only construction of any size was the long, flat rectangle of the processing facility known as a Depot. A small scout shuttle was already on its roof, and hers glided alongside to a landing.

Basu Hind touched the restraint foam of his seat and it subsided.

"Remember to stay alert for any signs of aggression," he said. "Our scouts have been watching and will have us under close surveillance at all times, but there will be a lot to look at. Don't let it distract you from being cautious." His last words seemed directed at Natira, and he gave her a smile. "I'll speak to the crowd from up here first; and if everything still looks welcoming, we'll go down among the people for a short visit. Let's impress the void out of them. Just keep a hand close to your shield activator. Here, breathe this." He passed through the cabin and sprayed a cloud of mist in front of each from a small cylinder. They inhaled it deeply. Natira felt a powerful tingle in her nasal passages.

"Germ shield?" asked one of the guards.

"That's part of it," Hind said with a lopsided grin.

With the opening of the shuttle door, Natira gasped.

Cold. Noise. *Smells.*

Cool moisture penetrated the light weave of her sleeves as they flapped in the light breeze. The fabric responded with an automatic rise in temperature that she hoped would be

43

enough to keep her from shivering. She didn't want anyone to think she was nervous or afraid.

By reflex, she put a hand to her nose. She couldn't fully identify any of the myriad odors, though some were almost certainly from vegetation, like the complex fragrance of the broad lawns of Sola Park and the great gardens of Capita Palace where she'd sometimes sifted rich soil through her fingers. Except this was a miasma that clung to the linings of her nostrils, and she tried without success to snort it out. She very much hoped the sourness wasn't the smell of the people themselves.

She shared a glance with Jalu Drake, Hind's first assistant. His arched eyebrows and the hand over his lower face mirrored her own. Hind shot them a frown.

"Imagine it without the nose spray," he muttered.

Chirps and chatters, buzzes and complicated strings of musical notes floated on the air. She realized that it was the sound of wild birds, responding to spring's warmth after the northern hemisphere's winter.

But the pleasant sounds were drowned out by a surge of rumblings and rustlings from the crowd itself—unbridled voices full of expectation. Clearly some had seen her group appear out of the shuttle.

Hind led his entourage slowly toward the edge of the roof in a shallow V-formation, a guard at either end.

Natira's first in-person view of the populace made her heart shrink. Cameras hadn't captured the grime on faces, or the slouch of shoulders. Expressions matched the dullness of their clothes, many of which showed ragged edges and obvious holes. Why? The Depot would recycle worn clothing and provide new apparel free of charge. There was no reason to wear anything damaged. Did they simply not care about their appearance? Yet most of the people had some form of adornment on their clothes. Maybe that was the answer. While the clothes themselves could easily be replaced, the individual enhancements required labor, or currency, or both.

A wave of restlessness spread through the crowd, accompanied by another swell of sound. Natira looked over the upturned faces. One very dark woman with white hair stood tall near the front, flanked on either side by men who didn't match her proud posture. That woman would draw eyes anywhere with the kind of classic beauty Natira had hoped to see in abundance on Earth, though not very evident in this gathering. Near the dark woman was a tall young man with black, shoulder-length hair and well-formed features. He seemed worth a longer look too, until Natira noticed that his clothing was among the dirtiest, heavily soiled up to his knees, and with splotches of filth all over. Did these people have no sense of *ceremony*?

She deliberately caught the young man's eye and was gratified to see how quickly he turned his face away.

Basu Hind raised his hands and the crowd fell silent.

"People of Borealis, and all our cousins of Earth . . . it is *good to be back among you!*"

The response was a roar of approval.

In one sentence Hind had answered their three most urgent concerns: he'd confirmed that he and his companions were human, that they were indeed colonists returned, and that they had not developed an incomprehensible language in the intervening half-millennium. Hind's rich voice filled the town.

"Yes, we are your cousins, the descendants of those colonists who left this planet five hundred years ago for your sake and for ours. Our forebears promised to return, because Earth is the ancestral home of us all. Well, now we have returned, and we have returned to *stay!*"

Another cheer. People hopped up and down in excitement, waving their arms and reaching out to *touch* each other. Some of them even embraced! Natira felt her throat tighten. All of these people surely could not be so intimate. It must be the delirium of the moment.

"My name is Basu Hind. I've been given the very great honor to be named ambassador to this part of the Earth on behalf of the Confederacy of Colonies. That's what we call

45

ourselves, we who live in communities near the Moon, on Mars, in the asteroid belt, and on the moons of Jupiter and Saturn. We live in peace and harmony *out there* . . . " he waved a hand skyward, ". . . under local administrations but one central government. I represent that government; but more than that, I represent a people . . . a people who have never forgotten where we came from and have always intended to rejoin you, our cousins . . . No—our *brothers and sisters* here on this beautiful Earth. That day has finally come!"

His arms shot above his head, and the accompanying roar was the loudest yet. Hind was a consummate orator, and this speech was his masterwork. Within minutes, he had measured his audience and told them exactly what they wanted to hear.

He told them more: about how ships had landed in a number of the most prominent Allocations of each continent; but even where they had not landed, his words were still being heard in the same NorthAm language from the Depots of every community. He told them about how each and every town would be visited in coming months and would be asked to accept a permanent contingent of colonists among them. And about how outstanding citizens of Earth would be invited to visit the colonies of their brothers and sisters in the sky.

There was a rustle of special excitement at that news.

Natira's eyes had again found the young man in filthy clothes. He'd disappeared for a time, but now the dark woman at the front had pulled him up beside her and was *holding his arm!* Could she be his mother? Natira knew that Earth people still bred directly and often kept their genetic offspring close, but there was no family resemblance that she could see. And she was certain that this woman must be a notable of the town. Surely a leader would not permit a member of her own family to present a disrespectful appearance at such a momentous event.

The man's face snapped upward at the mention of citizen-visits to Telluria.

Please no, she thought. *Not that one!*

She became aware that Hind had stopped talking and was looking at her. He exchanged nods with each of their group. They moved to the edge of the roof. Natira swept her left arm up her side and, as one, the five Confederacy citizens stepped out onto the air and slowly floated to the ground.

There was a collective gasp like a gust of wind and the crowd surged back, bumping into each other. A few fell over. Everyone else stood with their mouths open, some with pleasure, others in fear. All in awe.

Or nearly all. The dark woman just smiled knowingly. The dirty young man looked excited but not truly surprised. Natira wondered about that, but then thought it probably wasn't significant. She drew her arm down her side because her feet weren't making full contact with the ground. The lift vests worn under their clothing were controlled by a sweep of the left arm up or down, and adjusting their power would take practice.

At least, she wouldn't need a vest wherever the Confederacy constructed its Earth bases, and hadn't needed it on the Depot rooftop because a more elegant and comfortable technology was already in place. The bone structure of *Tantas* like her was augmented with millions of nano-modules of metal coated to keep them from interacting with her tissue, and these nano-modules reacted to installed repulsion fields to help to support her body against Earth's pull.

Eventually she would try to acclimate her genetically enhanced body to the full force of gravity. But not today.

Today was for showing off.

Hind immediately stepped toward the dark woman, his glowing clothes making her own light-colored robes look dingy. But if she felt outclassed, she didn't show it. The two bowed very formally, each for an exact and proper length of time, followed by an extended series of bows and exchanges of names among the three official Confederacy representatives and at least a dozen Earth elders, while the two Tellurian guards stood silently alert. Natira couldn't hope to remember the strange names, but there would be time to go over the vid recordings later.

To her dismay, she found the dark woman approaching her with the dirty young man in tow. Natira pretended to be distracted by something to her left, and then was saved by Hind himself who appeared beside her and indicated with a gesture that they would be pleased to enjoy a tour of the town core.

There were walkable spaces between buildings, but they could not be called streets, with no pavement but packed dirt.

The miserable dwellings she'd seen during the landing looked worse up close, their walls no more than bare sheets of plasticwood with no faux-brick or stone texture or even variations of color to relieve their drabness. The buildings were smaller than Natira's own rooms—single dwellings then, she assumed, despite what her research had said. As with the garments, there was some personalization among the lodgings, although a closer look revealed that the colorful circles, flowers, and vine motifs had been used to cover chips, holes, and long cracks in the walls. Was she imagining the slight movement of some of the rooftops? Surely they weren't *fabric*? The roofs of some of the largest structures appeared to be a kind of sunbaked tile. People had climbed onto them to get a better view, and she fervently hoped the structures were more solid than they looked.

And while her eyes were raised, she slipped on a patch of wet ground.

She tried to convince herself that it was mud, though the aroma reminded her of school trips to the agricultural bubbles beyond Telluria Prime's main habitat and a descriptive word she'd never understood before: *earthy*. Yes, this was a smell that was unquestionably *of the Earth* and nowhere else, probably because of the greater quantity of organic molecules than in the sanitized soil of the colonies. The scent wasn't wholly unpleasant. Much better than the acrid stink that came from the more muscular Earth men, and its mustier counterpart from the elderly. She was thankful again for Hind's protective nose spray.

The assault of a new stench made her recoil. Some thickly furred four-legged animals were tethered to a nearby hut. *Dogs*, she perceived, but not like any she'd ever seen. In Telluria dogs were hairless and fit in the palms of the most wealthy. These were not toys. The wall of the hut bore hundreds of deep scratches. One animal dug idly in the dirt, while another gnawed at something unrecognizable that might once have been alive.

"Wet dog," Hind muttered near her ear, unable to keep his hand from under his nose. "It truly is . . . indescribable."

It was clear that Natira's most intense experience of this place would come through her nostrils. The myriad sounds had fused into a cacophony, and the sights of the village provided no stimulation, only dreary sameness that included the faces. The anthropologists had been right: Five hundred years of indiscriminate interbreeding had brought about a homogeneity of racial characteristics beyond that found even in the Jovian moon colonies. She saw very few variations of skin color or eye shape. Some of the lighter hair shades included a reddish tinge, but dark hair was predominant and there were no blonds.

The dirty young man, only a few meters away, had eyes of a startling blue, more vivid even than her own, but he appeared to be the only one.

She tried to focus on the words that passed between the female elder—Momo . . . something—and Basu Hind.

". . . build a complex of your own?" the woman was asking.

"With your help we'll choose a section of land right away and clear it to make a landing area for our shuttle craft," Hind replied. "We don't want to keep landing on the Depot—that would be too disruptive to your community."

"And your own official residence? We would gladly make a dwelling available to you in this area, near our own."

"I'm honored by your thoughtfulness, but I'll live at the landing site. I don't want to interfere with your own government or inconvenience your elders in any way, I assure you."

Natira suspected Hind was as horrified as she would be at the thought of taking up residence in one of these hovels. From the knowing smile on the face of the old woman, she'd seen past Hind's conciliatory words but didn't take offense.

"For now," Hind continued, heading off further offers, "there are facilities for sleeping on our spacecraft. It will take us some time to fully adjust to Earth gravity, to the temperature and moisture content of the air, and other things. I'm sure you understand."

What Natira understood was that she'd be sharing a spaceship cabin with six men. Hind hadn't told her anything about that; but she should have guessed. It wouldn't be for long, though. No doubt hab modules were already on their way from Telluria.

Her thoughts were shattered by a harsh clatter from above. Before she could react, a male voice cried, "Look out!" and she was knocked sprawling into the dirt. Cries of shock and alarm mixed with a cascade of crashes and a heavy *thud*.

Dust filled her nose. She snorted, spat out dirt, then spat more frantically as awareness returned. The clattering noise had stopped. She blinked her eyes open.

There was a man arched over her, so close she could feel his breath. She screamed, saw that it was the filthy young man, and screamed again.

He clambered off her and rolled to his feet. A circle of concerned faces surrounded her as one of the Tellurian guards ran up. The blue-eyed young man reached down to grab her hand and she cried out again.

"Sorry! I'm sorry!" he blurted and backed away.

The face of Basu Hind appeared over her, filled with alarm and something more.

The lift vest was no help as she struggled to her feet, trying not to picture what she looked like with her hair and clothes askew. There might even be mud on her face! She wiped her sleeves over it, just in case.

"Why . . . why did he do that to me?" she gasped in horror, unable to fight the rictus of disgust as her lips pulled back from her teeth.

The woman elder bowed deeply.

"Our most profound apologies," she said breathlessly. "A man on the roof lost his grip and began to slide, knocking loose some of the roof tiles. Killian thought you would be hit. He tried to shield you." Her arm swept out and Natira could see scattered shards of broken clay tiles. A hazard for certain, but they would have missed her. Barely. The thought of the grimy man touching her was mortifying, and her face burned with shame.

Hind's expression was tightly under control. He wouldn't meet her eyes.

Instead, he proclaimed that his superiors were waiting for a report, so the Confederacy citizens would return to their shuttle for a short time. Numbly, she followed her companions back to the Depot, the roof, and into the ship. No one spoke. Everyone gathered near the rear of the craft to give Hind some privacy for a muttered report via the NEO station above.

When Hind, Drake, and the two guards went back out later in the afternoon for a meeting in one of the nearby dwellings, Natira wasn't invited. She almost wished the shuttle pilots would ask what had happened so she could at least defend herself to someone. She couldn't free her mind of the image of the man arched over her on hands and knees.

Heartsick, she reclined her flight chair and closed her eyes.

An aroma of cooked vegetables and curry roused her sometime later, but conversation stalled when she approached the floating table, so she took her meal back to her seat.

The night that followed was endless, her mind reliving her moment of humiliation over and over again before finally surrendering to exhausted sleep just before dawn.

Awakening with a start, she sat up to find Hind in the next seat facing her. They were alone. The look on his face was like a fist around her heart.

"I'm sorry," he said. "There's nothing I can do."

"About what?"

He looked away. "The Patriarch has ordered you home. He feels . . . your continued involvement in the mission would be harmful."

"What! Why? Because I was knocked down? How does that harm the mission?"

"It was a sign of weakness. You know how important it is to establish ourselves as benevolent caretakers to a planet of needy primitives. Like parents to awkward children. To affirm with our superior technology that we are superior. And then you let them see you knocked to the ground by some buffoon in muddy clothes."

"It wasn't my fault!"

He shrugged. "No one else received that kind of treatment. The man saw you as a female needing protection—it's their way. Clearly it was a mistake to bring a woman—I take responsibility for that. I should have understood their culture better."

"Their community leader is a woman."

He glared at her. "Your own Patriarch has ordered you to return. Gather your things and report to the scout ship. They'll take you home." He turned away. "I only hope my plan hasn't been completely ruined."

For a moment her hurt turned to fury, but she bit back angry words and stalked across the floor to retrieve her bag.

Not even the view of the receding Earth could draw her attention from her pain.

The dream was lost.

Her life's greatest moment had been shattered by a primitive brute who probably didn't even have the capacity to understand what he'd done.

As the stars began to appear, they dissolved behind a veil of tears.

6

A crack in the brown plasticwood wall admitted a ray of golden sunset light in the shape of a lightning bolt.

Killian barely noticed, his eyes unfocused, as he faced a corner of the hut. The wooden-slat floor his father had built so many years before bruised his anklebones as he sat cross-legged; but he relished the pain, and dug his fingernails into his thighs to produce more. If only physical pain could eclipse the mental kind.

"It ain't your fault," Grandmother said for the fifth or sixth time. "Go find Barton tomorrow and take it out on his hide—that'll make you feel better."

As unpardonable as it was that Barton had chosen that one disastrous moment to slide off the roof, giving him a beating wouldn't change anything. Killian had only his own clumsiness to blame, though he couldn't possibly have known how horribly offended the colonist woman would be. Maybe colonists were fragile, and she'd been hurt by the fall. But it was more than that. The mere thought of his touch had been loathsome to her.

Regardless of who was at fault, the punishment was all his. His lifelong dream that the colonists would recognize a kindred spirit and take him to live in the sky was over, destroyed in an instant. Himself disgraced, Momoko Quarry—his whole community—embarrassed and dishonored.

"The elders will not blame you," his mother said as if reading his mind.

For the first time, he noticed that, although Grandmother paced the floor in agitation, Summer, his mother, stayed seated, looking as if she didn't have the energy to do more.

"Who else would they blame? Barton? He didn't actually touch anyone. The tiles would have missed her. I just overreacted and ruined everything."

"You put your body in harm's way to protect the woman. In my day that would've earned you a kiss at least." Grandmother snickered.

"Not if you were pushed into the mud."

He saw again the look the blond woman gave him: fury and disgust—a look reserved for vermin. Nothing in his life had so quickly put him in his place.

He should go. Somewhere. Anywhere. The destination could hardly matter anymore.

There was a light gasp from behind him. His mother had her hand pressed against her side.

"Summer? Is something wrong?"

His mother wore an expression like someone caught in a lie. His grandmother looked worried.

"What is it? What are you not telling me? Is it worse than I thought? Have the elders already sent someone to make us leave town?"

"No!" Grandmother hissed. "It's not about you. It's *not* always about you." She gave Summer an apologetic look, then turned quickly toward the door as if to hide her face. "It's the wasting disease."

Killian's breath failed. He looked at his mother. She couldn't meet his eyes.

"No," he said. "You can't be sure."

"Sure as snow in winter," Grandmother replied, her voice cracking. "Seen it often enough."

He hurried to his mother's side and gently lifted her face. "How long have you been sick?"

"A few months." She shrugged. "Worse now, though. And I'm tired . . . tired all the time."

54

His burning anger at himself turned to fingers of ice wrapping around his stomach.

The townspeople could depend on the Depot for almost everything, including medicine. But not for the wasting disease. Sometimes it began as a lump, sometimes as a rough patch of skin, but the end result was always the same: a body consumed from within, and a terrible, drawn-out death. He should have suspected right away when he'd seen how thin she'd become, but he'd only been thinking about himself.

The colonists....

"They must have a medicine for this by now in the colonies," he said. "They'll know how to cure you. I'll go to elder Quarry right away." He started for the door.

"I thought you were sure she'd have nothing more to do with you."

"I'll beg her forgiveness if I have to. Anyway, as you said, it's not about me. Mother and father have done a lot for the people here—they're the next thing to the elders themselves, and Grandfather was chief elder for years. Of course, elder Quarry will ask the people from the Confederacy for help." He tried to ignore their exchange of glances as he left.

Quarry lived in one of the oversized shacks with red tile roofs closest to the Depot, though not the one whose loose tiles had caused Killian's grief.

As he approached the building, he heard cries like shrieks of pain. He broke into a run and flung the door open.

Even in the dim light his mistake was instantly obvious.

Three women were gathered around a bed on which lay a fourth, who was the source of the cries.

She was in labor.

The women snapped their heads toward the interloper at the door. The tallest, Momoko Quarry herself, shielded her eyes from the light from the door, and then gave a look of chagrin, thrusting her hands onto her hips.

"Killian Morningcloud, of all people! What in the world would bring you charging in here? Don't tell me you're the father of my granddaughter's baby."

Stunned, he was able to blurt an honest denial. In fact, Killian and Asha were old friends and had enjoyed sex a few times, but not within the past couple of years.

Whoever the father was, the man's reputation was made. Although the women of Borealis had no trouble getting pregnant, only about one in twenty were able to carry babies to term. When they succeeded, the credit, strangely, went to the father, who was praised for his tenacious "swimmers."

"Well now that you're here, make yourself useful and go fetch a couple of buckets of water," Quarry ordered. He nodded quickly and fled in the direction of the nearest community well.

Returning with the buckets, Killian was surprised to find a lot of water on the floor already. Then, with a lurch of his stomach, he realized that it wasn't water. He tried desperately to remember what else was involved when a woman gave birth. Not that he needed to know—the women in attendance had the situation well in hand. He set the buckets down near the bed and turned for the door.

"No, you don't," Quarry said to him. "It's about time you young men had a look at what you put women through, even if you're not the father this time. Come here and hold Asha's hand."

Killian was stunned that no one asked Asha's opinion, but he did as he was told, and as he entwined his fingers with hers, she gave him a flash of a smile before the next contraction began.

The half-hour that followed left a series of impressions seared into his brain: dark skin and dark blood; the odors of sweat and rust; sighs, cries, and grunts.

It was the most disturbing, frightening, uplifting and electrifying event of his life—a grueling ordeal that appeared in every way to parallel death, and yet its conclusion was life. New life!

Tears spilled from his wide eyes as one of the women lifted the newborn from the sodden space between Asha's legs and rested it on the new mother's chest. The tiny being was a mucus-and-blood-smeared mess, its skin the dark red of trauma and as wrinkled as an old man's. It kicked and squalled in outrage before its mother's caresses began to calm it.

"A little boy," the woman in charge declared. "With good strong lungs, too."

A good portion of Borealis had probably heard his arrival into the world. The squawks and yelps had set the local dogs to barking.

"Have you chosen a name?" the new great-grandmother asked.

Asha poured a look of purest love upon her child and then gave Killian a smile.

"Cloud," she said.

Momoko Quarry's slitted eyes made Killian laugh in protest.

"He's not my child! Really." He reached out to rub a knuckle against the little boy's cheek and said quietly, "Though I might wish he was."

He took a tiny hand between his finger and thumb. "Nice to meet you, Cloud."

It was only much later, as he was preparing to leave that he remembered what he'd come for, astonished that something so important could slip his mind.

Feeling awkward, he asked Chief Elder Quarry to give him a moment and explained about
Summer's illness. Quarry immediately agreed to ask the colonists for their help.

But when Killian returned the following day, he read the answer in her face as he knelt on one knee before her.

"I'm sorry, Killian. They said their treatment for the wasting disease is very complex and doesn't always work. Sometimes it makes things worse. They're afraid that if they give the medicine to someone like your mother and she died, our people might not trust them anymore, and they want our trust very badly."

"So instead, we can't trust them to help us!"

Quarry grasped his shoulder, stooping a little while he stayed on one knee.

"I'm sure they want to help. Maybe if it had happened a few months from now once they've had a chance to test us with their medical equipment . . . ."

"We're the same race! We can't have changed that much in five hundred years."

"You don't know that. They've been living in space, with less gravity, filtered air, different food and water. We've been exposed to the natural sunlight, breathing air and drinking water that may not have cleansed itself even after all these centuries. There was good reason for them to leave, you know. Humans had spoiled the Earth."

He looked into her dark liquid eyes. He'd always thought of her as wise, but did she have secret knowledge, too? That wasn't hard to believe, given her position.

"Maybe it's because of me," he said, clenching his teeth. "Embarrassing that light-haired woman yesterday. This is their way of punishing me."

"No! I don't . . . no, I'm sure they wouldn't do that. It's very important to them that our young people look up to them and want to work with them. And no one has been more enthusiastic about that than you, Killian. I told them so. You're just the kind of person they need right now to set an example for others. They would help if they could be sure of making your mother better—I know they would."

She gripped his other shoulder and guided him to his feet, his eyes only slightly above the level of her own. Her voice softened. "I will ask again in the coming days. Perhaps there will be a way to test the medicine a little at a time, or maybe they have something that can help your mother last longer . . . until they can be more confident about a permanent cure."

Yes, Killian thought, that was the best chance. If they wouldn't cure her outright, he would find a way to buy her more time and ease her pain. Whatever it took, he would at least do that.

# # #

For five days, time stalled—he had no place to go, nothing meaningful to do. The driving force of his life had evaporated. Yet his five days of darkness made the next step clear.

He had come to accept the fact that he was a nobody—he didn't matter to the town, the world, the universe. He would never be taken by the Confederacy to live amid the vastness of space; and if he died or was exiled from his people for the rest of his life, it would bring grief to his family but no real loss to anyone.

His mother, on the other hand, was a force for good. She counselled those facing hardship and pain and gave people reason to carry on when their own eyes saw only blackness ahead. She had prevented countless lost souls, many young but also many old, from taking their own lives, Killian included. When he had first gone to the secret school to learn about the colonists, the knowledge had left him feeling so terribly inferior that he'd wanted to die.

The people of Borealis had a special name for such self-destruction—it was called *"starwalking"*. Yet, it had been Killian's longing for the stars that had made him want to kill himself.

Summer had convinced him that his life would serve a great purpose one day, and he'd come to believe that it was connected to the return of the colonists.

If that belief had been mistaken, it was his mistake, not hers.

Disease must not take her from their people.

His own life was not too large a price to pay for hers.

#   #   #

Confederacy forces had easily negotiated a property arrangement with the town elders and cleared a large patch of forest about a half-hour walk to the west of Borealis. They'd chosen a site atop a high rise of ground with a small cliff at one edge, as if wanting a good view of the town at all times; though perhaps it just made it easier for their flying craft to avoid trees as they approached to land. The entire crown of the hill had been covered with a flat grey pad. Workers who had sprayed the pad onto the ground from large drums were able to walk over its surface only minutes later, carrying slim rods as if the objects would somehow tell them if their work had been done right. Within another twenty minutes a ship had landed, larger than the earlier shuttles; and from it crew carried a ball the height of a man that took on the colors of the landscape behind it. Placed toward one end of the pad, the ball inflated like a bubble with a flat bottom, growing until it was twice as tall as any hut in Borealis and even wider than its height. Men and women carried long shafts of a springy material into it through a wedge-shaped opening. After dozens of such trips, small sections of the bubble surface had grown transparent, like windows, but too high from the ground. Then Killian saw a face at a window and understood that the balloon structure included a second living space above the first one! He'd never seen such a thing before.

For most of a day he watched from the shadows of the brush that ringed the new launchpad, matching the arch of his body to a tree or bush. And although he could stay still for hours while observing deer or moose, the colonist workers became aware of him. Often one would stop, hold a small rod in the air, and then look straight at him. He knew better than to react, but he felt like a raccoon caught in torchlight while scavenging garbage.

At least they made no move to chase him away.

After a few days of steady work, the new settlement included four large bubble buildings, six smaller ones, and two or three spacecraft at any given time. The Confederacy citizens who stayed at the base did most of their tasks on the ground floor of the large bubbles but went to the upper floors after dark when the high windows appeared, and light spilled out. It seemed that they chose the loftier spaces for sleeping. Maybe that was natural for a people who lived in great cities that floated in the sky.

Killian remembered times that he'd spent the night in trees while traveling, as protection against prowling animals or a sudden flood. He'd never been able to sleep up there.

Twice during the landing pad's construction, he saw workers injured by debris, or caught by some of the grey spray blown off-target by a sudden gust of wind. The victims quickly went to the farthest of the four main buildings. If there were healers present, that was where they must be, and with them their medicines.

Killian made his choice. If the Confederacy would not give its medicine, he would have to take it. If he was wrong about that hut and it contained no cure, he would find a way to get aboard one of the spacecraft and go where it went. If he didn't recognize the cure when he saw it, he would make someone tell him. But he would not fail his mother.

Glancing at the sky, he knew that the clouds overhead were the long-lasting kind that would fill the sky all night. The Moon would set early.

Conditions would be perfect for his plan.

7

He'd meant to save a life, not to take one.

In the feeble light of pre-dawn, it was just possible to distinguish a darker shadow against the leaden landscape below him—a thing of motion that would move no more; a shadow that had been a man only moments before.

Murder had been the farthest thing from Killian's mind, but he'd been surprised in the worst possible place by a guard who must not have known how close they were to the cliff edge. Even Killian hadn't realized how far their grappling in the dirt had carried them; until, as each combatant tried to regain his feet, he had kicked out in desperation.

He'd heard the dull *crump* before he'd even noticed that his opponent was gone.

Lookout Cliff was not tall, but more than enough to snap the fragile thread of a human life.

The guard was dead—dead at Killian's hands. That appalling moment of realization would reverberate through Killian's mind for the rest of his life.

He stumbled halfway home in a daze before skidding to a halt and sprinting back to the cliff in the growing morning light. With some pine boughs cut well away from the cliff edge, he hurriedly swept the clifftop to remove the signs of struggle as well as his own tracks. He left the footprints of the dead guard untouched and muddled the ground that led right to the brink. There was just a chance that searchers would believe the man had unwittingly walked off the cliff in the darkness. At least they should have no proof of anything else.

But he would know, and others would guess.

Now Killian was a death-bringer, an assassin. Killian the Killer. And surely, soon, an outcast.

He would never go into space.

He would not get medicine for his mother. He had sacrificed his future for her, and now she would die anyway.

He should go to Momoko Quarry and confess his crime.

Would she exile him from their community according to the ways of their people? Or would she hand him over to the visitors—the ones he had wronged? He could no longer think of them as cousins. They were a superior race. But maybe that meant that their justice would be superior, too; that it would include mercy, at least enough compassion to let him care for his mother while she lived.

What if it didn't? Who would carry Summer from place to place when she could no longer carry herself?

Whatever punishment Killian suffered for his crime, it would not bring the dead guard back to life. And it truly had been an accident—if he had known that his plan would carry such a price, he could not have attempted it.

Would the authorities accept that?

No.

And it would benefit no one for him to sacrifice himself.

He returned to Summer's home as the sun rose, and said nothing.

# # #

When Killian was eleven or twelve years old, he and his friends had reveled in the giant snow drifts that the wind sculpted at the foot of Lookout Cliff. They'd taken running leaps from the cliff at the north end where it was only about six meters high, confident that the deep snow would cushion their fall. If you hit the drift on its downslope, the slide would reduce the impact even more, but if you overshot, you broke a leg.

The sickening lurch in his stomach at the beginning of each leap was something he never forgot.

Exactly the same feeling hit him that afternoon as he opened the door of his mother's hut and saw three uniformed men standing outside.

8

A glorious two-tone expanse of sea and sky filled Natira's eyes as the spacecraft climbed beyond the atmosphere. She felt like a microorganism in a drop of water, infinitely small and insignificant.

The black edge of space coalesced out of the haze, and she hung over a gigantic dome of swirling gauze: brown clay, and blue satin rimmed by flashing scales of silver reflecting the sun.

Gradually, the memory faded, and she blinked back tears as her mind returned to the present. Her eyes still rested on a half-lit Earth, but it was now only the distant ball viewed from one of the many observation galleries in the outer hull of Telluria Prime's vast cylinder.

Her throat ached with the beauty of that wonderful memory, and the understanding that she'd come to treasure that radiant blue orb more than ever, now that it was barred to her.

With a breath like a sob, she moved out of the glow toward the elevator that would return her to the cylinder's interior and the living spaces that had always been her home. A technician already stood inside and triggered the elevator mechanism for her. She offered him a practiced smile, then turned away to hide what she was really feeling.

Only a week earlier, she'd been on a marvelous pilgrimage.

How could such dazzling promise have turned into disaster so quickly?

All her adult life she had studied the Earth: its geography and geology, its weather patterns and water cycle, but most of all, its people and their history. It was her history too, though as far removed from the reality of her life as the home planet was by physical distance.

Raised like every other Tellurian child by a series of instructor holograms, one of her earliest memories was of running along a pathway in Sola Park, tripping and skinning her knee. The arms of Teacher Science had wrapped around her in an offering of comfort, a hand passed over her cheek as if to wipe away a tear—but there had been no actual touch, no touch at all. When she'd first heard about the primitives left on Earth who grew up knowing their parent, or maybe even two, she'd actually envied them. Then, as a teenager, she'd been taught the horrific reality of what mothers endured, carrying a whole person within their swollen bellies, and finally expelling them in a gruesome ordeal of blood and pain. A child surely must be marked by such trauma.

Natira's entry into the universe certainly wasn't traumatic, but she had often been lonely because of abilities that made other children avoid or mock her. That hadn't changed until her teen years when she was able to escape general studies and mediocre classmates and work with others who were equally gifted, led by brilliant mentors like Basu Hind.

He had personally chosen her to be his student, had stimulated her, challenged her, enthralled, and inspired her. Selected her to be his second assistant on Earth!

And it had all crashed down in one catastrophic moment.

No matter how many times the event replayed in her mind, she could make no sense of it.

The farce of fallen tiles, and a bedraggled crowd that had witnessed it, had no place in her conception of Earth. Those people were a grotesque antithesis of the noble primitives she had studied through stories and legends recorded centuries ago and validated by time: accounts of great actions, sacrifices, and battles won and lost. Surely those were the true barometers of a people's character. They were the reason the history and customs of Earth had become her life's work, both as a researcher, and then, as the return to Earth neared, in her role as a video presenter. When her supervisor at the CCC had approached her to prepare a series of programs about the people of the home planet, she'd readily agreed. Her small team of technicians had produced the main framework of six episodes based on her research, confident that they could be completed and distributed as soon as real footage from the ambassador's expedition was available.

It was only sheer, incomprehensible bad luck that the inhabitants of Borealis had been such a disappointment. Especially *that one*.

So much work would be wasted, and her reputation badly bruised, unless she could somehow find the *authentic* people of Earth.

Basu Hind had always laughingly insisted that such noble savages were no more—that Earth life no longer offered any challenges or conflicts to mold the natives in such a way.

If conflict were the crucible for character, such a crucible had cooled now that there were no more great battles. After the colonists' departure, the human population on Earth had plunged. In fewer than a hundred years, the inhabitants of flooded coasts, sand-scoured farmlands, and sunbaked, smog-smothered deserts of asphalt and concrete had all been forced to flee to the Allocations prepared for them, where all their needs were provided for. In fact, the Depot synth-factories were able to produce far more food and other goods than the shrunken populace needed.

The Depots and the pre-fabricated housing that accompanied them had been deliberately located great distances from each other to prevent territorial disputes. The result had been widespread peace, though some researchers weren't convinced that such peace was entirely a good thing.

According to Hind, with the loss of all necessity to fight nature or each other, the refugees had lost all of their ambition too.

The examples Natira had encountered in Borealis certainly seemed to bear that out. But they couldn't represent the whole population of Earth. She refused to believe that all humans had fallen so far. Had lost their proud heritage. Eagles in Telluria's zero-gravity zoo might molt, but did not lose their wings.

The people of the natural Earth had to have developed an intrinsic wisdom, and a bond with their mother planet that could not be so quickly set aside, she was certain. Such qualities would endure, if not in the Allocations, then perhaps among those few individuals who led deliberately isolated lives in the forests and hills. There were some, she knew. She had to find them. She *had* to.

But returning to Earth would not be easy. Her degradation at the hands of the muddy man not only reflected badly on Ambassador Hind but also on the Celestia family. Hind might forgive her, especially if his next weeks among the natives were fruitful, but her adoptive father, Patriarch Benjamin Tempest Celestia, was not so tolerant of failure. The family of the Confederacy's Prime Councilor had to be held to the highest standard.

Natira had always accepted that—had taken great pride in it. Being chosen to join the ruling family of Telluria at the age of twenty had been her life's brightest moment.

Would her acclaim among both the intelligentsia and the general public be enough to outweigh this one shameful setback? She didn't know the Patriarch well enough to answer that, despite living as his adoptive daughter.

She thought back to her first-ever encounter with the great man seven years earlier, on the day after her public claiming by the Celestias.

It was an unsettling memory. Part of her still wanted to believe that she must somehow have misunderstood the situation, unlikely as that was.

Family retainers had come to take her to the family baths and aesthetorium, where attendants had made her vibrantly clean with sonics as well as water, and then radiantly beautiful with exotic skin treatments, cosmetics, and a stunning outfit of color-shifting fabrics. The new clothing did not include any undergarments, and the one-piece leotard featured sheer panels that would have exposed her breasts and lower abdomen if not for a simple tunic worn over it, held closed by a single fastener. When she was finally brought before the Patriarch, she had never felt less scholarly. More like an offering.

The attendants quickly left them alone in the audience chamber. The Patriarch lounged in a single high-backed chair on a raised dais and invited her to sit on one of the thick cushions near his feet. She had expected to find him in a formal suit typical of Council meetings, but instead he wore a casual knee-length robe over bare legs and sandals. He made small talk, asking questions about her background and her work, the answers to which he'd certainly already been told. She answered efficiently, keeping any unseemly pride from her voice, and expressed her thanks for the Patriarch's implied support of her research as well as her video duties.

Then he invited her to move closer, to the space between his outspread feet, and made a comment about her exceptional beauty. Her stomach did a flip, but she saw no way to politely refuse. He casually loosened the tie that fastened his robe. Swallowing hard, she turned away, pretending not to notice, and contrived long answers to his half-hearted questions about her professional ambitions. She talked about the research that gave her life meaning and found herself trying to make it sound as boring as possible in the desperate hope that the tactic would bring their meeting to a swift end.

It didn't work.

The Patriarch gave a heavy sigh and shifted on his chair. She tried not to imagine what the movement might have revealed. Even then, the man did not dismiss her. After another deep sigh, he interrupted her mid-sentence and told her to stand before him. She did so, snapping her chin upward as her peripheral vision caught pale flesh tones below his waist. She'd deliberately stayed just outside his reach, but he stood to face her, and with a motion so swift she barely saw it, he unfastened and opened her own tunic. Cool air flowed through sheer fabric over the damp skin of her breasts and the tops of her thighs, and without thought her hands snatched the tunic closed.

"Your excellency!" she gasped. "I'm so ashamed that I permitted the staff to dress me in such a fashion, completely unworthy of a meeting with our Prime Councilor. I believed they were trying to keep me cool, but I should have realized the mistake and insisted on something appropriate, even underneath my tunic. Please forgive me. I'll remove myself from your presence immediately."

Without giving him a chance to respond, she bowed deeply and backed away, nearly breaking into a run as she approached the doors. In the hall outside, a lone retainer looked at her in astonishment but said nothing. After an awkward hesitation, he imperiously beckoned for her to follow him, and led her to a small anteroom where he left her alone on a short settee.

Heart pounding as if she'd run a race, she tried to make sense of what had just happened. Even with her lack of sexual experience, she couldn't have mistaken the Patriarch's intent. And while it surely was the highest flattery that he would be interested in her that way, Natira racked her brain to think of anything she had done to encourage him. Her clothing was certainly provocative, but it hadn't been her choice and was hardly typical. And his own attire seemed intended to facilitate sex.

Sex in person. Skin on skin!

She shuddered.

Were all new members of the family expected to submit to that? Or was Natira indeed exceptional in her beauty, and impossible to resist?

Nonsense. A man such as the Patriarch would be surrounded by beautiful women night and day. It was ridiculous to think that she would stand out among them.

A rite of passage, then. And she had rebuffed him. What would be the consequences of that? It was too much to expect him to be fooled by her dumb act.

She chewed at her lip, tasting the bitterness of the lip gloss. The opening of the anteroom door made her jump.

Through it strode a woman dressed in a deep blue pantsuit of the most gorgeous silken fabric Natira had ever seen. Her passage made her sleeves and leggings flutter like the wings of songbirds, and somehow their looseness emphasized her lithe form more effectively than tighter clothing would have. She came to a stop in front of Natira with hands clasped behind her back, accentuating perfect curves of waist and hips.

Natira's new 'mother', Matriarch Marissa Florentina Celestia.

There was nothing authoritarian about the Matriarch's stance, but Natira braced herself for an angry reprimand.

The woman slid gently onto the settee.

"You're Natira, our newest daughter. I've been so eager to meet you. And such a beauty, too." There was no insincerity in her voice. Her hand floated through the air over Natira's long hair, but didn't touch, though their hips were close enough that Natira could feel the other woman's warmth, and every breath brought a scent of clean skin with the subtlest hint of a flower garden.

Incredibly, the Matriarch made no mention of her husband and the debacle of moments earlier. Instead, she asked casual questions, nearly identical to those the Patriarch had asked, but in a tone of genuine interest; and she truly seemed to listen to Natira's answers.

Occasionally she would shift her position with the effortless grace of a sleek black panther Natira once had seen in a video. The silken leg touched the fabric of Natira's own tunic. She tried to edge away, covering the movement with an elaborate scratch of her knee. The Matriarch responded by leaning forward to adjust the cloth over her own ankle. The folded fabric of her top puckered open, giving Natira a generous view of smooth, tanned breasts exposed almost to the nipples. When the woman raised her head, her lips were only a hand's width from Natira's own.

Natira stood, then sat again, then jumped to her feet, babbling something that she could never remember afterward. What she did remember was the Matriarch's explosive laugh of surprise and amusement. There was no malice in it, but Natira still burned with shame to recall it.

Her escape—you couldn't call it anything else—was the worst moment of her life, at least until her recent humiliation in Borealis. She later heard that her adoptive parents had gleefully related the episodes to their friends, excusing her clumsy naiveté with the explanation that she was a 'Big One', as if her genetically enhanced physical body had been at the expense of her brain.

Deeply offensive as that was, their amusement had allowed her to escape the dual seduction without retribution, for which she was willing to swallow her pride.

Were Benjamin and Marissa typical of their peers in the Council of Five? She fervently hoped not. Maybe they were so libidinous that any novel sexual partner was irresistible. More likely, it was their bizarre way to establish a newcomer's place in the hierarchy; although to insist on *actual skin contact* was to reduce the sex partner to the level of a slave. Little more than property.

Natira preferred to believe that other members of the Tellurian leader class were not so debauched as her adoptive parents appeared to be, but she had no illusions that they represented the human race's brightest and best. After abandoning Earth, the leaders of her people had turned the race's energies toward material wealth and comfort, sacrificing a more pure search for knowledge. There had been no great adventures for discovery's sake alone; no outreach beyond the home solar system at all. The outer colonies were still mining colonies, first and foremost, existing to provide goods and gadgetry rather than to further any human destiny. Natira had recognized that at an early age, and the understanding still filled her with regret. She had been forced to hope that the noblest strain of humanity must yet be found on Earth, where humankind still struggled against a harsh environment without advanced technology.

Now, she shuddered at the memory of the dull and dirty sampling of humanity she had seen in Borealis. But she refused to abandon her belief in a subset of humankind refined by hardship.

She had to find those people. She had to go back. But how?

It would require powerful propaganda to erase the ignominy of being ordered home. And powerful leverage to overturn the decree.

Political leverage?

Personal?

Her throat tightened and her breath caught.

Could the mysterious data archive she'd found be the instrument she needed?

She still didn't want to believe that her report about the archive had anything to do with her being chosen for the Earth mission, but there was no question that the subject had made both Hind and the Prime Councilor uncomfortable. Would a subtle reminder convince them to send her back to Earth as a means to keep her from pursuing her discovery any further?

But an assignment to Mars or the Moon would serve that purpose just as well!

No, her knowledge of the archive's existence alone would not be enough. She would have to learn what was in it, and hope its secrets were valuable enough to be used as bargaining chips.

Could she do that? Could she really coerce two of the most powerful men in the human universe?

Her shudder made the technician across the elevator give her a strange look.

9

Killian felt his knees about to give way as he stared at the three uniformed colonists outside the doorway of his mother's home.

"Killian Morningcloud? I'm Captain Christopher. May I speak with you?" This tallest and oldest of the three men was certainly their leader. The other two gave Killian probing looks then turned their attention elsewhere, as if they expected trouble.

Who would dare cause trouble for a colonist? he thought, and then remembered a dark form at the bottom of a cliff.

"Is . . . something wrong?"

"We hope not. Do you know of something wrong?"

Hesitating a fraction too long, Killian shook his head. The pause that followed was awkward. To break it, he stepped toward the men, feeling a moment of alarm as the two subordinates reacted by stepping toward him. He swallowed and turned slightly to close the door behind him.

"My mother is sick. I don't want to wake her up. Let's talk across the way, there." He pointed. Christopher nodded, but neither of his companions moved until Killian did.

He stopped about ten meters away, conscious of the colonists behind him. Putting on a smile he hoped was welcoming, he turned to face them.

"What do you want to talk about? Is it about my mother—have your people decided to give her medicine?"

"No, that's not our department. The ambassador wants to meet you. We've been .. .asked to bring you to him. To invite you, that is." Christopher's mouth puckered as if the words tasted sour, although it may have been from the slight gust of breeze that brought with it the smell of the toilets. "Are you willing to come?"

Killian's stomach took another twist, but he simply shrugged and said, "Sure."

The officer's eyebrows furrowed as if he expected more enthusiasm, or maybe just more formality, then he turned and began to walk. Killian followed, but he would have felt better if the other two hadn't fallen in behind him. That was the way people were marched to the elders when they got into trouble. People would wonder what he'd done to anger the visitors, or maybe they would assume it was the result of his gaffe with the colonist woman on the day of their arrival.

That might be true, no matter what Christopher said. If so, it would still be better than the other reason they might have come for him.

He tried hard to remember the ambassador's name but couldn't. It was lost in the chaotic memory of that day.

Within a few minutes they reached The Road, which extended through much of Borealis past the Depot and out to the fringes. Confederacy forces had parked a large object there, shaped like a stretched egg. A uniformed woman stood guard next to it. As she saw Christopher's party approach with Killian, she straightened. Tall, and as bulky as the men, she might have been pretty if not for the sour expression on her face.

Killian mentally kicked himself for even thinking of her as a woman. That was a direction his thoughts must not go, as a toad must not think of a swan in case he ended up as lunch. Instead, he looked more closely at the egg. Its shape wasn't the only unusual thing about it. He bent over to look beneath it.

Nothing was holding the object above the ground!

Technology—that was the school word for things colonists made that worked like magic. It was no more surprising than craft that were able to fly, but he still found himself staring.

Portions of the shell slid open to reveal seats inside. Captain Christopher swept an arm toward them, but it took Killian a moment to understand what the man wanted him to do. He couldn't bring himself to move. With another frown, Christopher gestured at the woman, who looked uncomfortable as she stepped ahead of Killian and beckoned him to follow her in.

With a deep breath, he copied her motions and discovered that the cushion was softer than anything he'd ever sat on. He slid a little farther, which made the woman recoil against the far wall. Did all Confederacy women have such a revulsion toward Earth men? Or maybe not just the women. One of the men sat beside Killian but was careful to keep a half-meter of space between them.

The egg held another long seat with its back to him. There was no sign of the ambassador. Perhaps they were waiting for him to arrive.

Without warning, Killian felt his body pressed into the seat back.

The egg was moving. It was a vehicle!

Of course it was. Why else would it be on The Road?

Was he about to be carried off into the sky? He swallowed a surge of nausea and breathed hard through his nose, but there was no sensation of upward motion. Instead, the egg gently rose and fell and rocked very slightly, as if following an uneven surface.

So it was a ground vehicle. He'd learned about them at the Tech school, though the ones he'd seen in pictures had wheels and were called *cars*. His people had adopted that name for the small-wheeled carts that Killian and others pulled in exchange for goods or favors, transporting people who weren't strong enough to walk across town or to the nearest craft village. This car without wheels would almost certainly be taking him to the Confederacy settlement.

He clenched his lower abdomen and forced himself to smile at the woman beside him. She looked straight ahead, as if he wasn't there.

Hyper-awareness made the trip of a few minutes seem endless. He wished for windows and tried to picture landmarks along the route. The dryness of his throat made him cough, and the man and woman on either side of him shrank even farther away. He badly wanted to learn more about these people, but a closer study would clearly not be welcome; so he looked around the vehicle's interior instead.

The inner lining was a glossy pale-yellow material that he thought might be softer than plasticwood—certainly not metal. It had a fabric-like texture, but there were no loose threads, or tears, or even scuffs. It was seamless, too—he couldn't tell how the seats were attached to the vehicle because they looked to be all one piece with the walls. In the front of the egg there were some flashes of color that repeated in individual sequences, but he couldn't distinguish any overall pattern.

His ears strained for sounds. Was that a soft hiss in the background? Or was his mind only creating it to fill the silence?

The smell was odd, too. He took a slow, deep breath into his nostrils. The faint odor was a little like the scent of new clothing from the Depot, but somehow even more unnatural. There was a faint trace reminiscent of his uncle's homemade alcohol, and a subtle tang like hot plasticwood. As his nose processed those, he became newly aware of the musky smell of his own clothing. Perhaps that was why the colonists kept their distance from him. He could detect very little aroma from them, only a slightly sweet breath smell, along with an impression of soap. The woman smelled no different from the men and he wondered what that meant.

Their arrival at the base was anti-climactic. After a sudden stop, the doors slid open and everyone got out. Without words, his companions walked him to the farthest of the buildings, the one he'd planned to investigate two nights earlier—the healer's hut.

He took a sharp look around the moment they entered but was disappointed. A narrow corridor stretched ahead of them, but anything of interest was hidden behind its walls. Doors were marked by symbols that might reveal the purpose of the rooms behind them but the markings were meaningless to him. If he had managed to get this far on his own, he would have been hard-pressed to find what he was looking for.

Captain Christopher led the way to a flight of twelve stairs. The only other place Killian had seen more than four stairs at once was in the hut of an eccentric teacher who had built a small space on his roof from which he looked at the night sky through a tube-like thing he called a telescope. A few Borealans had built flat sections of roof on their huts for lying in the sun, but they used ladders to reach them.

There was a door at the top of these stairs. Christopher knocked on it, received an answering sound, and beckoned for Killian to enter as the door slid open.

The room inside was enormous—it must have taken up half of the upper level of the building. Cream walls were bordered in a dusty pink that took on a golden hue wherever it reflected more light. The floor was a uniform light grey and looked soft, like moss. Illumination seemed to come from the whole ceiling and not from the huge windows. He stared at those windows—he was certain there had been none in the building when he'd approached it. The buildings never showed windows in the daytime, and only rectangles of light in the dark hours. Yet now he could look toward the east and see the rooftops of Borealis in the distance.

For such a large room, the furnishings were few, including some that Killian couldn't recognize. One tall box was open at the front, showing shelves that held small rectangles standing on end. Those were in all colors, but most were dark, and he couldn't begin to guess their purpose. Other tall boxes had doors of their own as if to keep the contents hidden. In one of the near corners was a structure of bars at various heights with a sloping pad underneath that looked about the width of a man's stride.

At the far wall sat a large tabletop with the space beneath it enclosed by what looked like an imitation of wood, and there was only one chair pulled up to it from behind. Other chairs sat a meter-and-a-half in front of the table; and near one of the windows on the east side were two cushioned benches a little like the ones in the car that had brought him, as well as a pair of single padded chairs. The chairs and benches all had raised parts at the sides. Killian had seen such a thing at the home of an elder once, and again at the hut of an old carver. So, the person who used this room needed support for his arms. The ambassador, almost certainly. That could explain all the padding, too—old bones were brittle. Or possibly the arms of Mother Earth pulled harder than those of the stars.

A man entered through the opposite wall and Killian had a glimpse of blue beyond the door but nothing else. He recognized the ambassador and tried again to remember his name as the man approached.

"Mr. Morningcloud? I'm Basu Hind. I'm very pleased that you could come." He gave a slight nod of his head and Killian responded with a full bow.

The man's hair was white but abundant and healthy, and his light brown face had almost no wrinkles. Perhaps he wasn't as old as the leaders of Killian's people—he walked without any obvious pain, though his movements were otherwise spare and efficient like an elder's. He wore a loose-fitting garment that appeared to be one piece, covered by a long open cloak or robe, all in white with gold trim that sparkled when light caught it. Not for the first time, Killian reflected that such perfect white fabric without dirt or blemish would be impossible to find in Borealis. Its perfection spoke of power, prestige . . . a whole new level of authority.

Borealis's elders made a ritual greeting of clasping a visitor's right hand in both of theirs. This man kept his hands at his sides. Was it a deliberate rebuff?

"Am I in trouble?" Killian asked.

"Is there a reason you would be in trouble?" The man's mouth formed a gentle smile, but his eyes were half-closed, reminding Killian of a wildcat stalking prey. Yes, there was a reason—the worst reason of all—but Killian wasn't about to volunteer that information. Let them accuse him if they would. But perhaps he could deflect that line of thought.

"Maybe because of the woman. When I tried to protect her from the falling roof tiles. Was she hurt?"

"No. She was . . . unused to such rough treatment, but not injured."

"I only meant to keep her from being hurt. Could I apologize to her?" Killian had no real desire to debase himself again, but the gesture needed to be made.

"She's not here. She . . . chose to return to our home. You caused her to lose face—do you know what that means?"

"No."

"She was embarrassed. She believed your people would no longer respect her, so there was no point in her continuing to stay here. She very much wanted to stay." Hind's voice was like one of the teachers at the Tech school who tried to make Killian feel bad because he was bigger than the other students and tackled them effortlessly in kickball.

Remembering the look of disgust on the woman's face, he couldn't bring himself to feel sorry for her, but wondered if he was expected to make some kind of restitution. In Borealis, someone who had wronged another could be ordered to compensate the victim with goods or service.

"If I can make it up to her in some way, I will do so."

The ambassador's eyebrows rose, and his eyes widened a little. "Yes . . . . Yes, maybe you can."

The simple words were without menace, but Killian's throat tightened. He muttered, "Maybe it was not a good choice for her to come to Earth. Many things might be hurtful for those who don't know how to recognize the hazards."

"Indeed. One of our people lost his life only two days ago while guarding this compound."

There it was. Killian waited for the words that would condemn him. Should he appear shocked by the news? He didn't think he could make that believable. Instead, he frowned with real concern.

"There are dangerous animals in the bush, and they're hungry in the spring as they awaken from winter's sleep."

"This wasn't an animal attack. Or not a forest animal, anyway." Hind had a very mobile face that might have been showing regret, amusement, or something entirely different. He turned toward the window and rested a hand on the back of a chair, putting some weight on it. Perhaps it wasn't just a gesture, but a necessity—an older man not willing to show weakness to a younger one.

"This is a friendly meeting, I hope, Mr. Morningcloud. Please sit and be comfortable."

Reluctantly, Killian moved to one of the padded chairs and sank so deeply into it that for a breathless moment he thought it was a trap and he would fall through into a position of helplessness. He hoped his face hadn't betrayed his foolishness. The absurd softness wasn't comfortable and getting back up would require a real effort.

Basu Hind settled into the chair opposite with evident pleasure.

"Do you have any idea why I've asked you to meet with me?"

"I hoped you might have changed your mind about the medicine for my mother."

"No, I can't do that."

"Then I do not know."

"Elder Quarry thinks very highly of you."

"Elder Quarry is very gracious. She believes I should learn things I need to become a leader of our community when I am older."

"And isn't that something you want?"

Killian hesitated. He had no desire to confess his dreams to this man who could only be amused by them. But then, those dreams had been dashed and only time would take the pain away. The sooner he faced that fact, the sooner the healing could begin.

"I had . . ." He stopped to clear his throat. "I had hoped to learn about your ways—in the colonies—and perhaps be accepted to live and work there."

"To become a Confederacy citizen?" The pale eyebrows reached higher than before. There was amusement in the corners of Hind's mouth, but also something like pity in his eyes, which was more hurtful. "Well, to be honest, I don't know if such a thing has ever been discussed. But what if you could learn about the colonies and still become a leader of your people? That would be better, wouldn't it . . . for all of us?"

"I don't understand."

"We want to have a long and fruitful relationship with your people that will benefit all. Sharing and trading." Hind waved a hand toward the window and suddenly it wasn't a window anymore—the view of sky and forest became a flat grey sheet with horizontal lines of oddly-shaped marks across it, broken up by a few designs of straight and curved lines that might be very simple drawings of objects, though nothing Killian recognized. His bewilderment must have been obvious.

"Aah," said Hind. He leaned toward Killian in a posture of intimacy. "You can't read, can you? They don't teach reading anymore in your schools?"

"My father's father says that when he was a child there was a teacher who made marks that stood for words. There are marks like that on the Depot, too, but large."

"Yes, instructions. And warnings. The marks do stand for words, and numbers of things, too. What happened to the language teacher?"

Killian shrugged. "One day he did not appear at school, and he never came again."

Hind gave a thoughtful nod. "The hologram generator failed. Yes, we've heard about that in other Allocations as well. Some of them lost all their teachers. Five hundred years is a long time. How many of yours are still working?"

"The last time I was in school Teacher Math was there, and Teacher Geography. Teacher Arts would sometimes tell us stories, but then act as if she expected us to know many others, and she would draw on a screen once in a while, but never showed us how she did it. Teacher Science only talked nonsense—no one could understand it, so we left school whenever he came."

He said nothing about the special school he'd attended as a teenager, where records about the colonists were taught by real people. He had once been eager to show off the things he'd learned there, but that was before he saw the floating car and the buildings that grew themselves, with windows that really weren't. He hadn't learned about those, and now began to wonder what other gaps there were in his knowledge.

"It's regrettable that some of the systems failed over the years," the ambassador said, "but you're still young—you can still learn many things. And that's essential for the leaders of people. Humans fear what we don't know, and it's very important that your people know they have nothing to fear from us."

The words surprised Killian. He had never connected the colonists with feelings of fear until he had committed a crime against them. But he knew people who feared *technology* and the changes the Confederacy was sure to bring. His grandfather. His aunt and uncle. They certainly didn't trust the colonists to want what was best for the people of the Earth.

Teacher Arts had sometimes said that knowledge was the enemy of fear. Killian had never really understood that until now.

The ambassador waved his hand again, finishing with a supple curl of his fingers. The grey screen went blank, but in front of it spun a blue and white globe in mid-air. Killian had seen something like it before in Teacher Geography's class: a representation of the Earth. This globe was much more detailed, though. He could see that the white patches were clouds, and they moved over the blue and brown surfaces beneath. It made his breath catch.

"Yes, it's the Earth," Hind said. "And the moon would be over here." He stretched to the limit of his reach and seemed to pluck a grey-brown ball from nothingness and hang it in the air. After a few moments, Killian could see it move, just as the Earth globe was spinning.

"The Moon travels around the Earth in this direction." Hind gestured. "And following the Moon on the same path it takes and at the same distance from the Earth . . ." A shiny marble appeared a couple of arm lengths from the Moon, glowing with its own light. Hind reached toward it and spread his finger and thumb. The Earth and Moon shrank until they vanished, but the marble grew until it was a gleaming bubble the size the Earth globe had been, and kept growing until Killian felt he had fallen into the bubble and its skin had joined with the walls of the room. Now other large globes floated around him, many of them with reflective upper halves and dark bottoms; but what held his attention was a giant cylinder almost the size of a man. It was covered by wide bands of dull grey alternating with equal stripes of vivid blue that extended from end to end, and it was rotating along its length.

He gasped. The blue bands were windows! Through them he could see patches of green and brown as well as blue, and irregular shapes of gleaming white.

"Telluria," Hind said softly. "Telluria Prime, in fact. My home. There are four other colonies very much like her that float together forever, like children holding hands in a circle. There are farm and factory globes nearby . . . power stations, too. I thought you might like to see where we come from."

Killian tried to speak but couldn't. He only nodded, unable to look away from the magical vision conjured for him. But surely it had to be a creation painted by some artist—the real thing could not be so glorious. Then he saw a tiny white speck like a dandelion seed that moved on its own toward the near end of the cylinder.

"A shuttle," the ambassador said, amusement returning to his voice. "The very same kind that carried Natira home. That's the name of the woman you . . . embarrassed." Killian turned toward him, fighting hard to close his gaping mouth. Hind laughed. "Yes, you're seeing it as it's happening, right now. Actually a few seconds ago, but we won't get into that. So . . . what do you think?"

No words Killian knew could do it justice. Finally, he said, "I've imagined it so many times. but it was nothing like this."

"And . . . ?"

Killian's thoughts ran like tree sap in the winter, so very slow. Again, he felt his unworthiness.

"You really can't guess why I've asked you here?"

He shook his head helplessly.

"I want you to go there." Hind pointed. "To Telluria Prime. I'm offering you a chance to visit a colony to see it for yourself."

10

Killian trudged right past his mother's shack after the egg-car dropped him off. Trying to shake away a dense mental fog, he looked around in confusion, then retraced his steps. At the entrance, he took a moment to stand straight and take a deep breath before pushing through the door.

The startled faces of his Uncle Lewis and Aunt Regina looked up at him. Regina and his mother held each other, just separating from an embrace.

Then, Summer wrapped him in a hug, and it hurt to feel how frail she was.

"What happened? We heard that the colonists took you away."

"Yes, it's . . . I'll explain in a minute. Aunt. Uncle. What brought you here?"

"You left in such a hurry, without preparation. And then the storm came. Your Aunt Regina was worried." Lewis cleared his throat. "Then Jacob told us Summer was sick." He reached out to give her shoulder a gentle squeeze. Although Jacob was Killian's father, there were no distinctions of blood within the family. Summer had always been treated like a sister by birth.

Killian nodded. "I've been trying to get medicine for her from the colonists. They won't give her any because they aren't sure it will work on one of us."

The women lowered their heads, but Lewis's face turned grim. "As I've said, they are not gods. And they do not care about us." Although Lewis wasn't as outspoken on the subject as Grandfather, even the smallest mention of the colonists was enough to bring out an uncharacteristic bitterness inside the man. Killian was sure there must be a story behind it, but knew nothing more.

"Is that why they came to take you?" his mother asked, her face creased with concern.

"No, although I did ask again. It was . . . ." Killian badly needed to sit, but that would be disrespectful to the elders in the room while they still stood. "The ambassador sent for me. They want some Earth people to come to one of their colonies—to see how much they have to offer us." He bobbed his head. "He invited me."

"Oh, no!" Summer brought a hand to her mouth. "They won't take you from me! Will they?"

"Just what you always wanted," Lewis rumbled. "To leave us all and become one of them."

"No! It would only be for a short time. A visit. Just long enough to see some things."

"*Things* that will make you even more unhappy with your life here," Grandmother muttered, and turned to the bed to sit down. "Why you? I thought you insulted their woman."

"I don't know why. Maybe Elder Quarry suggested it—they seem to listen to her. After what happened the other day . . ."

"Jacob told us about that," Regina said. "It's the talk of the town. And all you did was try to protect the woman. Surely that should tell you how different we are. Why it's not a good idea to become too close to them, or to think they could ever be your friends."

"You don't understand."

"How soon would you go?" his mother asked in a soft voice.

"Soon. Tomorrow, perhaps." He swallowed as he saw dismay in her face.

"So that's why you're not jumping for joy. Because you know you'll be leaving your mother when she needs you the most."

"Lewis!"

"It's true. Look at his face. Since he was a boy, he's thought that the best thing that could ever happen to him would be to go out *there*, to one of their colonies, and forget that he was born on Earth. Now he has a chance, and yet he has the look of a beaten dog. Suddenly the wonderful colonists aren't the perfect beings he thought they were—they want him to abandon you in your last days."

"What do you know?" Killian snapped.

Except his uncle's words had hit the mark. It had not occurred to him that the price of going among the colonists would be to leave his mother when she had so little time left.

Unless . . . .

What if he could still save her?

He would be going to Telluria—the capital of the colonies, the heart of their technology. *And their advanced medicine.*

He'd tried and failed to steal the cure his mother needed. Now the colonists were offering to take him to the very place he might succeed.

"I know more than you, nephew," Lewis replied, though in a gentler voice.

"Why have you and Aunt Regina always hated the colonists so much? They've never done anything to you personally. Whatever they did to the Earth, that was five hundred years ago, and our ancestors were just as guilty! These are different people. What gives you the right to say they're evil? You can't know that."

Lewis glared back and seemed about to answer when Regina gave him a hard look. He dropped his eyes and spoke quietly, "That's not something I can say."

"Of course. Because there *is* nothing to say."

Killian turned to his mother and took her hands. "I'll only be gone for a short time. A week or two, probably. I will come back." He waited for her to give a little nod, then turned his head. "But I can't stay here right now."

He kissed her cheek and stalked out of the hut.

# # #

All but one of the confederacy shuttle's eighteen seats were full when Killian climbed aboard, occupied by people from other Allocations. Borealis was the last stop before the spacecraft set its course beyond Earth.

Though not as ridiculously soft as the ambassador's chairs, the shuttle seating was shaped to support every curve and hollow of the human body. Its covering was not skin from any animal, and odd spots of different texture and strange shades of orange seemed placed for a purpose, but an unknowable one. Few of the occupants could sit still for very long anyway.

The last available seat was beside a young woman who wasn't quite pretty but had an impressive figure. He refrained from staring, though, since her face already wore a scowl she probably put on just to discourage anyone from sitting beside her.

Two of the people in the craft were obviously colonists, with slender frames and silver clothes exactly alike. One was a flat-chested woman who came to stand beside him. In an equally flat voice, she instructed him that something called a *restraint field* was controlled by moving his left hand along the edge of his seat, and a *vomit funnel* could be pulled to his mouth from the back of the seat in front of him. Then she returned to her own seat at the front of the row, and the white-haired man in front of Killian turned around to give him a smile.

"The restraint field is some colonist magic that holds you in the chair, and the funnel is in case you feel sick and have to throw up," the man explained. "I was the first one to get aboard—I've heard the explanation more than a few times." He lowered his voice to a whisper. "Before she began to cut it short." He winked.

Killian thanked him but was shocked that the journey would be rough enough to make someone throw up. He vowed it would not happen to him. He glanced at the woman beside him and caught her eyeing her own funnel.

Across the aisle was a thin girl, barely more than a teenager, who looked scared to death. Another two or three people might have been in their thirties. The rest were all quite a bit older—elders of their communities, probably. Killian wondered why Momoko Quarry hadn't arranged an invitation for herself—why she would feel that it was more important for Killian to have the experience.

All the passengers were nervous, some giving themselves away by appearing too calm. One heavyset man had his eyes closed and was snoring softly, but Killian didn't believe the act. Anyone willing to take a journey beyond the Earth's atmosphere would be excited about the prospect, even if they'd already flown across half a continent.

While they waited for the craft to launch, a few people were talking. To try to distract the frightened girl, Killian asked her where she was from.

"Rillya," she said. "My name's Jee-an."

He'd heard of that Allocation. It was many days' travel south of Borealis, on the northern edge of an uninhabited zone once called Tronna, devastated by plagues in the first century after the Divide.

"How were you chosen for this?" he asked.

"My mother is our head elder. She insisted, and she always gets her way. Especially with me." Her eyes became glassy, and she shuddered, then looked at him and giggled. "I don't want to be here. I smoked some weeds before I came, but that's already wearing off."

"Don't be scared. The colonists must travel like this all the time and they're no different from us, in spite of how they look." An inner voice denied his words. What if Confederacy citizens had become so used to space travel that they were no longer even aware of effects that might hurt a human from Earth?

The white-haired man in front of him was listening to the conversation.

"My name's Raymen," he said. "An elder from Minnsoda. We have so many elders, they were glad to get rid of me." His laugh was infectious. "I promised them to find out if there

90

really is a Man in the Moon. Plus, I heard that, out in the colonies, you're not weighed down, so you can fly like a bird. I always wanted to fly."

"It's called zero gravity." The woman next to Killian made her words sound sullen, as if annoyed to have to say them. "Gravity is a force that keeps us pulled down to the Earth. Once you're out in space you're too far away for it to pull you. That's why they have restraint fields to hold us in our seats." Some of her NorthAm words were pronounced strangely with odd twists to the vowels, and her 'th' sounded more like a 'd'. She must have come from an Allocation very far away.

"Ya mean we'd fly around the spacecraft?" Raymen asked. "I just might shut mine off and give that a try later."

"Please don't," came a voice from the front. It was the colonist woman.

Raymen gave a sheepish look and dropped his voice. "Maybe they have better hearing than us. Or maybe we old guys just talk too loud."

Suddenly the blank walls on either side of them lit up, filled with an enormous vista of brown and green below them and shades of blue above. Windows, like the ones in the ambassador's room, Killian realized. Someone had just decided to turn them on, revealing the craft to be already well above the ground, suspended between Earth and stars.

There were gasps from every direction. Jee-an frantically reached for her funnel and threw up, then leaned back, her face white and her eyes closed. But everyone else eagerly shifted position to get a better view.

Killian found he was holding his breath, and released it in a whistle of amazement. He'd stood on cliffs much higher than Lookout Cliff and never got tired of seeing huts like pillboxes and people the size of beetles. But this . . . . He couldn't make out any detail at all. It was if he was standing on a bald hillock and someone had thrown buckets of mud and pond scum over the ground below, poured melted clods of clay over parts of it and then scattered scraps of blue and silver cloth everywhere else. He must be looking at the Earth from high above, but he couldn't make the vision real in his brain.

The green areas . . . those must be forests broken up by rocky outcrops and chiseled gorges. So, the patches of silver and blue . . . could they be lakes? They were so small. But if that true, Borealis itself would be much too tiny to see, even if he knew where to look. For the first time, he felt a moment of dizziness and a twitch in his stomach. Yet he had no fear of falling—the perspective was too alien for his mind to connect it with danger.

The view blanked out for a minute or two, replaced by a flat color a little lighter than the grey of the craft's walls. Then, with a brightness that hurt his eyes, blue sky returned in the top half of the windows. Below it lay a landscape of white, as if the whole world had instantly been buried beneath a hundred meters of snow. There were hills and valleys, plains and rifts, alternating patches of dazzling sunlight and blue-grey shadow.

"A cloud," he breathed, and heard Jee-an throwing up again.

Stunned, Killian watched as the cloudscape became more distant, and finally he could see around it again to the ground and water beyond. But what arrested his attention was the horizon. It showed an unmistakable curve. Above the far distant land surface was a hazy band of white topped by increasingly darker shades of blue, and the canopy overhead was now nearly black.

Space.

He truly was leaving the Earth.

His stomach did another flip—he fought to ignore it. Twisting his head, he saw the colonist at the back of the other row casually reading from a rectangle of words that floated in the air in front of his face and paying no attention to the scene outside. If that man had no concern, then Killian would not give in to fear either. He turned back to the window view and told himself to enjoy the changing vista, as the rich blue darkened and pinpoints of brightness appeared amid the blanket of midnight.

Stars—they had to be. Changing the tilt of his head, he thought he could make out shapes he recognized: the bear, the hunter, a few others. Yes, this was the night sky he'd always known, except that these stars did not sparkle. Maybe it was only natural that they would lose some of their mystery as he ventured among them, and with it, their spark. He was no longer a simple man of Earth: He was a voyager of space and must see its splendors with new eyes. The thought made his chest swell and his throat tighten.

"Shit! I think I missed the funnel. Does anyone have a cloth?"

Jee-an's tiny voice made Killian laugh—he couldn't help it; and the hurt look on her face only made him laugh harder.

Raymen passed a kerchief to her, and she half-heartedly rubbed at her shirt, occasionally glaring at Killian. The sour woman next to him cuffed him on the side of the head.

"Asshole!"

He laughed harder still, and gasped apologies when he could catch his breath. Finally, the fit subsided and he tried to tell Jee-an that he was truly sorry, but she wouldn't look at him.

"Asshole," he heard again.

"I didn't mean it. It's all . . . too strange, I guess." He twisted toward his name-calling neighbor prepared to offer her an apology, too. Instead, he just said, "My name's Killian. From Borealis. What's yours?"

He'd begun to think she wasn't going to answer, when she said, "I'm from Kaybekwest. My name is Aylenn." She crossed her arms. "Quit staring at my tits."

"What? I . . ."

"Don't bother saying it. All men stare. You should have seen the first colonists I met—you'd have thought I'd grown another head below my chin." Suddenly she laughed, and her surly face was transformed. Maybe she was pretty, after all.

"Fair's fair," she said. "I did my share of staring at you."

"What do you mean?"

"Ah, you're one of those guys, eh?"

"What guys?" Killian frowned.

"The kind who doesn't notice that girls go fawn-eyed over him."

He snorted. "I notice . . . sometimes. But whatever they think about the way I look, I know I'm not what they're imagining. They'd be disappointed."

Her eyes narrowed with skepticism, but she didn't look away. Feeling himself begin to blush, Killian searched for a way to change the subject.

"Do you know a lot about colonist things, like that zero..."

"Zero gravity," she said. "I don't know as much as I'd like—who does? But I know that our people are fools to think that the colonists have magic. It's not magic, it's science."

"I thought it was technology."

"Science is knowing how things work, and why. Technology is using what you know to make things do what you want. They have both. We have neither."

Killian objected to that, but he didn't want to reveal his secret schooling, especially not within the hearing of colonists. On the other hand, what the school had taught him were all things that the colonists had learned and developed. Did Killian's own people have any actual science of their own? He couldn't say that they did, and the thought saddened him.

Something had changed while they were talking. The windows now showed nothing but black scattered with flat, white pinpoints. They were truly in space. His stomach felt strange. Come to think of it, his whole body felt strange. He looked at Aylenn. Her shoulder-length hair no longer rested on her shoulders. And...

"Your breasts," he said in a whisper.

She looked down and brayed a laugh. Her ample chest was much higher than before. She pushed both breasts down with her hands, but they just bobbed very slowly. With another laugh, she did it again.

It was a struggle to pull his attention away and look around at the others. Any hair longer than a few centimeters floated lazily around heads like the petals of flowers. A tall man in the middle rose improbably high in his seat and began waving his arms as if trying to push at the air to get back down. The woman colonist sprang from her place and actually *flew* to the man, gripping the back of his seat with one hand and pushing him down with the other. She must have done something to his restraint field because he didn't rise again. But as Killian continued to watch in astonishment, there were sounds of vomiting from all around. It reminded him of the queasiness in his own stomach, and he swallowed hard.

"Zero gravity," Aylenn said with a smirk, and looked down at her chest again. "I kind of like the look, don't you?"

Killian turned away, flustered.

"It's like falling, except it doesn't end." His stomach protested again, but he remembered all the times he'd hung upside down from tree branches, swung through the air on ropes, and leapt from cliff faces into deep water. None of that had made him sick, and he wouldn't allow it to happen now. Besides, Aylenn didn't look bothered at all. It was only a kind of floating, not much different from swimming in a lake. His stomach began to settle.

"It's like my body does want to fly," Raymen said in a hushed voice.

"Well, don't, because I don't feel like being kicked in the head." Aylenn said the word like 'edd', and Killian smiled. He twisted in his seat to see how others were coping and was astonished to find that there was a window in the back wall, too. It showed a large, bright ball against a wall of black.

His breath caught. The ball must be the Earth. The world on which he'd spent his entire life, far too large for him to ever explore, was a mere bubble on the surface of a black lake—a tiny globe of milky blue and white glass set in an unthinkable vastness around it. Why was it blue? His world could not have so much water. There must be another explanation.

He thought of the Moon, much bigger than the stars, but still no larger than an apple held at arm's length. His teachers had claimed that was only because it was so very far away. He'd accepted their words without really absorbing what they meant. Could it be that the Moon was another whole world, as large as the Earth? He looked for it in the side windows but couldn't see it. The ambassador had said something about Telluria being the same distance from Earth as the Moon was, but that explanation, too, had been no more than words until now.

If it was true, then the people of the colonies always saw the Earth this way: a ball floating in the night sky like a second Moon, but with textures of vibrant blue and white.

More than anything else, that view confirmed the superiority of the colonists over his own kind. Remembering how he struggled to pull a cart along packed dirt paths to carry people from place to place, he thought of this craft, bigger than three huts, being flung in only minutes across a distance greater than he could travel in many lifetimes. And it was going to a place of wonders, created out of an emptiness so vast that whole worlds were only pebbles in comparison.

His uncle was wrong. The colonists *were* gods.

## 11

Killian's first voyage beyond Earth's sheltered garden was a transcendent experience. The magnificent void through which they were travelling conveyed the vastness of the universe as no mere description could ever have done. Yet, once distance had reduced humanity's home world to a glassy blue ball, the view did not change for many hours.

His chin had just slumped to his chest when there came an ear-splitting bang, and the interior of the shuttle was plunged into utter blackness. It only lasted a few seconds, but it took his breath away—he'd never experienced such darkness, not even on the cloudiest winter midnight. Light returned as a deep red color that almost seemed to make the compartment darker instead of illuminating it. Worse, it let him see the people around him, shock on their faces ready to become outright fear and even panic. Some were rising out of their seats, no longer held in place by colonist magic.

"*Power failure!*" cried a voice—the woman colonist. "If we start to lose air, special bags will pop out of the ceiling. Pull them over your head and press the edges as tightly as you can against the skin of your neck until it seals and sticks on its own."

Lose air? How could someone lose air?

He turned to Aylenn, but before he could ask the question, she said, "There's no air in space, you idiot. Only what we bring with us in this ship. She's saying something may have made a hole in the walls and will let the air out. I don't hear anything, though."

What was she expecting to hear, he wondered, and how could it possibly be heard over the increasingly frantic voices of the passengers? The two colonists hovered higher than the rest, waving their arms in a downward motion, but if it was an effort to calm people, it did no good. The colonist toward the back gave up and repeatedly struck a small red square on the wall with the palm of his hand. That had no effect, either.

The tall man who'd risen from his chair earlier did so again, this time banging his head. In anger, he shoved at the ceiling and came down hard on top of an elderly woman in the seat behind him. Killian heard her cry of pain, but his attention was distracted by Jee-an throwing up again. There was nothing left for her stomach to eject but the sound was contagious. Others began to vomit, desperately aiming mouths at funnels they hurriedly clutched, except the funnels weren't working, and their spasms of vomiting only served to launch them from their seats. In the lurid red light, the scene became a nightmare of bodies tumbling and twitching, while streaks and blobs of liquid sprayed through the air.

In horror, Killian heard someone choking. A white-haired man near the front frantically clutched at his throat. The woman colonist was right next to the man but clearly didn't know what to do. She twisted her head in every direction as if searching for someone to call or a panel to hit.

Uncle Lewis had once taught Killian a trick he'd claimed would save someone from choking. He tucked his feet against the chair back and launched himself through the air as if diving from a cliff. Too late, he realized that the comparison to swimming was a bad one—with no water to push against there was no way to slow down. He hit the white-haired man with more force than he intended, knocking him into the forward wall of the compartment. But as the man rebounded there was a rattling gasp, and suddenly he could breathe! The collision must have knocked something free and allowed air into his lungs.

A woman to Killian's left grabbed at her throat and her body jackknifed.

This was insane. Zero gravity was trying to kill people!

He stretched an arm toward a chair below him and accidentally grabbed the hair of a red-faced woman who screeched her objection. Finding another grip, he shoved his body through the air toward the new choking victim. Her terrified eyes locked onto his, her hands like talons as they reached for help. He used them to spin her around and their bodies came together with an audible thump. As his hands locked together against her abdomen, he gave a sharp thrust inward and up.

Nothing happened. The woman struggled to escape. In desperation, he tried again, even harder. With a wet, explosive noise her head snapped forward, followed by the harsh rasp of a sucked breath, and another, and another. She moaned and began to cry.

Killian would have stopped to comfort her, but a strangled gargling drew his attention yet again.

Raymen.

The man's thrashing arms pushed him from his chair. The compartment was already clogged with floating bodies. Two older men flailed right in front of Killian, trying unsuccessfully to regain their seats. How could he get to Raymen in time?

Then he saw *Aylenn* rise into the air. With a nod to Killian, she wrapped her arms around Raymen as if to give him a fierce hug. A cloud of something flew from the man's face, but Killian's view was blocked by two women who clumsily batted at each other for some reason.

The male colonist near him was still futilely banging at a panel in the wall.

Suddenly, white lights came back on. People reacted to the painful brightness with a collective groan and then exclamations of shock and disgust at what the lights revealed.

If they'd 'lost' any air, no-one said; but the two crew members began to shout commands to someone unseen, which triggered a sudden chill breeze through the cabin. Everything loose was sucked toward an opening in the ceiling—globules of liquid and other matter first, and then scraps of cloth people had used to clean themselves, and even a piece of fake hair from one elder's head. The wind drew hapless passengers toward the center, too, until the colonists shouted again, and the commotion stopped.

It took a long time to get everyone back into their seats. Killian managed on his own, but the woman colonist gave him a strange look as she came by to check his restraint field.

He turned his head to find Aylenn smiling at him.

"Nice trick you knew," she said. "And by the way, you can put those strong arms around me anytime."

His blush embarrassed him, but it wasn't entirely unpleasant.

Neither did he mind when other passengers began to call him Killian the Life Saver. There was honest gratitude in the nickname. It didn't erase his guilt about the life he had taken only days earlier, but it was a good feeling all the same.

12

In an artisan's village a half-day's walk from Borealis, Killian had once seen a man who made treasures out of glass. More fragile than the plasglas used for windows in Allocation housing, it had a special clarity that caught the eye and held the mind. According to one of Killian's teachers, humans had used glass in hundreds of ways in centuries past; but hardly anyone believed that, pointing out that most people rarely stumbled across more than half a dozen pieces of true glass in their lifetime. A few argued that it might be much more common in once-heavily-populated areas like Tronna, but no one ever went there to find out.

Killian had found bits of glass from time to time—most brown and one green. The artisan in the village melted such offerings down over a ferocious fire to make astonishing creations by twisting the softened material and blowing into it through a long tube. One of his unforgettable pieces—not for sale—was a globe a hand's-width across, nearly perfectly round and beautifully clear. He'd filled it with the purest water in which lay thin bits of polished metal of various colors. If you gave the globe a gentle swirl, the small amount of trapped air would foam, and the metal fragments would dance. It had held Killian's attention for so long that the artisan had finally laughed and told him he could make such a thing himself if he devoted the rest of his life to learning the skill.

Killian's first glimpse of Telluria was like that globe brought to vivid life.

Baubles danced a slow parade inside it, lit from within and sparkling like tiny stars or glowing with bands of bright blue and yellow. But somehow, he knew right away that these baubles moved with purpose, like bees in a field of clover.

That such a fragile work of art could be home to teeming thousands, he couldn't immediately accept. This place was the universe in miniature; and for a time, his mind couldn't decide whether he was seeing multi-colored candle flames floating against a blanket of black, or a manifest darkness punctured by pinpoint holes into glorious brilliance beyond.

The female colonist was suddenly happy to talk. Perhaps she hoped that showing off her home would make them forget her ineffectiveness during the power loss, and the uncomfortable fact that even colonist technology could be damaged by a pebble if its speed was great enough.

Like the glass-artisan's masterpiece, the Tellurian colony was also a globe filled with water, but only to a depth of ten meters from the outside surface, to provide protection from the harmful energy of the sun and stars. Inside the water-filled shell was an ocean of air. The small spaceship had to negotiate a complex series of tunnels past enormous baffles to make its way inside, a short distance, but one that took most of an hour to transit.

Inside the bubble floated five lozenge-shaped objects mottled with blue and green against a white background, and about a dozen balls of varying sizes. Complex mathematics and technology kept all the objects from bumping into each other. Some of the balls were farms growing food, others were processing plants that refined ores from the Moon or asteroids. Still more were *factories* that made manufactured goods—like the Depot, Killian thought. One was even dedicated to making air and water from moon dust!

Seen closer, the balls weren't complete spheres—the bottom half of most seemed to be dirt or some other solid with an upper half that was open. Killian thought they looked like boats adrift on a calm lake.

The spacecraft passed near enough to one of the globes for the passengers to make out boxy shapes and domes and tubes that twisted like snakes beneath a dingy grey-brown haze that clung to the surface. There was no sign of people. Aylenn said it was because humans didn't work there—the factories ran by themselves, like the Depots did. She didn't explain how she knew that.

Of the five enormous white-mottled lozenge shapes, one of them was more irregular than its siblings. What had first appeared to be a fuzzy covering turned out to be a grid-like cocoon with dozens, if not hundreds of small objects clustered around it. In a flash of intuition Killian asked, "Is that a new colony that's not finished yet?"

The crew-woman answered with shining eyes, "Actually it's the opposite in a way. That's Telluria Quinta, one of our five original habitats. As we became more efficient with our population control it was decided that Quinta's populace could be resettled in the other four communities so the habitat itself could be put to another purpose. It's being entirely refitted to make humankind's first colony ship to the stars!" The pride in her voice was obvious, and her audience responded with the appropriate gasps of wonder.

Killian stared wide-eyed. There before him floated the very embodiment of his childhood fantasies: to join the god-like colonists as they ventured far from mundane Earth to voyage interstellar seas. Nothing could take him farther, literally and figuratively, from old Borealis—*Boring*-alis, as his friends called it. The very stuff that dreams were made of was now so close he could almost reach out and grasp it.

His chest ached as he watched Quinta recede, but it was not their destination.

Instead, another of the lozenges grew large, revealing it to be a huge cylinder like the barrels his father and uncle made to store their home brew, except much slimmer and elongated. The end they could see had a rounded cap with a protrusion in its center that reminded Killian of a breast. He had a sudden vision of his uncle putting a big nipple on his beer keg, and had to suppress a laugh. But as their craft moved so he could see the whole length of the cylinder, he gasped.

It was just like the one he had seen in the ambassador's office, divided along its length into three solid strips of a white metal alternating with three clear strips that could only be windows. Through them he saw green landscapes with patches of blue, and thin streaks that looked like the Earth clouds he'd recently seen from above for the first time.

"Telluria Prime," announced the woman colonist. "The first of our five cylinder-colonies, and the most important. Also, the most beautiful." She went on to explain with pride that large areas of the first colony had been returned to parkland. Killian didn't know what that meant, but he did appreciate the green of growing things amid the silver-and-black-latticed places that made up most of the land area. The woman called those "cities" and said that the Earth visitors would be staying in Capita, the most prestigious one, where the government of all the Confederacy colonies made its home.

Fins like those of a fish extended outward from the "nipple" on the end of the mammoth cylinder. They reminded Killian of a windmill that one of the village elders had made to pump water. But he couldn't guess at the purpose of such a thing here. That the colonists could create something as gigantic as these cylinders and then somehow entice them to spin in a volume of air was completely beyond his comprehension.

The next few hours condensed into a series of vivid images: the cylinder growing larger and larger until the spacecraft stopped with a noticeable jerk; he and the other passengers getting out and stumbling through long tunnels brightly lit by the walls themselves, then being led into cold, clinical rooms of spotless white. There, a whole series of strange new experiences awaited them. The spacecraft crew coached them through the incomprehensible questions of three official interviews, calmed them while bizarrely shaped pieces of metal and plasticwood circled their bodies with threatening noises, separated them by sex and instructed them to remove their clothing, then hustled them through scorching, brightly-lit showers that didn't feel like water. Leaving his worn old clothes behind gave added significance to the experience—Killian's life was at a turning point. He wondered if the discards would be saved for him, and found that he didn't really want them.

Finally, the visitors were given pant suits of a rich blue to wear and an attendant pressed a device against the inside of their left forearms which left behind a small light-blue tattoo shaped like a globe. Once that was done, their trek toward the surface of the manmade world resumed.

The tunnels became crowded with people—so many people—until the flow brought them at last to a large opening and beyond.

The Tellurian sky opened to them like a lily greeting the daylight. Several of the Earth natives grabbed the arms of others for support. Three fell over.

Killian's heart raced as his eyes traced an unimaginable view—not a blue sky, nor a cloud-filled one, but *two other land masses hanging over his head!* Upside-down cities, poised to fall on him. He felt Aylenn's hand in his and clenched it tightly.

Separating the stripes of land were three bands of black that stretched away into the distance. Those must be the windows he had seen from space, except this time he was looking out into the void of space; but he could see no detail because the massive windows were bordered on each side by thin strips of incredible brightness. He'd encountered artificial lights before, especially around the Depot, but his mind was hard-pressed to associate those dim things with these ribbons of liquid sun.

And that's what they were, he realized. Sun substitutes. Although real sunlight would shine into the giant windows as Telluria Prime spun, sunbeams would sweep over the landscape much more quickly than the sun travelled over the surface of the Earth. The bright borders must be there to even out the light and keep the days to a length humans could live by.

Their widespread luminance at first kept him from seeing threads of even more intense light, drawn in perfectly straight lines from the exact center of one cylinder end to the other. These were so vivid that they left afterimages in his vision. He thought he could count five of them, and then he noticed dark objects at intervals along them, like beads on a necklace. After a few moments he could tell that the dark things were moving. Then it came to him how distant the things must be, and he realized that they had to be travelling at incredible speeds.

The whole vista made his head swim.

When he could finally pull his eyes back to ground level, he saw that his group was surrounded by buildings, but buildings as unlike those of Borealis as the spacecraft was to Killian's wheeled cart. Still bemused by the two-level huts of the colonists on Earth, he now stood before buildings that rose *ten levels and more* above the ground in shapes that ranged from rectangular blocks to cylindrical towers to swooping structures like the necks of swans. Most were in shades of white, black, or silver, and often in combinations of all three; but there was very little color. Splashes of red and yellow and purple appeared here and there, but only on ground-floor walls. Perhaps those were signs explaining what each building was, but he couldn't read them.

He glanced at Jee-Ann and Raymen standing nearby, their wide eyes and stiff bodies expressing not only wonder but fear. Was that how he looked? He consciously relaxed his muscles—he didn't want to appear like a child lost and confused among the marvels of a grown-up world. He wanted to show himself worthy of living among these people as an equal.

Strange music came from somewhere behind his left shoulder. He turned and saw a woman walk past. There was no question that the sound came from her because the air around her body pulsed in changing colors to the rhythm of the piece. The Earth people turned as one to watch her go by.

Killian noticed another woman apparently waiting for something. From a pocket she pulled a tube that looked like a bottle made of paper and gave it a squeeze. Within moments steam spurted from the spout and she tipped it to her mouth to drink.

A chime sounded and the woman bent her body to sit on the sleek outline of a chair that hadn't been there seconds before. Body and chair rose into the air a few centimeters and were suddenly surrounded by a mirror-like shell in the shape of an egg that launched forward and disappeared around a corner.

Killian's knees felt weak, and he wasn't surprised to feel Aylenn gripping his shoulder to steady herself.

From the time they had entered the colony, it was a real struggle to walk without falling forward. Somehow Killian's body was too light for the strength of his muscles. That was exhilarating in a way—he felt energized and powerful. But his legs had a terrible time finding their rhythm. It was only a small consolation that most of the others struggled even more. Raymen fell often, though his tumbles didn't take the silly grin from his face.

None of them could keep their eyes from the threatening masses of metal and soil that loomed above them. And then there was the mind-cracking sensation of seeing streaks of moving cloud *below* those distant lands.

Their guides led them to a tall structure about a hundred meters away. Climbing the stairs to the building's grand entrance was the most difficult challenge yet. Whenever Killian raised a leg, his foot took a path of its own, lifting much higher than he intended. Several of the elders fell and had to be supported the rest of the way. The impatience of their escorts also rose to new heights.

When they finally passed through doors a meter-and-a-half taller than needed, the space within was so vast that Killian almost went back out to confirm that the building's inside wasn't actually larger than its outside. It was filled with a swirling mass of humanity as if the whole population of Borealis had been brought into that one room and set in motion. His small group huddled together, so thoroughly awed that even Jee-an stopped talking. That made it easier for the spacecraft crewwoman to get their attention.

"This is the Hall of Gathering," she said. Looking over their heads with obvious relief, she added, "And here comes the escort who will accompany you during your time in Capita."

Killian twisted his head around. The perimeter of the hall was a spiral of walkways that rose up and up until they blurred with distance. There were people on all of them, but none stood out.

Then he heard a woman's voice behind him say, "*Devils of the void!*"

The words were nonsense, but the dismay they expressed was clear.

He spun around and immediately recognized the white-blonde hair and flawless features.

Not just any woman. *The* woman.

The woman he had knocked over while trying to protect her from the falling tiles.

"God *damn!*" Killian breathed.

13

She must be mistaken.

Out of the millions of people still left on Earth, he could not have been one of the select few chosen to come to Telluria Prime. Not such a boor, such a clown. Such a . . . savage.

For the first time, she realized that that term no longer signified something noble to her.

The void-headed fool had shattered her most cherished dream, and now he was back again like a monster in a nightmare from whom there is no escape.

She cursed her luck. With Earth itself barred to her, the highly anticipated reciprocal visit offered a chance to at least meet some of its most exceptional citizens. So, she'd agreed to cover the story for the CCC while assisting the official guides. Certainly, those chosen for the honor of visiting Telluria would be among the best the planet had to offer.

Or not.

For an instant she wondered if she could pretend not to recognize him, but it was clear from his shocked face that he'd recognized her and found the reunion no more welcome than she did. At least that meant that he hadn't deliberately arranged the encounter to add to her suffering.

Could she ask for a second escort and pawn him off on someone else? That would happen the next day anyway—each individual visitor would be paired with a Tellurian guide of their own from the Ministry of Intercolonial Affairs to provide a more personal experience. But to call for help at the very first meeting would imply that she couldn't handle the job, and she wasn't about to let one clumsy brute derail her chance to get back into her government's good graces.

Natira glanced at the man again while appearing to survey the whole group. A woman stood very close to him—no, she was actually *touching* him, pressing a grotesquely heavy breast into his arm. They were probably lovers. In Earth terms that would mean that they performed sex with each other's physical bodies, rutting like animals on a farm asteroid. The image made her feel queasy. But it wasn't any of her business, and she couldn't allow herself to react like some squeamish schoolgirl.

The woman wasn't even pretty.

Could it be that Basu Hind had deliberately sent this man to Telluria to punish Natira? The ambassador had recommended her as chief escort for the Earth visitors, making it sound like a generous opportunity to redeem herself; but what if he planned to avenge his own humiliation by setting her up to fail?

That was not going to happen.

She would be the perfect escort, a role she'd performed dozens of times as a favor to Hind. He never greeted his guests himself—it was important for him to appear too busy for such a task. Tours always began in the Hall of Gathering because its enormous spaces were intimidating, especially to those from the outer colonies where habitable space was at a premium.

Swallowing her annoyance, she launched into her welcome; and, keeping her face turned away from the man and his heavy-breasted sexmate, she drew the group over to a holographic map of Capita to point out a few landmarks.

Foremost was Capita Palace, the seat of government for the Confederacy, where all the city's roadways ultimately converged. The Palace was a four-lobed structure surrounded by lush green-space, each of its lobes a soaring tower of offices and meeting places. Privately, all government workers considered it a monument to excess, with most of its office space superfluous. But in public, they unequivocally declared their admiration for its bold architecture, unique heritage, and masterful technology. Natira was no different. Part of her was proud of it, but she was glad that her own work time was divided between the much more practical Ministry of Earth Studies building and the spartanly efficient CCC studios.

"Because Telluria Prime was the first space colony of this design, its creators chose to use a familiar system of reference for navigating," she explained. "They decided that the cylinder end that originally faced Earth would be its south end, and the outward-pointing end would be north. The cylinder spins on its long axis—if you look northward from the south end you would say it turns 'clockwise'." She'd never seen a rotary clock except in history archives and didn't know if the Earthers used them either. Her guests' faces were discouragingly blank—she began to wonder if they ever looked different—but she pushed on.

"Technically, if you face north and hold your arms straight out from your sides, your left hand will be pointing 'spinward'—that is, in the direction of Telluria's spin—and your right hand will point anti-spinward. But those are clumsy terms so, as on Earth, the direction of your left hand is called west and the other east. That should make it easy for you to find your way around."

They looked doubtful. She pointed out some other highlights in the hologram including Sola Park to the south, marked in green, Capita Wellness Centre to the southwest, the Ministries of Earth Studies and Colony Studies to the northeast, and their present location in the Ministry of Colonization building three blocks east of the Palace.

Although she was glad to see them paying attention, she wished they'd close their mouths once in a while. It would make them look more intelligent. And the brute man and his female companion still stood as if bonded. What could the woman possibly see in him? His physique was impressive in the form-fitting pantsuit, but his facial features were too . . . forceful to be truly handsome.

The Hall of Gathering offered exhibits showcasing all the colonies within the Confederacy; but rather than overload the visitors with information on their first day, Natira opted to take them back outside for a slow walk to see some of the city's landmarks up close. They should be impressed. With a pasted-on smile, she led them back to the entrance, shocked to see how awkwardly they moved down a simple flight of stairs in the lower gravity.

The boorish man and his companion were last. He stopped in front of Natira.

"I was only trying to keep you from being hurt. You know?" His voice was husky and soft. She merely shrugged.

"I'm Killian. Uh, this is Aylenn." He shifted his body slightly away from the woman, but she quickly closed the gap again.

"My name is Natira. You'll have a different guide tomorrow. Each of you will have your own." She thought a trace of a smile crossed the other woman's face, but she couldn't decipher Killian's expression. He nodded and said, "I'm just really sorry—that's all I wanted to say."

They moved down the stairs. The weaker gravity that caused the others to descend so cautiously didn't seem to bother Killian quite as much, or maybe he just tried harder not to let it show.

The walking tour lasted no more than an hour. The Earth people used short strides, as if on ice, yet still bumped into one another surprisingly often. The effort tired them, and one of the older men pleaded that they'd already been through a lot on the journey from home, which, for some, had begun in the earliest hours of that morning. She was more than happy to cut things short and show them to the Visitors' Centre where quarters had been prepared for them, and a small meeting hall had been reserved for their meals.

112

At the Centre, she led them to a lounge with soft music playing, and demonstrated controls for a display wall that could not only provide entertainment, but also show them nearly anything they wanted to know about Telluria. Then a staff member announced that their rooms were ready, and most of the guests moved quickly toward the hallway she indicated. Only a handful remained in the lounge. Among those were Killian and Aylenn, though Natira sensed that it was at the woman's insistence, and she tried not to imagine what would happen when the couple was finally left alone. Whenever Natira had looked at Killian that day, Aylenn had been conspicuously in between.

Now, as she said goodbye for the night and gratefully turned to go, Natira felt both sets of eyes on her.

14

Before the excursion to Earth, Natira had almost never needed serotonin stimulators. Now she used them almost every night, yet her sleep was still disturbed by raw images of that one indelible day, sharp flashes of detail she'd barely noticed at the time or may even have imagined. Four dogs barking in sequence. A flock of crows berating her as they wheeled above. Muddy ruts littered with discarded possessions: a single blue sock, a fork with a bent tine, a jar lid licked clean. And the faces—especially his face—looming over her.

She awoke with a start, an hour or more before the sun lights lit. As she shifted to the edge of the bed and tasted the sourness in her mouth, there was a lingering image in her mind of a naked Aylenn with her excessive breasts pressed hard against Killian, skin against sweaty skin. Natira's stomach twisted, and she commanded the wall to display the morning announcements—anything to clear the dreamtime trash from her mind.

Instead, the broadcast gave her a hollow feeling, knowing she should have been the one describing the key events of the day to millions of people across the solar system. But she'd been expected to spend weeks on special assignment recording the Earth delegation and its mission, and her temporary replacement was an ambitious daughter of the Corona family, not to be denied the opportunity to prove herself. So Natira's humbling recall had put the program's producer, Roja Manno in a very awkward position. He'd graciously given her a chance to save face by doing interviews and reports with the Earth visitors instead. She'd agreed and worn her head-cam to meet the guests.

Then, against all odds, she'd come face to face with Killian Morningcloud.

She'd hurriedly shut the camera off in case the audience might make the connection that would humiliate her all over again.

Now what? The production team could certainly alter footage to remove him, as long as she kept the man at a distance, but it would be deeply embarrassing for her, knowing they had to do so.

Thank the stars that she could pawn him off to another guide.

Wearily, she rose from the bed and summoned her shower stall.

#   #   #

"But I don' want to 'ave a different guide! Killian and I 'ave decided to stay togedder."

Aylenn's accented speech became even more pronounced when she was angry.

Her neck was nearly as stiff as her unbreakable grip on Killian's arm. The man himself looked flustered but hadn't managed to get a word in to make his own feelings known. Natira suspected he wasn't the talkative type, but Aylenn more than made up for it.

"As I've tried to explain, the Ministry insists that everyone have their own personal guide, not only so your guide can learn the things that most interest each of you and provide the best possible experience while you're here, but also so that our people can learn to understand each other better. That's the whole point of this visit—to bring Earth citizens and Tellurians together so we can get to know one another. And that works best one-on-one."

Aylenn's arms folded rigidly across her chest. Natira scowled at the nearest guide, named Tod, who was unabashedly staring at the Earth woman's upper body.

It would be disastrous to lose her composure—the end of her involvement with Earth or any of its people, she was certain. With a deep breath she took a step to the side and raised her left hand up to her chin.

Speaking to the air, she said, "I'm sorry, Commander. It appears that one of our guests feels she's misunderstood the purpose of their trip and would prefer to return to Earth after all. Could you please arrange that for me?"

There was an explosion of breath behind her.

"*Merde!* OK, *fine!*" Aylenn snorted. "I go wid 'im."

Natira caught a withering glare from the other woman who immediately grabbed Tod's arm and stalked off with him. Despite the objectionable contact, the guide looked indecently pleased.

Not bothering to suppress a sigh of relief, Natira turned back with a forced smile and said, "Now we'll just get another guide for you . . . ." But as she looked around, the words died on her lips.

There were no others. Her dispute with Aylenn had lasted so long that each of the other escorts had been paired with a visitor, and most had already left the building. She turned her head to Killian, her mouth falling open in dismay. His obvious discomfort turned to hurt as he registered her expression.

"Sorry. I'm . . . I'm very sorry," she stammered. "Of course, I will be your guide."

"No need," he said, thrusting his chin forward. "Call someone else. I'll wait."

"No, that's . . . I'm not going to do that. This is my assignment and I'll do it."

"Very noble of you to make the sacrifice."

Anger flared in her chest, but she forced it down. He had every right to offer insult for insult. She was being unprofessional. How could she complain about him being ill-bred when she behaved so badly herself?

Still, the first thing she did was to touch the jewel-like camera on her forehead to switch it from standby to video-only mode. At least that would capture some views of the tour that could be edited together with footage of the other guests to make it look like she'd been with them. Her producer was sharp—he'd get cameras to some of the other guides and arrange interviews for the evening or something. She hoped he'd understand and forgive her.

Killian gave her a puzzled look, but she wasn't about to explain. Instead, she gestured for him to follow her, and they stepped out into the light.

Her plan for the first day had been to take her assigned visitor through several government buildings, culminating with a short visit to the Palace itself. But the situation had changed. On impulse, she turned in the direction of Sola Park. It would be satisfying to show this man that growing things weren't confined to the Earth alone, and that they could be managed and still be beautiful.

"Were you really talking to someone through your hand?" he asked quietly.

The laugh escaped before she could stop it. "No, that was just for show. I just didn't know what else to do to convince her. Although I do have a . . . device with me that allows me to communicate with others at any time."

He gave a half smile. "You don't need to worry about being alone with me. I promise not to push you into any mud."

"No, that's not what I . . ." She shook her head. After they'd walked another block in silence, she tried again. "I can accept that you pushed me because you thought I might be hit by those falling tiles. I'm . . . sure that you didn't mean me harm."

Was that the truth? She tested her feelings and found that it was. This man might be badly behaved, but she was becoming convinced that his action came from ignorance rather than ill will.

"But you have no idea of the harm it did cause," she continued. She stopped and looked into his face. "I've worked most of my adult life studying Earth and preparing for our return there, and when you . . . knocked me down to *protect* me, it made me look weak. My superiors were very upset about that. They ordered me back to Telluria, and my lifelong hope of exploring Earth was over. Maybe for good."

"Because of what I did?"

She simply nodded.

"That's not fair," he said in a soft voice, his head lowered. She had a strong sense that he wasn't speaking only of her, or to her, but he didn't elaborate.

"No, it's not fair," she said. "And I don't need protection, Mr. Morningcloud. Not from you or from anyone else."

He gave a nod in return and then they just walked.

While he craned his neck around, unwilling to miss any of the sights, she watched him.

Time after time their progress came to a halt as he looked up and become lost in the view, the arc of his head trying to take in in the full length of Telluria Prime's cylinder world. It was a typical day, a few clouds overhead in layers, some near, some very far, and still others appearing as if on their sides where the cylinder walls curved upward. Searing across everything were the fiery threads of the central transport corridor, where zero-gravity trains shuttled goods from one end of the cylinder to the other along beams of light.

Natira could understand intellectually that it would be a difficult view to process for someone who'd only ever seen the unchanging globes of Sun and Moon and the horizontal strata of Earth's atmosphere, but for her, the view gave a comforting sense of completeness. A circle meant closure, and a contentment that comes with full control. The arch of the Doran Peninsula across the Sagan Archipelago, and the sweep of continental Planitia above her was reassuring.

The wide-open Earth sky was too unpredictable for her—it could lead anywhere.

Killian's arm shot upward. "Birds! Upside down!"

The specks were just visible against the distant landscape. Their track curved slightly anti-spinward as they flew from point to point. Would they follow a straight line on Earth? Or would the curve just be less obvious?

As if he were wondering the same thing, Killian said, "It's strange. We both live on worlds that spin. The movement of each day brings us around to the same place as the previous day, as if everything we do is a repetition of something done before. Yours is a world of progress while mine feels ... stuck in an endless loop. But seen from inside, it is yours that has the appearance of never moving, never changing. My sky changes with the seasons but yours never would. Only passing decorations over its surface would change, like paint on a face at festival time."

The observation surprised her, both for its length and its depth. Maybe he wasn't a man of few words after all, once given a chance to speak.

"We don't see it that way. Things do change within our lifetimes, as buildings are replaced, and landscape features restructured." She waved a hand overhead and toward the south. "That rectangular lake was an agricultural center with plowed fields when I was a child, but it was decided to experiment with rice and other marsh crops instead. Sometimes I wonder if colony planners make such decisions for purely aesthetic reasons once in a while, just to change the view." She cocked her head. "Our life is circular, I suppose, but we plan its cycles well ahead."

He gave a thoughtful nod, not making a value judgment one way or the other, then took a startled step backward as a man swept past them quickly on a hovermat. The rider was obviously reading a message on his corneops while the mat carried him smoothly around any obstacles.

Since focusing her research on the Earth, Natira hardly ever used the mats anymore. She enjoyed the feel of her muscles in motion and the texture of grass under her slippered feet.

From the beginning of the colonies, much of the vegetation in Telluria had been deliberately cultivated in a simulation of Earth's seasonal cycles, synchronized with a location about thirty-five degrees north of the equator. So, Spring had already come to Sola Park. The northern perimeter through which Natira and Killian entered frothed

119

with cherry trees in bloom. The profusion of pristine pink petals in every direction made Killian stop in his tracks, eyes wide.

"Don't they have cherry orchards near Borealis?"

He shook his head. "No. Apple trees and crabapple trees look something like this but not so . . ." Words failed him, and he could only shrug. Natira understood.

"This is one of my favorite times in Capita. And one of my favorite places. Many of the trees have white petals, but most of the ones in this area are pink, and they're such a . . . joyous expression of life . . . ." She turned her head to him suddenly. "You probably think that's a girlish thing to say."

"Yes." The corner of his mouth wrinkled. "But it's not a bad thing that a woman will speak words that a man will not. It's the man's loss, I think."

She wondered if he was subtly mocking her. Or just trying extra hard to earn her forgiveness.

She wasn't ready to give it. Not yet.

"Let's keep walking. The rest of the park is very impressive, too."

She pointed to a grove of trees a little farther on that featured larger white blooms and some others nearby with flowers not fully opened that were pink at their base and white toward their tips. The very air was charged with scents that spoke to her of beauty, of renewal, of hope. "Magnolias. Several different varieties. And those are crabapples over there." She glanced back to see if he was actually interested or just pretending to be, but his appreciation appeared genuine. It wasn't fair of her to judge him, but the boorish image of him in Borealis was still sharp in her mind.

"When you . . . came to see us—the colonists—in Borealis." She gave him a sidelong look. "I don't understand how you could have come to such an occasion looking so . . . well, so *dirty*. That was disrespectful to your elders, wasn't it? And to us, too?"

He sighed and his shoulders drooped.

"Yes, it was." He cleared his throat. "I'd just walked for two days through the bush to see you, in a snowstorm, because I'd

120

heard that a ship had landed. An earlier thaw had made the trail pure mud. I was planning to change my clothes at my mother's house, but then your craft flew overhead and . . ." He shrugged. "I couldn't wait. I should have. It was wrong."

"Yes," she said after a moment, but didn't trust herself to say more. Instead, she moved along and pointed out the purple cones of some grape hyacinths and, a few meters farther, a large bed of vivid red and yellow tulips that were just beginning to open. She beckoned him closer, but for a moment a trace of musky sweat obscured the perfume of the flowers, and she drew back involuntarily. He looked vaguely annoyed, but she wasn't prepared to explain her reaction.

Small objects floating in lazy patterns around the flowers made Killian bend closer.

"These aren't bees."

"No, they're drone bots—small cameras that take pictures of the blossoms so people everywhere in Telluria can look at them."

He was confused. She did her best to explain about holo displays and then about cerebra-links that people could wear to override the input from their eyes and ears with transmitted information.

"They would miss the fragrance," he said, leaning over some late-blooming lily of the valley.

"No. Cerebra-links can provide that too. Through stimulation of the olfactory centers . . . ." At his skeptical look, she said, "It's complicated."

They spent a couple of hours strolling around the park, resting occasionally on the grass, and then moving on. At one point she caught him looking at her with an amused smile.

"Is something funny?"

"I just didn't expect my visit to Telluria to be about seeing flowers and trees from Earth."

"I thought you might enjoy it. I thought you should see that we brought many of the best things from Earth and made the rough things even . . ." She stopped herself.

"Better? Or more civilized? That may not always be the same thing."

Was he talking about the flowers?

Feeling unjustly chastened, she turned away and began to walk quickly back north. "That's fine," she said. "I can show you our buildings instead, or our system of government, or our technology. All you want."

He caught up to her and touched her arm. She jerked away as if stung.

"I'm sorry. I wasn't complaining, and I didn't mean to insult you. In fact, I was enjoying myself. Very much," he said in a softer voice.

It was hard for her to read emotions in his sharply etched face, but he seemed implausibly sincere and open by nature. Every time she wanted to hate him for his crudeness, her feeling rebounded into a pang of remorse. She was the civilized one—she should be more ready to make allowance for his deprived upbringing. But she couldn't bear for him to suspect her inner conflict. With shoulders pulled back like a shield, she continued forward, but didn't try to outpace him.

After an awkward silence that carried them past a half-dozen shrub sculptures she'd wanted to show off, he cleared his throat.

"How were you chosen to go to Earth?" he asked.

Her lips puckered. "I was chosen for it before I was even born." She hadn't been "born" in the sense that he understood it, but she didn't feel like getting into that.

"What's that supposed to mean?"

She sighed. For a total stranger, he had a startling knack for finding the sources of her greatest pain. Was it worth explaining to him?

Yes. He should know how committed she'd been to the resumption of relations with Earth.

"When our people knew we'd be returning to Earth within the lifetime of the next generation, our scientists made sure that some of our children would be adapted to function there, with Earth's higher gravity and denser atmosphere. We're called, uh . . . well, we're called the *Tantas*. It means . . . well it more or less means Big Ones." She fought off a blush. "That means that things like my leg muscles, hip

122

structure, lung size are all more substantial than those of most people. It's . . . not a pleasant thing, but it's a burden I'm willing to bear for the sake of knowledge."

"Not pleasant . . . you mean it hurts you?"

"No. It's just ugly, that's all. But I've made my peace with it."

"Ugly?"

He turned his head to look more closely at the other people they passed, and then unapologetically drew his gaze down her body. She squirmed a little.

Just then she heard her name being called. A tall dark-haired man moved swiftly toward her across the park on a mat.

Gram Jaxon.

She winced. Gram had been a co-worker of Valenti's before her intended was assigned to the Ministry of Justice and was still one of his best friends. But the attention he gave Natira was entirely unwelcome. Unfortunately, his high rank within the Celestia clan made it unwise for her to rebuff him.

"I thought it was you," he said, with an overdone smile. "You're unmistakable. And unforgettable."

Natira kept her face expressionless. His corneops would have identified her from half a kilometer away. In fact, he could have located her from anywhere and sought her out.

"What's this," he asked, looking at Killian. Then his eyes opened wider. "A man from Earth?"

Killian's face tightened but he extended his hand and gave his name. Gram ignored the gesture—and the hand—and turned back to Natira.

"I'd heard you had some kind of . . . misunderstanding with one of the brutes. Oooh, wait. Don't tell me *this* is the one." He shifted his gaze back and forth between them, his smirk far more genuine than his smile, and Natira wished she could slap it from his face.

"Gram, it's nice to see you but I'm on official business . . ."

"I know, I know. But you're not always at work. And I can think of a pleasant way to spend some of your free time. Maybe tonight?"

"Valenti is my Intended."

"I won't tell him if you won't." He stepped uncomfortably close. She darted a glance at Killian, who stood stock-still wearing a look of disbelief. Was that a touch of anger, too?

"Gram, I've told you I'm not interested. Now please let me get back to work."

She stepped to the side, but he blocked her.

"You know it would help your standing in the family to be nice to me. And right now, you can use all the help you can get."

His grin made Natira shudder.

Suddenly he was flat on his back in the grass with Killian standing in front of her.

With a look of shock and then fury, Gram struggled to his feet and stepped forward.

"Listen, brute man . . ."

Killian effortlessly shoved him back onto his ass.

"Killian!" Natira gasped. "Don't . . ."

But Gram was up and charging. In a move too fast for Natira to see, Killian had the other man face down on the ground with his arm twisted behind him.

"This woman doesn't want to be with you. I think you should listen to her and let her get back to *work*." On the last word he gave Gram's arm a twist, eliciting a gasp of pain. Then he stood, looked at Natira, and began to walk northward. She was utterly certain that Gram would get up and attack Killian from behind, but he did no such thing. Eventually he rolled over and sat up, his face a sorry mess of grass and dirt and rage. She pretended not to see and hurried after Killian, who didn't even look back.

"In the name of the Void, *what were you thinking?*" she shrieked at him.

"I only promised I wouldn't push you into the mud."

She darted in front to block him.

"This isn't funny. You can't imagine the trouble he could make for me. And he could have you arrested for assault. I'm certain he will."

124

"No, he won't. Because then he'd have to admit to everyone that he was beaten by an Earth man. And even if he tried to claim that I used dirty tricks or a weapon, he knows that you would tell the truth."

His words were spoken with such conviction that she had no response to them. Finally, she hissed, "I told you I don't need protection. Not from you or anybody else."

He looked at her with an expression of honest puzzlement. "Needing protection is one thing. Deserving respect is another." He paused and then resumed his stride.

She could only shake her head and follow him.

As they drew close to the Visitors' Centre, she wondered if she should continue the tour to the government buildings, or just call it a day and return Killian to his quarters. Who knew what more trouble he might cause? But then, if Gram did call the security forces, they could locate Killian anywhere in the world by his visitor's tattoo. They might behave more discretely in the halls of government.

"I just don't know what makes Gram act that way," she said, almost to herself.

Killian gave a snort. "I'm not surprised at all. Ask him if Big Ones are ugly. The women here all look like skinny boys. You look like a woman."

He walked purposefully toward the gleaming medical complex ahead of them.

Once again, he'd left her without words.

15

Mechanical bees. Mats that carry people. Clothes that reflect their surroundings or change color at a whim. Exotic foods offering any flavor imaginable and available anywhere, just for the asking.

Telluria was unquestionably a world of wonders, but Killian was truly puzzled by Natira's complacency about some elements that disturbed him.

On Earth, men had no greater influence on family or community decisions than women had. Either sex could perform any kind of work or service they were capable of doing, without judgement. And if couples chose monogamous bonds, it was out of real affection, no other incentive.

Natira spoke of her "Intended" as if their pairing brought one or the other special status. She didn't boast of his looks, or his devotion—she barely mentioned him at all. The jerk in the park had clearly assumed that she would have to give in to his seduction sooner or later, and she should have kicked him in the balls. Instead, she was afraid to make him angry. And she was obviously, willingly subservient to the Earth ambassador, Hind.

It wasn't personal weakness that accounted for such things—he sensed a core of strength within her.

So, then it must be a reflection of her society. Which of the two cultures reflected the ways of Earth at the time of the Divide, he wondered? Or did neither of them?

He wasn't likely to find an answer.

In the meantime, the marvels of Capita were entertaining, but his mind kept returning to his most important reason for being there: to find medicine that would cure his mother.

The Confederacy wasn't going to give it to him—he'd become convinced of that. He would have to steal it; but he had absolutely no idea where it was kept, or how to find out.

Until the information fell into his lap.

Natira was proud to show off Capita's special place of healing that she called the Medical Centre. She explained that most Tellurians hardly ever needed direct medical intervention because their health was constantly monitored by technology and automatically treated through the food distribution system. But Capita was the heart of the Confederacy's government—the home of its most important people, and some of its most elderly, who needed more medical care.

He was dumbstruck by the exotic machinery and what she claimed it could do, but what impressed him most was the cleanliness of the place. Every surface gleamed—every corner and entranceway was dust-free. Clothing worn by the staff looked new and immaculate. Such spotlessness could never have been possible in Borealis, or anywhere on Earth that he knew about.

Even the air smelled clean, reminding him of the freshness after a thunderstorm.

"Which of these machines cures the wasting disease?" he asked as casually as he could.

"The wasting ... do you mean cancer? Well, none. I mean, cancer comes in many forms and curing it requires several types of treatment. Some machines help, though most of the ones you see here are only for scanning patients and gathering information. Each case is different and needs individualized treatment."

Killian's heart missed a beat. "You mean there's no medicine that can cure everyone's ... cancer?"

"I'm sure there are some that help a great deal in a general way. Our medicine has made huge strides in the past five hundred years. Let's see."

He followed her toward a nearby wall. She seemed to welcome the chance to resume her role as a guide after the encounter in the park, especially to show off her people's technology.

Citizens in white uniforms performed various tasks nearby. He thought she would ask one of them for assistance. Instead, she made some motions in the air and asked her questions to the wall, and it lit with a display that she seemed to understand.

"Here's one," she said. "It's called Fulvizyme. It . . . well, it helps the patient's own body fight the cancer. It's not a cure; but in most cases, it improves the chances that other treatments will work. And they do. Almost no-one dies of cancer in Telluria. Doesn't your village factory, your Depot, provide this?"

"No. The Depot has no cures for the wasting disease. At least, they aren't given to us." He tried to keep the emotion from his voice, but she gave him a probing look. He cleared his throat and said, "Something like that must be valuable . . . kept secure in a special place."

She gave a light laugh. "Not at all. If someone needs it, they get it. Most times it would automatically be added to their food or drink; but if not, they'd come here and ask for it. Medicines can't be used for anything else, so why would we lock them away?"

He shrugged. "Is everyone treated the same in the Confederacy?"

"Of course. Well, as much as possible. In the outer colonies some resources are much harder to get, so living conditions can be more of a challenge."

"But leaders and important people get medical facilities right where they live."

Her face pinched closed. "Maybe it's time for us to see something else." Without waiting for an answer, she strode toward the building's entrance.

Killian cursed himself. He'd meant to change the subject, not to antagonize her, but he couldn't seem to help it.

She was such a strange woman, telling herself that all people were equal, but not hearing her own way of speaking to him, as if to a child. And avoiding his touch as though he were a rattlesnake.

He expected better of gods. Natira seemed as flawed as anyone he knew, and that man in the park . . . . But then, they were only workers, after all.

Or were they? The obnoxious man had spoken about Natira's family as if it was important. The jewel she wore on her forehead might be a sign of that. He knew that some settlements of the past had been led by chieftains whose family members were designated by ornamentation. Maybe she was some kind of princess of Telluria?

Such a question would sound stupid if he was wrong

Instead, he said, "My grandfather has been an Elder of Borealis. Does your family include Elders of your . . . city?"

"When I turned twenty, I was adopted into the Celestia family, one of the five most . . . influential families of the Confederacy. The head of our family, the Patriarch, is currently Telluria's Prime Councilor, the top position in our government."

He was stunned. She *was* a princess, in every way but name! But while he would have expected her to proclaim such a thing with pride, she seemed a little embarrassed.

So, who were the truly influential people of the Confederacy? Presumably he would meet some when she took him through their government buildings.

He didn't. They met almost no one, as if the word of their coming had gone ahead to warn everyone to avoid them. Was the presence of an Earth person so very distasteful that he wasn't even an object of curiosity? Or was idle curiosity satisfied by cameras hidden everywhere, like the flying ones he had taken for bees?

They stopped to eat in a small room of an administrative building, and the rest of the afternoon passed by looking at different variations of building styles. Only the Palace itself stood out, mainly because it exhibited a range of decorative materials luxurious beyond anything Killian had ever seen. There were fabrics that looked like silk but could be walked upon like boards. Zones of colored lights that cooled or warmed with a touch. Tiles in the floor that rose when stepped on and carried him around rooms while floating a few centimeters in the air. Clear vertical tubes the width of a human body that lifted him to higher levels of the building on a puff of wind.

He barely spoke a word—could not think of words to say. And if there was a trace of smugness on Natira's face, he did not begrudge her that. To be one of a people who could create such things . . . well, not to feel pride would be impossible. Especially compared to the run-down and backward habitations of his own people. He tried not to feel resentment. The colonists had made their own way into the great void, had challenged the cold menace of space and conquered it. They deserved the fruits of their labors.

Natira herself seemed to need some means to restore the self-esteem Killian had damaged so badly. So, if she had to regain it at his expense, he wouldn't complain.

They returned to the Visitors' Centre, and he voiced his surprise that he hadn't seen any of the other Earth people all day. Surely, they would have been taken to see the same sights.

Natira raised her forearm, and a patch of skin began to glow. It was like the tattoo they'd put on the inside of his own forearm when he'd arrived, but larger and more complex.

"We guides can see where each visitor is at any time, thanks to your tattoos. I didn't think there would be any advantage in coming together . . . with the others." Her smile looked a little uncomfortable. "But I expect you'll want to share your experiences this evening. You can gather in the lounge, or easily find each other's rooms." Her eyes darted away. "If you need any help finding your way to your quarters, the walls will show you the way."

He shook his head. "Will they show me how to get to my quarters without being seen by Aylenn?"

They laughed. It was a moment of closeness that took them both by surprise.

16

Aylenn clung to him that evening like a hawk to a fish, and it was all he could do to prevent her from coming to his room for the night. Barely restraining his impatience, he waited until the line of visitors' rooms had become completely quiet and then another two hours beyond that. He'd discovered that he only had to speak the single word "Time" in a certain way to light up a display in the air in whichever direction he was facing. No doubt other words could produce a whole host of results, but he didn't need anything else right then except to make time pass more quickly. The room was no help with that.

He had a moment of concern that the doors might lock on their own to keep guests from wandering, but his opened when he approached it. The hallway flared with light when he stepped out, but no one came to check on it. The exit doors of the Visitors' Centre weren't even locked for the night.

Doors in Borealis were left unlocked too; but then, no one had reason to steal from others when the Depot supplied almost every need. The few acts of malice that did occur were impossible to hide in a community of that size. He'd expected Capita to be different, if only because there was so much wealth. But maybe Natira was right. Maybe people were so near to being equal that they had no reason to want what others had.

He took a deep breath. Nighttime on Earth smelled very different from the daytime, with scents more pronounced because of the moister air. Not here. Outside air was almost indistinguishable from building air, with distinct smells only if you were near vegetation or some new construct. One pervading scent was familiar but took him some time to place. It was the smell of the Depot in the spring.

When winter ended, his people flocked to the Depot to get new clothing for warmer weather. The air surrounding the building developed a sharp tang that lasted for a few days. Killian had been told it had to do with electricity, which he'd learned about in school, though none of the settlement's own buildings were supplied with it.

The faint aroma was common in Capita City, especially as he passed transport tubes or sidewalks that moved by themselves.

The street was not dark—some sunshine came through the giant windows in the sky, though the dazzling lights that rimmed them were shut off for the night. He had no trouble finding his way to the Medical Centre. Three times he encountered other people on the street—one passed right by him in the opposite direction. But if they were curious, they did nothing about it. He copied their behavior, looking straight ahead without any acknowledgment.

Even the Medical Centre entrance was unlocked, and the lobby area empty. There were voices in the distance, but no one came into view. He went straight to the counter where Natira had consulted the wall about the medicine, but didn't know what to do once he got there. She seemed to have drawn a response by making a gesture in the air, but he hadn't noticed what it was. Anxiously bouncing on his toes, he leaned over the counter.

"Can I help you?"

His head snapped up, searching for the source of the female voice. There was no one.

The words came again, from the air itself. He cleared his throat.

"Fulvisine," he said, and flinched at the loudness of his voice.

"Did you mean Fulvizyme?"

"Yes. I need some Fulvizyme. For ... cancer."

"Dosage, please."

He didn't know what that meant. Did it mean he had to pay money? Natira hadn't said anything about that. What if someone couldn't pay?

"It's, uh ... it's for a woman. An adult woman," he hedged.

"Course of treatment?"

What was that? What else would a healer need to know? How long to administer the medicine?

"Two months."

"Name of patient?"

Shit! He'd desperately hoped he wouldn't be asked that.

"Natira ... Natira Celestia."

"Upon notification and confirmation, a course of Fulvizyme will be added to Natira Celestia's diet."

"*No.* No, I need to take it with me. She's uh ... she's going to be away from Telluria. On Earth." It sounded plausible, he thought.

For an endless moment nothing happened. Then, with a soft hiss a panel beside the counter opened and a small round box slid out. Killian snatched it quickly and began to turn away, but straightened again and said, "Thank you."

"We are pleased to be of service. Good night."

He felt a shiver of relief; but before he could hurry to the door, he heard voices in the nearby corridor. Very close.

There wasn't time to escape. He had to hide!

A second hallway led away from the lobby. He dashed along it, clutching the box to his chest. The colonist technology in the walls didn't seem to distinguish between Tellurians and Earth people; but other humans certainly would, and they would want to know what he was doing at a medical center all alone in the middle of the night.

The corridor was almost exactly like the one in the ambassador's building on Earth with its identical doors and unreadable markings, except this one had many more branchings. If he took one, he might get lost; but if he kept going straight, he would still be visible from the lobby, and for a long way. Finally, he risked a left turn and tried to memorize some symbols on the wall to identify that same corner when he returned. If he was very lucky, the new hallway might lead to the outside. He thought he would be able to orient himself under the open sky.

There was no exit, though, and the voices became louder, as if they were following him. Sooner or later, he would be seen.

Then his attention was caught by a slight scuff mark on the floor in front of one of the doors. Maybe something had been dragged through it. That could mean a place for equipment instead of people.

He cautiously waved his hand. Nothing happened. He tried waving over different spots until, at last, the door slid open to a little room, but an inner light came on—not the concealing darkness he'd hoped for. The interior of the room was very narrow and filled with strange boxes, drums, tubes and other shapes. He clambered behind a large cylinder. The door closed on its own, and he desperately hoped it could be opened from the inside.

With his back against the wall and legs tucked under him, he tried to get his breathing under control. In his ears, it was frighteningly loud. But as he calmed down, he could hear the voices again. Or maybe not the same voices. These sounded different, and they got quieter if he moved his head.

After some experimentation, he found the voices were coming from a ridged oval in the wall. Maybe it connected to the next room. He placed his ear against it.

There were two voices—both men—but one of them sounded just slightly flattened. It reminded him of the speech of the display walls, or a conversation he'd heard in the spacecraft from Earth. Voices from people who were not in the same room. Maybe the room was occupied by a patient, while a healer talked to him from another place.

It wasn't right to eavesdrop, but the situation was desperate. Anything he could learn might be important. He

135

pressed closer to the wall. Fragmented words became sentences.

". . . thought you were starting to get soft about these people. Even getting to like them."

"Coming to confirm their potential would be more accurate," said the flattened voice. "We were right. They are primitive and are barely educated, but with proper training they can be turned into useful workers."

"I still don't know why you're so sure they'll agree to work for us."

"What choice will they have? They've become totally dependent on the Depots in every Allocation. When we shut the Depots down, they'll either come to work for us or they'll starve. And once they come, they will not leave."

Killian had to bite his tongue to keep from crying out.

The men must be talking about one of the outer colonies. It couldn't be about Earth.

". . . would have heard how the planet was spoiled before. They'll never allow it to happen again."

"Nonsense. Humans only care about what they see. Keep the mine sites and smelters away from their little settlements and they'll ignore the problem. Just like before. They'll turn a blind eye until their sky turns on them and the rivers run black. Only the workers will see the truth and they won't escape to tell anyone."

The man in the room next door gave a laugh that made Killian's skin crawl.

"You're a devil," he said. "I knew we picked the right man. And you won't feel the slightest twinge of remorse at exploiting the recovery of the past five hundred years while making the Earth an ash heap again, will you?"

"It's either that or bow to the demands of the outer colonies. You know that. No, I have no sentimental attachment to Earth. It's not *my* home. Merely a particularly useful and convenient collection of resources, to be expended and then discarded."

"You're still certain that the plan can't be discovered by our own authorities? Or even that the real reason for Telluria Quinta's refit will leak out?"

"Most Tellurians never look beyond our Halo shield, including our government officials—maybe *especially* them."

The dark laugh came again.

"Keep me informed," the first man said. The conversation was over.

Killian swallowed saliva as he fought the urge to vomit.

What he'd heard couldn't be real. It must be a colossal joke being played on him. Or one of the 'prepared entertainments' offered by the display walls. That was it—the man in the next room was playacting a scenario with someone in another place!

Or, if it was real, there had to be another explanation. There were bound to be some Tellurians who hated Earth and didn't want the Confederacy to restore relations with the planet. Maybe one group had gone so far as to make plans to prevent it. Or worse. But the Tellurian government would stop them if they knew. He'd tell Natira—she would know what to do.

Except then he would have to explain where he'd been, and why.

He made no move to leave. His entire body was shaking. It took a long time to get it under control.

He was still in a daze when he left the small room and staggered toward the lobby.

Which was why he ran straight into the security team.

17

It wasn't bad enough that one of the Earth visitors had broken his leg trying to 'fly' from a rooftop, and the junior guide, Tod, had been reprimanded for unsuitable behavior with Aylenn. When Natira was summoned to the Ministry of Justice because of Killian, she wanted to scream. First her humiliation on Earth, and now this.

Valenti met her at the building's entrance—of course he would have been alerted.

"What's this about?" he asked, matching her brisk stride across the lobby with a flash of irritation.

"It's nothing. I'm sure it's nothing. Just one of my Earth 'guests' wandering some place he shouldn't have."

"It has to be more serious than that or they wouldn't have ordered you here in person."

"How else would I come to take responsibility for him?" She stopped at the entrance to the air lift. "Look, I'll handle it— you don't have to become involved."

He frowned but nodded slowly and took a step back. "OK. Just try to keep my name out of it, all right?"

She didn't roll her eyes until the rush of air had lifted her most of the way to the third floor where the security forces temporarily detained citizens. It occurred to her that Killian wasn't a citizen, so she had no idea what security protocols would apply to him.

Opposite the lift, the wall was mirrored, and a brief glimpse of her reflection made her scowl. Despite her reassuring words to Valenti, the early morning call about Killian had disturbed her enough that in the rush to get here, she'd neglected to wear her restraining bodice, and some of her hair had straggled free too. She looked like . . . like an Earthwoman. But it was too late to do anything about that now. The security forces' reception holo appeared before her.

"What can I do for you, Citizen Celestia?" A calm voice matched an eminently proper female image.

"I've come to see the Earthman Killian Morningcloud, who was detained last night."

"Certainly. Please follow me."

The hologram rotated and moved along the corridor, its legs moving appropriately but making no sound while Natira's own slippers scuffed a soft rhythm over the polished floor. The area for detainees was not far. A man in the dark blue jumpsuit of the security forces took over from her holographic guide and led her to where Killian paced back and forth in a small room with three walls. The fourth wall was durafilm, barely visible except where an overhead light reflected from it. It allowed air and moisture to pass through, but nothing more solid than that.

Killian started when he noticed their approach, then openly stared, his eyes traveling down her body from head to foot. The twitch at the corner of his mouth brought an angry flush up her neck to her ears. She covered her unbound chest with crossed arms. She would not be provoked—she would be professional.

"You're just determined to bring me grief, aren't you?" she said. Her quick look at the security man made him step back a few paces, but he didn't leave.

"It isn't like that." Killian looked at the other man, too, but the guard ignored them both. Killian hesitated, then said, "It's my mother. She has the wasting disease. I . . . I asked the ambassador for medicine, but he wouldn't give it to her. So, when you showed me where it was yesterday, I . . . decided I would have to take it myself. I can't let her die," he finished quietly, eyes on the floor.

Swallowing hard and darting another glance at the guard, Natira said, "I was just showing you what our medical facilities are like. I had no idea about your mother. I'm sorry. But why did you think you had the right to just . . . steal it?" The words felt strange in her mouth. She'd probably never used the word 'steal' more than a dozen times in her life.

"You said that if a citizen needed it they would just get it. How can it be so wrong for me to take what any citizen can get just for asking?"

"You're not a citizen. You haven't given a lifetime of work to benefit our society. And you were directly refused by the ambassador—he must have had his reasons. Yet you felt you could just ignore them?"

"Like his reasons for sending you back to Telluria when your place is on Earth?"

The words were like cold water in her face. She took a step back and began to turn away.

"No, wait! I'm sorry. I didn't mean to insult you. I've just . . . got a big mouth. Blame it on my culture or whatever you want. But please don't make my mother pay for something I've done wrong." He paused and looked between Natira and the security man. "So, I've . . . committed a crime. What happens next?"

Natira looked the question at the man next to her. He shrugged.

"This week's magistrate was alerted at the same time you were, and he immediately spoke with the ambassador on Earth. Now he wants to speak to you." He waved toward the wall and gave a name. There was a pause of nearly half a minute before the air filled with the image of an older man seated at an invisible desk, who ran his fingers through greying hair as he looked around at them.

"Citizen Celestia," he said in a voice that was deep with a slight rasp. "And this is the Earth man in your charge, I take it? In fact, isn't he the one responsible for your recall to Telluria?"

Natira cleared her throat. "Yes, Magistrate."

He gave a slow smile and a shake of his head. "I'm interested . . . now that he has committed an unsociable act against our society as well as your own person, what would you do with him? What sentence would you impose?"

Killian looked alarmed and appeared about to speak, but a glare from Natira kept him silent.

Blood burned in the skin of her face and neck. *Void's perdition*, she hadn't expected this. What was the magistrate playing at? Of course, she'd love nothing better than to see this crude Earth man pay for the way he'd wrecked her dreams, but what payment would suffice? What punishment could he suffer that would make things right? That would make her feel . . . whole again?

Nothing could do that. Nothing at all.

"I would send him back to Earth," she said in a near whisper.

"Just send him back? Nothing more? No punishment?"

She hesitated. "No, nothing. He doesn't really understand what he's done." She looked into Killian's face but couldn't read the emotions there.

"The ambassador told me you would say that." The magistrate's throat rumbled with something like a laugh. "Which, he said, would show that you still don't understand the bigger picture." His head turned toward Killian. "The Confederacy is embarking on a new relationship with these people of Earth, a relationship that must be based on strength. We can't afford to look weak. We can't let them think they can do whatever they choose without consequences. So, examples must be made, right from the start. Do you understand what I'm saying, man of Earth?"

Killian nodded, then lifted his face and said, "My name is Killian. I don't represent anyone else from Earth. Only myself. Any punishment should be for me alone, not them."

"Don't be melodramatic. We're not going to punish your people. But you . . . *you* must pay a price. You will be sentenced very publicly for willful behavior against the common good."

Relief radiated from Killian's face. "I accept that. Do what you want with me."

The response was a snort of disbelief. "It isn't up to you to accept or reject anything. But if you cooperate fully when the proceedings are recorded for broadcast to Earth . . . we will see that your mother is given the medicine she needs. Enforcer? Please make the arrangements." With that command, the image of the magistrate vanished. No one in the room moved. Killian was clearly stunned. He looked at Natira.

"Does he mean that? Will he give her the medicine?"

"Of course, if that's what he says."

"But what about the rest? What's my sentence?"

She tried to speak but had to cough and couldn't meet his eyes.

"Mars," the security man answered for her. "Or possibly one of the outer colonies. A work gang. You'll do labor for the government, maybe for as long as five years."

"*Five years* . . . ! All right. And then I'll be sent back to Earth?"

"No." Natira looked into his face. "You won't."

He tried to respond but couldn't, his skin the color of ash. The security enforcer beckoned her away with a jerk of his head. She followed numbly.

"What now?" she asked him.

"Well, we almost never keep citizens under guard, so we don't have the facilities for an extended stay. He'll be released with restraint bracelets. But he'll be in your custody."

"Mine? I don't want him!"

"Who else? Our people have other duties."

She gave a string of curses under her breath. Was this another test arranged by Basu Hind? Or just the latest manifestation of her horrible luck?

"For how long?"

"They haven't told me. But how long could it take for them to record a broadcast for Earth and ship him off to Mars? Three days? A week at most. Who knows, maybe they'll have you record the announcement." His smile probably wasn't

142

meant to be cruel, but it was like she'd been hit in the stomach. Yes, that was exactly what Hind would do.

She presented her palm to a scanner and was led back to Killian. Once a pair of shining silver bands had been sealed around his wrists, he was released to follow her out of the building. He didn't say anything until they had walked two blocks down the street.

"They're just letting me go for now?"

"You're my responsibility. Lucky me." She threw him a glare. "Which means I'll lock you in your room when I want to, and you won't give me any trouble about it."

He just nodded. "But I didn't think our rooms had locks."

"Every room in Capita has a lock if you're wearing restraint bracelets. The security forces have given me the command code. You can go almost anywhere you want. Until I say you can't."

"I won't cause trouble. I've never meant to bring you trouble—I truly haven't. I'm so sorry that it's worked out that way." He hung his head as they walked. "I couldn't understand why you were so disgusted by me from the very first time you saw me. I swore you were wrong, and I'd prove it to you. But you weren't wrong."

He turned his face away and they walked on in silence, his words like hot brands on her cheeks. Had she really been so judgmental?

Yes, she had. And yet now he had justified her scorn. He was a criminal—nothing less. Maybe she hadn't known that at first sight, but her instincts had been proven right. Hadn't they?

She looked up at the looming walls of the Ministry of Enterprise building as they passed it, and beyond to the continent of New Europe stretching overhead. It all shone with good order and careful planning. Civilized. What place could a man like this have in her society? He should be sent back to where he belonged.

Not to Mars, though, or even worse, to one of the outer moons. He was a product of his heritage—banishment was too high a price for what he'd done. After all, no one had been hurt.

She was surprised to notice how close they were walking. Almost touching. She edged away and looked up to find him staring straight ahead. His jaw was set hard, but a world of emotions played in his eyes.

"What are you thinking?" she asked, not quite knowing why.

It was a long time before he answered, in a voice almost too quiet to hear.

"I was thinking about the colonists leaving Earth. Leaving my people behind. I've never blamed them for that—I thought they were wise to know that the Earth needed fewer people in order to heal, and courageous to make the sacrifice of going out into the great blackness and cold to face such hardship. They couldn't have meant us harm—they left the Depots for us. They weren't quite wise enough to prevent the coming of the great plagues, and the Depots had no medicine against those—not everything can be foreseen. Only . . . I could never understand why they had to destroy all of the knowledge when they left. Why they wiped out every storage place of information, removed every trace of technology, and wrecked all the schools except the Depot enclaves they put in place."

"That's not true."

"It is. They did. Oh, they left behind Teachers in Depot classrooms who were permitted to teach us simple things. To carefully answer so much, but no more. And certainly nothing that would help us rise again. Nothing that could allow us to follow them into the sky."

"You said it yourself: The world was damaged and needed to heal. Technology was largely to blame. It would have been wrong to leave behind the tools to continue that destruction."

"That's what I told myself, too. But who were they to make *that* judgment?" He looked at her. "To decide that they were fit to use such technology, but the ones they left behind were not."

144

They said nothing more as she led him back to his room in the Visitors' Centre. They met no one, and she was glad of it. With the reassurance that food would be brought to him, she left him alone, staring at a wall.

Perhaps leaving him isolated was unkind at such a time, but she had some investigating to do.

18

Natira closed the door of her quarters and leaned against it, marshalling her resolve.

Killian's words had stung her. If he was right, her people's self-image as a benevolent race was a lie. Other principles she'd taken for granted might have to be re-examined too. Like most Tellurians, she'd simply accepted the account of the Exodus from Earth as it had been told to her and never looked deeper. Now she would.

Was that the unpalatable information held in the secret archive she'd found?

That week before her trip to Earth seemed so long ago now, although her turmoil about the discovery was still fresh in her mind. She'd been surprised to find an unaddressed and unlisted data archive deep within Telluria's computer network—she'd only stumbled onto it by pure accident while doing some research. But more disturbing was the evasive reaction of both Basu Hind and the Patriarch when she had reported it to them. She still couldn't help wondering if that event had influenced her assignment to the Earth contingent, as a means to get her away from the city for a time. Because when she'd looked again to confirm the existence of the archive, she'd found it heavily encrypted—a new development that proved that someone didn't want it read.

Well, she wasn't ready to risk trying to penetrate it just yet. The public archives should provide enough of the true story of how her ancestors had left Earth.

She hesitated before activating the display wall. Maybe she should go somewhere else, where the search couldn't be so easily traced back to her. But she wasn't doing anything wrong. As a researcher who specialized in Earth studies, an interest in the Exodus was perfectly legitimate.

She called forth the genie in the wall and put it to work.

It quickly found what she wanted, but she immediately wished it hadn't. The words and images burned into her very soul.

Five hundred years earlier, the Earth had indeed been ecologically damaged, and far worse than she'd ever understood. The creatures of the land, sea, and sky had been decimated by human encroachment on their habitats and by pollution of the environment. Species extinctions were a daily occurrence. Ocean reefs were scourged by water that had become too warm and too acidic, and when the coral died, whole ecosystems went with it. Eventually, even sharks were wiped out, too, and the entire hierarchy of the sea devolved into chaos.

On land, there was nowhere that humanity had not tamed, and then despoiled. Mountains were ground down for coal and ore, rivers diverted to provide irrigation but then tapped too often to endure. Irreplaceable underground aquifers were drained forever, and glaciers that might have replenished them had already melted away. An atmospheric warming effect triggered by humankind's industry and voracious hunger for energy had pushed Earth's climate past a tipping point that left millennia-long weather patterns in tatters. Devastating droughts, catastrophic freezes, and storm after punishing storm wreaked havoc with human populations and their food crops. By the time of the Exodus, nearly half of the eight billion humans on the planet had become refugees—nomads without a place to call home, because that home had been burned or flattened or flooded.

Humanity had tolled its own death knell. There had been no question that "something must be done." The quandary was no longer *how* to save some of those teeming billions, but *who* to save.

For almost all its history, the human species had allowed itself to be divided: by close family ties, broader genetic links, tribal relationships, racial characteristics, then larger and larger geographical divisions. But it had also allowed divisions in a more consequential way: into the haves and the have-nots—those with wealth and power, and those ruled by them.

In the final two centuries before what came to be called the Divide, various permutations of government had paid lip-service to the idea that all people were equal, but equality was never anyone's reality. For short periods of time in various places, political experiments made the dream of equality seem within reach. But as technology had enabled larger and larger business conglomerates, quicker and more clandestine transfers of wealth, those with currency and influence were able to increase their holdings exponentially while the average person sank beneath obligations and debt. Most of the world's wealth was controlled by a few thousand people; and in the fifty years before the Divide, the wealthiest had holdings that were small countries of their own in everything but name.

It was a chaotic time. For many decades, private industry had performed most of the exploration and exploitation of the solar system beyond Earth. Since the depleted home planet was still host to a race of rabid consumers, the resources of the Moon, Mars, the asteroids, and the moons of the gas giants were in high demand. Mining and processing outposts were built in far-flung places, followed by small colonies for the workers, and eventually their families. It was a hard life, and a grim one for workers, though not for the resource-company owners who had special, private quarters built onto the worker domes. In such places the elite enjoyed luxury the working caste would never see, and indeed were not meant to know about. It became fashionable for the ultra-wealthy to use such extraterrestrial facilities as vacation homes, and sometimes even host extravagant parties, spending sums that were truly astronomical.

Whether this flaunting of wealth was the result or the cause, there came a time when the have-nots arose in a monstrous retaliation. They could not openly rebel— punishment for rebellion was swift and relentless—so, anonymously, via the worldwide public communication networks, they helped each other identify the richest of the rich, the location of their homes and workplaces, their travel routes, and their daily schedules. Armed with that information, an outrageous new 'sport' sprang up: Thousands of the disenfranchised became hunters.

The rich became their prey.

A common bullet that cost almost nothing could end a lifetime of selfishly accumulating wealth.

The ultra-wealthy reacted by isolating themselves more and more within fortresses and heavily guarded communities in remote places. Humanity's great Divide began decades before the wave of spaceships left Earth during the Exodus.

Yet Natira found a gap in public records at that point. Little was available about the final few years, or the planning and execution of the Exodus itself. There were official statements from the time that suggested all people had been given an equal opportunity to migrate from Earth, but that narrative didn't mesh with the preceding course of events.

Neither could Natira refute Killian's assertion about the destruction of knowledge in the wake of the outmigration. The terrible plagues of ten years later were a matter of record; but presuming that the colonists still closely observed the planet they'd left behind, they preserved few of those observations for later generations.

Unless all of that was in the secret archive.

Part of her yearned to test its armor of digital code; but if she simply blundered into safeguards, that would only alert those who'd tried to keep the contents hidden. Her attempts might bring punishment, subtle or overt. Worse, it would mean that she'd never learn the truth.

The Patriarch and Basu Hind knew that she'd found the repository, and then it had been deliberately secured so as to be beyond her reach. There would be no way to pretend innocence if they caught her. She would have flagrantly defied two of the most powerful men in Telluria, including the very leader of its government, her own adoptive father. Her entire social standing lay in the hands of the one man, her academic career in the hands of the other.

She shuddered.

No. She couldn't risk so much out of mere curiosity. Trying to access those records was a step too far.

19

Killian couldn't resist trying the door.

It didn't move when he approached it, touched it, tried to slide it using the pressure of his palms. There was no give at all—it had simply become part of the wall.

He banged on it in frustration, but had to admit that his confinement was no more than he should expect. He had broken their laws. By any measure, there would have to be consequences for doing that. And he was willing to pay the price, now that he knew his mother would be given the medicine she needed. He had failed in his plan, but succeeded in its goal. His only regret was that his mother and his family would suffer when they saw him publicly sentenced to banishment and hard labor on Mars or elsewhere. They wouldn't blame the Confederacy—the sentence was not so different from what Borlealis's own council of elders might pronounce for a similar infraction. But his crime and punishment reflected badly on all of Earth's people. He'd been selected to represent his planet to the colonies, and he'd repaid the honor with an act of theft. Such an act tainted all his kind.

His body slumped in shame. The motion triggered the bed to rise from the floor, and he sat down on it heavily.

As he stared into space, a second regret came to mind. He had made trouble for Natira. *Again.* Why did that keep happening? It wasn't something he'd ever meant to do. Quite the opposite. From the first time he'd seen her and felt her scorn, he'd wanted nothing more than to prove to her that her contempt was unfounded. Despite his impulse to run away and hide his shame that very first day, he had stayed by Momoko Quarry's side to meet the colonists face to face, and then had tried to shield this strange woman from harm with his own body. Later, in Capita, he'd yearned for a chance to prove that he too was fit to be a citizen of the Confederacy.

All his good intentions had backfired disastrously. Who knew what damage he'd caused this time to her status and reputation?

He couldn't say that he liked her—it was hard to like someone whose every action betrayed her disgust. But he didn't wish her harm.

Was she right that he would never be allowed to return to Earth? Probably. But maybe he could turn that into an opportunity—a chance to prove his worth to the people of the Confederacy and earn a place among them. With hard work and persistence, it just might be the answer to his lifelong dream.

Somehow that possibility didn't comfort him as much as it should have.

He lay down on the bed and closed his eyes.

Sleep was a long time coming, and was troubled when it did come. He dreamed that he was in a dark closet listening to menacing voices of men who argued about how they were going to tie someone up and then carve him into pieces to be shared among them. With sickening certainty, he knew they were talking about him. He tried to get out of the closet and run away, but there was no door. He flailed blindly forward only to run into a wall each time, driving whimpering sounds from his throat. Then, all of a sudden, the wall opened and light dazzled him.

He jerked awake to discover that the lights in his room had come on. They must have reacted to some motion of his. A quick look confirmed that he was still alone, and that the door was still closed.

He lay back down and tried to calm his breathing.

It wasn't hard to figure out that his dream was about the conversation he'd overheard in the medical center. The turmoil of his subsequent capture and sentencing had almost knocked the bizarre event from his mind.

The exchange still made no sense to him. What could the Confederacy possibly need that the inferior people of the Earth and their already-ravaged planet could provide? And why would anyone be talking about such a secret in a treatment room of a medical center instead of in some hidden refuge?

Because it wasn't official, only the idle scheming of some unbalanced Earth-haters. The disgust that Natira could not hide was bound to be even more pronounced among a self-righteous few.

And his own actions had only justified such contempt. If there were Tellurians who sought to undermine what little confidence remained within the people of the Earth and make them slaves to a foreign will, Killian had played right into their hands.

He snapped upright in the bed.

Great Earth Mother. Could that be true?

Memories of the past few days twisted in his brain.

From his act of misplaced gallantry in Borealis, to the fight on the clifftop, to his quick arrest in the medical center. Did it form a pattern? A plan?

Yes. He *had* played into their hands. In fact, he had danced to the strings of a master puppeteer.

Someone had recognized him as a perfect pawn for their scheme. Knowing about his killing of the guard but being unable to prove it, they'd found another way to entrap him and use him for their own ends. They'd known how desperate he was to get medicine for his mother, so they'd taken him right to the place it was kept. Had even shown him how easy it would be to steal, confident that he wouldn't be able to resist.

Hadn't Natira said that his location was known at all times thanks to his visitor's tattoo? Yet he'd been allowed to go straight to the medical center and carry out his crime. From

153

then on, he was theirs, caught red-handed by guards who'd known exactly where he was.

It was a brilliant scenario. He had bitten the hand that had reached out to lift him up. So, what could law-abiding Tellurians expect from the rest of the rejects on Earth?

His own people would be eager to make up for his indiscretion. Eager enough to ignore any signs of betrayal, and fatally misplace their trust. Easy pickings.

The images that played out in his mind were horrific. He desperately hoped that he was wrong. But if not, there was one more painful implication that he couldn't ignore.

One person had led him right to the bait.

Natira Celestia.

"I'd have thought that you, more than anyone, would be eager to see this man get what he deserves."

The Patriarch's image was a study in irritation, his arms tightly crossed, his chin stiffly pointed. It looked as if he was speaking to her from a clinical setting somewhere—perhaps a longevity treatment, if she were to believe family gossip.

"I don't like him," Natira said, "but he isn't fully to blame for his actions. His mother is dying, and we unwittingly placed the very thing he most wanted right within his reach. While their devotion to genetic parents seems pointless to us, it is a very real attachment and stronger than almost any other impulse they have. Of course, he couldn't resist. You don't have to be a criminal to give in to a temptation like that. I'm not even sure he knew what he was doing was wrong. Their primitive culture . . ."

"Has laws against theft, just like ours does. Banishment, usually. Exile from their settlement. His punishment from us won't be any worse than what his own people would give."

Banishment from the very planet of his birth was a whole other level of penalty, but she didn't say so out loud.

"Then why don't we banish him from Telluria back to Earth? That's where he belongs."

"That's not enough. We have to send a strong message to anyone else who might think we can be victimized. It's important that they understand their place."

155

"Yes, so I've been told. And this whole mess turns out to be a perfect way to get your message across, right from the very beginning."

Suddenly her own words exploded in her mind. *It was true.* The situation was perfect. Too perfect.

Her hand rose to her chest, her next breath almost a gasp.

"You knew he would steal the medicine. That's why he was chosen to come to Telluria in the first place."

She expected the Patriarch to deny it, but he only smiled.

"Diplomacy takes many forms. And the stakes are high. I don't apologize for using one primitive Earth man to gain a favorable position in our future dealings."

"You used me, too."

"You exist to serve your family and your society, as I do. I'm confident that you welcome the chance to be of any service you can. And will continue to do so." He made a motion to break the connection.

"Wait! Please. At least you will see that his mother gets the medication she needs, won't you?"

"Medication would only buy her a few months. She would need full treatment, and I'm not about to set a precedent by bringing an Earth woman to Telluria to cure an illness. All of them would expect the same. Where would it end?"

"The magistrate promised."

"If the Earth man gives his full cooperation. Who's to say that commitment doesn't extend for the full term of his sentence?"

She was too stunned to answer. Her adoptive father's image vanished leaving her to slump against the wall, as badly winded as if she'd just returned from the *high-g* exercise room.

She had been used. What's more, if she could figure out that Killian had been set up by her government, he would almost certainly come to the same conclusion. He might be uneducated, but he wasn't stupid. And he would blame her for playing a key part in his betrayal.

So what? Why should she care? He'd wrecked her own dreams and derailed her life. Now the tables were turned, even if her revenge was totally accidental. And the Patriarch was right—the issues at stake were much bigger than the lives of one man, or one woman. She had played her part unwittingly, and that soured her stomach, but she should be pleased that she had served 'the greater good.'

She went to bed that night trying to picture Killian's mother.

# # #

Her efforts to put a positive face on the situation had evaporated by morning and left behind a smoldering resentment. She probably would have done almost anything the Patriarch had asked of her—if he *had* asked. The fact that he had callously used her as a pawn filled her with a need to express her independence. She was also tired of blundering in the dark.

Breaking into the locked archive was still too risky, but there might yet be more information to be found in deeper levels of the public record—archives hidden from general queries but not expressly forbidden. Except it would require greater technical knowledge than her own to uncover them.

Wait. There was someone she knew with skills like that.

It made her blush to think of him.

Even in the unflinchingly dispassionate Tellurian education system, the flood of hormones at puberty was impossible to ignore. For Natira, the focus of that torrent had been a boy named Reece Tellurian: as awkward as any teenager and even skinnier than most, but still fairly good looking and as driven as Natira herself to succeed in his studies. His favorite subject even then had been mathematics and related intricacies of codes and cyphers. Reece hadn't been adopted by one of the powerful families despite his impressive academic record, but he had been offered prestigious work in the Ministry of Communication. Though their emotional entanglement had lasted less than six months, she and Reece had remained friends; and when her role as a video presenter allowed their paths to cross a few times a year, it was a pleasure for both of them.

He might not be so pleased this time.

She pulsed a message to him using a childish code they'd once created. It would pique his curiosity; but, more importantly, it might keep him from being implicated in her plans if he chose to refuse.

Three hours later he was leading her through an unfamiliar part of the city. A nondescript grey building opened its wall to them, and they marched for five more minutes through a succession of downward-sloping corridors. He didn't explain until they'd passed through a small doorway at the end of a hall, which had been invisible until it opened.

"You wouldn't have asked me for help with any ordinary search," he said. "Which means you want to know something the government wouldn't sanction, and you want anonymity. This is where you can get it."

"What is this place?"

"The building is just a residence for older citizens who need extra support. But this room was created five years ago by a small group of very private people."

"You mean . . . rebels?" Her eyes opened wide.

"No." He laughed. "Except in the sense that they rebel at the idea of someone in the government watching everything they do on the networks."

"The government doesn't have enough staff to do that."

"Well, most monitoring is done by artificial intelligence. But a live person can look at anything you're doing at any time. We don't like that. I don't like it, and I work in the Communications Ministry. The links to and from this room are specially shielded, and are also disguised as other nodes. In fact, in a random sequence which changes every thirty seconds, it will eventually use the network address of nearly every network node in Capita."

"Is that legal?"

He gave the half smirk she remembered so well from the rare occasions when she missed a math question in junior school.

"Do you really want to know?"

"No, I don't. Let's just get down to work."

"Good. I hope its juicy."

In a gesture that was surely just a peer-group affectation, he pushed back the sleeves of the stretchy blue shirt he wore, revealing pale brown skin that had almost no hair. As the space in front of the room's end-wall began to glow, he swept his arms outward, curled his wrists, and extended his fingers in a series of movements too fast for Natira to follow.

"Just making connections," he said with a smile. His left hand swept a lock of sandy hair from his forehead, and he rotated his shoulders as if in preparation for a workout. She'd seen athletes do the same thing, but Reece was no athlete. His arms were still as skinny as ever. She idly wondered what it would have been like if their relationship had escalated, but the image was too strange.

"So." He finally stopped and looked at her. "Did you say you want details about the Exodus?"

"The final month or two before it, and the first few years after, yes. Did you know that almost all the wealth of the planet was controlled by only a few thousand people at that time? They were called the ultra-rich, and because they didn't share their wealth, Earth's common people began to hunt them. *For sport.*"

"That can't be true!"

"It is. That much is in the public records. And it may have been the final incentive for the Divide, I don't know. Accounts become vague at that point. We know that thousands of spaceships were launched on a single day, but who was aboard them? How was the choice made? When were the ships even *built?*"

"So, let's find out."

The search took the rest of the morning, not because it was difficult, but because Natira and Reece were so stunned by what they learned that they read many of the entries more than once. Very gradually, pieces of a new picture came together.

It hadn't been difficult for the world's wealthiest to build spaceships of their own. They'd controlled the planet's space industries for half a century. Their launch ramps used electromagnetic tracks up the sides of mountains, enabling multiple launches within minutes of each other. With the vast number of factories controlled by the wealthy all over the globe, huge numbers of vessels were built and made ready without the general population knowing a thing. But when amateur astronomers began to notice large structures taking form between Earth and the Moon, an explanation was needed. Official proclamations from the world's governments declared that these were a response to the Earth's disastrous conditions. Giant spacecraft were being built beyond Earth orbit that could take immigrants to other star systems so as to preserve humanity. That such a voyage would require centuries was rarely mentioned.

The news was explosive. Citizens were assured that everyone would have an equal opportunity to take the journey if they were truly willing to leave their home planet behind—forever.

In earlier times, there might have been few takers, and only from among the most adventurous. But an imminent collapse of world order was plain to everyone. Humankind had finally turned the planet's own weather against themselves, and billions of homeless had little to lose in seeking a new home among the stars.

The charade was maintained for two years. Then, unannounced, came the day of the Exodus itself, and the world's teeming masses watched in dismay as thousands of spacecraft rode trails of smoke and flame into the sky. Without them.

They'd been left behind.

The escapees refused all communication with the planet they were abandoning, but it took only a few days to confirm that all the world's wealthiest were gone, along with everyone in key leadership positions. Having prepared their flight for years, they'd taken most of the Earth's remaining wealth with them in the form of art treasures, antiquities, and precious metals. But worst of all, they had taken the planet's best and brightest people, too: top experts in every field that mattered, and thousands upon thousands of the lesser lights who might have replaced them. These most ingenious and dynamic minds, and the knowledge they carried, were the Earth's true wealth, and it had been stolen.

Such callous cruelty on the part of their ancestors was hard for Natira and Reece to accept. They checked multiple sources—but the answers never varied.

And there was more.

Killian had told the truth. On the day of the Exodus, data centers, libraries, even schools were wiped out in an unprecedented display of coordinated destructiveness. The worldwide web of computing networks was eaten from within by viruses and worms of malicious code—poison spread throughout a vast circulatory system. Nothing was left functional. All electronic records and most physical records were eliminated; and although some private homes managed to retain printed repositories of information such as books, such repositories were few. Almost everyone in the world had chosen long before to store and access data electronically.

Technological infrastructure was eliminated with equal thoroughness. After all, since every complex device had been manufactured by one of the mega-corporations, it could be equipped with any one of dozens of methods of self-destruction, from deliberate short-circuits, to vials of corrosive substances, and even explosives. Everything from mammoth machines of transportation to personal care items was disabled—if it ran on electronic circuitry, its circuits were melted into slag with a simple coded command. And then, when the fleeing spaceships reached beyond Earth's atmosphere, the planet's surface was bombarded by electromagnetic pulses of frightening intensity as ultimate insurance. No circuitry could have survived outside of especially shielded Depots.

This plan had been in the works for years and was carried out with utter ruthlessness. Those who left their homeworld had determined that not only would they never be followed into space, but that the technology with which the planet had been ravaged could also no longer be used to pollute the skies, land, and water.

A technological Dark Ages had dawned.

Natira could barely breathe as she tried to picture the days after that great destruction. How could anyone carry out such a ruthless campaign of carnage? But equally incomprehensible was why the departing colonists had bothered to build the Allocations and Depots for the wretches they left behind.

"Maybe there were some who couldn't handle the guilt," Reece said. "Providing Allocations and Depots eased their consciences a little."

"But they built them in remote places, not where people already lived. And from what I see here, the Allocations and Depots could never have supported all the people left behind."

"I don't have an answer for that. Or maybe I just don't want to think about the answers." Reece's mouth was tight. Natira knew that expression. He wouldn't say more even if she asked. He coughed and looked at her directly. "So, is this what you wanted to know?"

"This is not something I *ever* wanted to know," she said, looking into his eyes. His brown irises were deep and liquid. Filled with hurt, like the day he'd come to congratulate her on being chosen by the Celestia family, though he had no prospects of his own to celebrate.

She turned away from the display. "I'd also planned to find out what happened in the first decade or two after the Divide, but I don't know if I can handle any more . . . shock right now."

"I can't bring you here too often. People would notice."

"No, that's why I brought this data unit." She nudged the squarish pouch she carried on a strap over her left shoulder. "Could you please copy as many of these history files as we have time for, so I can look them over later?"

Reece nodded and she held out an optical connector for the data port. A hard connection would be best for such a large transfer. More secure, too.

While they waited, Reece tried to make small talk, asking about her life within the Celestia family and her commitment contract with Valenti. Where she once would have poured out every trivial detail, she found that she didn't want to talk about that life anymore, especially to someone like Reece who didn't have access to the ridiculous luxuries and privileges of the leading families. Hearing about them could only invite comparisons with the monstrously selfish ancestors they'd just been reading about.

She thought about Killian Morningcloud and the people of Earth who'd been deprived of even the most basic technology. Schooled by holographic teacher-algorithms programmed with a bare minimum of knowledge most likely shaped by Confederacy propaganda. Why? To keep them properly subservient for when the people of the colonies chose to return?

A nebulous plan beginning to form in her mind provoked a shudder, and she was glad Reece didn't see it.

There might be a way to make some small restitution to the people of Earth, though it would be horribly risky. She released a deep breath. Reece looked up.

"That sounded like a tough decision."

She shrugged and gave a half smile. "Would you be able to copy over some other files, too? I'd like as many practical engineering databases as we can get—diagrams and instructions for tech students, historical records of inventions, basic principles of machinery and electronics. Not modern level. More like what technology was like when our people left Earth."

The puzzlement on his face was tinged with apprehension. "Why would you want that?"

"There might be clues to what I'm trying to figure out," she said. "You know, to give me a better understanding of what our ancestors were trying to keep to themselves, and why. Can you do it?"

"I think so. When I was a kid, I was interested in all kinds of primitive tech so I found some old data aggregators, if I can just remember them. It'd be a pretty big package though."

She looked at her Synappt portable processor. "This was a gift from the family when I was first adopted. I'm told that even the processors on shuttles don't hold as much as this one."

He looked suitably impressed, rubbed his chin and launched into more hand motions, grabbing projected icons from the air and placing them onto the symbol for Natira's unit.

Silences were becoming awkward. She could tell that he was trying hard to decipher her motives, and did her best to look nonchalant.

"So far, what we've been doing might puzzle people if they stumbled onto it," he said, "but considering your field of research, there wasn't any real need for secrecy. What *aren't* you telling me?"

She hesitated. The last thing she wanted was to bring Reece the kind of trouble she might be courting, but his look of sincere concern made up her mind.

"Earlier this month I stumbled onto an archive that wasn't like anything I'd ever seen before. From a handful of tags, it looked to be a government record from the time of the Divide, but it was encrypted like no other historical record I've found, and it wasn't coded to any index either. Like a package of raw data just dropped into a library with no way to know it was there. I didn't try to decrypt it right away, but I decided to tell Basu Hind, my mentor, and then spoke to my Patriarch. Both men tried to slough my discovery off as a programming mistake or a bunch of random code orphaned in the system during some transfer or other. But I could tell they were surprised and uneasy. And then when I looked for the archive again it had been placed behind new walls of sophisticated encryption."

"What are you trying to say, that it's some kind of deep, dark government secret? They have special databanks for that, with ridiculous amounts of protection. Why would anyone just leave something dangerous lying around in the wild?"

164

"Any layer of protection can be hacked—people in the outer colonies do it just for mischief, to thumb their noses at us. And security measures announce that you've got something to hide. But what better way to hide something than to leave it with no labels or indexing or anything that could possibly call attention to it?"

"So what were you hoping I would do?"

"I wasn't. I don't want you getting involved in any way—it might get you into trouble."

"You can't expect me just drop it now!"

She balked, but he wouldn't be dissuaded. Taking the risk, she told him where she'd last found the file. He let out a low whistle when it appeared in his display.

"I see what you mean. Yeah, that spells bad news, no question."

"So, we're not going to try to break the security measures, right?"

"Right. For now."

"What's that supposed to mean?"

He laughed. "I know you won't be able to leave this alone forever. Maybe there'll be a time when you can take a crack at it somewhere safe. So, we won't try to open it. We'll just copy it."

"What?"

"Sure. It's not big—I'd guess it's just text and maybe a few images—and while they've smothered it with armor to keep it from being opened, I would guess that they didn't shield the raw data from being copied." He looked the question at her.

A chill ran up her spine, but she bit her lip and nodded. He was the expert.

"I just wish we could be sure this won't get you into trouble," she breathed.

His forehead furrowed as he forced a grin. "So far, this node has been totally successful in staying anonymous. But I don't think I'll use it again for a few months, just in case."

The copying process took longer than she'd expected. Finally, he made another series of hand movements and the display vanished.

"I did one more thing that might help you out," he said. "The security lock was set to automatically delete the files after three unsuccessful attempts to access the archive, but it's three times per user per day. I've set it to cycle through different user identities to give you a lot more chances to crack the codes."

"Whose identities?"

"Every citizen of Telluria. That should confuse things a little!"

They shared a laugh, then walked in silence back through the sterile corridors into the open air and stood awkwardly in the artificial sunlight.

"Thanks," Natira said finally. "I'm so sorry for . . . for putting you through that. And please be careful."

He shrugged and gave her a smile that made him look like a teenager again. "Let's get together for a happier reason sometime soon."

"I'd like that."

With a nod they turned and went their separate ways.

21

Killian had paced for more than an hour when the door suddenly opened.

Natira stood there looking distracted. Then her nose wrinkled.

He probably smelled bad. Apart from the pacing, he'd been exercising to burn off energy. She should be thankful that the room provided toilet facilities. She'd left him alone for thirty-six hours.

After a marked hesitation, she stepped into the room and closed the door.

"How is this better than the cell your police kept me in?" he blurted.

"I'm sorry. I never meant to leave you for so long, but a lot has happened."

"Of course. Your leaders must have taken you to celebrate how well your plan worked."

She looked startled, then cast her eyes toward the floor.

"Yes, there was a plan, but they didn't tell me about it. I didn't know any more than you did." Her discomfort seemed sincere. "You don't have to believe me. But you will have to give me some trust if I'm going to get you free."

"What? Have they decided that I'm not a criminal after all?"

"It's . . . not that simple. How badly do you want to get home?"

The question took him aback. Only days earlier he'd wanted to be anywhere but Earth. Even now, the prospect of forced labor on Mars wasn't unbearable if it meant he'd be able to become a citizen of the Confederacy afterward. He said so.

Natira's shoulders slumped.

"I'm not sure that would happen."

"Not sure?"

"All right, I'm certain that you would be kept as a laborer with no rights and no chance to come to live in Telluria. You'd have to take a chance that one of the outer colonies would accept you. Is that what you want—a short life of hard work in a mine, on a world where you can't even breathe outside a dome?"

This declaration took something out of her, and she began to walk the perimeter of the room with her hands clenched together in front of her. Killian was shocked at the difference in her from just the day before. The lithe, overconfident, perfectly dressed woman now seemed smaller, her clothes slightly askew and locks of flowing blonde hair out of place. She had some kind of satchel slung around her neck over one shoulder. He hadn't seen her wear such a thing before, and she kept nervously fingering the strap.

"So, you're offering to somehow get me home, but that isn't official, is it?" He raised his eyes to the ceiling and balled his fists. "No, I can't do that. If I try to escape, they won't give the medicine to my mother."

"They're not going to give it to her anyway."

"What did you say?"

She finally looked into his eyes. Her own were ready to spill with tears.

"They have no intention of curing her. The Patriarch told me so himself. That was just a false promise to ensure you'd cooperate."

Killian had to sit down. The bed rose to meet him. He looked at her but couldn't think of anything to say.

She gave a wave in the air and a chair extended from the wall. "I'm so, so sorry. There are plans in place that don't include me, and maybe never did. But I had no idea they were using me to trap you." Her eyes fell and she swallowed hard. "Today I learned that my ancestors were greedy, power-hungry people who not only left Earth in a crisis of their own making, but took away any chance for the ones they left behind to be able to rise above the disaster on their own. They might just as well have killed them."

"They didn't have to. The great plagues did that for them. My uncle told me that the human race nearly died out on Earth because very few plague survivors could have babies."

"How does he know this?"

"I'm not sure—I've often wondered, because my parents never told me any of that. But he also said that in the early years, some people did try to get off the planet in flying machines, but they were destroyed by lightning."

"After the plagues the people left the cities and went to the Allocations?"

"That's what I was told. Where else could they go? The colonists had forbidden us from hunting our own food."

"What?"

"People who killed animals sickened when they ate the meat. Boats that sailed out to gather fish were sunk by lightning." He shrugged. "There are some people who do hunt now, but they are very few and are very careful."

"Did people try to grow their own food?"

"Many still do, on the fringes of the settlements. But it's mainly for variety and to give them something to do. The weather makes it hard . . . ."

"Droughts, and floods, and storms. Yes, I know. Even after five hundred years."

He nodded again, and they retreated into their own thoughts.

"How would you help me escape?" he finally asked. "And why would you take the risk?"

"The how is the easiest to explain. I'm a video presenter—I help present information to people through the networks that the display walls use. When something important or interesting is happening I may be sent to . . . describe it for

169

anyone who watches the displays. This afternoon my producer asked me to go back to Earth to show Tellurians what's being done by our people there."

"That must mean they've forgiven you for my behavior. Why aren't you happy?"

A smile flashed across her face, but it was gone as quickly as it came. "I'm convinced that the reason I've been offered the job isn't because of their renewed confidence in me. I think it's because of things I know and things I might find out. Potentially embarrassing things. Including your situation."

"So, it's to shut you up."

"A reward for my silence, yes, and a promise of more rewards to come if I behave myself and play along."

Killian frowned. "Are you sure it's not a plan to send you into danger? So you might not come back?"

Her mouth opened in shock.

"*No!* No, they . . . they just wouldn't. But they *are* willing to bribe me for my cooperation, just as they were doing to you."

"They were lying to me."

She waved a hand to dismiss the implication. "The point is, I'm going to be sent to Earth, and I was invited to take along one of the Earth people who've been visiting Telluria, so I can record them telling their family back home all about it."

He eagerly sat forward.

"When would we go?"

"Tonight. It has to be right away because they'll come to take you as soon as they can stage a trial. There's a shuttle leaving in four hours. I'll come back to you before then."

"What about these bracelets?"

She frowned. "We can hide them with long sleeves, and I can control whether doors let you pass or not, but an alert might sound when we go into the shuttle zone."

Killian thought a moment. "Give me the strap of your bag."

It was fastened with clips. With her help, he threaded it through the bracelets several times to draw his wrists as close as possible and joined the clips together. Then he drew his knees up. With an explosive motion, he flung his arms down toward his shins and straightened his legs.

170

An instant of pain made him grunt, but the broken circlets slipped to the floor. He rubbed the bones of his wrists while an astonished Natira retrieved her strap.

"I can't believe that!" she said. "I guess they don't have to be strong because Tellurians would never think of trying to escape."

They looked at each other and laughed, but it was short-lived.

Killian's heartbeat quickened at the prospect of danger. He thought that Natira stood straighter too. She tugged on the refastened strap of her satchel to settle the bag just above her left hip.

"You still didn't say why you're willing to do this."

She sighed. "Maybe I'll tell you on the way. If I can figure it out myself. First, I have to get you some clothes."

He glanced down at his drab outfit. "Why? Because I smell?"

"Yes, you do. But that might actually work in our favor. The other clothes are part of my plan." A smile flitted across her face again. "And you're not going to like it."

22

Killian caught sight of his reflection on the way to the departure zone and it left him speechless.

There had to be a reason for the ridiculous clothing Natira'd given him to wear, but he couldn't imagine it. He'd certainly never seen any Tellurians dressed this way.

A fabric that simulated buckskin in a light tan color had been cut into a pair of very loose pants that were laced up the sides. Over that, a kind of tunic in the same material draped like a sack from his shoulders and was open most of the way down the middle of his chest. The bottom edge of the tunic was fringed with thin dangling strips of buckskin. Decorations made of tiny red and blue beads were stitched onto the clothing in seemingly random places. Both pants and tunic were too short for him. Natira had also insisted that he tie a band of the same tan cloth around his head to hold his long black hair in place. Getting everything just right took longer than it should have because she still couldn't bear to touch him and appeared repelled by the smell of his sweat. But she claimed that other Tellurians would feel the same and that would be a good thing.

He saw what she meant when they approached a pair of security people at the entrance to the shuttle gangway. The man reacted with a sharp step backward, but the woman raised a hand to her face and walked away a short distance, pretending to consult a display that showed rows of black scribbles. Another man and woman came out of a tunnel and stopped nearby, dressed in the silver uniforms that signified a flight crew.

"This is one of the Earth men," Natira told them, then dropped her voice. "He was going to be part of an exhibit; but this one's too stupid to learn what he's supposed to do, so I'm taking him back with me."

She'd warned Killian not to speak, but it was a near thing. He struggled to keep his face blank.

"It would be a great favor to me if you didn't record his description in the ship's log," Natira added. "It's completely my fault for not making sure all our selections could be trained, and I couldn't bear it if the great Basu Hind was embarrassed because of my mistake. I'm hoping to get to Earth and bring back another one before anybody notices he's gone."

"I've heard they all look alike," the security woman said, not concerned that Killian could hear her.

"No, there are differences." The shuttle crewwoman smiled. "This one is bigger and better looking than most. But he still has that Earthborn *smell*." She waved a hand in front of her face. Killian bit his cheek. "I think I'll stay in the cockpit and leave the passenger zone to the two of you. There's no one else going down. Just cargo."

"We won't bother you. He's actually pretty well-behaved." Natira darted a glance at Killian then gave a nod to the others and pointed toward the tunnel from which the flight crew had come. He took the hint.

He vowed to give her an earful once the shuttle was on its way; but by then the Moon had come into view beyond the floating colonies, many times larger than he'd ever seen it from Earth. To him, the mysterious cratered face had always symbolized the limitless potential of everything beyond the Earth, and consequently his own personal potential to rise above his station in life. He'd sometimes talked through his troubles to that magnificent presence that presided over the night.

It hurt to think that his closest view of the silver orb had only come as he was being exiled from its realm forever.

In vain, he searched for Telluria Quinta, the habitat being converted into humanity's first-ever star-roving vessel, but it was obscured by floating farmlands and factories.

His eyes fell on the ridiculous clothing he wore, and he plucked at it in disgust.

Natira held up a hand. "Before you say anything, maybe all of this was a bit excessive, but as you saw, it gave us a much better chance of getting away."

"Tellurians hate the way I smell and think all Earth people are morons—I get it—but what were these bizarre clothes supposed to do?"

"That's what Tellurians think Earth people of the wild look like. In fact, this is a costume that my Intended, Valenti, wore to a party."

He blinked, trying to tell if she was serious. "They've forgotten about the Depot clothes they gave us to wear?"

"Most people don't know, and don't care. Be thankful. Those security people would have talked about us anyway, but this way they'll make a joke out of the story, and no one will think of Killian Morningcloud when they hear it. That will buy us some extra time."

"Time for what? You haven't said what we'll do when we get to Earth. Won't we be landing right where your lying snake of an ambassador works?"

"Please don't talk that way about him. Ambassador Hind has been a friend to me most of my life. I wouldn't be where I am if it weren't for him." She frowned at Killian's raised eyebrow. "We have no proof that he knew about the plan to entrap you any more than I did. I prefer to give him the benefit of the doubt."

"Whatever you say. But he'll still be able to see us walk out of this spacecraft, and I don't think your boyfriend's costume will fool him. Is there some way we could . . . take control of the vehicle and land it somewhere else? Maybe somewhere out in the bush?"

"Absolutely not! These shuttles are tracked at all times. If we went off course, alarms would sound, and security forces would be on us before we even touched the ground. Besides, being alone with you in 'the bush' is the last thing I'd ever do. Borealis is the only choice. You'll at least have a chance to disappear among your own people. Or escape into the forest if you have to. Maybe if I stick to my story, the flight crew will help us avoid Ambassador Hind."

Killian was deeply skeptical, but it turned out that she was right. Not only did no one question Natira's explanation, but they were even able to get a ride into Borealis with a security contingent.

"Why are you still coming with me?" Killian whispered in the car. "You should have hidden among the Tellurians until the next shuttle back."

"I want to go with you to your mother's. I have something for her."

Killian was afraid to ask more because the security men in the forward seats stopped talking and turned around to look at them.

They arrived at the worn door of Summer's hut and the contrast of its shabbiness with the gleaming vehicle that had brought them made Killian's head swim. What was he thinking, bringing Natira Celestia, adopted daughter of the Prime Councilor of Telluria into such a place? Now, having witnessed the splendor and prosperity of Capita, the squalor of his mother's home struck him like a blow.

His mother and grandmother sat near the bed, frozen in the act of drinking tea. Their fleeting smiles at seeing Killian turned into gasps when they realized who this visitor must be.

They quickly stood and gave small bows, as they would to a village elder.

"Welcome! Welcome to our home," Summer said, managing to produce a warm smile despite her obvious shock. She looked around for a suitable place for such a guest to sit, but failing in that, she waved Natira toward her own chair.

The Tellurian woman declined the offer respectfully.

"I can't stay for long, and I know you're ill. Please sit."

Killian wished for more chairs, but there was only the bed, and that would be much too intimate.

An awkward silence was finally broken as Grandmother asked Killian, "What in the name of the ancestors are you wearing?"

It felt good to laugh. He stepped forward and reached for the hands of both women. Their smiles soon vanished as he quickly related the details of his troubles in Telluria.

"The bastards!" Grandmother said, then put a hand to her mouth and looked apologetically at Natira, who couldn't help but laugh again.

"So, I can't stay long," Killian finished. "I'd better disappear into the bush before they come looking for me. But this woman helped me escape, even though she risks losing the work that she cherishes. Maybe even her freedom." He looked at Natira who kept her face impassive. "Coming here is even riskier. I don't know why she did."

"I came because I have something for you, Summer." She drew her hand from a pocket of her tunic and held out a clear vial filled with an amber liquid. "This is medicine. Put one drop into a glass of water at each meal. It won't cure you completely—that would take treatment you can't get here— but it will make you feel better, and help you live longer than you would without it. I wish I could do more."

The women and Killian were stunned. Summer slowly reached out a hand for the gift, as if it were an item of fragile magic that might disappear at her touch.

"But how . . . ?" Killian began.

"You'd already told the medical system that I needed it. The amount you took was re-entered into inventory, but no one cancelled the requisition. I just had to ask for it."

"This is more . . . more than I could ever have expected," Killian said, his voice cracking. He turned away slightly. His mother and grandmother looked at each other with wet eyes.

As Summer stepped toward Natira to speak, a loud whooping noise interrupted from a distance.

Seeing alarm on Natira's face, Killian said, "It's the Depot. It only makes that sound when there's an important announcement."

He gave his mother a lingering hug then hurried Natira out the door as Summer called out her thanks.

It wouldn't be wise to take the most travelled paths to the Depot. He knew a route dense with clotheslines that might hide them if security forces were on the pathways.

A small crowd was already on hand by the time they arrived. The Depot's last summons had been many months ago, and that had been to warn the people to collect extra supplies ahead of a fierce early-winter storm. As Killian and Natira approached furtively, they heard an emotionless male voice, while red symbols that Killian couldn't read flashed across a black surface.

The voice was repeating a message about a fugitive who had committed a crime against the Confederacy and was being sought by their security forces with the permission of Borealis's Council of Elders. When a picture of Killian flashed onto the black wall, he flinched and hurriedly looked around to confirm that he was hidden from most of the crowd. A picture of Natira came next. The Depot voice said that they might be together, and the colonists were concerned about the woman's safety. Citizens were urged to report to one of their elders if the pair was seen.

Killian turned to her, reading utter dismay in her eyes.

"You can't read the red words, can you?" she asked. "They're intended for any Tellurians nearby, I suppose, though security officers would also have aural implants for communication," she added, then swallowed. "Those words say that I may have *helped* you escape."

"Oh, no."

He wanted to touch her in some way, to comfort her, but knew it would only make things worse.

"We have to hide! Maybe back at Summer's house."

"No!" She shook her head violently. "They know it. They probably just missed us there."

"Then there's no choice—we have to hide in the forest." He began to move toward the nearest stand of trees. She started to follow, but stopped, head and shoulders slumping.

"They'll see us—with infrared sensors."

"What?"

"Heat—our bodies give off heat, and special equipment can see that. We'll stand out brightly in the forest because we'll give off much more heat than the trees and soil around us."

"The ground vehicles and shuttles have this?"

"Well, no, probably not. But there are satellites—equipment that circles the Earth high in the sky and watches the surface. Security forces will use those."

Killian looked up. "They're watching us all the time? Right now?"

Her face lit with a faint hope. "Maybe not right now. There are only six satellites that stay in a synchronous orbit to relay communications, the rest travel in fast orbits." Killian just shook his head, not understanding, but sensing her urgency. "Odds are that none of them will be in just the right spot. The security forces will have to wait until a satellite passes over Borealis, or they might even have to change the orbit of one of them." She began to walk again, then broke into a run in the direction he'd been heading.

"How long do we have?" Killian caught up and took the lead.

"I have no idea."

"Could we hide in someone else's hut, or even burrow into the snow to block our heat?"

"Huts like these? No, they wouldn't hide us. Snow probably wouldn't either."

"Then there's only one place nearby that we can go." He thought back to the obsessive cleanliness of Telluria. "And this time you're the one who's not going to like it."

PART TWO

23

It took all of Natira's willpower to enter the cave.

At first, she couldn't believe there was really an entrance in front of her. It was hidden by evergreen shrubs and twisted cords of dead vines that dangled from a rock face. But as Killian's feet disappeared from view, she knew she would have to follow.

Lowering herself gingerly to her hands and knees, her fingers recoiled in shock from the cold of the mud and snow mixture. Her knee pinned the bottom edge of her tunic, nearly sending her face-first into the muck.

Her lift vest was partly to blame. Strapped around her waist and chest, it was meant to resist gravity in a standing position—on hands and knees, it made her hips lighter than her head and shoulders, which made crawling incredibly awkward. She shifted back onto her haunches and tried to roll up the tunic bottom. It wouldn't stay—she could only keep tugging it out of the way. With teeth clenched, she ducked under a pair of shrub branches and knocked a flurry of snow down her neck. The icy jolt impelled her through the grasping vines, which caught her hair and brought down a cascade of dirt from the rock face. She scuttled forward, spitting grit and some of the foulest language she knew.

The low tunnel extended only about five meters, every part of it dripping meltwater. There wasn't enough room to stand upright. Killian shuffled hunched over for a short distance then turned to wave her toward one side—she was blocking the entrance and its stingy light. Finding what he was looking for, he reached out for her arm but stopped himself at the last moment and only beckoned her closer.

"I've been here a few times before and dragged in some branches and fern fronds to sit on," he said. "They're still fairly dry."

He motioned for her to go first. Reluctantly, she put an arm out to feel for obstacles and stepped past him. Her fingers confirmed that there was a thick mat of piled material up against the cave wall. It did seem drier than the rest of the surroundings; though as she sat down gingerly, she immediately felt dampness soaking through her pants.

Void's perdition! Could he have picked a more disgusting place?

"Sorry. Your white clothes are probably filthy now," he said.

"The dirt will fall out of the weave once it dries. But not your clothes. They were meant to simulate animal skin."

He grunted and sat down a meter away. "Then I probably look the same as the first time you saw me. Maybe that's my fate. Anyway, we don't have a lot of choice if we have to hide our body heat." A reflection glinted in his eyes as he turned toward her. "Is it really true that Telluria has things in space that watch us—have been watching us all this time?"

"Yes." She didn't want to elaborate.

"You could see how we live, but you've never done anything to help us make our lives better?"

The question caught her by surprise. "You were given the Depots."

"Sure. Just enough of a handout to discourage us from doing anything for ourselves."

"On a wrecked world, that seems pretty helpful to me. But from what you say, you don't depend on the Depot yourself."

He shrugged. "My aunt and uncle have different ideas than most people. They wouldn't let me stay in Borealis and do nothing all day."

"Does that mean they don't live in the settlement? I've read that some Earth homes once had rooms underground. Rooms like that might hide us from the satellites."

"Their cabin isn't like that." He shifted position. "Can these satel..."

"Satellites. It means they orbit—travel around— a larger body. The Moon is a satellite of Earth, though a natural one."

"I do know about satellites—I went to a special school to learn some colonist science. I've just never had to say the words before." He sounded irritated, but he forged on. "I was going to ask if these satellites can tell the difference between you or me or other people?"

"Not by infrared, I don't think. Oh, wait!" She pulled her Synappt case in front of her and opened the flap. The display projection filled the air with light for several meters around, enough to show the consternation on Killian's face.

"What's that? I thought you'd brought food, or ... women's things."

"It's a Synappt—an information processor, also called a computer. There was some important knowledge that I didn't want to leave behind. But I have to make sure the machine is not sending out a signal, trying to connect with other information networks." The function was easy to switch off, and she did so, but then pulled up her left sleeve. It wasn't so easy to defeat her Tellurian citizen ID, the glowing blue and red oval clearly visible under the skin of her forearm in the relative darkness of the cave. The colony's central computer could track her anywhere, but it depended on Telluria's omnipresent network of linked nodes to detect her signal and pass it along. Surely the transmission from the ID tat itself couldn't be strong enough to reach space from Earth's surface. And any overflying craft would have to approach within a few hundred meters, she thought.

Killian would still have his visitor tat, as well. Two electronic tattletales. That probably explained how his escape to Earth and her role in it had been revealed so quickly.

"I think we're safe from electronic detection, at least until they send shuttles to look for us," she said. "As for infrared tracking, I'm pretty sure most people would look about the same to the sensors, especially at a distance."

"So we should have stayed in Borealis, among other people."

"No. Could you trust that none of your neighbors or friends would give us up? Eventually the security forces will check every hut—the village isn't that big. But if we could get to your aunt and uncle's . . . ."

"No, I . . . I don't want to do that. They don't like colonists—we had a big fight about that just before I left."

"You think they'd hurt me?"

"No! Of course not. I just mean that they're already angry with me, and they'd be furious if I brought colonist trouble down on them after trying to warn me away from you people my whole life." He tossed a pebble across the cave and was silent for a few minutes. Then he lifted his head and asked, "What will your government do to you if they find you?"

"The security people wouldn't dare harm me—I'm a member of the first family of Telluria. Although maybe not for long. The Celestia family might disown me for something as serious as helping a prisoner escape. Especially when your punishment was an important part of their plans for Earth." Her voice cracked a little, and she coughed to cover it.

"Some Tellurians have plans that are even worse."

"What's that supposed to mean?"

He shook his head. "Will they keep you locked in a room? Or exile you to another colony?"

"If they were angry enough, they might choose exile. There aren't any prisons in Telluria."

"You would walk free?"

"Remember, I told you that every door can be locked if you're wearing restraint cuffs. I would be allowed to go some places but not others, entirely at a magistrate's choosing, with whatever restrictions might be considered suitable punishment. And the punishment could change at a whim, from day to day. But it is social stigma that would be the real punishment. I would lose all the status given to my family, my work, my friends . . . ." She stopped, not trusting her voice to go on.

"I'm ruining your life again."

"No . . . ." But she couldn't protest with any force. There was too much truth in what he said, even if it had been her own choice to help him escape.

"There's only one thing we can do," he said after a silence. "Can you talk to them with that thing in your satchel?"

"Talk? No, it's mainly for data storage and display." But there was something else that could reach the security forces. "My ID tattoo has an emergency function that can send a much more powerful signal than normal if it senses I'm badly hurt or in deadly danger."

"You *are* in deadly danger. Because if the security forces come within half a kilometer of us, I will kill you."

Her blank look turned to uncertainty, then fear, and her attempt to scramble away from him was brought up short by the wall.

"Seriously?" He snorted. "Do you really think I would do that? It's what *you* have to tell the security forces. Say that I forced you to help me escape and you've been afraid for your life ever since. If it's really necessary, we can scratch you or cool your body down in a creek to make them think you're injured."

"If they believe I'm in serious danger, they might swoop in with guns blazing."

"What kind of guns?"

"The security forces carry hand weapons called stunners—they incapacitate you for an hour or more and it's not pleasant."

"Would they take the risk that I might kill you before they could stop me?"

"I don't know. They probably won't believe that I didn't help you willingly anyway, once they talk to the shuttle crew. But if you threaten me with death, they'll never let you get away. They'll punish you very harshly."

"At least you won't suffer for something that was my fault. Besides, they'd have to catch me. And in the meantime, the threat might make them keep their distance—give us a chance to get away for good."

"Us?"

"Well, you have to go back to Telluria . . . of course. But only when you can be sure your name has been cleared. For now, I'd just like some kind of plan that would get us out of this damned cave."

He looked surprised when she laughed, and kept laughing.

But her laughter stopped instantly when she turned her head to find a more comfortable position, and put her face into a spiderweb.

24

"I still think we should go to your uncle's," Natira said into the darkness of the cave. She had no way to know how long they'd been there, but with the dim light from the cave mouth gone, it must be night. It seemed like forever. Without her Synappt's glow she couldn't see a thing. "Our people probably don't know him and wouldn't know it isn't normal to have four heat sources in his hut."

After a long silence, Killian said, "All right."

"There's another thing. Do you remember how light you felt in Telluria? The colony's spin only gives it about three-quarters of Earth's gravity. So that's what my body is used to. I have to wear a lift vest here—a device that supports some of my weight. But I have no idea how long its power will last."

"And if it stops?"

"Well, I told you how my body was . . . modified so I could come here. And I exercised in higher gravity all my life. My heart, lungs, and organs can cope if I don't push them too hard, but if the lift vest fails, I won't be able to walk far." She hated admitting weakness, but he accepted it without stating the obvious. He was certainly strong enough to carry her for a time, but if she couldn't walk, it would probably end any chance of escape.

"If it can be turned off and back on again, maybe you should only use it when we're moving."

Of course. She should have thought of that. She drew her hand down her side and immediately felt her muscles sag. Her mood was dragged down with them.

"It's not like we'll be going anywhere soon," she complained. "They'll be scanning the whole area with infrared by now."

"Hush. Listen."

There came a flash of light she could see even through closed eyelids. It was followed a few seconds later by a deep rumble that she felt as much as heard.

Had the Confederacy found them already, and brought heavy machinery?

"Thunderstorm," Killian said. He sounded pleased. Natira only groaned. She could hear the hiss of the droplets now. It must be one serious downpour, which meant that water would again come sluicing into the cave before long.

"How will we stay dry now?" she asked.

"We won't." He laughed. "Come on, we have to go."

"*What?* Why? Will the cave flood?"

"Probably not, but the storm should hide us from Tellurian satellites, shouldn't it?"

She pictured dense clouds shot with lightning. Tree branches blowing overhead. Millions of water droplets spreading and refracting their heat signatures.

It just might.

With a groan, she reluctantly reached out to grasp his clothing and followed him to the cave mouth.

"Wait a minute. How will you see where to go? Don't try to tell me you can find your way through a forest by lightning flashes."

"Well, first we're going back to Borealis so you can use your tattoo to call for help. I'm betting your machines won't want to fly a search in weather like this. From there I know a trail that we should be able to follow even in the dark."

"You can't be serious."

"When I'm joking, you'll hear me laugh." Which wasn't true. She could almost never tell whether he was being sincere or sarcastic.

The full force of the storm was even worse than Natira imagined. Her clothes were thoroughly soaked within seconds. If she raised her face, the storm's flat-out assault took her breath away; but if she hung her head too far, water ran from her hair into her nose and mouth and threatened to drown her. After a bad step brought her hard to her knees, she remembered to reactivate her lift vest. Its buoyancy was a great relief. She only hoped it was waterproof.

Between lightning flashes, she could see nothing except outlines of tree limbs etched into her retina. She kept a desperate grip on the back of Killian's tunic, though even that was far too personal for comfort.

They walked through a nightmare. At every moment, she hoped that the storm would end, but feared that her wish would be granted. Surely even a Tellurian punishment couldn't be worse.

She didn't know that they'd reached Borealis until Killian told her, his voice sounding far away. The next flash of lightning revealed boxy outlines amid spreading pools of water. Sheltered from the wind behind a hut, she pulled back her sleeve and tapped out a code on the glowing oval, then held her wrist toward her mouth and yelled out the message she'd chosen. It sounded garbled even to her, but with luck they would understand enough.

When she was done, she looked around only to find that Killian had vanished. Had he abandoned her? What could she do?

But then she heard a small noise, and soon saw a dark form solidify from the gloom.

"We're going to need coverings to keep us warm," Killian said. "I got lucky. These were being aired out after the winter."

He pulled something like an absurdly heavy fabric over her shoulders, except that while the inner surface was smooth, the outer felt like very coarse hair.

She gasped, then blurted in a harsh whisper, "Is this from an *animal?*"

"Muskrat. Very valuable. I've just stolen someone's prized possessions. I'll have to find a way to get these back to them."

Killian was already on the move. Whoever lived in the hut might have heard them and could come out to investigate.

Her nose recoiled at the smell of the covering, even though it wasn't completely unpleasant. It was the thought of the dead animal that made it repulsive.

But not repulsive enough that she refused to wear it. She already had spells of shivering from the cold and wet.

Knowing she'd be going to see Killian's mother in primitive Borealis, she'd worn her toughest shoes, but by now they were a sodden, slippery mess. Some of the puddles on the edge of the settlement had to be waded, and she felt Killian stumble time after time as they forged on into the forest. He staggered from one side of the path to the other, only detecting its edge by the scratch of shrubbery and the treacherous miniature crevasses where softer dirt had washed away. She could tell that he was indeed trying to navigate by the lightning, so it perversely chose to appear less and less often.

There came a time when the rain eased, and finally stopped. Killian looked at the sky anxiously, but black clouds still roiled overhead, and lightning flashed within them.

Hours later, Natira heard the rush of water again. It wasn't a return of the rain—the world had begun to lighten. Dawn must be near, though the storm clouds showed no sign of admitting the sun. Now, she was able to follow Killian without clutching his clothing. But where was the water sound coming from?

A shout from Killian startled her.

"Great Mother Earth, it's the raft!"

They'd come upon a river—an expanse of black water that wasn't terribly wide but moved with dangerous speed. After a moment she saw the thing that had caught his attention: a flat deck of logs lashed together in some way. A raft? Her mind associated that word with boxy floating platforms that were sometimes pushed out into Capita Lake to shoot off fireworks. In this dim light, it looked as if a rope extended from the far side of the raft into the river, and a second rope to a nearby tree.

"My aunt and uncle must have left it for me—pushed it back across after they used it, in case I came this way."

Left it for ...?

No, he couldn't be planning to ....

No. No! *"No!"*

"What do you mean, no? How else do you think we can cross? I used a fallen tree the last time I came this way, and believe me, you wouldn't be able to do that."

"I won't be able to do *this*. There's no way you can make me get on that thing."

"No," he said. "There isn't."

He took her cloak and folded it with his own at his feet, then simply stood, waiting.

She screamed when the raft came loose from the shore and hated herself for it. Of their own will, her fingers scrabbled until they felt cloth and then gripped for all they were worth while she kept her eyes tightly shut. The jerking and bobbing of the platform made her stomach heave. Through her knuckles she could feel the muscles ripple in Killian's back as he pulled fiercely at the rope, arm over arm, fighting the current of the river to bring them to the other side. But each pull tugged his edge of the raft downward; and, as freezing water flowed over her shoes, she was sure they would capsize.

Terrified into senselessness, she had no idea how long the ordeal lasted. Killian must have yanked her ashore by the arm, but she didn't even notice. She only knew that she was on land again, and the relief made her drop to her knees in the mud sobbing for breath.

When her pounding heart had begun to slow, she leapt to her feet and charged at him, beating at his chest with her fists.

"Why do you keep doing this to me?" she shrieked. "Why do you hate me so much?"

He let her pummel him until eventually her arms tired and fell to her side. Then he simply wrapped her muskrat cloak over her shoulders again.

"I don't hate you at all," he said in a voice almost too soft to hear over the wind. "I don't . . . I've never . . . ." He turned his face to the sky and walked away. After a moment she stalked after him.

"So, what's next? What new torture have you come up with? You seem to want to prove you're better than me, so bring it on!"

He turned his head, but his only response was a look of hurt and sadness. At last, he said, "Next, we rest. Just ahead are the ruins of an old, abandoned homestead. There's a lean-to over there. We'll have to spend the daylight under it, I guess. The roof is metal, so I hope it will block our heat from the satellites. It's all I can think of."

When they arrived, he trudged into the dense trees and brush and returned with an armful of evergreen boughs that he spread over the floor of the shelter—no more than a metal sheet leaning against a pile of cut logs—then repeated the trip several more times until, apparently satisfied, he ducked inside and lay down on the ground. He'd left plenty of space for her, but she refused to join him. Instead, she paced outside and scanned the forest, not even knowing what she was looking for. The sky grew lighter by the minute, the clouds finally showing signs of breaking up. If she didn't get under cover soon, their ordeal of the night would be in vain.

With an inarticulate bellow she vented her fury at ground and sky, then clambered into the shelter to lie with her back as far from Killian as she could get, hugging her anger to her chest. She pretended not to notice when he carefully spread his muskrat cloak to cover her more completely.

After a few moments of cold silence, he spoke in a flat voice.

"I don't suppose you'll want to hear this, but your lift vest probably could have carried you over the river."

Thunderstruck, she suddenly remembered that he would have seen her float down from the roof of the Depot on that first day.

With a grunt of rage, she snatched a handful of dirt and threw it at him.

25

As Killian slowly came awake, it took a few moments for him to identify the vibration that had roused him.

Natira was shivering. In rain-soaked clothes, that wasn't surprising, yet he could hardly risk a fire even if he were able to light one. The fur cloaks were excellent at trapping body heat, but couldn't create heat on their own. He and Natira should be huddling close to share their warmth. But he suspected she'd rather die than do that. It was as if the merest contact with him defiled her.

Yet she'd risked everything to help him escape and to bring medicine for his mother. Those weren't the actions of someone with hate in her heart, despite the havoc he'd brought into her life.

Uncle Lewis had warned him that nothing good could come of his obsession with the colonists, but Killian had never imagined that someone else would pay the price. He had to get Natira back where she belonged and draw the blame upon himself.

He took the fur cloak warmed by his body and spread it over her, hoping it might ease her shivering a little. Certain that he wouldn't be able to sleep, he sat and tried to make a plan.

Maybe the Tellurians would heed the warning Natira had sent and keep their distance, but Killian didn't want to give away their location regardless. He especially didn't want to lead pursuers to Lewis and Regina's.

"You're not going to sleep anymore?" Her voice quavered with the shuddering of her body.

"I've been trying to decide how to move on. When you're ready."

"I'm as ready as I'm going to be. If we don't get moving, I think we'll freeze here."

"It's the water in your clothes evaporating next to your skin . . . you've probably never been this cold before, have you?"

She sat up, with needles and bits of twig protruding from hair that stuck out in surprising ways. He chose not to mention it.

"Now I know what it must be like on Mars." Her stiff lips could barely form the words.

"Mars . . . I can't imagine it. Even your colonies hanging there in black space . . . spooked me, to tell you the truth. I always dreamed of going to one of them, but when I finally did, well . . . I feel more comfortable in a thunderstorm." He gave an awkward laugh.

"I'd feel a lot more comfortable almost anywhere but here. Let's get moving. How do you propose we do that?"

If they couldn't risk leaving their metal shield, that left only one choice.

The sheet was thin enough to lift, but Killian knew that his shoulders wouldn't bear the constant strain for long. Staying undercover as much as he could, he scrounged through the nearby remains of the collapsed cabin and finally wove together a framework of branches and thin boards that would distribute some of the weight onto his hips. A belt would have helped. He tried to tear a strip from off the bottom hem of his false-hide tunic, but the material wouldn't part, even when he tried to shred it over a corner of metal. The most he could cut off were bits of the fringe dangling from the hem. He painstakingly knotted them into more useful lengths and used those to lash his frame together.

With an effort, he hoisted the panel up, then directed Natira to stay close behind him under its trailing edge. It was a poor solution, but all he could think of.

Natira fretted that a computer analysis of the satellite imagery might detect a rectangular shape warmed by their bodies moving through cooler vegetation. But there was nothing they could do about that.

When they finally approached Lewis and Regina's home hours later, Killian's shoulders felt like they were on fire. He stopped twenty meters from the cabin, knees nearly buckling.

Lewis stepped through the door. His voice rumbled like distant thunder.

"Do I even want to ask what you're doing?"

"The Confederacy is probably tracking us from above the sky. Trying to see our heat."

Lewis's eyes widened. Regina appeared at his shoulder, and he held an arm out to keep her back. "Go to the woodshed," he said. "It's got a metal roof."

Killian staggered toward a structure of rough log posts that sheltered ten neatly stacked rows of split firewood. To call it a shed was overly generous since it had no walls and so, fortunately, no door. Once beneath its corrugated roof Killian let his shield slide to the ground and collapsed with his back against a wood pile, groaning as he tried to bring life back to his abused arms.

"Why in the Earth Mother's name did you bring *her* here?" Lewis glowered just beneath the edge of the shelter. At least Regina looked glad to see her nephew.

"Lewis Partridge, Regina Oak, this is Natira Celestia. Obviously, you recognize her, but what you probably don't know is that she's the daughter of the Prime Councilor of the entire Confederacy."

"A princess, no less. Even has a tiara on her head."

Killian looked at the jewel in the center of her forehead, which hadn't even shifted during all they'd been through. Its band had to be fastened to her in some way. But slumped in exhaustion on a pile of split logs, she certainly didn't look like a storybook princess.

"Being rude only makes you look bad, Uncle. Natira doesn't deserve it. In fact, she helped me escape from Confederacy security and brought medicine for Summer." As briefly as he could, he explained their predicament.

Lewis opened his mouth to speak but Killian waved him off. "I know. It's all my fault for worshipping the colonists. I'm an idiot. I should have listened to you. Is there anything else you really need to say?"

The big man was taken aback.

"Yes, there is. What can we do to help?"

It was Killian's turn to be at a loss for words.

"If you can think of any way we can get back to the Confederacy base near Borealis without Killian being captured, that would be a great help," Natira said.

"Why would you want to?"

"Her whole life is in Telluria," Killian answered. "A good life, with the potential to do great things. I refuse to be the cause of her losing all that. Our story is that I forced her to help me. I'll give myself up if I have to. But if they capture us first, we won't have any leverage."

"They'll know it's not true." Regina spoke for the first time. "They'll have medicines—drugs—that will make you tell the truth, both of you. You'll be surrendering yourselves for nothing."

"How do you know what they'll have?"

Husband and wife looked at each other but didn't speak.

It struck Killian that it would be hard to find two more different examples of womanhood than Natira and his aunt. Regina was a full head shorter, with shoulders almost like a man's and a stocky frame to go with them. She was strong in many different ways, but could also be surprisingly gentle. And wise.

"We've got to try," he said with less force. "In fact, maybe I need to be captured."

"What did you say?" Fire sparked in Natira's eyes.

196

"I need to speak to someone in authority. Maybe being captured by the security forces is the best way."

The faces of the others showed only bewilderment. He took a deep breath and told them about the conversation he'd overheard in the medical center in Capita: the plan to despoil Earth a second time, and force its people to work for the Confederacy.

"You never told me about that!"

His head slumped under her glare. "I didn't know if I could trust you. You might have been a part of it. You were part of the plan to entrap me."

"Not knowingly! They used me as much as they used you."

"I know that now. And now I'm telling you what I overheard. But don't pretend I'm the only one keeping secrets. Something happened to you between the time you left me locked in my room and when you came back for me. What was it that suddenly made you willing to break your laws and help me escape?"

She tried to hold onto her anger, but her eyes teared up and she turned her head away.

"It wasn't something that happened. It was something I learned."

She told them about the history archives, and the way the Divide really came about—how the wealthy and powerful had tricked everyone else into believing they offered a way out of Earth's crisis. The great betrayal. And then their malicious destruction of tools, technology, and all depositories of knowledge.

"They knew about the plagues, and they didn't help. All these centuries, they've watched and left you struggling even to keep some purpose in your lives. I . . . can't do anything to make up for all that, but I can refuse to be a part of it. And I brought as much of the old technical knowledge as I could with me. To share." She held the Synappt satchel up for them to see. "Only now it sounds like their scheme to use Killian might be just one of many." Her other hand pressed against her upper lip, and she couldn't look at any of them.

"There is more about those days that you still don't know," Lewis muttered. But when pressed, he only said, "No, it shouldn't come from me. You need to discover it for yourselves."

Natira narrowed her eyes, then seemed to make up her mind.

"This Synappt portable processor includes a copy of a hidden information archive from Telluria that I think may contain the most important secrets of that time. With proper equipment, I might be able to get into it; but there's no technology like that on Earth outside the Confederacy bases."

"I'm not so sure that's true," Lewis said cryptically. "But that's going to have to wait. First, we've got to deal with this pursuit. I have something that might help."

Killian had never seen his uncle act so mysteriously, and the man was clearly enjoying it. He walked off into the trees and was gone for about fifteen minutes. He returned with something like dull silver in his hands.

It was a kind of filmy material in two pieces. He gave one piece to Killian and one to Natira.

"What are they?" she asked.

"A kind of survival suit. Tech from before the Divide, from what I've been told. They're meant for cold weather—they reflect virtually all of your body heat back at you. But it seems to me they ought to hide your heat from prying eyes, too."

The one-piece body suits included boot covers and tight-fitting hoods, shiny silver on the inside with a dull outer finish, but so thin the whole outfit felt as if it could blow away on a breeze.

"Where did you get these?" Killian asked breathlessly, but Lewis only shook his head and said, "Another time."

"Then if I can ask another favor . . . ," Killian began. "The muskrat cloaks we brought—I had to steal them from a hut in Borealis. You know how valuable they are. If you could find some way to return them, I would be very grateful."

Lewis just nodded. The fugitives began to pull the strange suits on over their clothes.

"Don't think you're going to just dash off," Regina warned. "You can wear those to the house, but then Lewis is going to build a big fire and you're going to stay until your clothes are dry and you've had some food." She snorted. "And Killian is going to change out of that ridiculous clown outfit."

#   #   #

The radiant heat from the wood fire, familiar surroundings, and tantalizing smell of Regina's cooking all made Killian more relaxed than he'd been in weeks. As he slouched in a well-worn chair, he looked at Natira sitting even closer to the fire, bowed with worry but also rigidly uncomfortable, fingers pressed tightly together.

He tried to see the scene through her eyes, every single thing around her strange and primitive. Humans react to the unknown with fear, and she must be filled with it. Her comfortable life had come crashing down—all her hopes smashed. He could identify with that to a degree, but at least he was on his home planet. Natira even had to rely on technology to fight the Earth itself pulling her down

"Can you eat our food?" Killian asked her.

"Right now, I feel like I could eat anything." She tried to smile, her knee bouncing a little with tension. "Actually, the planners of our return to Earth recognized that we might need to attend ceremonial meals and special events, so they prepared our digestive tracts with bacterial flora from Earth. But I think they still expected most of the food to come from settlement Depots. Did you . . . gather this food yourselves?" she asked Regina, who stood on the other side of the room in the open kitchen. "Are there any . . . animals in it?"

"No animals," the older woman said with a reassuring smile. "I was pretty sure you wouldn't like that. But yes, we grew most of this food ourselves, or gathered it from the forest. Except for the flour, sugar . . . milk, I suppose. Do you know that it takes more persuasion to convince the Depot to give us ingredients than it does to get whole meals? Where's the fun in having everything prepared for you?" She laughed.

Natira was at a loss for words. From what Killian had seen in Telluria, she'd probably never prepared a meal for herself in her life. She stared at the cooktop on the wood stove and nibbled at her lip.

"Only eat what you want," she said. "No one's feelings will be hurt."

"It does smell wonderful."

"That's mostly the bread," Regina said. "Nothing like the smell of fresh-baked bread. Our Killian here is actually a pretty good bush cook himself, except his specialties are mainly roasted rabbit and fish baked in clay. It might be a while before you're willing to try that."

Killian gave a sheepish smile, but Natira's vanished completely.

Regina's vegetable stew was accompanied by some early greens from the woods, including wild leeks that were among Killian's favorites. Natira tasted everything, but filled up on the bread and sprouts. He was relieved to see that she didn't suffer any ill effects. Dessert was cornbread washed down with mugs of mint tea. She had second helpings of that.

When the tea was gone and conversation began to falter, Killian announced that they should be going.

"We'll need darkness when we get close to the Confederacy base."

"You'd never get there before dawn," Lewis protested. "Even you need to slow down in the dark, and you're not traveling alone. Besides, didn't you say that the colonists would see you by your heat? So even with the silver suits you'd be better off traveling in daylight when the sun heats the ground and the bush."

Natira looked at Killian. She tried to keep her face impassive, but he could sense her fear at the thought of another night journey through the unnerving forest.

"Take the time to pick your way carefully tomorrow, and then wait until dark to make your final approach."

He nodded at his aunt. "OK."

Natira was caught in a huge yawn, provoking a laugh from the others; but she refused the offer of Lewis and Regina's bed in a loft above the kitchen.

200

"But there's only one other," Regina said. "Killian's bed." She pointed to a narrow cot beside the box of firewood.

"I'll sleep on the floor," he said quickly.

Some extra cushions were put down beside his cot, probably closer than Natira would prefer, but there wasn't room anywhere else.

The only walled-off corner of the building enclosed a toilet. Natira had already used that room to change into some of Regina's clothes, but now that her own pants and tunic were dry, she put them back on for sleeping. Killian idly wondered what she normally wore to bed in the perfectly even warmth of Tellurian rooms, or if she wore anything, then tried to think of something else.

When his aunt and uncle had extinguished the candles, his quiet "Good night" went unanswered.

26

Watching Natira make her way through the dense brush, Killian yearned to help her avoid raking branches; but knew that she'd resent what she might see as coddling. He also wished he could shield her from prying eyes. The tarnished silver of their heat-masking coveralls gleamed alarmingly in the patchy sunlight.

So graceful in her home city, she clumped awkwardly in a pair of heavy boots that Regina had lent her, her Tellurian shoes destroyed. Long sunlight-blond hair occasionally strayed from her hood, and the ornament that Lewis had called her tiara was still visible on her brow. The combination of elements gave her the look of a royal waif from a melancholy fairy tale. Yet, to Killian, she was more appealing now than the stunningly perfect goddess who had floated down from the Depot roof on that momentous first day. Where that Natira had been untouchable, this one was undeniably human.

Downtrodden and heartsick, she resolutely pushed herself to match his pace, and refused to complain. If they'd been lost in a maze of streets in Capita, he wasn't so sure that he would have remained as stalwart.

He was proud of her, and he didn't know what to make of that.

Her worst moment had been re-crossing the river. This time she knew that she could use her lift belt to float across, but it would be an extravagant waste of power when she didn't know how much remained. It might even run out of energy mid-stream.

So she went with him on the raft again.

It took real courage to do that.

At Killian's urging, she climbed onto the platform first and huddled into a ball so he could stand over her to control the craft's balance. They'd hardly tipped at all, and were across the river in less than two minutes; but she'd needed much longer than that to recover, taking deep breaths while bent over her knees. He gave her all the time she needed without saying a word, wishing he could do more to help. When she was ready, she simply straightened and began to walk again.

From the first time they'd seen each other at the Borealis Depot, he'd experienced a whole range of emotions—shame, guilt, and regret foremost among them—but what he felt most now was sympathy. He would never understand her. She was much too judgmental and over-indulged, along with the rest of her society. But she didn't deserve what she'd suffered in the past weeks, so much of it at his own hands.

She glanced up at him and he quickly turned his face away, afraid of what she might see in it.

After another hour of travel, he left the path and struck out into the bush.

"Are we close to the Tellurian base already?" she asked.

"Not yet. I just want to show you something."

He wondered if she'd noticed the music that had called to him. In a few more minutes he pushed through a clump of spruce trees and held aside the branches for her to pass.

Before them was a broad vertical rock face about thirty meters high over which dozens of miniature waterfalls leaped and splashed, twisting, trickling. They filled the air with song as the droplets drummed on stone and scurried through pipe-like channels beneath melting ice. The rock faced north, so ice still clung to it like haphazard windows— windows in a rainstorm—and now and then small shards broke loose to shatter tinkling below with the sound of chimes. Some of the rivulets were already bordered with green, lush moss; and where isolated ledges captured layers of spongy soil, there sprouted small flowers of liverleaf—some white, some lavender—and blossoms of spring beauty with its pink-veined petals.

At that moment, sun broke through the clouds and pale yellow shafts of luminous glass gleamed through the forest canopy, giving the panorama the quality of a dream.

Natira gave a soft gasp.

"It's so beautiful!"

"These waterfalls only last for a week or so, as if the Earth Mother knows that the sweetest things should also be short. Soon, the last ice will be gone and most of the running water with it, and this will just be another rock cliff. Until next spring."

Her reaction pleased him. When she was finally ready to move on, her face seemed brighter, her step lighter. That was all he'd hoped to accomplish.

When they stopped for a rest a couple of hours later, Natira said, "I know you planned to approach the base through the bush, but let's go to Borealis first. I have an idea."

He waited for her to explain further; but when she didn't, he simply nodded.

Opinions in Borealis were weighed according to experience, not gender or even age. So, if Natira thought she knew the best way of dealing with her fellow Tellurians, he wasn't about to argue.

His stomach churned whenever he thought about giving himself up. To do it, he had to believe that forced labor on a colony world could eventually lead to Confederacy citizenship. But to accept that meant ignoring every warning voice in his head,

Regina and Lewis hated the idea too, of course, and Lewis had insisted on pressing a scrap of paper into his nephew's hand that morning. It was a small hand-drawn map of a triangular bluff about a two-day walk from the cabin. The map showed a rough X at the foot of the cliff at its northwest corner, but no indication of what was to be found there. Lewis's cryptic warning to "Go there if you can escape!" didn't help. Killian had committed the directions to memory and left the paper behind. Now he wondered if he'd ever get the chance to find out what it signified.

Their pace brought them to Borealis just as full night took hold.

"We want a place close to dense bush and not too close to any main pathways," Natira said in a hushed voice, her gaze darting nervously along huts revealed by cracks of coppery light that escaped between poorly fitted panels. Killian didn't reply but began to skirt the northern edge of the village in the direction of the colonist base. He thought he might know what she had in mind, so he led her behind a trio of huts where the two of them were hidden from view in most directions.

After a shared look to confirm they were ready, Natira raised her forearm and triggered the emergency beacon of her ID tattoo again and spoke in an urgent whisper.

"This is Natira Celestia. I'm being held in a hut somewhere in Borealis. Please help!" She tapped the tat and rasped, "Let's go!" breaking into a clumsy run toward the trees.

Killian heard a door open behind them and wondered what the hut's inhabitants thought of the charade.

He jogged after her, catching up easily. Though her lift vest supported her weight, it didn't provide the right balance and traction for efficient running.

They had to slow to a half-jog once they reached the bush to avoid the noisiest bushes and most hazardous overhanging branches. In less than ten minutes, a hoarse *swish* cut through the sky, and he reflexively pulled Natira under a dense spruce tree.

She yanked free and said, "I hear them too."

After that, he went more cautiously, pausing from time to time to make sure of his bearings. At least one more craft passed overhead.

"I thought they'd use ground vehicles," she rasped.

"Maybe you're more important than you know."

"Or they consider me a criminal now, too."

"I won't be very popular after they've barged into every home in Borealis for the second time."

"They won't. They'll have taken a fix on my signal, so they'll focus on that area first. That's why we really have to hurry—the distraction might not draw the guards away for very long."

"I thought you'd just run onto the base, claim that you escaped, and then tell them where to find me."

"If they catch me too soon, I lose control of the situation."

The argument didn't convince him, but by then the lights of the base were in view. From the edge of the trees, he pointed out a distinctive clump of closely packed cedars where he would wait for her to return with his captors.

Watching her walk away from him toward the glaring lights and foreign shapes produced a mix of feelings that left him nauseated. He should be glad to be rid of her, in spite of her help. He'd brought her trouble, but it went both ways. He wouldn't be under the threat of exile and forced labor if she hadn't come into his life.

An inner voice told him to run. He ignored it. Without his 'confession', the security forces might not believe Natira's innocence in his escape. He had to give himself up and then withstand the interrogation that would certainly follow. But it might not be too rigorous. There was a good chance that official Telluria would prefer to believe that their prodigal princess had been coerced.

The sky in the direction of Borealis was lit by occasional flashes. How long would it be before one of the tadpole shapes slid through the air to land in front of him? Or were there still enough guards left on the base to come for him on foot?

At last, a hint of movement drew his attention. A dark figure was silhouetted against the lights. One soldier? Was he such an insignificant threat that they only sent one?

Then he recognized the clumsy gait.

Natira! What was she doing?

She didn't even slow as she passed his hiding place.

"Come on—the troops will return any second!" Cedar branches swished and cracked as she blundered into them. He hurried to keep her from injuring herself.

After a half-hour of pushing westward into a series of rugged, heavily forested gullies, Killian sensed a change in air pressure and motioned for Natira to scramble under a rock overhang. A dark shape passed swiftly through pitch darkness overhead, the searchers confident in their technology. In minutes, it passed by again farther to the south.

He brought his mouth close to Natira's ear so she could hear him over her own panting.

"What happened? Why didn't you give me up to the ambassador?"

"The ambassador wasn't there. His personal shuttle was gone—probably called back for a consultation with the Council. I didn't want to give myself up to just anyone in case the security forces had me listed as an accomplice in your escape."

She was a terrible liar.

"What are you carrying?"

She thrust the small package at him. "More medicine for your mother. The ambassador's quarters are also the medical building, so while I was there . . . ."

A rush of emotions made his throat tighten and he didn't know whether to thank her or to scream at her for putting herself at risk again. In the end, he only said, "But we can't get it to her! We're heading in the wrong direction. And your people will be more determined than ever to find us."

"Don't worry. The amount I gave her should last for a month, and its effects will keep her alive quite a bit longer than that. But you'll have to stay free to make sure she gets this dose."

"What about you?"

"I should . . . I should leave you and make my way back to the base once you've had time to get clear. You're in more danger as long as I'm with you, and I'll only slow you down."

He waited for her to look into his face.

"Something's happened. You don't think they'll just let you go."

"It's nothing. They won't hurt me." But her voice didn't have the same certainty as before.

"No. Come with me. We'll think of some other way to convince them you're innocent. I don't want to go back to Lewis and Regina's—it's too dangerous for them—but Lewis told me about another place. It's a long walk, but he thought we'd be safe there."

Even in the dark he could sense her conflict. Something had upset her badly, but against that was the prospect of days or even longer alone with Killian in a trackless forest where she'd be completely dependent on his bush skills. And totally at his mercy.

"Look," he said softly. "I'll take you back right now if that's what you want. It's not safe for you to try to find your way on your own. Or, if you decide to come with me, I make you this promise: If there's ever a time that you feel afraid of me, send your emergency signal and leave it on until they find us. I won't stop you."

After a hard swallow, she said, "I'm always a little afraid of you. Aren't you a little afraid of yourself?"

He had no response to that.

The night hid her face, but he imagined the emotions that would be written there: the fear, but perhaps also the need to trust.

After a long moment, she took a deep breath and said, "Lead the way."

The Void take men and their secrets!

How much of her torment of the past weeks had been part of a plan by her own government?

No one could have foreseen that Killian would knock her into the mud, but someone powerful had been looking for an excuse to engineer an advantage over the Earth people, probably since long before the Confederacy's return. Fortuitous opportunities had been put to instant use. And she had been one of the pawns pushed into play.

Now she had to decide how she would deal with that.

She wasn't ready to tell Killian about it, but an image on the holo display at the base headquarters had burned into her brain as an indictment of her own people. She'd only seen the image for a few seconds, but long enough to recognize it as a strategy chart. Long enough for certain words like 'generals' and 'governors' to shock her psyche.

'General' was a military title and nothing else—even the Confederacy's Outer Planets Security Service didn't use the term because of its combative connotation. And governors? She knew from her Earth studies that, historically there had been some jurisdictions on Earth where the position was an elected one; but most often it was appointed, and usually by a colonizing power, a hallmark of empire. And why wouldn't Basu Hind object to meddling in Earth's governance? He was a man of principle, and the planet already had governments of its own, albeit local ones. Surely that was all that was needed for the benefit of Earth's scattered and primitive peoples.

Unless the intended benefit was not for them.

Somehow Hind was being tricked by the Patriarch and his cronies, but he wouldn't just accept Natira's word for it. She'd need proof. If such proof existed, it must be in the archive they had been keeping so secret—she felt sure of that. But she'd lose any chance to investigate that archive if she turned herself in.

She couldn't bring herself to explain what she'd seen to Killian. It wasn't as if he could do anything about it.

Somewhere on this forsaken planet there had to be the wise leaders she'd dreamed of meeting—the 'noble savages' who were her intellectual equal. Such people—those with a will to resist the seductive dependency fostered by the Depots—might live in hiding. If so, where? In Earth's long-deserted cities? Or in hidden settlements of their own, far from their apathetic cousins?

Maybe Lewis Partridge's map was leading them to just such a place. The man had secrets—he'd produced infrared-shielding suits in the middle of a wilderness, like a magic trick. There might be much more to his knowledge. It was worth enduring some hardship to find out.

Except Killian said that their objective was a two-day walk away! And that was without the extra effort of hiding from patrols while dragging along a pampered princess from space.

He hadn't used those words, but she could hardly blame him for thinking them. She couldn't even walk without a mechanism to help to support her weight. Her pride urged her to experiment without the lift vest, to put her genetically enhanced muscles to the test. But not yet. It would only make her more of a burden—Killian might even leave her behind!

No. Somehow, she knew he would never do that. And that was a shift in her own attitude toward him that left her confused.

The first night, they had no choice but to get as far from the Tellurian base as possible. For endless hours, glimpses of the lights of shuttles on the hunt taunted them, like frenetic fireflies darting through the night. She'd thought that nothing could be worse than their trek through the torrential rainstorm, but this journey was torture at a different level. Their coveralls made her skin and scalp sweat without relief—she'd never experienced such sticky discomfort. Though Killian made every effort to prevent the branches he pushed aside from whipping back into her face, she blundered into other trees on her own. Her clunky boots found every rock and root, and though the lift vest kept her from falling hard, her palms and forearms were scratched and bruised. A cool wetness on her upper lip might be blood from a nostril assaulted by a hooked twig, or it might just be mud from a landing in a puddle. Both tasted salty, though mud had an extra hint of vegetable rot.

Odors were everywhere—the less her eyes could see, the more her nose made up for it. Some were pleasant; many were not. Occasionally a breath of wind brought a hint of Killian's musk to her nostrils. It still made her nose recoil, but also evoked something less identifiable deep within her.

Raw pungency of wet soil predominated, full of apple-like sweetness from last year's leaves now uncovered. She began to relish the resiny aroma of spruce and pines as if it tapped into a reserve of racial memory; but the slightly duskier aroma of cedars was even more welcome. Especially when Killian chose a tightly clumped stand of them on a small hillock as a good spot to rest for the night. He gathered armful after armful of cedar boughs to make a bed for her, and she was relieved beyond words to shut off her lift vest and sink deeply into their embrace.

After a dreamless sleep of a few hours, she awoke with a desperate need to empty her bladder, and though she tried to wait longer, the dawn refused to come to her rescue. The crackling of the branches as she climbed out of them awoke Killian, forcing her to explain her predicament. Worse, the night had become darker than ever, and she didn't dare go more than a few meters away for fear of getting lost. He must have heard every sound. She stumbled back to her bed of boughs thankful that at least the night wouldn't reveal the shame that burned on her face. He'd stayed awake to make sure she returned safely, then rolled over without comment.

Arms wrapped around her chest, she hugged to herself all her hatred for this garbage heap of a planet. No punishment from the Tellurian government could be worse than this. In the morning she would insist that Killian take her back within walking distance of the base so she could surrender.

But when she awoke again in the rising dawn light, she was horrified to find her chest touching Killian's back, one of her knees resting against his. She pushed away with a shockingly loud crackle of branches, then tried to keep perfectly still.

"It's all right, I'm awake," he said. "I have been for quite a while."

"What? You let me just lie there like that?"

He rolled over, his face lined with confusion. "I thought you must have been cold. It didn't bother me."

"No, I'm sure it didn't!" She jumped to her feet, but had forgotten about the higher gravity and tumbled into a clump of juniper that raked her face, her arms too slow to catch her. Instantly Killian pulled her up by an arm, but she jerked free and fell again.

"Don't touch me!"

She staggered to her feet, this time sweeping her hand up her left side. It was such sweet relief to feel the support of the lift vest that she set it too high, her feet barely touching the ground. Which left her utterly unable to stomp off into the woods in indignation.

After a moment's adjustment she strode into the trees but realized that she had no idea which way to go. Her throat exploded with a howl of rage.

"I have to *pee* again!"

Killian just said. "Me too. You stay there and I'll go over this way a little." He stepped beyond some trees, and she angrily squatted behind the offending juniper bushes; but this time her embarrassed bladder refused to cooperate until she heard his stream strike the ground. It was prodigious. She'd once witnessed a horse urinate at a mammalian preserve in Telluria Quartus and that had been no louder. Or longer.

Forcing her own body to fulfill its need under cover of Killian's noise, she still finished before he did. An unsullied patch of snow on the other side of the junipers let her clean her hands a little.

As she stood, she realized that every part of her *hurt*. Her neck was the worst—she could barely turn it, but her shoulders radiated a constant ache, and pain stabbed her lower back with every step. What was wrong? Was she sick? Could she have contracted some virulent Earth disease in only a few days?

It would hardly be a surprise. Hunkering down in dank caves, eating unprocessed food prepared by people who had been repudiated by civilization and its medical safeguards. Sleeping in piles of twigs on the filthy forest floor. She was supposed to have been inoculated against all disease carried by humans, but how could the Tellurians be certain of that without actual contact? And who knew what vicious bacterial strains might lurk in raw soil or rotting vegetation?

When Killian returned, he seemed about to say something but stopped and just looked at her.

"What? Am I covered with filth?" she asked with a glare.

"No! I was just feeling sorry that you've had such a hard time here. I'll take you back now. It was stupid of me to drag you deep into the forest. Your own people won't treat you as badly as this."

It was no more than she'd been thinking herself, but it rankled to hear him say it.

"No. I can handle this, and worse. Don't think that just because we're born under weaker gravity, we're not strong. In the long run, mental strength counts for more than large muscles."

To his credit, he only nodded.

"Except . . . ." She hesitated. "Except I might be sick. Every muscle and joint in my body hurts."

His first look of concern gave way to a smile, and she felt heat rise up her neck.

"That's probably just from sleeping on the ground," he said. "It's cold and hard. Even when you're used to it you can feel pretty stiff first thing in the morning, until you get your muscles moving again."

Could that be all it was? She'd had her lift vest turned off all night for the first time. Even the previous night she'd set the vest to keep her barely touching the mattress after ruefully noticing that the bedsheets did not float above the bed on their own.

"So, the pain should go away? Soon?"

"Well . . . probably not all of it. Walking through the bush you're using muscles in new ways. They're going to complain until they adjust to it. So, a few days at least. Your colonist base would have medicines to take the ache away."

"No, I can stand this."

Could she? She hadn't even tried walking without the lift vest yet. So much for her genetic enhancements.

"OK. But the going will get worse. Rougher terrain. Bad weather. We could still have a snowstorm or ice storm. And in a few more weeks we'll be into fly season."

"*Fly* season?"

"Insects. Black flies and then mosquitoes. So thick they'll cover every bit of exposed skin day and night, hungry for blood and flesh."

She backed into the trunk of a tree in horror. Then she realized that he must be playing with her—exaggerating to scare her off. Well, that wasn't going to happen.

"I don't care. If we turn around now, everything we've suffered already will have been for nothing, and I won't have learned a thing. We need to get to that place your uncle told you about. I need time to find hidden information in this machine I'm carrying. It could be crucial to your people." She rubbed her throat. "Maybe my people, too."

He sighed. "I wish you'd change your mind."

214

"So you won't have to drag me along? Baby me? Well don't, then. You just . . . point out some landmarks for me to follow, or draw a map. I'll make my own way." It sounded ridiculous, even to her.

His face was inscrutable, but after a few moments he simply shrugged and began to walk. He wouldn't abandon her in a trackless forest, she knew. So, what was making her say such things? She was embarrassed by her weakness and even more ashamed for being so unreasonable, yet she couldn't bring herself to apologize. Instead, she followed him and hoped that the lift vest would last. Most Tellurian devices made for use on other worlds used radioactive materials as a power source; and as long as it didn't get damaged, it might still function for quite a while. She had a strong feeling that she'd need to conserve her own energy.

That thought made her realize how hungry she was. But if Killian could go without food, so could she.

Sometime later—it felt like hours—she said, "It was stupid of us not to bring food, wasn't it?"

"This is one of the worst times of the year for gathering food in the bush. In a few weeks there'll be plant sprouts and buds all over, but not yet. Hunting or trapping animals takes time, more time than we can spare with your people after us." He looked back at her. "But we do need to eat. Regina sent some trail food with us."

From a pocket he took out something that looked like strips of bark wrapped in a light-colored cloth. It was as stiff as a stick as he held it out to her, and the texture was rough but more slippery than bark.

"What is it?"

"Meat. Mostly. This is venison—meat from a deer, if you know what that is. Good eating. Plus, there are some berries mixed in. We mix it together, pound it flat, and then dry it for a long time. It can last for weeks without spoiling. We call it *pemmican*. This is Regina's recipe—a little drier than some."

He probably thought that would impress her, but he shouldn't have put the idea of spoiled meat into her head. She'd never eaten the flesh of an actual animal and her mind rebelled at the thought. Then the faint scent of the pemmican reached her nostrils, and she was suddenly ravenous. He mimed biting it, and she put one end of the strip between her teeth, hoping he wouldn't see the tremble of her fingers.

It was like biting the arm of a chair! She clenched her teeth harder and harder, but they refused to break through. Was this a joke? Killian was struggling to control his face. Finally, he gave a small cough and said, "Hold it in your mouth for a while to let your saliva soften it, then try again. I've got another piece for myself."

He turned away—to stifle a laugh, she suspected—and at long last she was able to tear a piece from the leathery substance. It took a major effort of will not to picture a living creature, but she had to admit that the taste was more than acceptable, if only because of hunger. Chewing what she'd bitten off into a consistency she was willing to swallow took forever—and it was salty! Her thirst became urgent, and she had no idea where they'd find drinkable water in such a place.

Wait, though. Would Killian have forgotten such a basic need? No. She'd have to ask him for a drink. *Void's breath!* She hated having to depend on him for everything.

Just then he stopped, slipped a flat gourd-shaped object from under his jacket and pulled a plug from its slender neck as he handed it to her. The water was cool and one of the best things she'd ever tasted. And the fact that he'd thought of her need himself instead of forcing her to ask, turned it into an act of nurture. That felt good too, but she couldn't explain why.

It was one of the only good moments of that trying day. Though she'd noticed the aches in her upper body first, her legs soon protested fiercely. Sometimes an extended stride would send a jolt up the nerves of her leg, like when she struck the unprotected part of her elbow against something hard. When that happened, she would falter, and need a moment to marshal her resolve before carrying on. The first time it happened, Killian asked her what was wrong and received a sharp "Nothing!" for an answer. After that, he tried not to let on that he noticed, as if attempting to spare her pride.

That was wasted effort. She had no pride left. The food he'd called 'pemmican' had eased her hunger and revived her strength, but had disagreed with her digestion; and the lack of privacy was appalling—the worst part of the whole horrible ordeal. Part of her hated Killian for being a witness to her humiliation yet again.

Before the day was half done, her knees had developed a tremble she couldn't suppress. Increasing the lift of her vest helped, but not much. She was forced to rest often, and could only assuage some of her self-disgust by being the first to rise and resume the march. Even so, she stumbled on in a daze, her mind seeking escape from the pains of her body by taking refuge in abstract thoughts.

She thought of her life in Telluria—every need provided for, every discomfort quickly relieved. The physical ones, at least. Her job and social position brought stresses of their own, but complaints about those at this juncture seemed ludicrous. She'd always believed she was strong, but maybe what she'd really been was resolute. To achieve the excellence she demanded of herself had required sacrifice, but she couldn't say that she'd ever really suffered. Determination wasn't the same as bravery. Social ostracism had brought her pain, but never lasting damage. And then her life path had veered into the territory of ancient fairy tales: the ordinary girl who becomes a princess.

Common life and all its discomforts had been left behind.

Or so she had thought.

The man who walked in front of her—what had his life been like?

This journey through trackless wilds didn't seem to cause him any discomfort at all, but she was somehow sure that he was no stranger to pain. He couldn't be. He'd lived with Earth's relentless gravity all his life, where muscles protested from everyday strain, and simple falls could break bones. For him, the cold of winter was relieved by heavier clothing and the heat of physical effort. The adequate but never-appetizing food provided by the Depots made the simple fare of his aunt's kitchen a feast by comparison.

Yet, for a man like him, the worst trial of all would be living with such limited potential. To know that he had no hope to achieve anything of real meaning. And would get no support if he tried.

No wonder the exotic realms of the Confederacy had called to him so strongly. He would never understand why they couldn't be his.

As much as she resented him—maybe even hated him—there was pity in her heart too.

# # #

Near mid-day they stopped for food. Killian had some rock-hard biscuits to go with the nearly inedible pemmican, and Natira had to drink a lot of water. He gave the water gourd a rueful look and declared that they'd make a small detour to a fast-flowing stream that had been on his uncle's map.

The long hours wore on, though not in silence. It wasn't the humans, but birds that filled the air with speech: trills and warbles that were mostly mating calls, she'd once been told; but she'd never imagined such a variety of sounds. Killian said that most bird species travelled south each fall and only returned to the north once the waterways had shed their ice. Then they were unflagging in their vocal attempts to lure a mate, but even success didn't halt the music. Only once the first full heat of summer came to stay would they stop their nearly constant singing.

To Natira, some of these songs sounded like water running over pebbles, while others were like sonic representations of sunshine itself.

Killian called a halt long before sunset. Natira had fallen twice within a few minutes and couldn't even summon more than a grunted response when he told her to rest. She slumped onto a rock, not caring that its edges dug into her flesh. He urged her over to a worn-down stump with part of its remaining trunk making a crude backrest. The seat had a cushiony cover of dry pine needles that she suspected had not been there a moment before. Her whole body trembled with fatigue, but she was helpless to stop it. She caught a look of pity in Killian's eyes before he could turn his face away but didn't even have the strength to snap at him.

A sour smell floated on the air from time to time—the scent of a marsh, though it wasn't visible through the trees. Killian told her to stay where she was—a wholly unnecessary instruction—and disappeared into the woods. A long time later he came back dangling a sizable brown and white bundle.

"Is that a . . . a bird?"

"A goose. I got lucky, very lucky." He began to pull the feathers from the creature and then hooked it on a low branch while he went to gather sticks and larger branches he could break beneath his foot.

"You're going to light a fire? What about the satellites?"

"There hasn't been any sign of searchers all day. Either they're looking in the wrong places, far away, or they're not in any hurry to capture us. Maybe they're waiting for you to contact them again. Or maybe they'll just lie and tell people we were caught and punished." He shrugged. "It doesn't matter. You need nourishing food. I'll build the fire under this rock overhang. That won't hide it completely, but the heat will reflect from the rock and give us more warmth during the night." The overhang had been carved well into the yellow sandstone of the rockface by a long dried-up river. It seemed deep enough for a fire inside it, and for both of them to sleep near its widest end.

Before they'd left Lewis and Regina's home, Killian had been deeply touched by a gift from his uncle: a small packet of tools for bush travel that included a sharp knife with a carved wooden handle, loops of twine, and what looked like a chunk of rock and a small rod of steel that Killian called a flint and striker. His expression had signaled that the items must be very precious.

Lewis had grunted, "You'll need these." And Killian had merely nodded. But a look of great affection had passed between the two men.

Now, Killian coaxed a handful of very fine dry moss into flame by striking sparks from the steel with the rock. Natira's stomach rumbled, but she didn't know whether it was from hunger or revulsion as she looked at the pale corpse of the bird. When the moss finally caught, he carried it to the pile of twigs he'd arranged, tending the fledgling flames with all the attention of a nursery attendant soothing a baby. At last, he took the goose out of her sight, presumably to save her from seeing the messy preparations, then returned with the meat skewered on a green stick, and carefully placed it on a makeshift framework over the now-crackling fire.

Natira found herself fascinated in spite of herself, listening to the sizzle and spit of dripping fat, and watching the outer skin of the bird grow dark as Killian occasionally turned it. She knew she could never bring herself to eat a creature that had been alive only an hour earlier, but she couldn't resist taking deep breaths whenever the shifting breeze carried the smoke—and the aroma of roasting goose—in her direction.

At some point, Killian declared that the meal was ready, but she shook her head at the offered serving and only accepted another of the hard biscuits instead. He left the pieces of flesh he'd cut for her on a slab of birchbark at her side, and bit into his own portion with unmistakable relish. His chin quickly became shiny with grease, and Natira shuddered. Some of the liquid that dripped onto the ground was unquestionably blood.

Swallowing hard, she looked at the meat by her side. Perhaps if she picked it apart with her fingers, she could find a piece or two that wasn't too bloody or fatty. One piece looked nearly white—it shredded without difficulty, releasing only a hint of steam. She raised it to her lips and sniffed it, then reached out her tongue. The taste was much like its smell—rather strong but not unpleasant, though certainly not like anything she'd ever eaten. She would just eat a few shreds of it and then see if it upset her stomach.

When she finally looked down and found that all the meat from her birchbark dish was gone, she had to fight a surge of nausea. But the queasiness wasn't real—it was only in her head. A surreptitious glance at Killian found a pleased expression on his face, but no hint of mockery.

"More?" he asked.

She quickly shook her head but found that it was bobbing up and down instead.

"There's no shame in eating whatever's available when you're hungry," he said as he served her a piece cooked golden brown and kept a blackened chunk for himself. "It's how the world is. My mother says that long ago, people would say thanks to an animal's spirit when they took its life; but my father says that's only a foolish story. I know I'm grateful to the Earth Mother when I'm fortunate enough to catch a good meal like this."

Natira thought of glistening dishes of lightly sautéed greens, buttery lobster, and flaky pastries that dissolved when you bit into them. Shrimp cocktail, bouillabaisse or vichyssoise, eggs Benedict, spicy pâté, and stuffed crab. None of it from actual living creatures, of course—all of it at her slightest whim. Would this man even be capable of comprehending a good meal?

Yet she chewed thoughtfully on another morsel of goose and felt a growing contentment in her stomach. Clearly the appreciation of food could be affected by circumstance. An ancient truism declared that 'Hunger makes the best sauce' but she'd never understood it until now.

Evening's twilight lasted a long time. They were both too tired to make conversation. In the long silences Killian went off into the trees to gather more firewood and boughs for bedding, while she looked up at the sky and tried to name all the different shades of amber and ochre, russet and rose in a vivid sunset painted across the horizon.

Though the sky stayed luminous well after the sun had gone down, Natira could barely keep her eyes open. Killian had spread an extra thick layer of boughs on the ground near the fire. Was he trying to ease her pain?

"Would you rather I slept over there?" he asked, pointing four or five meters away and outside the rock overhang. At that distance he'd barely get any warmth from the fire at all.

"No. Just . . . let's keep to our own space, that's all."

"I will if you will." He smirked, but she was too sleepy to retort. With her eyes closed, she heard him settle himself on the crackly boughs as a trace of sweat and smoke reached her nostrils.

She breathed it in deeply, breathed out, and was asleep.

28

They reached the destination marked on Lewis's map just before midday, and Killian realized that he'd been there many years earlier with his uncle. At least twice, if his memory was accurate.

It was a place of magnificent beauty: a pointed promontory that reared above a wide, flat-bottomed valley with a river winding through it. There was a clear view for kilometers in every direction but south, the way Killian and Natira had come, which had been an arduous struggle over steeply rising terrain. The top hundred meters of the promontory was a sheer cliff whose crest overhung the rest of the face. From the base of the bluff, a steep slope of tumbled boulders, gravel, and scrub growth swept down into the valley.

Instead of climbing to the top of the plateau, Killian took a side path that he vaguely remembered from his uncle's map. That brought them out at the foot of the cliff face along the top of the scree, but the footing was treacherous. He badly wanted to be able to take Natira's arm for her safety; and a few times she even seemed to reach out, herself, but always withdrew her hand quickly. After her foot slipped on a patch of gravel, he stopped, fished around in his pack, and drew out a tight coil of rope.

"Tie this around you and hang onto it with one hand." He showed her a knot that would not slip and demonstrated by

223

fastening the rope's other end around his own waist. "It'll let you feel a little more secure."

Her expression was a mix of relief and doubt. "But if I fall, you'll fall with me."

"I won't fall. I've been here many times." That was an exaggeration, but he had climbed rocky northern crags all his life and felt at home among them. Assessing a field of rubble and recognizing rocks that were secure enough to take his weight took almost no conscious thought. Which left too much of his mind free to imagine Natira tumbling down the jagged slope. "If you can watch where I step and try to copy me, that will help too."

He'd given her a little more than two meters of free rope, but she stayed closer than that, with a firm two-handed grip on her lifeline.

He remembered his own experience of floating helplessly mid-air when power had been lost on the Tellurian shuttle. Natira probably wouldn't have been phased by that at all. She likely visited weightless parts of Telluria for recreation, as Raymen had so badly wanted to do.

But Earth's gravity was her worst enemy, a personal nemesis she must continually battle for supremacy.

"Could your lift vest keep you from falling to the bottom?" he asked. "I remember you floating down from the roof of the Depot."

Her face brightened. "It can give me that much lift for short periods of time. The problem would be controlling it as I fell. Now that you mention it, the engineers probably built in an automatic response for falls."

"Let's not find out the hard way," he said.

"Yes, sir. I'll be careful. Sir!"

He was taken aback and didn't catch the significance of her hand raised to her temple. But it was the first time she'd ever joked with him. He took it as a good sign.

From time to time as they made their way around the triangular base of the cliff, he paused to let her rest while he scanned the sky and the forest beneath it. The spot gave a perfect view to the east. Pursuing craft from the colonist base wouldn't be able to approach unseen from that direction unless they could make themselves invisible. Was that possible? Maybe the reason he hadn't seen any signs of the searchers for more than a day was because they chose not to be seen and flew high enough that the noise of their passage didn't reach the ground. Disturbed, he asked Natira about it.

"Invisible? Our security forces certainly have that capability," she said. "But we wouldn't bother to install such equipment on a regular shuttle. I guess it all depends on whether they felt the need to bring stealth ships to Earth."

He nodded. After all, the very suits he and Natira wore could help prevent some forms of detection, and they had to be very old tech. By now the colonists would have learned how to hide bigger things and hide them completely.

Suddenly the view from the cliff left him feeling dangerously exposed. He hurried on.

They passed around the northernmost point of the promontory a few minutes later and found what they were looking for only minutes after that. It was a vertical cleft in the rock too regular in shape to be natural. Killian had never seen this opening on his previous visits. It *couldn't* be seen from more than a few meters away. From almost any direction, a wall-like rock formation in front of it would hide it with the opening mistaken for a shadow.

Before they entered, Killian removed their rope, coiled it carefully, and stowed it in his pack. The gap was about twice Killian's height and wide enough to walk through single-file. After a passage of several meters, it opened up.

Into a huge— and artificial—cave.

Natira gasped. Killian felt his heart pound.

Even in the dim light that filtered through the passage he could see box-like shapes with rounded tops as large as a Borealis barracks, but much too uniform. Several had tubes and bulges covering one or more sides, as if they were being eaten by monstrous snakes. To the left were four big globes on cylindrical stalks; to the right was a thick vertical panel that partially extended from the wall. It was the color of dull metal. A door? A barrier to close off the cave?

After allowing his eyesight to adjust, Killian walked slowly into the twilit space.

He'd only taken a few paces when sudden brightness blinded him, and he dropped to the ground in a defensive crouch.

The whole cave lit up with illumination coming from the entire ceiling about ten meters above their heads. His eyes darted around the room, trying to see who'd turned on the lights.

"Motion sensors," Natira said. "It doesn't mean that anyone is here. All rooms in Telluria have them so we don't waste power lighting empty spaces."

Killian remembered his room in Capita. He stood slowly, feeling foolish.

Now that he could see everything, he noticed a thick layer of dirt on the floor—maybe centuries of dust and silt blown in through the opening, though the box-like structures and their appendages were strangely free of it. The dirt stopped about five centimeters away from them. When he pointed, Natira said, "Static repulsion. It's electrical, but takes very little energy."

"If this cave was made before the colonists left Earth, that . . . static whatever has been running for a long time."

"Well, there's nothing complicated about it. Solar energy collectors or a small radioactive power source could keep it going for centuries. The bigger question is, what else is running in here?"

She moved among the structures while Killian followed cautiously behind. In this place, she was in her element and he the clueless interloper.

As she stepped close to one of the box shapes, an entrance slid open, the space behind it lighting instantly. There was a room inside with many tables and countertops, most covered with objects Killian couldn't begin to recognize. There were also a few chairs. At least they looked like chairs. He couldn't be certain that anything in this cave was what it appeared to be.

226

"Laboratories," Natira said. "Separate small laboratories, enclosed to keep out the elements or to shield the work from the effects of other projects." She looked at him then added, "Laboratories are workspaces for scientists, with special equipment they use to investigate things, or do experiments with substances, or test inventions."

"I've heard the word. I couldn't picture one before."

"Well, every lab is probably a little different and yet they all have similarities too." She approached a nearby table. There was no dust on anything in the room—the bright colors on some of the surfaces looked fresh, almost new. She didn't touch anything, only passing her hand close to a few of the objects. Killian braced himself for a sudden noise or another burst of light, but nothing happened.

"I don't think any of this equipment is still active," she said. "Maybe it really has been here since the Exodus."

"How could it be newer than that?"

She didn't answer but continued her inspection. After a time, she moved into another room, and then another. The shapes of the objects differed in each, but Killian came no closer to understanding what purpose any of them had once fulfilled.

It was in the fourth that she gave a cry of excitement.

A small, flattened cube about the width of Killian's hands lay on one of the counters. Four tiny points of blue light gleamed from it.

"A network receptacle!" she said, hurrying to it. "A power source for my Synappt, but it'll also be linked to storage and maybe even digital archives." She was already unpacking the satchel she carried. "I don't know if any storage media from back then could have survived five centuries, but if there's been power all this time it's worth a look."

Killian came closer. "Before you get too involved, we should probably have something to eat. We still have some pemmican and biscuits, but I won't find any game on this slope."

She turned to him with a smile like a child on a feast day.

"If this was a working science outpost, there'll be supplies, including food!"

"After *five hundred years?*"

She walked quickly from the room. "Whatever you do, don't forget the location of this lab. But for now, we're looking for a room that has tables with no equipment covering them."

Killian found the room at the back of the cave, right beside a box that contained dozens of stacked beds. Natira pronounced the room with tables a 'mess hall', though it seemed perfectly tidy to him. She hurried toward some handles embedded in the right-hand wall and pulled one of them. It was a simple cupboard with nothing strange about it except its contents, which were rectangular packets about twenty centimeters by fifty in many different colors, stacked to fill the space. When Natira pulled a few from the top of one stack he saw that there were marks printed on it—words that he was unable to read but that caused her no difficulty.

"Beef Wellington. Rotini Bolognese. Oooh, Lasagna!" She turned the packet over and back, obviously looking for a way to open it.

"But we don't dare eat these things after all that time!"

"Yes, we can. I've heard of these. Early colonists to the outer planets used them almost exclusively until they could set up greenhouses and yeast processors. The food inside has been completely sterilized and vacuum-sealed—there are no live bacteria or anything like that to make it spoil, and the covering keeps out air and moisture. They can last forever. These will have picked up a little radiation from the rocks and maybe from whatever's powering this place, but I'm sure it wouldn't be enough to hurt us. Ah!" She slid her forefinger and thumb along one edge and the package peeled open. She held it out to him and he took a step back, unable to suppress a shudder.

"What's wrong? I ate your dried pemmican. *And* the dead bird you burnt over a fire. But you're not willing to trust me?"

"I trust you not to poison me on purpose. But you can't know that these things are safe."

With a look of defiance, she peeled the covering back some more and took a large bite of the contents that were reddish with layers of something creamy white, and a smell that reminded Killian of cooked tomatoes. Whatever it was, Natira ate it with obvious pleasure and finished it as quickly as she could swallow.

"It might take a while for you to die," he said. "I can wait."

She snorted. "You're the one who's spent your life obsessed with colonist technology. Now you have a chance to experience it firsthand and you're too . . . cautious to even *try* it?"

He knew the word she'd chosen not to use. And he couldn't even deny it. When she opened another package and held it out to him, he took a deep breath and bit into it.

It tasted like cooked meat—beef, most likely—with a thick, flavorful sauce. A little chewier than he would have preferred, but he detected none of the sourness or sharp aftertaste that might have indicated spoilage. He took the packet from her and ate some more, ignoring her self-satisfied smile.

They didn't die. They didn't even suffer indigestion. But Killian was still skeptical that something . . . *ancient* . . . there was no other word for it, could still possess the nutrition they needed; so, while Natira located some carry-bags of tough cloth and filled them with as many food packets as she could, Killian vowed that he would still hunt to keep his strength up.

Either way, there was no reason for them to move on unless forced to. A small waterfall tumbled spring melt-water down the cliff nearby, and if that water source dried up, the wide river at the bottom of the valley passed just beneath them. They would have food and water to last a long time. The well-hidden cave should shield them from prying eyes both human and mechanized. Bad weather could not touch them. And, just as important, his long-suffering companion would have a bed on which to rest. She deserved it.

Lewis Partridge had chosen well. Killian couldn't help but wonder when the man had found this place, and how he had kept it secret for so long. How many other secrets did his uncle conceal?

Natira quickly returned to the lab with the network receptacle and placed her own Synappt next to it. Apparently, no physical connection was necessary—the device could connect to any other functioning processors nearby through the air and draw power the same way. They might not know the source of the cave's electricity, but what counted was how long it would last. With a sudden smile, Natira pronounced that her lift belt should be able to automatically recharge its power too.

She radiated excitement as she began to work with her computing device. To Killian it was just markings floating in the air—he couldn't read them and wouldn't have known their context if he had. So, after watching for a few minutes, he went off to explore the rest of the cave.

They'd already found six separate laboratories or workspaces, but if those contained anything useful to fugitives in bush country, Killian couldn't recognize it. In a back corner, though, was a large storage area packed with equipment with more obvious functions. He decided that a large cylinder with a masterfully rendered spiral blade on the front must be for digging. A square platform held above four giant wheels by a cleverly arranged metal lattice appeared to be for lifting heavy things into the air. There were also extendable rods with lights at each end, reels of rope and cable that unspooled or retracted with a touch, and a roll of some incredibly thin, shiny material that was so slippery he couldn't stand on a patch of it without falling.

The most exciting discovery of all just looked like a bundle of rods and fabric at first, but one section of cloth was covered with diagrams—pictures that showed how to put it together.

It was a flying machine.

The largest image looked like an eagle in a dive, with a pair of wings fused together into one large V with a half-cylinder framework suspended beneath it that held two small seats. It reminded him of a flying model his uncle Lewis had once made from Depot cloth carefully shrunk by heat over carved pieces of dry cedar wood. Even unpowered, the model could glide for a considerable distance. In fact, its final flight had been from the top of a cliff as high as this one, floating so far on currents of air that they'd never been able to find it again.

From what he could discern, this colonist machine was primarily a glider too, but also had some form of motive power that could lift the craft to a substantial height so that its slide back to Earth could extend over a great distance. It was capable of carrying two people, but not much else; so Killian couldn't immediately see what use it would be to a race that could make machines that flew without any wings at all.

Then he noticed that the fabric was like the cloaks he and Natira wore except that it took on the color of its surroundings. *Of course.* A silent, hard-to-spot glider at a great height could be very useful for watching people who weren't meant to know they were being watched.

His assessment was confirmed when he rested his palm on a hand-shaped yellow patch and the entire glider vanished from sight.

He yanked his arm away, realizing too late that if there was any way to make the thing visible again, it would probably involve the same hand-shaped symbol. Natira would call it a 'switch'. His body hadn't moved, so he was able to place his hand very close to the same spot it had left. Fingers touched fabric. He shifted a little to the left—yes, there was just the slightest indentation. With another small movement he conjured the glider out of empty air like a magician's trick.

An invisible flying machine that would carry two people. Now *that* could be useful.

So useful that he couldn't believe finding it was a coincidence. Again, he wondered how much Uncle Lewis knew.

The assembly diagrams showed the craft in various stages of completion, but not any specific steps to link the parts together. He'd have to hope the word markings were more instructive. It was annoying to have to depend on Natira for that. He felt a swell of resentment toward his instructors at the secret school. They'd been so eager to show off their knowledge of colonist tech—why couldn't they have just taught him how to *read*? But then, in his everyday life, there was nothing that required reading, except a few markings on the Depot that no one seemed to consider important.

There wasn't enough room to assemble the glider inside the cave The top of the cliff would be the best launch point anyway. He only hoped they wouldn't have to carry it up there in a hurry.

He found Natira so immersed in a cloud of text that she wasn't aware of his presence until he spoke her name.

Her half-smile was at odds with her wrinkled forehead.

"Did you get into the archive?"

"I managed to access the first level. It's arranged in layers like an onion, with each layer having its own encryption. It's going to take time—a lot of time."

"Have you learned anything?"

She sighed. "Mostly confirmation of what I'd found before. The Divide was planned and carried out by the Earth's richest people, and it's clear that their plan included the Tellurian system of government, which is still based on succession amongst the wealthiest families. There are clear records of knowledge and technology on Earth not only being destroyed immediately after the Exodus, but also suppressed for decades afterward. Any aircraft that took to the sky were shot down from orbit. Large watercraft designed to harvest fish or carry cargo were all sunk. Even methods of personal transportation were eliminated. Every facility for processing fuel or energy was systematically wiped out. Earth's people had no energy supplies to maintain life in their cities, but no means to go anywhere else."

"People went to the Allocations."

"Yes, but on foot over great distances, and not until much later—not until after so many had . . . died." She turned her face away. "I can't understand why the ones who went into space couldn't have just left the rest alone."

"We were all told it was done to let the Earth heal. The laws still say we aren't allowed to kill animals or do anything that might pollute the air and water."

"But the suffering it caused . . . . My whole world was built on such devastating cruelty!" She couldn't speak for a moment, then she pointed at some of the floating marks. "This part describes the building of the Allocations and the Depots, but I still can't discover why. There must have been some rival faction that disagreed with the callousness of the leaders and tried to help the abandoned people, but I can't find any evidence of that.

"And there are other things . . . I think I must be reading them wrong. There are references to events involving Earth people a long time after the Divide. Maybe centuries."

"Well, Tellurians must have been watching from space."

"Of course; but these reports describe direct interaction with Earth as if the recorder was right there. And I've been wondering about some of the equipment in this cave. I'm almost positive some of it hadn't even been invented at the time of the Exodus. I don't know what to make of it."

"Maybe your people didn't keep their distance as much as we've been told."

Killian scrutinized the floating words, willing them to give up their meaning, but looked away in irritation.

In a soft voice, Natira said, "Would you like me to teach you to read?"

He snapped his head toward her, prepared to reply in anger. Instead, he paused, and said, "Yes."

"OK. Do you want to start right away? I can't get any farther into the archive for now anyway, and I need a break."

"In a little while."

Instead, he led her to the glider and waited while she read the instructions. Her laugh made him scowl.

"No, it's a good thing. We don't have to know how to put it together—it will assemble itself. You just touch this blue symbol over here. Once the framework is in place, an electrical charge stiffens the fabric. Solid; as strong as metal. This indicator light shows that the original power source still has enough energy to form the glider, and then the wing surface itself will gather enough sunlight to maintain it."

"It can become invisible," he said, trying to redeem himself a little.

"Yes. In fact, when the material of our suits is in contact with it
. . . ." She leaned against the bundle and pressed the yellow palm print.

Both glider and woman disappeared.

"*Goddamn.*" Killian blurted, and Natira laughed as she reappeared.

"If we'd only had an energy pack, we could have been invisible all this time," she said. "I think I saw some that would probably fit into these inner chest pockets." She went to get them.

He couldn't help but smile. For two people on the run, it would have been hard to think of a more valuable find.

While she hunted for power packs, he left the cave to search for the path he and Lewis had taken all those years ago that led to the clifftop. He hadn't gone far when he found a broad ledge above the rubble, about eight meters long and five wide. Maybe just large enough for the glider, and certainly closer than the peak. He looked up at the sky and changed his mind about exploring further. Dark clouds approaching from the west threatened rain or even late snow. Maybe both. The glider could wait until morning.

He returned to find Natira going through the labs with a bag slung from her shoulder.

"Are you finding useful things?"

"A few," she said, and held up a black rectangle about as wide as her hand, half again as long, and the thickness of a finger. "This looks like one of the medical scanners they use in the med center, except more basic. If I can get it to charge at the network receptacle, that could be helpful."

"Why?"

She smiled. "I thought you'd want to know if the food was making you sick."

"I'm not sure I do. Could it also tell me if the food's doing me any good?"

"Yes, over a week or two. It can show if you're getting enough nutrients or if you've developed any deficiencies."

"Good. Do that. In the meantime, I'm going to find us a shower."

"Are you implying that I smell now?"

"No. I think Tellurian bodies must have been changed to keep your sweat from smelling. But obviously I still do—I can see it on your face every time I come close."

"Sorry. It's not really so bad."

"Uh huh. Well, I'd rather smell good than 'not so bad'." He turned away before he could blush.

Hygiene facilities were in the back corner opposite the storage area, and the shower was the best Killian had ever had. Even in Telluria, showers had been miserly with water, using instead what Natira had called "sonic pulses." Maybe he'd misunderstood. Noise to shake dirt off? Give him good hot water and soap any day.

He took so long to come out that Natira asked if anything was wrong. Or maybe what disturbed her was that he hadn't put his shirt back on, to enjoy the feel of the air on his skin while his hair finished drying. After her first wide-eyed glance, she looked away and pretended to search through the room's cabinets.

They ate some more of the packaged dinners. Then Natira invited him to sit next to her and used her Synappt's display to draw letters and finally small words in the air. Killian was surprised to find that he knew the letters and even many of the words after all. What had kept him from recognizing them in the Tellurian markings was something Natira called the *font*—slight differences in the shapes of the letters. Tellurian print was blocky and densely packed, with none of the embellishments Killian's eyes expected. He must have been taught the basics of reading in his early school years, but had eventually lost the skill for want of anything to read. Teachers had delivered later lessons verbally with the help of pictures and video.

The reading lesson went on for an hour or so until they both felt sleepy. The sleeping room held only double bunks. Killian chose one near the door and automatically climbed into the top bunk, even though they had seen no sign of rodents or snakes. He expected Natira to pick a bed as far away as possible; but after she dimmed the lights, she went to the top bunk right next to his.

He kept his surprise to himself.

29

A crispness in the air drew them outside the next morning. A few centimeters of snow had fallen, and the frosted forest looked newly-made. Natira was awestruck, casting her eyes from place to place as fresh vistas caught her attention. When she walked to the point of the promontory to look east toward the risen sun, Killian followed out of concern for her safety. Although the wind had swept most of the scree free of snow, there was still enough moisture on the rocks to make them slick.

He'd just opened his mouth to call a warning when she slipped.

It was hard to follow what happened next, whether she somehow triggered her lift vest, or an undiscovered automatic function did it. After the first tumble to the ground, she rose to half a meter or more above it—but that eliminated her traction on the steep slope, and the motion of her fall began to build serious momentum. She might as well have been on glare ice, eventually stabilizing face up but powerless to slow herself. Frictionless. Unstoppable.

With a cry, Killian launched himself after her, leaping from rock to rock, desperately seeking those that looked not only firm but sufficiently free of ice. Some broke loose and left him sliding for a few meters before he could leap again. A trip would send him into a deadly tumble over every jagged point and spur.

Natira hurtled downslope with frightening velocity. If she hit one of the half-dozen larger boulders among the rockfall, her lift vest wouldn't save her.

And at the bottom of the slope was the river.

Somehow, she missed all the obstacles, if only by an arms-length. As Killian watched in horror, she reached the bottom and shot across the surface of the river in a great gout of spray, carving a trough a hundred meters long before shedding the last of her speed. Then she sank instantly. Either the vest had been damaged or could not repel water the way it did earth.

Killian staggered to the shoreline just in time to see her head pop up. Even at that distance he could hear her desperate gasps for breath. The water would be icy. Could her off-world constitution stand the shock?

He was about to dive in when he realized that swimming that distance would be the wrong choice. He'd reach her much more quickly on foot through scrub-growth to the next bend, where the river current was carrying her.

Already winded from his charge down the mountain, he somehow found the strength to sprint, dividing his attention between tripping hazards and Natira bobbing farther away by the minute.

At the riverbank he only paused to tear off his boots, then dove into the dark water.

The cold was like hitting something solid and knocked his breath away; but he surfaced with arms already windmilling and legs churning the water. When he lifted his head to judge the distance, he was amazed to see Natira swimming toward him. In a few more seconds, he'd wrapped a strong arm around her, turned her onto her back, then stroked hard for shore.

When she was finally safe on land, he was alarmed to hear her make a choking sound, her body spasming convulsively. In a panic he dropped to the ground and bent over her, but she pushed him away.

She was laughing.

"Oh . . . oh shit," she gasped. "I must have looked so ridiculous. But what a ride! *Void's piss*, I've never felt anything like *that!*" She fell into another fit of laughter while Killian looked on, mystified, wringing out his hair and retrieving his boots. Had she lost her mind from shock? He knew that even ten minutes in such cold water could seize a person's muscles. Could it scramble their wits, too?

He touched her face with the back of a hand to see if she was dangerously cold. She didn't jerk away but managed to get her laughter under control.

"Seriously," she said, "I'm all right. Cold as space itself, but all right. It was actually . . . exciting. Really exciting. Do you want to give it a try?"

"No! I'd like to live a little longer, thanks. I just about killed myself coming after you as it is."

"Oh, sorry. Uh . . . help me up, would you? This vest . . . ."

He offered his hand, but she only held it long enough to get upright. Judging from her straight stance, the vest was working as it should. Her feet were firmly on the ground.

"We were right—it does have an automatic fall response; but I don't think the makers ever thought about it activating on a slope as steep as that. And its effect over water is almost nil. If I'd known that when we used that void-cursed raft, you could never have made me cross that river a second time." She took a few deep breaths. "Am I babbling?"

"You're probably suffering from mild shock, no matter what you say. We've got to get you warm, but the fastest way will be to climb back up to the cave."

"Up that slope?"

"No. Although Lewis and I never found the cave, we did travel along the southwest edge of that slope. It won't be an easy climb, but safer than the loose rocks. Can you manage, or do you need me to carry you?"

"Don't be ridiculous. I can walk as well as you can." Her first step proved the lie as she almost fell on her face. Killian didn't pick her up, but she allowed him to take her arm until they'd reached the forest edge. Then she used saplings and tree branches to pull herself up the steep path. The effort couldn't have warmed her very much. She hadn't dared to kick her boots off in the river—she had nothing else to wear on her feet—and although they'd been emptied, Killian could hear water squish between her toes with every step.

The warm air that flowed over them the moment they passed into the cave was pure bliss.

They hurried toward the hygiene area eager for a hot shower, but as they passed the lab where Natira had been working, she gasped and staggered against a wall.

A new display hung in the air slowly pulsing red and orange.

"What does it say?" Killian asked, his throat tightening with dread.

"It says 'Connection made with outside network'."

She turned to him, her face losing color.

"They know we're here."

30

"Our arrival must have awakened the whole complex and it automatically looked for a connection with the rest of the global network." Natira shuddered, not only from cold. "I wouldn't have believed that Tellurian equipment would recognize such old protocols—unless the message only means that it's connected with some other ancient base no one knows about."

"Can we take that chance?"

"No, we can't. We've got to go. Now." She turned back toward the entrance.

"Wait. You can't go anywhere as wet as you are. You'll freeze. You've got to get warm and dry first. Use the air heaters in the shower area, and don't forget to dry out your boots. I'll gather up the supplies you collected, and your Synappt. Maybe I can drag the glider to the entrance on my own."

"You must be just as cold as I am."

"No, I'm not. I generated a lot of body heat going after you." After a moment's pause, he began to strip off his clothes, his face turned away. Their stealth suits didn't hold water, but his own clothing did. He handed the garments to her, except for the small pair of shorts he wore. "Dry these if you can, but warm yourself first."

She couldn't help staring at his nearly naked form as he ran toward the back of the cave. With a shake of her head, she hurried to the hygiene room and shed her own clothes. A movable rack against a wall allowed her to spread their garments in front of one of the heaters while she took a quick shower. Its blast of warmth felt unbelievably good.

As she dried herself afterward, she caught her reflection in a mirror. Had the struggles of the past few days made her lose body mass? She thought so—it would be surprising if they hadn't. And Killian must already think she was too thin compared to the women he was used to. Not that she cared about that.

His own physique didn't appear to have suffered at all.

Despite the urgency, it was all she could do to pull herself from the stream of hot air. She told herself she had to make sure their clothing was thoroughly dry—her boots took the longest. When she couldn't stall any longer, she dressed and hurried to find Killian.

He'd managed to drag the flyer most of the distance to the cave mouth. She helped him the rest of the way to the ledge on the western cliff face. In several more trips they brought her Synappt and other equipment, plus two large bags of food packets, though not as much as she'd wanted. A wire cage under the passenger seats served as the glider's baggage carrier, and it was full to overflowing. They could only hope the extra weight wasn't too great for the machine's lift.

Having placed the rods and fabric bundle as close to the center of the ledge as he could, Killian looked stricken.

"I don't think there's enough room to extend the wings all the way."

Natira took a calming breath. "We'll . . . just have to get off the ground and trust that it can finish its extension in flight."

He took a doubtful look at their baggage. "Can you use your lift vest to make you lighter?"

"It would just push against the glider framework. Like standing on something while you try to lift it."

She reached into the bundle and pressed the blue icon. Immediately the rods and wing membrane began to move forcing them to jump out of the way. Killian had been right: the wing tips caught on rocks bordering each end of the ledge and the motion began to push the little craft's nose over the lip. Natira hurriedly ducked under the wing and climbed onto the rear seat.

"No! You should fly it," Killian cried. "You've probably flown in Telluria. I don't know how the controls work. I don't even know where they are!"

"I've flown in the zero-gravity zone of our sky with *wings* that I flapped like a bird. Nothing like this. And the glider is controlled by your mind—put that blue circlet around your head. It'll make you feel as if the glider is just an extension of your own body."

"But I've never . . ."

"You've watched birds glide. And you have much better muscle coordination than I do on Earth. You'll do fine. I trust . . ."

Suddenly she stopped to listen. Yes, there was a high-pitched rush of sound, growing in volume.

"We don't have time to argue. They're almost here!"

Killian grunted and climbed onto the front seat, quickly slipping the control circlet over his head. Straps automatically slid into place around their waists. The wings twitched again, as if answering an unheard command. With a muttered curse, he stretched out his legs and pushed the contraption forward while Natira copied him. Her stomach lurched as their center of balance shifted and the glider tipped over the edge.

Killian gave one last prodigious push, then stretched his neck upward as if willing the machine to follow. There was a loud clack as the wings completed their extension and then a softer snap from the fabric as it became rigid.

The frame gave a violent wobble—the wings catching the wind—but it continued to fall, less than two meters above the rocks of the slope. Then the nose suddenly swung upward and Natira could feel the tiny craft begin to stall.

"Don't pull up so much!" she yelled. "Let it follow the slope and pick up some speed!"

The nose dropped—too far—then levelled out. She could see Killian's shoulders shaking with effort.

"Don't fight it, just *feel* it. As if the wings are your arms and you're doing a graceful dive into the water."

The ride smoothed out, but they were still low and approaching the bottom of the valley much too quickly.

"How do I start the motor?" he cried.

"Run your left hand up that green stripe just in front of you."

There was an unmistakable shove from behind and the glider pitched nose-down, but Killian recovered, and it swooped upward just before they reached the river's edge. From there the craft gained altitude slowly but steadily, a meter or two every few seconds.

She couldn't hear their pursuers over the rush of wind in her ears, but they couldn't be far.

"Don't forget the yellow icon!"

With another curse, Killian pressed his palm to the flat plate in front and vanished from sight.

Even though she'd known what to expect, Natira gasped. The sudden unobstructed view of her surroundings made her feel as if she was falling from a great height. The flyer was nearly even with the cliff top by then, about half a kilometer west of it, and still climbing. With a prickly feeling at the back of her neck, she looked behind her.

Five shuttles rose over the far side of the promontory and began to move in a coordinated circle. None came in her direction.

Would they find the cave? It seemed inevitable. Her reawakening of the site's network had probably delivered a very precise location.

The glider continued to gain altitude, but much too slowly for her peace of mind. Soon she was able to watch the shuttles from slightly above, and they looked terribly close. How could they fail to discover their quarry hanging helpless in the sky, even with the stealth screen?

Small shapes dropped from some of the shuttles—men and women tasked with searching on foot. A number landed at the bottom of the cliff. It was only a matter of time before they found the cave opening. Knowing it was there made all the difference. She could tell when it happened because dozens of the small dots swarmed together at the top of the slope and then disappeared.

It was a long time before anything more happened. The glider had almost reached the bottom of some low clouds when she heard Killian ask her if they should go in. She told him not to—it was better to see the pursuit, and the cloud cover wouldn't offer any extra protection. In fact, the flyer's motor might be giving off heat the stealth field couldn't mask.

He shut it down, and there was a noticeable shift of balance as the forward thrust fell off. Whether instinctively or from recent experience, Killian nosed the craft down slightly to regain some speed, eventually finding the best compromise between forward and downward momentum.

The landscape spread before them like a rumpled white cloth but with dark blemishes from exposed rock, wind-swept clumps of trees, and the meandering river. It was a stunning view, and floating above it all gave an indescribable feeling.

"Look!" Killian cried.

She turned her head in time to see a gout of flame spew from the cliff face, then three more before the sound of the first reached them: a deep crack and rumble, like thunder, repeated four times. When the last had died away and columns of smoke climbed into the sky, she could just make out a mass of debris sliding down the slope, raising a cloud in its wake.

The Tellurians had blown up the cave.

"They don't plan to let us use that again," Killian muttered. "I wonder if they would have done that if we were still inside."

"Of course not." But her declaration wasn't because she trusted the compassion of their pursuers. The fugitives would be much more useful alive if only so they could be put on display, as a warning to all.

Awed by the destruction in spite of herself, she couldn't look away. If the flyer was spotted, she and Killian would be helpless; but she had to watch, desperately hoping that the searchers would give up and leave.

They didn't. Instead, the five craft resumed their circling, gradually expanding the pattern. Its perimeter grew until one of the shuttles passed right beneath the glider, though hundreds of meters below. Natira realized that she was holding her breath.

After that, the search grid shifted back toward the south. Perhaps the leader felt that anyone sensible would instinctively travel in the direction of warmer weather or the nearest habitations. They didn't know Killian.

When the pursuit had moved sufficiently far away, he finally spoke.

"We should get as far away from the Tellurian base as possible, right?"

"Of course."

"But there are two problems with that. For one thing, we're also getting farther and farther from my mother, with the medicine she badly needs. For another, one of us has to contact the higher Tellurian authorities to tell them about the con . . ."

"Conspiracy?"

"Conspiracy to strip the Earth of resources again and use my people for forced labor."

She nodded, even though he couldn't see it. He was right, of course. But it didn't matter.

There was no higher authority than her father the Patriarch, and she couldn't be sure that he himself wasn't involved in the conspiracy. Even if he wasn't, he might not care about a plan to enslave Earth people, unless it interfered with his own interests. It wasn't as if the average citizen of the Confederacy had any interest in Earth politics. And if the security forces decided that she'd helped Killian, he wouldn't listen to anything that she said.

"Of course, we want to get the medicine to your mother, although she'll be well enough for a month, or even two. I'd like to talk to your uncle again. If he knew about the cave, what else does he know? Did these stealth suits come from

246

there, or is there another hidden cache of equipment somewhere? That could be a big help."

"I've thought the same thing."

"The good news is that my Synappt is fully recharged, so I'll be able to work with it for a few weeks, I think. And it was the computer at the cave, not mine, that gave us away."

Without further comment, Killian swung the flyer slowly toward the north. An hour or so later, he used the motor to regain lost altitude. Thin clouds passed enough sunlight to replenish the engine. In another twenty minutes, he returned to a powerless glide, gradually turned eastward, and pointed out that the landscape in that direction was flatter and more heavily forested. Once they did land, it would be difficult to find another launch point.

This would almost certainly be their first and last flight.

It was an incredible experience, drifting high above the world with the only noise the wind in her hair. Gusts tugged at her cloak and occasionally stole her breath, but also brought the scents of the land: the perfume of a cedar grove, the crisp ozone tang of fresh snow, the ever-so-slightly fishy odor of lake water. Even, one time, an astringent whiff of a creature Killian called a skunk, probably in its death throes at the teeth of a predator. From that height she felt detached from struggles of life and death, and even from her own troubles. For this moment, she floated above them all, a little nearer to the vast spaces of her birth, and temporarily freed of the Earth's dreary pull.

Her feeling of transcendence was all too brief. Exposed to the wind, Natira steadily grew colder. The cave's heaters hadn't quite restored her body's core temperature. Shivering progressed to chattering teeth. She gripped the glider's framework in an effort to stop it, but knew it was a losing battle.

"Is that you, shaking?" Killian asked.

"I'll b-be ffff-fine." But her stuttered words gave the game away.

"Shit, I should have realized." He immediately nosed the flyer downward.

"No. We have to make as much distance as we can."

"I hate to tell you, but I can't figure out where we are from up here. I'm guessing—that's all. From high enough, we'd be able to see Borealis; but these clouds are too low—and if we keep on flying blind, we really will get lost. We might end up farther away than ever."

Neither said anything more, and within another quarter hour Killian had picked a light green clearing as his target. There weren't many alternatives within reach.

A hundred meters above the ground Natira called out, "But that's a marsh!"

"I know, and I wish there was someplace else—but there isn't! I'll get us as close to the forest's edge as I can."

True to his word, there was only half a meter of water under them and ten meters to the shore when they splashed down. Killian coaxed the flyer into one final moment of lift, allowing them to hop off and land on their feet. Natira was just about to praise him when a groan came out instead. Her boots had sunk into the muck and filled with brackish water. Bubbles rose to the surface, giving off one of the worst smells she'd ever known.

"Sorry about that. But if there's any chance we might be able to use this glider again . . . ."

She only nodded and helped him drag the craft to dry land. Once out of the water, they collapsed it and looked for a secure hiding place with landmarks they might recognize if they ever returned this way.

"Not much hope of that, though. Swamps all look pretty much alike."

"I have an idea." She unpacked her Synappt. As she'd hoped, its network finder located a signal from the flyer. "I'm not sure of the range, but if we ever come close enough, this will let us know."

They found a clump of small spruce trees up against a cleft in some rock a short distance along the shore. Those hid the glider fairly well.

"Which way from here?"

Killian looked up at the sky. Natira found it hard to even pick out the sun's location behind the clouds, but Killian didn't hesitate before pointing.

"Let's go south for a while. See if I can recognize anything. Your people were searching west of here, but we'll have to listen closely, just in case."

As they entered the shadowed world among the trees, the memory of the bright, warm cave was a weight on Natira's heart. The fleeting interlude among familiar comforts had only made her exile on Earth harder to face. For a time, she'd felt in control of her fate again. Now, once more, she'd placed her life in the hands of a man she barely knew.

And among all the reasons she gave herself for doing so, she would dearly love to know which was the real one.

31

It took them five days to find Borealis.

It took the black flies two days to find them.

After the snowstorm back at the cave, Natira couldn't believe how quickly the weather had warmed. Since they felt compelled to wear their stealth cloaks and she refused to shed any other clothing, her body poured sweat, and Killian's long hair looked as if he'd just been dunked. And dunking was often the case. They took every opportunity to immerse themselves in the many small lakes and streams. But after one such swim, Natira felt a sudden pain on her face. Her hand flew to the spot but found nothing. The sharp prick was repeated moments later on her forehead. She slapped at it.

"Black flies," Killian proclaimed. He showed her one of the tiny things, and she found it hard to believe that something so small could produce such a surprising sting. Then he brushed a finger over her neck and showed her a trace of blood.

"Sometimes you don't feel them. Then they get the time to bite deeper. We'll have to watch to make sure the bites don't get infected."

Horrified, she pulled the hood of her suit as close around her face as she could, though the sleeves still left her hands as fair game. Something bit her every few minutes, and she didn't know how she could stand it. Now that they had portable power packs, she even tried making her suit invisible, but the pests still knew exactly where to find her. That night, on Killian's advice, she sat in the smoke of their fire, though it made her throat and nose burn. To sleep, she pulled her hands into her sleeves and her arms over her face.

By the next afternoon, it was a hundred times worse. The tiny biting flies crawled over her face constantly, no matter what she did, with a special preference for her ears, the corners of her eyes, and the back of her neck. She found some relief whenever she and Killian came across a body of water, and kept herself beneath the surface as long as she could. Then, too, in moments of hot sunshine or in a strong breeze, the evil pests retreated for a time. Those moments were heavenly.

The next morning, Killian laughed at her in surprise, declaring that her puffy eyelids made her look like his friend Zhana. She didn't see the humor.

He told her that the open spaces of settlements like Borealis provided some relief from black flies, though not mosquitoes; but his distant ancestors had lived among the trees all the time, suffering from both kinds of pests and more during warm months. She didn't believe him; but, to her chagrin, he wasn't bothered by the bugs as badly as she was. It should have been the other way around, thanks to his gamey smell. Instead, he declared that for the bugs, she was 'sweet meat.'

Within another two days, even wetlands and clearings didn't provide any escape because now mosquitoes had arrived, noisier insects that sank needle-like proboscises deep into her flesh to draw blood. They even injected a venom to keep the blood from coagulating quickly. Her disgust with the creatures bordered on outright fear, even finding herself waving her arms non-stop in a frenetic reaction she could barely control.

Killian called a halt at the next stream. He opened his stealth suit, stripped off his shirt, rinsed it several times and wrung it out, then cut a pair of slits with his knife. Natira couldn't believe that he'd willingly expose so much skin and couldn't imagine why.

"Here," he said. "Wear this over your head and neck." And slipped on the top of his stealth suit.

"But you won't . . ."

"I'll be fine. Just try it."

She did, positioning the slits over her eyes and pulling her suit tight. Almost immediately she felt her body begin to relax. The evaporation of the moisture in the cloth cooled her face a little, and only a few mosquitoes managed to penetrate at points where it touched her skin. She could handle that. But she knew that Killian's suit top alone wouldn't protect him from marauders entering at the neck and cuffs. The thought made her shudder. When she thanked him, he only nodded and resumed his walk.

Even after its thorough rinsing, the shirt was still redolent with his male animal scent, but that was no hardship compared to the biting bugs. The more serious drawback was that it impaired her vision. It wasn't easy to follow Killian and watch her footing at the same time. And it was just bad timing that she'd lowered the power of her lift vest in a first attempt to accustom her body to Earth gravity.

A loop of exposed tree root caught her foot like a trap.

She gave a cry of pain as she fell.

Killian was at her side immediately to help her up, but she almost collapsed again when he released his grip. Her left ankle wouldn't bear her weight.

She cranked up the lift vest and tried to walk, insisting that she'd be fine.

She wasn't fine. She couldn't go on.

It was only midday, too early to stop for the night; but they took a long break for food and water while Killian examined her injury. He was almost sure that it was only a sprain. Natira remembered the med scanner she'd found, and it confirmed that nothing was broken. But her ankle still caused some of the worst pain Natira had ever known, and it showed no sign of easing. She'd brought the scanner but hadn't thought to bring pain killers or antibiotics.

Killian took his shirt from her, tore a wide strip from its hem, and used that to bandage her ankle as tightly as he could without cutting off circulation.

"I'll carry you," he said.

"You can't do that. I'm as big as you are."

"But not nearly as heavy. Especially if your lift vest can push downward and not against me. Look, you're going to need to rest this foot for a few days, and I think we're only about a day from Regina and Lewis's."

His plan made logical sense, but she was horrified at the thought of hanging over his back like captured game.

So she tried to walk again, but failed

Submitting to the inevitable, she gritted her teeth, clambered onto his back, and wrapped her arms around his neck, loosening them a little when he protested. They'd strapped as much of their baggage as possible onto her own back, and with her lift vest set fairly high, it relieved him not only of the weight but also most of the pressure on his torso and shoulders. Even so, her skin shuddered at every point of contact as she tried to reassure herself that there were always several layers of cloth between them.

Lost in her own indignity, it took some time for her to notice that the arrangement left Killian without full use of his arms to keep bugs from his face, though he suffered without complaint. From then on, she was diligent to swat the invaders away as much as she could. He thanked her and said nothing if her skin occasionally brushed his.

The hours that followed were a new form of torture for both of them; and when they finally came in sight of Lewis and Regina's cabin, Natira could scarcely have been more pleased at seeing Capita itself.

Rough-cut walls and imperfectly fitted windows couldn't keep every mosquito out, but Natira sighed with relief and unabashedly slumped in a chair while Regina tutted over her swollen and bruised ankle. Killian's aunt replaced the makeshift bandage with a poultice that contained pungent herbs and took some of the pain away.

253

Over the next few days, both couples took turns grilling each other. Regina was dismayed to hear about the close call at the cave, but Lewis admitted that he'd known about its contents and was pleased that they'd been of use. He clearly had mixed feelings about its destruction.

"I never felt it would be right to show you the cave when you were young, Killian, but those suits of yours did come from there," he said. "There are other stockpiles, too—some I've seen; others I've only heard about. But there's something else you should know."

"The Confederacy has been coming to Earth all this time," Natira said.

He looked surprised but nodded. "In great secrecy, but some . . . people I know found a hidden landing site. We think it might be their base of operations for the whole continent."

"Where?" Killian leaned forward.

Lewis shook his head. "Don't think I'm gonna help you go *there*. You'd never get past all the security, and they could do whatever they wanted to you without anyone ever finding out."

"But that's exactly why we have to go," Natira protested, surprising them all. "Most of my people know nothing about this. And they need to know. I'm an information presenter by profession. If I can record evidence of what's been happening, I think I can persuade my bosses to show it throughout the colonies." The jewel-like camera she wore on her forehead had prodigious storage capacity, and automatically linked with her Synappt.

"What good would that do?"

"I don't know, to be honest. Earth isn't a big part of our lives, but Confederacy citizens do like to believe that the Earth was left alone to heal, and they don't like their government to keep secrets from them. I think they'd object to this . . . interference. Especially the citizens of the outer colonies who battle with interference all the time. And your people certainly should know what's been going on."

Killian shook his head. "I don't understand. Why would the colonists come here all these years? To stop us from killing animals and polluting the Earth?"

Lewis gave a dark frown. "To keep us in our place. Make sure we don't develop technology of our own—to keep us dependent."

Natira wanted to deny it. Instead, she whispered, "To make you compliant workers." She and Killian exchanged a worried look.

After dinner that night Killian took a small vial from his pack.

"It's more medicine for Summer. Natira got it from the Borealis base after we were here."

"Summer's being watched closely in case you show up," Regina said. "But we'll get it to her. The watchers will be distracted by the big ceremony."

In answer to their puzzled looks she explained, "The ceremony to appoint that ambassador, Hind, as governor of NorthAm. Three days from now."

"The whole continent?"

"Why would people agree to that?"

Regina only shrugged.

"I don't understand why Hind would do it, either. It's not like him," Natira insisted.

Killian raised an eyebrow at her but said nothing.

"This second dose of medicine will help Summer a lot," Natira said, changing the subject. "The effects are cumulative. If I can get more, it might give her another two or three years."

Killian's face was a study in conflict. "That would mean you going back into the Tellurian base. They'd arrest you on sight."

"Most of the base staff will be at the ceremony to put on a good show, and the ones still on duty will watch it by holo. We couldn't ask for a better distraction."

He said nothing, his lips pressed hard together. She took it as tacit agreement.

Regina got to her feet and asked Natira to come into the kitchen to help with the cleanup; but when they were alone, the older woman waved away her help and said, "I just want to talk." She picked up a dishcloth and gestured for Natira to sit on a chair by the counter.

"You know that Killian looked up to the colonists all his life—obsessed over your technology, wanted to be one of you."

"I think he still does, in spite of the way my people have treated him. He wants to believe it's all a mistake that will be corrected, and then he'll come to live in Telluria or on one of the colony planets, happily ever after. But that doesn't make sense to me—he's so at home on *this* world, as if he understands every plant and animal."

"I'm glad you agree. And I hope you care enough about him to help him see reality."

"Care enough about him?"

Regina just gave an amused look. "Tell yourself what you want about your own feelings, but I can tell you that our Killian has fallen for you. Though he may not know it himself, yet."

"*What?* No, he hasn't. He thinks I'm a pampered princess who's a royal nuisance to drag through the forest. And he's not even wrong." She tried to make her smile casual.

"Killian's a good man. He'll go out of his way to help anybody—he always has. But he bends over backwards for you. And it's never been easy to read his feelings. Not until now. You just gave him a choice between his mother's health and your safety, and he was like a rabbit between a fox and a cliff."

Natira felt a ridiculous blush warm her cheeks. "I never meant to make him choose. And I'm . . . I'm sure you're wrong. But I'll do everything I can to . . . set him straight about things between us." She nodded hard to emphasize her words. It was absurd to think in those terms about Killian. He'd ruined her life, and she'd ruined his. If it weren't for her, he wouldn't be a fugitive facing exile on Mars. Surely no relationship could be built on that much mutual resentment.

Regina just said softly, "Two different worlds, yes. You belong in Telluria. He belongs here. But if you have to let him down, Natira, please do it as gently as you can."

Natira didn't trust herself to answer.

When they returned to the main room Killian had convinced Lewis to sketch a map to the secret Confederacy operations base, although the older man wasn't happy about doing it. Natira was surprised to recognize a few of the landmarks from the countryside they'd passed through to the north. But their destination was far beyond those, through territory even more heavily pockmarked with small lakes and rivers they'd have to cross.

"Maybe we can build a raft," Killian said with a smirk.

She shot him a glare that could have melted him.

The next three days passed too quickly as Natira enjoyed the company of Lewis and Regina. They weren't the all-wise chieftains she was still hoping to meet, but they had a deep stock of everyday wisdom and knowledge of simple things. She could see why Killian had spent so much time with them. And she was disturbed to find that she envied him the close relationship with his aunt and uncle, as well as his devotion to his mother and other family members. That was so far from Natira's own experience that she hardly knew what to make of it. What would life be like with actual genetic relatives to share it with you, helping you through difficult times and caring about your happiness?

The Tellurian way of genetic selection and manipulation, and ruthlessly impartial nurture, was clearly superior. At least, more efficient. Random sexual intercourse, nine months of pregnancy, and live birth through hours of painful labor was a revoltingly crude way of replenishing the species. But it was hard to deny that the resulting connections could provide real benefits. She had only to look at the happiness on Killian's face as he joked with Regina and Lewis to see that.

When they set out early on the fourth morning to retrieve medicine from the base, Natira's ankle was still very tender. Lewis had made her a short cast of plasticwood that he'd carefully heated and re-shaped. Even a layer of padding couldn't prevent her skin from chafing, but with help from her lift vest she could walk without much of a limp. He'd also given her a stout staff to lean on as she walked, smoothly stripped of its bark by an animal Lewis called a *beaver*.

They were better equipped for a journey through the wild this time, with tent, knives, and even some lightweight cooking pots that nested together.

They reached the base near Borealis about an hour before sunset and she waited with her foot raised on a stump. Killian tried one more time to persuade her not to go into the base. He insisted that they'd stand a better chance of getting medicine from the secret installation to the north, where they would not be expected.

She held her ground.

The induction ceremony for the NorthAm region's new governor was scheduled to coincide with the setting sun as part of a feast and celebration that would last all evening in the plaza surrounding the Depot. As Natira had predicted, the base was nearly deserted. Even better, one shuttle had been parked within only twenty meters of the trees on the eastern edge of the pad. It provided a long shadow that Natira used to approach the craft and enter it. In a crew locker, she found a spare uniform and put it on, counting on the fact that the base guards wouldn't know every spacecraft crew member that came and went. Half an hour later, she hurried through the gathering dusk to where Killian crouched among some juniper.

"The dispenser would only provide one vial at a time," she said. "But that will still go a long way. Should we take it back to Regina and Lewis's now?"

"Does it work better if she takes larger amounts?"

"No, she still must take only a drop with each meal. This would just give her an extra supply on hand."

He hesitated, probably weighing the chances that they would be captured. "No, it's not worth the risk right now. Most people never go far into the bush, but some do, and they all know the Confederacy is looking for us."

They skirted the outpost as quickly as they could and headed north.

# # #

The warming of the days benefitted insects more than humans. Regina had provided cowls made of loosely woven threads like a screen to protect their heads from mosquitoes, and a tent-like shelter of the same material; but when they travelled through open areas in hot sun, larger insects Killian called deerflies and horseflies were easily able to bite through where the screening touched skin. Those bites really hurt and drove Natira to distraction. Once the cool of evening chased the flies away, mosquitoes took their place; and during night hours, even the fine mesh was unable to keep out scourges of tinier, biting *no-see-ums*.

Natira had once read of the ancient human concept of Hell: a place of endless torment for the wicked. Now she'd discovered its inspiration.

"You said your people once lived in the bush all the time," she said to Killian accusingly. "They couldn't have done that without some protection from these void-cursed insects."

He actually laughed.

"My teachers said that before the Divide there was technology that used sound, and strong smells, and other strange devices for that, but I'm not sure I believe it. Grandmother claims people once covered themselves with bear grease. Would you like me to ask a bear to sacrifice himself for us?"

"You mean there could be bears in these woods?"

"Of course. Bears, moose, wolves. Lynx, too. Lots of coyotes and foxes. But don't worry—the amount of noise you make, they hear us coming a kilometer away!"

She knew she'd just been insulted but wasn't sure how. Scaring wildlife away had to be a good thing. Unless he was trying to say that he wanted to hunt, and she was spoiling it for him.

Too bad.

32

Returning to camp from a foraging excursion one evening, Killian was startled to find Natira standing with her back to him, surrounded on three sides by what looked to be full-length mirrors. He had only ever seen such a mirror in the house of an elder. But these didn't show Natira as she was—in the reflection, she wore pants and a light tunic or jacket of a very light beige with fringes hanging from the forearms. The clothing reminded him of a fancy beaded costume that his aunt Regina had inherited from her ancestors and saved for special dances at the peak of summer and the beginning of autumn. The dance costume was made of carefully preserved doeskin, he knew. Why would these floating mirrors show Natira wearing something like that?

He carefully walked into her field of vision, trying not to startle her, but did anyway. She blushed, and with a motion of her hand the mirrors disappeared, but not before he saw that there had been a mirror behind her too, though invisible from where he'd stood.

"What was that?"

She reluctantly held out a small tube in the palm of her hand before returning it to her bag.

"It's a style projector. It shows us different selections of clothing, to help us choose what to wear for the day."

"It changed your hair, too. It gave you a ponytail."

She gave a stiff nod. "It can show us with jewelry, or decorations on our skin . . . . Very useful."

"But you don't have clothes like that with you."

"No."

He wanted to ask more, but the expression on her face told him such questions wouldn't be welcome. With a shrug, he showed her what food he'd gathered: some cattail roots, wild carrots, and plantain leaves. They wouldn't make much of a stew, but he'd sneak some earthworms and wild leeks into it for flavor.

She nodded and turned away to gather dry sticks, her neck more rigid than usual.

He could understand that she wanted to be somewhere else. *Anywhere else.* But the scene he'd witnessed suggested that she also wanted to be some*one* else.

In a mirror that almost seemed to grant wishes, who did she see?

#   #   #

During the long hours of breaking trail, Killian felt a profound gratitude to Lewis and Regina for the way they'd prepared him for such an ordeal, though they could never have envisioned his current need.

He was also surprised by how much he missed Borealis. Wherever he went in its shabby labyrinth of rough pathways, hands waved and people called out greetings. Of course, he'd lived in the same small neighborhood most of his life—his father's shack was only a couple of rows away from Summer's—but it was more than that. Perhaps because of the attention he received from Momoko Quarry, people believed that he was being groomed for leadership. Their quarter of town was represented on the Allocation council by a couple of elders, but one of those was very old and would eventually pass on the responsibility. Killian had more schooling than almost anyone in the quarter and rarely caused trouble, so many people pushed him toward the council position.

He had little interest—as far as he could see, the council never did anything. Besides, he had always hoped the colonists would return and take him back with them into the sky. But he hadn't resisted the efforts too much because he was sure that community leaders would have the closest access to the colonists, and a good record of service might even make him more attractive to them.

More than that, he'd learned from his father that helping other people was good for everyone. Jacob Horsetail never said no when someone needed a helping hand, whether it was nailing a shack together, fixing a water pipe, chasing bears away from a friend's maple syrup pots, or herding unruly children to school. In that fashion, Jacob had learned nearly every skill there was, and everybody liked him.

Killian often went along with his father to help; and later he spent even more time helping on his own, including pedaling a pedicar he had found on the far edge of town and fixed up. A healthy person could walk anywhere in Borealis, but it was a serious challenge for some of the oldest people. With the pedicar, Killian drove the elderly, the sick, and expectant mothers around town with no expectation of reward. For other passengers, he traded his service for future favors; or, if the trip was to one of the tiny artisanal settlements farther from Borealis, craft goods or homegrown food. Garden food was his favorite payment. Well, perhaps not quite—he sometimes transported young women, too, and their company was a pleasure all its own.

As that memory came to him, he couldn't help comparing those women to Natira. The contrasts were many, not least of which was the beauty of her radiantly blond hair and perfect, fair skin. But her appearance, pleasing as it was, was almost inconsequential. It didn't begin to explain the vast difference in the way he thought about her compared to other women in his life. Resentment and indignation clashed constantly with more pleasant feelings that were harder to define or, at least, harder to acknowledge. She challenged him, exasperated him, and left him utterly confused. Yet now that she was in his life, he couldn't imagine that life without her, a circumstance that seemed exhausting and energizing at the same time.

One thing was certain: he couldn't picture her ever making a life in backward Borealis.

33

The urgency to find the colonists' outpost, and the endless trials of the journey didn't allow for much sightseeing; but sometimes Killian chose to stop and make camp in the late afternoon because they'd come to a good source of clean water and signs of game.

One such evening near sunset, they sat at the edge of a tiny lake like a bowl scooped out of hard rock. Unlike so many other ponds that were rimmed by marshes, this one had walls that rose straight from the water, rugged and patched with shades of ruddy brown and grey.

As Natira gazed at a nearby promontory, she sat up straight and said, "It's a face."

"We do call them rock faces," Killian said, earning a cuff on the arm.

"No, I mean it looks like a face. See, there's a big nose with a bend in it. And stern eyebrows, and dark grey eyes looking out over the water. Don't you see it?"

"Sure, I guess. But if you like that, try turning your head sideways and look at those rocks over there with their reflections."

She gave him a look of skepticism, but then she tried it. The water was as still as a mirror, every feature of the shore reflected perfectly in it.

"Beautiful. But why sideways?"

"Sideways, the rocks join to their reflections . . . people see images in them. Sometimes faces. More often body shapes, with legs and arms, or even wings and horns. Angels. Demons. Spirits of the lake. Who knows?"

She tried to let her mind run free, and before long, she saw what he meant. The rocks opposite now looked to her like an ancient Earth hunter carrying his catch in each hand. Another image might have been a dancer with outflung legs and crossed arms. A third had smooth, flowing lines in muted shades: a head with long hair and a billowing dress with sleeves draped from slender arms—a female form, certainly. The spirit of the lake? Or the spirit of the Earth itself?

Natira couldn't help but wonder what Killian saw. The spirits of more accomplished ancestors? Or the things he'd always dreamed of: trappings of an imagined utopia with exotic spacecraft and sculpted asteroids, and maybe even aliens from other worlds.

She looked at him expectantly, but he only shrugged and answered her unspoken question with, "I never see anything but rocks."

She didn't believe him.

#   #   #

Five days north of Borealis, they found the house.

With slumped walls and a roof that sagged like a bow, rimmed with evergreens, it was so thoroughly covered with moss and rotting pine needles that from above it would probably be indistinguishable from its surroundings. It also stank of rotting logs and mildew. Plates of fungi protruded from the walls outside and in. Natira's mind quailed at entering the decrepit building, but at least it provided some shelter from the biting bugs. Killian assured her that he had no plans to sleep there.

It wasn't a family home—more like a schoolhouse or other meeting place, with one large central space flanked by smaller enclosures. In some of the small spaces they found desks and tables that had collapsed, and shelving now crumbled into pulpy shards. More surprising, there were many clumps of a substance Killian called paper that bore little resemblance to the reusable cellulose known by that name in Telluria. Its matted sheets could not be pulled apart without crumbling, and they smelled very bad when he made the attempt. After searching the place for a half-hour, they returned outside.

"You think it was a school? Way out here?"

"No, I said it's like a school, but this building was deliberately hidden."

"How do you know?"

"Look how the forest comes right up to the walls with trees that are older than the cabin. People don't build that way—we like some cleared space to let air circulate and sunshine to get through. And the moss on the roof is too even, like it was placed there. So, who would the builders have been hiding from, and why?"

"Someone looking for them from above," Natira said, and he nodded. "My people? Maybe from the secret base north of here?"

He nodded again. "If you wanted to keep an eye on a base like that, or even if you wanted to meet somewhere without your neighbors knowing about it and knew that you were being watched from the sky . . . ."

"You'd need somewhere far enough from Borealis and not too close to the base."

"Right. There are some very small villages to the south and east of Borealis where artisans and farmers offer their goods for trade. They'd provide enough of an excuse to be gone from home for a few days at a time without making anyone too curious."

"So, some of your people knew about the Confederacy's presence on Earth and got together to talk about it. But what good would that do them?"

"I don't know. This cabin . . . the smaller rooms are too big to be closets. They almost remind me of those laboratory rooms in the cave. But I can't imagine what they would be used for."

They'd been walking through the trees in a slow circle around the building. Killian jerked to a stop, rocked from foot to foot, then knelt on the ground.

"What is it?"

Without answering, he dug at the dirt with his fingers until they penetrated to the wrist. Reaching both hands into the depression, he gripped and pulled hard with his back. A thick disk of soil about an arm's length in diameter tugged free, with something rigid on its underside. Metal?

Natira leaned over and saw that the disk had covered a deep hole. She thought she could see the bottom. The width and depth looked about the size of a standing person.

She gasped and stumbled back. "Is that . . . a burial hole?"

"A burial hole? You mean a grave?"

"Your people often bury the dead, don't they?" Did the dark shadows obscure some rotting corpse?

"Some used to. But not standing up. Not our people, anyway."

"Then what's it for? To preserve food? Or hide valuables?"

"Not bad guesses." He replaced the disk, roughed up the dirt and grass around its edges, and began to walk again, paying close attention to the ground in front of him. "Hiding is right. But the valuables were themselves."

"What?"

"Think about it. If you realized your secret gathering place had been discovered and you expected to be raided at any moment, you could try to run away into the bush . . ."

"And be seen by infrared instruments."

"Or you could hide. Under the ground, with a metal lid to block your pursuers' technology."

"Unless they used penetrating radar or metal detectors."

"Pene—what? Anyway, would you use those to find *primitive* humans?"

"I suppose not."

"These people didn't think so either. And if they made a hiding hole for one person, they made more." He picked up a stout, straight branch like a pole and began to prod the earth with it as he went. By the time he'd made a full circle around the cabin he'd found six spots he believed were holes and was sure there'd be more at various distances throughout the nearby woods. He only opened one other that was particularly well-hidden and left it open, but when Natira asked why, he just shrugged.

Walking back slowly toward the cabin he said, "I don't trust this roof enough to sleep under it, but we can probably take a break from the bugs for a few hours." He closed the rickety door behind them, pulling it hard but carefully. Natira sat down in a corner and took her Synappt from its satchel.

"Without so many bugs to swat I might be able to make some progress with this," she explained.

The hottest hours of the afternoon passed. The air inside the ruined cabin was still and stuffy, but the number of flying, stinging, and biting creatures was almost tolerable. While Natira worked to crack the next level of the archive, Killian sat against the opposite wall with his eyes closed. He said he was thinking about the best place to make camp for the night, but it looked like he was sleeping.

Natira's stomach had begun to suggest it was near dinner time when Killian suddenly sat up.

"Do you feel that?"

"What? I don't feel anything."

He paused for another moment then jumped to his feet and said, "Come on!" nearly pulling her out the door. "They're coming!" He looked around them frantically.

He darted to his left through the trees and Natira followed. In dismay, she realized that he was going to the hole, largely hidden under some spreading bushes.

"No! I can't get into one of those!" she shrieked.

"It's either that or get caught. Maybe you've got some clout with the people at the top, but the ones who'll find us will be lowly guards who just might not have been told how special you are."

She glared at him but slid into the hole, terrified that something would happen to him and that she might not be able to get back out on her own. Now she could hear a rush of wind, though there was no wind.

"Isn't there anywhere else to hide?"

"There's no time to get anywhere else," he said.

In a flash of understanding, she opened her mouth to yell an objection, but it was filled with his hair as he slid into the hole with her. Before she could even free her arms, he'd pulled the lid into place and wrestled it back and forth a few times, presumably to stir up the ground-cover of pine needles and dead leaves to disguise their refuge. They were plunged into blackness.

There wasn't enough air. She gasped for oxygen and her hands flew up to claw at the lid. Killian snatched her wrists and pulled them down to his waist, but she yanked them away and held them rigidly to her side. It took all of her will not to shriek.

"I can't do this!" she hissed. "I'll scream." The hole was bigger than she'd thought, but their bodies were pressed together, and his face was only centimeters away from hers.

"Why? I won't do anything to you. Do you still not trust me?"

"It's not that. I don't . . . we aren't . . ." In a voice on the edge of hysteria she hissed, *"We don't touch each other in Telluria!* We almost *never* touch another human being. *Haven't you noticed?"*

His gasp was real. "I thought . . . I thought maybe someone had abused you and that's why you couldn't stand to be touched."

"No! It's just not done. We're not . . . ." She stopped herself, but he completed the thought.

"You're not animals. I know. But, still, that can't be . . . . Not even for sex?"

"No! That would be the most disgusting of all!" She couldn't repress a shudder.

"Goddamn . . . ." he rasped. "You're a *virgin.*"

"I am not!" she spat, then cringed, afraid that her voice had carried. There was no sound from above. If Confederacy shuttles were overhead, they hadn't yet landed. She should just let the subject drop, but she continued in a whisper, "I've had sex dozens of times. My Intended and I . . ."

"How? With holograms? Mechanical equipment?"

"They're called coitusuits. Fully linked to our own nervous system, and to each other's. It's the closest experience two humans can share."

"Without touching each other. Unbelievable. And you think *we're* pathetic!"

She could feel the angry rigidity of his body mirroring her own, smelled his sweat pungent from adrenaline. It was amazing to realize that she could now distinguish his fear sweat from that of normal exertion. And it was probably getting all over her!

"Well, I promise you we won't be having sex," he continued, "but if you insist on me climbing out of here ..."

"Don't be stupid. But you're crushing me. And how can we know this hole won't collapse on us?" she asked.

"The walls are reinforced with plasticwood. You can feel it."

His hands reached under her arms to shift her upward and her breath caught at the sensation of his palms so close to her breasts. Then they were gone. Her chest was still squeezed tightly against his and the rigid wall held her immobile, but she had to admit that it wasn't the pressure that was affecting her breathing.

"*Calm down, can't you?*" he snapped. "You're making as much noise as a sow in heat."

The insult rekindled her anger, but she pushed it away. Instead, she began to shiver. He must have thought she was cold—he put his arms around her. She gave an involuntary whimper, and his arms withdrew.

"*Souls of the ancestors!* You'd think I was a swamp slug. Keep yourself warm, then."

She felt him try to pull farther away, but it wasn't possible. Her breasts were flattened against his ribs, her chin pressed between his shoulder and neck. Self-reproach made a sour taste in her throat—she should have been stronger than this. She couldn't fall apart just because her body was in contact with a man's. And there was clothing between them.

Except for the stubble of his cheek on hers, and his breath rustling her hair.

Disgust swelled up again.

"You probably planned this," she hissed.

"Don't flatter yourself. I'd be afraid to have sex with you—I'd break you in half. Now *shut up.*"

For the first time she could hear a hum through the closed lid. The searchers must be right above them!

She clenched her lips together and tried to control a new round of shuddering, as if the vibration might transfer to the ground around them and give them away. Perhaps thinking the same thing, Killian pulled her tightly to him and buried her face in his hair. She had to distract herself, had to think of other things than the desperation of their plight and the revolting nearness of this arrogant man. Maybe she could imagine ways to get even for his wounding words.

Except she knew that his words were only because she'd wounded him first. She'd studied his people—she knew that they touched each other without reservation, as if to reinforce the familial ties that she so admired. Such a thing was a deep part of his being; and by attacking that custom, she had attacked him and those he loved. Of course, he had lashed out.

Minutes passed. She was tempted to count the seconds, but it would only make the ordeal seem longer. At least she couldn't hear the hum anymore. Instead, she was astonished to hear what had to be the rhythm of Killian's heart. It beat far more slowly than her own and the sound gave her unexpected comfort. First, she listened to it, then tried to sense it with her own flesh.

She could.

It was as if, for a time, they shared the pulse of life itself; and the strength of each pulse flowed from him into her.

The tempo of his breath was a counterpoint as it ruffled her hair. She could smell it over the odor of damp earth—not unpleasant, perhaps a little metallic—along with the musky scent of his body, probably affected by their closeness. She thought again of his sweat soaking through his shirt and then hers to touch her skin—the stealth suits were selectively permeable to allow skin to breathe, and though they could block rain and retained heavy sweat, moisture could slowly pass through. It made her swallow hard. Yet the warmth of his taut muscles against her chest and belly felt . . . good. Reassuring, but also something more that she couldn't identify.

Her own heart beat much faster than his. Would he feel it? Almost certainly. What would he think? Would he be disappointed by her fear?

The hum returned. She felt his body tighten, and he held his breath, so she did the same, expecting at any moment to be struck by bright sunlight as the lid of their hiding place was ripped away. That would be an exposure far worse than what she was experiencing now. That was truly to be feared—the touch of this man was not.

After a long, long time the hum faded, but then returned at random intervals, and Natira wondered if Killian was keeping track of the gaps, calculating the pattern of the search. How much time had passed? Her chronometer lay under the skin of her wrist; and, with a start, she realized that it was on the far side of Killian's back.

Her arms were around him, as his were around her!

Unthinkable! When had that happened?

But she didn't move them. Instead, she flexed her foot to ease a slight cramp and noticed that their thighs were touching, and her knees rested against his.

The thought made her slightly dizzy; but she didn't quiver anymore, didn't shake. She sent her thought into her fingertips, identifying the various sensations of warmth, texture, vibration, and the dampness of their skin. In that position, she fell asleep.

34

Killian was forced to raise the lid of their hiding hole in the middle of the night. Natira had fallen asleep, and he was afraid that lack of air might be to blame. The cool, fresh flow through the small opening tasted wonderful and quickly helped to dispel his grogginess. But then he detected a trace of something else in it.

Smoke?

Sudden fear gave him the strength to shove the lid completely off, and he struggled to clamber out of the hole without hurting Natira.

As soon as he was free, he rolled to his knees and bent over to grasp her arms, but they'd slipped to her side and she still wasn't awake. He shook her by the shoulders, softly calling her name. Their pursuers probably weren't far away.

She awoke and started to protest, but he hushed her and helped her out of the hole. She put her mouth next to his ear.

"What's wrong?"

"We've got to go. I smell smoke," he replied, as he bent to re-cover the hole and disguise its lid.

The breeze was from the northwest, and even as he determined that, he felt it rise in strength. Was the sky lighter in that direction? He couldn't be sure, and didn't dare wait to find out. Beckoning Natira to follow, he plunged through the trees toward the south. They made far too much noise crashing through the brush in the dark, but there wasn't any choice. Besides, if what he feared was true, the Tellurians would be aboard their craft high in the air.

As he paused to find a way ahead, there was a harsh sound like a rush of wind from behind them. Except it wasn't wind, he knew. A glance back confirmed it. The trees were backlit by a ruddy glow.

Fire. And it was gaining on them.

He forged ahead, constantly checking to make sure Natira kept up. He didn't think she'd be able to for long, with her injured ankle. They would not escape on foot. A forest fire at the height of summer could outrun fleeing deer. They were still alive only because the dampness of the springtime forest slowed the progress of the flames.

Would they have been safer in the hole? No, they would have been cooked like a bush roast. But he had to find refuge. The fire would keep coming unless a change of wind turned it back on itself or it encountered a body of water too large for it to leap across.

He didn't remember any lakes within their reach, but water was their only hope now. He closed his eyes and took a deep breath, trying to detect scents beyond the smoke.

Yes, there was a marsh nearby, if he could only be sure of its direction. So much of the terrain looked the same.

He felt heat on the back of his neck, and quickened his pace. Then he forced himself to stop and wait for Natira to catch up. She grabbed his arm, eyes filled with fear.

"We've got to get to water," he said. "We passed a pond not long before we found the cabin. I think it's this way."

Trekking blindly through dense forest toward an uncertain destination, it seemed as if they were standing still. The fire pursuing them was not. Faint crackling punctuated a constant low rumble, with the occasional whoosh Killian knew was a pine tree going up in a fountain of flame.

The light increased at the same time his boots splashed into water. They were at the verge of a marsh and soon came through dry rushes into the open. Although the night sky was mostly overcast, a partial Moon behind the clouds and the glow from the fire gave enough light to show an expanse of water ahead. It wasn't large, but it would have to do. They slogged through the sucking marsh as quickly as they could, Killian pulling Natira closer to help her balance. When the reeds ended, he waded until his chin was barely above water. She flailed with her arms for a moment, then stabilized on her toes.

Killian turned to look the way they'd come and sucked in a breath. A single row of trees was silhouetted between the shoreline and a wall of yellow and orange flame. As he watched, the fire engulfed the line, and billows of spark-filled smoke rose to the sky.

"How well can you swim with your arms alone?" he asked. "We should get farther out but I don't want to give up our boots."

"I'll do what I have to do."

He took her at her word and made for the middle of the pond with strong strokes, his stealth suit adding only a little drag. In his peripheral vision he could see the fire spread along the shoreline, surrounding its prey. This time the heat on his neck was not his imagination. He scooped handfuls of water over his hair and told Natira to copy him. The splash of her arms was almost obscured by the roar of the fire, its scorching heat creating its own windstorm to suck in oxygen. Shifting funnels of wind carried thousands of glowing cinders through the dark sky and over their heads like living rivers of stars. Some of those cinders began falling.

"Duck under the water!" he cried, and didn't wait for an answer before filling his lungs with smoky air and submerging.

Muffled by the liquid, the crackle and roar of the inferno sounded like some monster of the deep rising to devour them. His water-blurred eyes marveled at the silvered surface above, dancing with swirls of yellow and orange and red: a glorious spectacle, but he didn't want it to be the last thing he would ever see.

Something bumped into him, and he realized it was Natira. He put an arm around her and lifted her to the surface.

"Do you need help swimming?" he called over the fire's roar.

"These boots are pulling me down. Should I take them off?"

"No. Wrap your legs around me."

To his surprise, she did it without argument. He'd always been a strong swimmer who could float vertically with most of his head above water on a full breath. Now they slid beneath the surface together and each time they came back up, Natira sculled with her arms behind his neck. He was confident he could keep them both afloat for a long time.

He had to. The fire raged for hours. Sometimes they could rest for a few minutes on the surface, then every so often he would warn Natira and plunge them back under if a sudden flare of sparks and flame came too close, or just to wet their hair as a precaution. Once she gave a cry, and he ducked her under immediately to quench a fallen cinder. She sputtered a little upon surfacing but didn't complain.

While the fear and exertion sapped their strength, near-constant coughing drained it further. Every breath seemed to be filled with more smoke than oxygen.

The dawn, when it finally came, looked sickly through towering curtains of smoke and steam, the sun's wan light befitting the devastation it revealed. Rank upon rank of blackened tree trunks stood like an army of crooked black skeletons. The underbrush was gone, the ground a dreary grey peppered with carbonized debris. Killian had seen fire, and knew that new life would poke up through the cover of ash over in coming months, and a few more years would see the area busy with regrowth; but for now it looked like the end of the world.

Utterly exhausted, they swam to a nearby stretch of shore that was free of marsh and stumbled onto the scorched earth, needing their soaked boots to protect them from the heat. After surveying the destruction in silence, Natira stepped into Killian's embrace and softly cried.

"Why?" she asked finally. "If they wanted to destroy the cabin like they did with the cave, why didn't they just blow it up?"

"Because they knew we were nearby and wanted to flush us out. Or, if that didn't work, to at least make sure we were dead."

She looked into his face, her own eyes the blue green of old ice, her jaw rigid. "Do you still think you want to be one of them?"

He hesitated, then gave a small shrug.

"Their society also produced you," he said, and turned away before the moment could become uncomfortable. He immediately missed the warmth of her body, but they should get moving. The searchers could be overhead soon, perhaps expecting to spot two charred shapes that looked different from the rest. He and Natira still had their stealth suits, surprisingly clean despite the soot, and patchy heat from the torched landscape would obscure their movements.

They returned to the collapsed and blackened remains of the cabin. The very image of abandonment before, now it was barely recognizable as an artifact of human effort. Its smoking timbers smelled even worse than burned forest. More like death.

The quick collapse of the structure had made a dense pile that kept the flames from penetrating completely. It was impossible to move the heavy tamarack timbers of the main roof, but their belongings had been left under a table in a side room, and an hour of digging through debris rewarded their efforts. All their food had been ruined by the heat, but their bug-screen tent and extra clothes had been protected by the thickest remains of a crumbled wall and were only scorched. The Synappt and other Tellurian equipment, buried under everything else, looked unscathed. Natira was eager to check it, but that would have to wait.

"You know it must have been the Synappt that gave away our location."

She nodded. "But I don't see how. I won't use it again until we're somewhere shielded, maybe underground, and the first thing I'll do is make sure all network functions are disabled." She stood wearily and, after a moment's hesitation, reached out to grasp his hand. "Thanks for saving my life. In the hole and in the water."

Her liquid eyes drove any worthy words from his head. He couldn't even come up with a witty reply. He only nodded, and they staggered back to the pond where he could refill their water skin, swirling the surface with his hand to clear away sooty scum. Then he shouldered his charred pack and walked away toward the north.

35

After two days of denial, Killian was forced to admit that he was sick. He picked himself up from the patch of mud where he'd fallen and slumped onto a nearby log. His head spun, his throat burned, and his limbs were so weak they trembled.

When the first symptoms had appeared—light abdominal cramps and a sore neck—he'd blamed it on the forced immobility of their time in the hole followed by all the exertion of swimming and digging. It might even be hunger pangs—he'd only managed to chase down two small grouse; and, although spring shoots had just begun to appear, edible ones were still sparse and difficult to identify. Since leaving Borealis, he'd made a point of teaching Natira about the kinds of plants that were safe to eat and those that were not. She'd paid attention, but there were few examples to show her—it was too early in the season. In any case, he knew she didn't ever expect to need the knowledge.

She didn't expect to stay on Earth.

"What's wrong?" she asked, squatting beside him.

"I don't know. It may have been the water. Some still lakes have bad germs in them and can cause something called beaver fever. Are you feeling all right?"

"I feel fine. Just a second." She undid her pack and pulled out the medical device she'd found in the cave. She held it briefly to his temple, his ear, and his wrist. "Breathe onto it."

He watched the play of emotions on her face. It wasn't encouraging.

"Oh, no."

"What?"

"You're infected with a virus. But it's a Tellurian virus—something that first appeared not long after the Divide and quickly spread through the whole population of the colonies. Our medical people got it under control, but it was never entirely eliminated. We developed an immunity instead. For generations now everyone in the colonies has carried traces of the virus, but it's harmless."

"If you're a Tellurian."

"Yes."

"We spent a long time very close together, breathing the same air."

"I know." She looked hard at the ground. "But even so, it's only contagious in someone who has symptoms. I'm not sick. So, there shouldn't have been enough of the virus in my body to infect yours. Unless . . . ."

"Unless someone deliberately added new virus to your system."

She could only nod.

A sudden chill made Killian shake so hard he had to clutch at the log for balance.

"I'm not going to get much farther until this passes," he said, clenching his teeth to keep them from clacking together. "We have to find shelter." He forced himself to his feet and nearly toppled over. Natira caught him and pulled his left arm over her shoulder. Then she swept a hand up her side to boost her lift vest.

"Why would anyone want to make me a carrier?"

"You were coming back to Earth as a public communicator, right?"

"So?"

"You'd be going to lots of places, meeting lots of people."

"But the virus transmission requires close contact. I think that's one of the reasons my people stopped . . . stopped touching each other. Anyway, it wouldn't make us look good to spread sickness everywhere we went."

"Then maybe whoever it was had something more specific in mind." When she only looked puzzled, he sighed and continued, "Maybe they saw us spending time together in Capita City. You and me."

"And you were the target? So you'd get sick and die at a labor facility on Mars? But justice officials would make sure you got medicine."

"Not if I escaped."

She shook her head slowly, unwilling or unable to absorb the thought. "That's crazy. You couldn't escape without help, and I couldn't infect you without . . . ." Her mouth opened wide. "You think they assumed we were . . . ."

He squeezed her arm. "You're right—it's crazy. I don't know how your people think." He pointed toward the right. "That overhanging cliff face. Cliffs often have small caves or hollows at the bottom."

Though the slope wasn't steep, it took the last of Killian's strength to climb it. They did find a fairly dry cavity, but it was barely large enough to let him stretch out. Not that he could do much of that with the vicious abdominal cramps that struck every couple of minutes. Natira quickly gathered what tree boughs she could and helped him roll onto the improvised bed. By then his vision seemed to be closing in, and he struggled to remind her to get water from fast-flowing streams, gather the fiddlehead-shaped sprouts of fern clusters, and not to trust fungi or berries.

A tide of pain swept upward from his gut and made his body spasm.

Then everything went dark.

# # #

He was awakened by a violent shudder that lifted his body from the ground, and he gave a cry like a wounded animal. The forest fire must have returned—he was burning up. He had to get away from the flames.

With eyes closed, he tried to push up from the ground, but something held him back—a weight on his chest. He tried to protest, but couldn't understand his own words. There were other sounds too, but they were far away and made him wonder if he was underwater. His head rocked back and forth all on its own, and he gagged once as his tongue blocked his raw throat.

The fire must be all around him, but someone was touching him with ice—on his cheek, his forehead, the side of his neck. It both shocked and soothed him. He tried to reach for it, but firm hands gripped and held his arms. Then a fount of fire surged up his neck into his brain; and with exploding sparks, it faded into darkest night.

# # #

Someone was trying to pour liquid between his lips. It was hot and stung them, but then a few drops got by and tasted ... kind of mossy, but not bad. He allowed a little more to dribble into his mouth; but when he swallowed, the claws of an animal ripped at his throat from inside and he clenched his teeth tightly, struggling to get away. The liquid in his mouth drooled out, and he coughed, whimpered, coughed again. Coughing sent his abdomen into spasms, and he rolled sideways just as a flood of lava erupted from his throat. There was no light, or maybe there was, but it fluttered on and off, on and off, leaving him in black emptiness that became red, then faded through brown to dark grey to black again, repeating until the pulses eventually receded in the distance.

# # #

He must have been on a shuttle bound for Telluria. Floating, for certain, staring at his feet over his head. Then the ceiling of the shuttle was gone, and stars took its place. Stars everywhere, cold, lifeless, as if he'd been imprisoned in a black bag with holes poked in it, and someone was trying to stab him with an ice-pick. He became a giant and the tiny lights only pinholes. But then, in an instant, perspective reversed and he was an insignificant speck in vastness he couldn't comprehend. Arms flailed for support, struck something solid, and he clutched at it: a ruddy silver globe covered in scabs and blemishes of every size. He pulled it to his chest to keep afloat on the endless sparkling sea, but the ball wanted to roll out of his arms. As he bobbed there, a perfect soap bubble floated past, full of gems that danced and swirled inside. It was the most beautiful thing he had ever seen, and he reached for it desperately.

He could nearly touch it, but someone was pulling on his legs. The pull grew stronger, and the bubble slipped past his fingertips farther and farther from his grasp. He kicked out in anger and looked down to find his tormentor, but no one was there, only the spinning blue orb of Earth. At first, windswept clouds dashed against his ankles, but the orb quickly grew larger. It became a landscape in map form that furiously unrolled away from him in all directions, and he realized that he was falling. Until then, he hadn't noticed the silence, but then there came a whistling hiss, a rush of wind past his ears. Raising hands to his head to block the sound sent him into a tumble—no, he stayed still, but the world began to spin around him, over his head and under again. Where there had been blotches of brown and green and white, now there was only blue . . . cerulean, cobalt, aquamarine, wrapping around him like a striped blanket.

It felt so welcoming that he closed his eyes and slept.

#   #   #

Something touched his lips, and he opened his mouth like a baby bird anticipating a worm. Instead, it filled with a warm broth that tasted of roots, and leaves, and lichen, and grass, and needles, and fronds . . . tasted like all the forest elements in turn as it seeped into every hollow and crevice of his mouth, washed over his tongue, trickled down his throat, and spread from his stomach to infuse every part of him. His body was a desert and the broth, rain; every tiny drop was absorbed to cement his dry and crumbling shell into a smooth adobe tower. He swallowed the broth greedily, opened his mouth for more, and his body took it and rejoiced to have it. Its heat filled him and grew and grew until he understood that he'd had too much, and he was on fire again, radiating heat of his own like the fierce embers of a campfire on an exposed hilltop. His body was a beacon in the night—his arms lifted and pivoted, shooting curls of smoke like tossed plumes of grass. A shower of fireworks flew from his head into the ebony void, and he understood that they were his thoughts fleeing, scattering, leaving his mind empty.

#   #   #

His fire had been quenched. He was surrounded by water, blue and cool. Cooler, and more chilling. Cold. He was too cold, and still growing colder, shedding heat like a spray. Ice crystals formed on his eyelashes, the hair of his arms, the stubble of his cheeks . . . crystals filled his navel, eye sockets, hollow at the base of his throat—then joined together into an ice-shell that fractured as his body began to shake. Again and again, his skin of ice would re-form and shatter, meld and fracture, as waves of vibration passed through him, until every part of his body shuddered. He fluttered like maple keys in a tempest. Shook until he knew that his bones would crack and dissolve into dust and scatter in the wind.

Something warm pressed against the length of his body, wrapped around him, and filled his nostrils with a scent as warming as the touch itself. It was wondrous. But it was not enough. The ice re-formed, and its grasp tightened. His shuddering increased.

The warm presence drew away and left him more exposed than ever. He felt a damp second skin being pulled from his chest, arms, legs. For a frozen moment he knew himself abandoned and about to fly apart.

Then the warmth was back, more glorious than ever! A skin of pure fire pressed against his own, smooth and soft. It wrapped around him tightly as if to fuse a single skin from two. They pulsed together as one—one living rhythm. He breathed in a fragrance that held both longing and healing. And slowly, slowly, the ice within him began to melt. His violent shudders eased. Teeth unclenched. The twitch of muscles became more sporadic, grew gentler, then stopped completely.

284

Fragments of light and sound and smell and touch all began to swirl then, mixing in a frothing vortex that plunged into a bottomless well.

# # #

Killian winced as light stabbed him. A flood of pain nearly burst his head, but it only lasted a moment. Shielding his eyes with his hands, he tried opening them again. Gradually, he made out his surroundings.

A small hollow at the bottom of a cliff—he remembered the rough rock. The air was thick with a damp mustiness, but also a sour smell that he was afraid was coming from him.

Raising his upper body, he discovered that he was lying nearly naked except for his small underclothing on the mesh tent atop a pile of tree boughs. The rest of his clothes and his stealth suit were pulled over him like a blanket.

Where was Natira? He couldn't see or hear her, yet he sensed she wasn't far away. As he thought of her, he could smell the sweet fragrance of her skin and hair, the natural perfume that was so unmistakably hers and hers alone. With a shock he realized that the trace of scent came from his own hands, arms. Chest.

He tried to call her name, but his voice wouldn't work. He needed water, and then he needed food—his gut was an empty pit. Rolling to his knees brought a swell of dizziness. There wasn't enough room to stand up—he had to crawl to the cave opening, dragging his clothes.

The bright world outside dazzled his eyes and took a long time to come into focus. It was sunny, and the cave mouth overlooked a gentle slope of maples, birches, and poplars, the very first traces of leaf buds giving a pale green sheen to otherwise-bare branches. At the bottom of the slope, a few hundred meters away, lay a small body of water—a beaver pond, probably—fed by a creek that gurgled down from the cliff about fifty meters to his right. His eyes followed the creek upslope and he found Natira, wringing out her silver blonde hair. Her back was to him, and with a shock he realized that it was bare.

He swallowed and tried to turn away to spare her embarrassment, but he couldn't. The vision held him helpless.

She slipped her tunic over her head without turning, replaced the tiara she always wore, and plucked the full water gourd from the ground before she stood to make her way uphill. Her face looked calmer than he'd ever seen it. Then she caught sight of him, and her dazzling smile bathed him in warmth. It lasted only seconds before concern took its place, and she clutched the water gourd to her chest as she hurried to him.

"I didn't see anything except your back," he said hoarsely.

"It's not that. I don't know if you should be up. Are you sure you feel strong enough?" Her face pinched together. "You nearly died."

"I can believe that. Obviously, I would have if you hadn't stayed with me. What did you do?"

She shrugged and looked away.

"You . . . warmed me when I was freezing, I know that much," he prompted. She couldn't look at him, but a blush came to her cheek. He cleared his throat. "You fed me, too . . . gave me broth or tea."

"I couldn't find much, I'm sorry. And you couldn't keep it down at first. I was nearly useless at lighting a fire, too. Then I was afraid to build it close to you, and sure that the satellites would see it. But maybe they aren't looking for us anymore."

"How long was I . . . ?"

"Five days."

"*Five* . . . and you managed to survive on your own and keep me alive, too? You're . . . amazing!"

More color rose in her cheeks, but she didn't turn her head.

"What's wrong? What else happened?"

Her throat bobbed. "I had to give you medicine."

"*My mother's medicine?*"

She nodded. "It doesn't just fight cancer. It boosts the body's immune system to fight off any cells that don't belong."

"How much?"

"Most of it. You would have died."

"You can't know that!" He wanted to stand and give full reign to his anger, but his body was too weak, which made him angrier still.

"I *do* know that! My med scanner showed that your vital signs were fading—the virus was just too strong for a human body to defeat on its own." She finally looked at him. "I couldn't let you die."

"Why not? I'd say you've learned enough to make it back to Borealis without me. And then safely back to Telluria."

The hurt in her eyes shamed him. They both looked away.

"Anyway, you didn't have the right to do that without asking me."

He struggled to his feet and stood panting. It was a stupid thing to say, and as he admitted that to himself, he also knew that if the tables were turned and Natira was sick, he would have done the same thing. Use the medicine. Without hesitation.

The understanding left him rattled. He gathered his clothes and shuffled unsteadily toward the pond. He was badly in need of a wash.

As impatient as he was to resume their journey, he knew his body needed at least one more day of rest. He couldn't just lie there, though. Instead, he set a snare along a nearby animal trail then slowly searched for any edible shoots Natira might have missed. He found quite a few, not because she had done badly, but because each day brought a new tide of life to the forest floor. By late afternoon, the snare had trapped a rabbit and Killian roasted it over a fire at the mouth of the cave hollow. The flames would warm the rocks and make their sleep more comfortable that night.

He hadn't seen Natira much that day, and they ate in silence. After the meal she rose to leave but he called out her name.

He stepped very close to her, and she didn't back away. Tentatively, he raised his left hand to her arm and his right hand to her face. She took a hesitant step forward. And then their arms were around each other.

287

"I'm so sorry." The huskiness of his voice surprised him. "I was talking like an idiot, and you deserve better. You saved my life. I just . . . ."

She put a finger to his mouth.

Their foreheads touched. Their noses.

And then their lips came together.

He inhaled her sweetness in a rush. Drank in her warmth. The taste of her was like berries, and mint, and wine, and he wanted to swallow her and be swallowed. He'd never wanted anything so fiercely but for that moment to go on and on without end.

Finally, he pulled away, with a gasp. He took a step back and her face wrinkled in confusion.

"I . . . there's something I have to tell you," he said.

"I think you just did." But her smile faltered.

"No. You deserve to know what I really am. What I've done."

She searched his eyes then slowly let her hands drop to her sides and nodded. They sat together on a fallen log.

He told her about his attempt to steal medicine from the base.

The lookout. The cliff. The guard.

The crumpled form on the ground.

The shock in her eyes made him feel sick again.

"Oh no, no!" Her body crumpled inward. Her hands flew to her face, and she began to rock back and forth. "All this time I thought . . . I thought you were an innocent victim. A pawn. Persecuted for no fault of your own."

"I never meant to hurt anyone. If that possibility had even crossed my mind, I couldn't have gone to the outpost at all. But afterward . . . I think maybe your people knew it was me. Or at least, guessed. And when they couldn't prove it, they looked for another way to punish me." He choked. "I deserve to be punished. To be sent to Mars."

He looked into her face for any sign of forgiveness, but the muscles there were taut, and tears filled her eyes.

"You should have told me!" she rasped. "I've given up my career—my whole life—because I thought you were wronged, and I felt ashamed for how my people treated you." She shot to her feet and the tears spilled. "Well don't worry—the whole story will come out. Your confession has just been recorded, like everything else while we've been together."

"What do you mean by that?"

She touched her tiara. Its presence was so much a part of her, nearly hidden in her hair, that he'd almost forgotten it was there.

"This is a camera," she hissed. "I wear it to document my experiences—it records everything, and then I make reports from the highlights. I turned it off during our escape from Telluria so it couldn't be used as evidence, but then I thought a few days alone with an Earthman on the loose was bound to produce something interesting. And it has. It certainly has."

Killian felt like he'd been punched in the gut. His breath wouldn't come.

He wanted to be furious, but he couldn't even do that—he was utterly numb.

When his open mouth refused to produce any words, he simply turned away and staggered into the dark forest. Eventually, a long time later, he chose a clump of spruce trees to spend the night.

36

Natira was sure she was going to throw up.

Could she have caught the boosted virus from Killian? No, she was a carrier—immune—she couldn't get sick from it herself. The med scanner didn't show any sign of pathogens, only elevated stress hormones.

That was no mystery.

How had her life come to this: exiled on a primitive world with a killer as her only companion? Dependent on him for survival, no matter what he said.

The whole situation was unfathomable. Where had Natira Celestia gone? Who was this woman who had taken her place? The one who had touched and been touched—pressed tightly against a man in a dark hole for an entire night. The one who had warmed this man with her naked body to help him battle for life. Had kissed him, skin to skin, wanting him desperately.

That woman was no one she knew. She had betrayed herself and her kind—had drawn punishment down upon herself. Had foolishly given in to a yearning she could barely comprehend, only to learn that it was horribly misplaced.

She'd given up everything for a fraud. Worse, a killer.

Was there any way back?

The cave rocks had been warmed by the fire, but she shivered anyway. A low moan startled her until she realized it had come from her own throat.

A night black as space. An empty bed in a cave in the wilderness. Could anywhere be more lonely?

The coming of dawn was wondrous. She walked cautiously among the trees searching for new sprouts at a handful of locations she'd marked, and stuffed the greens into her mouth, washed down with water from the gourd She tried to keep herself from looking for Killian, or even wondering if he had passed the night safely. Exposed to the night air in his condition, he could easily have had a relapse.

Why should she care? The gnawing hurt in her stomach was only hunger.

After a time, she returned to the mouth of the cave and sat there, numbly staring into the forest. At some point she became aware of Killian standing a meter to her left, watching her. Without words, she gathered her things and started down the slope in the direction she thought was north. He waited a long time before following her, but soon passed by her and only altered direction slightly. He was carrying her Synappt satchel—she had forgotten it in the hollow.

They didn't speak for a whole day.

Even so, she could sense his frustration, unable to catch any game while they travelled; but he managed to gather some plants as food, including several roots that looked and tasted like miniature carrots with very lacy tops. Nutritious but not very filling. They certainly wouldn't replace energy burned during a day's strenuous walk. What Natira really needed was protein to build muscle as she relied less and less on her lift vest. She was proud of her firm legs and abdomen but knew that some of her curves were melting away. On Telluria, her breasts and hips had been considered larger than was tasteful.

Killian probably wouldn't notice.

Or maybe she was wrong. That evening, when they stopped for a break, he tromped through the woods nearby searching higher places than usual. He reached his hand into holes in the trunks of some of the trees. At the fifth one, he gave a cry of satisfaction and pulled his fist out full of some

291

rounded nut-like things he called *acorns*. He soon found more lying between layers of broad leaves beneath a large tree but kept those separate from the first.

Back at their campsite he cracked open the acorns from the tree hole with a rock, ground them up into a powder between two flatter rocks, and put the result into one of the nested cooking pots they carried. After adding water, he hung the mixture over the fire. A good while later he poured off a yellow liquid, added more water, and repeated the process several more times. By then, Natira was hungry, the greens she'd gathered not very satisfying, especially compared to the smell of Killian's cooking. At last, he allowed his mixture to boil into a gruel and gave it to her to eat.

The nutty flavor had just a hint of bitterness, but she ate it all and found it made her stomach feel more satisfied than it had in weeks. Killian promised he would leach more of the bitterness from the acorns in the future.

Those were the only words spoken that night.

The next day they passed a grassy open field, and he dragged their anti-bug mesh through it. Natira thought she saw occasional specks dart through the air near him, but he didn't show her what he'd caught. As they made their way along, she bit her tongue to keep from laughing at his outlandish headgear: a shallow bowl of bark with mesh over it to hold down a cargo of acorns that he hoped would dry in the sun. The nuts were easier to shell when dry. In the meantime, he made a point of searching under fallen logs and picking up some whitish objects he found. A short but heavy rain shower sent him scurrying over a patch of muddy ground plucking at things that sometimes appeared reluctant to let go of the soil.

When he finally prepared another batch of acorn gruel, he sprinkled the results of his gathering into it and mashed them up before letting it all cook to an even consistency.

Natira couldn't bring herself to eat it.

"It has things you need to build up your body," he said. "Green plants are not enough."

"You mean protein? Fat?"

He shrugged. "Like in meat or fish, but I haven't had the time to hunt for those."

"I saw some of those things wriggling."

"So does a rabbit. Or a bird." He made a show of scooping a handful into his mouth and chewing with satisfaction. A growl from her stomach made the decision for her.

The flavor was still nutty but much richer. As hard as she tried to put aside the mental images, she couldn't quite enjoy it, but didn't stop eating either. He left more for her than he ate himself. She couldn't bring herself to refuse it.

Instead of the tea she had seen him make from tips of pine boughs, he boiled new leaves from a green plant that looked like a flower. It had a pleasant taste that made a good contrast to the nut porridge and seemed make her aching muscles feel a little better.

"It might help your aching joints and muscles," he'd said, and it had.

That night was colder, so they slept with their backs close together. She wasn't about to forgive him, but she wasn't going to suffer the cold just to show anger. He didn't take advantage. Not even when she awoke with her arm draped over his hip.

It was hard to believe, but such contact didn't make her recoil anymore. Though they rarely spoke, there were many times they brushed together as they went about the tasks of staying alive: gathering kindling and building a fire, bending large saplings into the framework of a shelter. One day when Killian's snare caught three rabbits, he boosted her up to a branch to hang the leftover meat for the night, even though it meant his face was at the level of her hips. She felt a shiver for just a moment but shrugged it off.

She still had nothing to say to him. She had sacrificed so much in the belief that he was totally innocent. That was a wound that wouldn't heal, even though she knew him well enough by now to believe his claim that the guard's death was a tragic accident.

Could he ever let go of his own anger? Keenly aware that his people were a source of derision and even cruel amusement to Tellurians, he would see her act of recording their time together as proof that she felt as they did. That he was no more than a potential means to save her career.

Could it *be* saved? Could her life be restored?

She didn't see how, but she had to find some way back into Tellurian society, even if only as a common worker. She certainly didn't belong on Earth.

It was painful to acknowledge that, though she didn't know why.

In any case, their days as companionable travelers were over. Though their bodies might accidentally touch, they were worlds apart and always would be.

A week passed, and then another. The assault of biting insects eased a little, or she was becoming hardened to it. But still the boundless forest stretched on with no sign of their goal. Her life had become an endless struggle for survival, every trace of excess fat and soft living burned away.

One day, while making some notes on her roll-up notepad about how to prepare unripe heads of cattails for cooking, she caught sight of her face in the screen's reflection. Her skin was no longer as pale as bullrush root, but a more golden color. Concerned, she checked herself with the med scanner. Killian laughed and said that her face and hands were just tanned by the sun. Tanning was a word he'd used to describe processing animal skins for clothing—the tanning of her own skin couldn't be good! But he insisted that it wouldn't harm her as long as she didn't let her face and arms get too red, which would make them sting for a few days. It made her wonder if that was the explanation for his own dark color. She'd assumed it was genetic, but maybe not entirely.

Their days had fallen into a pattern: a messy, smelly, difficult routine. How had she ever thought that such a life could be 'noble' in any way? It was subsistence living at its very worst, and getting enough nutrition was a constant challenge. She thought her own body had stopped losing mass, but she was sometimes a little concerned when she looked at Killian, especially when he had his shirt off. His ribs were more prominent than ever before, though his arms and shoulders were still corded with muscle.

Then came the day when she found her underclothes covered in blood.

37

Killian caught her crying.

"What's wrong?"

She wiped her tears from her cheeks with her palms but couldn't bring herself to answer.

He grasped her shoulders ever so gently and asked again.

"I'm bleeding."

"Bleeding! Where? Show me."

"*No!* I'm bleeding . . . between my legs." She turned her face aside in shame.

"You mean it's your woman's cycle?"

The words struck her like a blow. *Was that possible?*

"I . . . I don't know! I didn't think of that. I've only had it once, when I hit puberty. Tellurian women receive medication in our food to suppress it. I never thought about it coming back."

"Is it hurting you? Are you weak from loss of blood, or are the cramps really painful?"

"They were for the past day or so. I thought I was just dehydrated. I can manage."

Could she? If it really was her menstrual cycle, at least that was better than some injury or disease.

"Then it's just a normal thing. It'll pass. Nothing to be afraid of."

"*I know that.* But it's disgusting. I know you'll be disgusted by me."

He sat back on his haunches, and she wanted to knock the smile from his face, but he held up a hand of truce.

"I'm not disgusted at all. In fact, it makes . . . . Well, never mind. But you'll cope—I'll help you. When people like my aunt Regina live in the bush and don't eat much Depot food, they have strong cycles every month. Dry moss between layers of cloth works well, or cattail fluff once they flower. And there's lots of water around to wash clothes, so it's not a problem unless it's hurting you or it doesn't stop after a few days. If that happens, we can just give in and make sure the Tellurians come to get us."

Did he really mean it? There was no revulsion in his face. Even his smile was more pleased than amused.

She wiped the last of her tears away and got to her feet.

"Show me how to find the moss."

A few hours later, they stopped for a rest. Natira opened her mouth to speak but couldn't, embarrassed to have to ask a question about her own body. Killian looked at her expectantly.

After a deep breath, she said, "Earth women still have babies this way, don't they? I was never sure I could believe what I read about that."

"Well, I'm sure you know the blood means you're not pregnant this month. But yes, if your monthly cycle has come back, then I assume it means you'd be able to get pregnant."

Natira hoped he couldn't see her hands tremble. She'd come to the same conclusion.

"Which also means," he continued as he turned to walk away, "that you'd better keep well away from me."

"What do you mean, 'well away'?"

"Three or four meters at least. At all times. No touching, definitely no kissing. Probably shouldn't sleep on the same bed in case we breathe the same air."

For a moment she almost believed him, but even from behind she could tell that he was smiling.

That's when she hit him.

# # #

As they were getting ready to sleep that night, she asked, "What were you going to say?"

"When?"

"You said my cycle wasn't disgusting, and you were going to add something else but then you said, 'Never mind'."

He sighed. "I was going to say that I thought it made you even more human."

"Are you saying that Tellurians aren't human? Just because we don't push babies out of our bodies like . . . ."

"Like animals, right. And your people don't touch each other either, or kiss with their own lips. They think my people are little better than beasts, and mine think yours are . . . altered so much as to be a little inhuman. You and I know better. Isn't that a good thing?" The words could have been sarcastic, but his voice sounded sincere. He gently took her hand. "Among our people the ability to have babies is a very special gift. It's not disgusting—it's wonderful."

She looked deep into his eyes and there was no question that he was telling the truth as he saw it.

Her own feelings were a mess.

"Shouldn't we put out the fire?"

"No, I think I'll keep it going to discourage any animals that might smell . . . us."

"You mean smell *me*. Can they really smell that? Wait—don't tell me. *You* can smell it, can't you?"

When he hesitated too long, she said, "Oh shit. That's just terrific." She began to get up to find another place to sleep but he grabbed her arm.

"It's not that strong—most people would never notice it. I've spent a lot of time out here, deliberately learning to smell things. Anyway, it just smells . . . female. It's part of you. It doesn't bother me at all. How can I make you believe me?"

After a moment she gave in and threw herself back down on the bed.

"Now I'd never dare to go back to Telluria."

"That would be their loss." He turned his face away before she could see it.

She was only being melodramatic. A monthly flow of blood wouldn't keep her exiled—it would certainly stop again as soon as she received the proper chemicals in her diet.

Wouldn't it?

She'd never heard of a Tellurian or colony woman whose cycle had returned, even when some had been trapped in a disabled spaceship or remote outpost for many weeks. Maybe it wasn't only the lack of regular chemicals.

And suddenly she knew the answer.

Killian.

It was his constant presence over a long period of time. Especially the close contact. Maybe his body's odors, too—especially ones the texts had called *pheromones* that she couldn't even consciously detect.

Without her knowledge or permission, her body reacted to his. *Remaking* itself according to eons-old imperatives that neither of them had any control over. Transforming itself for a mate!

Devils of the void! Maybe she really should sleep somewhere else. She couldn't get pregnant without actual physical intercourse; but the evidence was convincing that their closeness had changed her; and if it continued, there might be no going back to the Natira Celestia she once was.

How could such a thought be so terrifying and so exciting at the same time?

38

"Can we keep watch for a deeper cave?" Natira asked.

"Why? Anything substantial might have an animal living in it. And if it's a bear just out of hibernation, they tend to be hungry."

Her eyes widened a little, unsure if he was joking. He wasn't.

"I'm convinced that the archive in my Synappt is really important. I know it probably gave us away back at the cabin, but I can defeat those functions. Except it would be safest to be somewhere shielded before I start it up."

"Is it more urgent than getting to the Tellurian base? I can't help feeling that there are big things happening while we trudge through the bush."

If not for that conviction, he would have taken the time to do more fishing and trapping, maybe even made a bow so he could bring down bigger game. He'd caught a half-dozen good-sized bass a couple of days earlier, but he and Natira still weren't getting enough of the right food to make up for the energy they burned. He'd especially been concerned about her loss of blood from her monthly cycle, though it had ended as expected after a few days.

He grudgingly agreed that keeping an eye out for a large cave wouldn't add much time to their journey.

They found a suitable place two mornings later: a large crack where part of an eroded cliff point had broken off eons in the past and the top three-quarters of the gap had filled with fallen rock and dirt. The remaining opening was just below man-height, but the space inside extended about ten meters back. He loudly smacked a pair of rocks together as he approached the cave, and again when he decided to enter it.

"A bear was here over the winter, but it's gone now."

"Will it come back?"

"They need to range pretty far to find enough food at this time of year, just like we have. It might have been the one that followed us for a little while yesterday."

"*What?* And you didn't tell me?"

"We've crossed paths with four of them since we left Borealis. Did you really want to know?" She didn't answer. He grinned. "Why do you think I don't complain about the amount of noise you make? Animals hear us coming and get out of the way. Bears and wolves in these parts don't attack humans unless they're starving or cornered. The one yesterday probably just thought you smelled good. I don't blame him."

She gave him a sour look then settled at the back of the cave and pulled out her Synappt. After a few minutes, she said, "It's safe now. Computers automatically try to connect with each other, so I've set this one to receive input but not talk back. I should have thought of that before."

"You've never had to hide before."

She shrugged, then took a sharp breath.

"There's a message. For me. From . . . the ambassador. It was delivered . . . ." She had to think hard to work out the timing. "While we were in that hole at the cabin." She beckoned him closer. Sitting next to her, he could see the man's head floating in the air. Its smile was friendly, but a shiver ran up Killian's spine.

"My dear Natira, your family and I have been terribly worried about your welfare since you were kidnapped. My troops have been searching the whole countryside." His face grew larger. "Except it wasn't really a kidnapping, was it? I can't begin to understand what hold that man has over you to persuade you, not only to help him escape, but to steal government information too? Did you think about the implications of that for your parents—and for me, as your mentor? I'm very disappointed.

"But perhaps he told you a fiction about something he supposedly overheard while in Capita City. A couple of the other Earth visitors in his group have admitted that they planned to embarrass the government of Telluria with a story about some kind of a . . . conspiracy against Earth. As you probably know, there are many Earth citizens who don't want us back because their primitive state has provided them with power and influence that would be threatened by our presence. Others fear us because of some ancient beliefs that can be quite fanatical. Your . . . friend appears to be one of those. You should ask him about his contacts, the dissidents who call themselves 'Keepers'.

"I know you're intelligent enough to see that embracing such unfounded beliefs is not worth giving up your standing in Tellurian society. Maybe even your Confederacy citizenship. It's clear to me that you've been misled; so although your reputation has been hurt by these events, once you've returned the information you took and helped us to apprehend the criminal Killian Morningcloud, the Prime Councilor and I will be able to repair the damage. We can make all of this disappear. And if your companion is unwilling, remind him that I will see that his mother gets treatment—a full cure—in exchange for his surrender and an admission of his part in the efforts to sabotage Confederacy relations with Earth.

"You have three days to consider your position." The face vanished.

"That was more than two weeks ago!" Natira blurted. "We've got to reach him!"

Killian's hand closed over hers as she reached for the device.

"We can't. Not from this. They'll know where we are, and this time they won't give up until they've found our bodies."

"You don't know that. The fire was probably a misunderstanding—some security officer acting beyond his orders. Basu . . . Ambassador Hind wouldn't condone something like that. Besides, can you tell me what he said that wasn't true? About the . . . Keepers, or whoever they are?"

He looked into her eyes and read doubt there. Of course, she doubted. Hind was obviously a friend, maybe even more than that. She trusted him, and such trust was hard to give up.

"If there is such a group, I don't know anything about it. If there was a plan to embarrass the colonists, I was never told. I only know what I overheard, and I don't see how Earth people could have arranged that little scene in the middle of Capita just to trick me. You know I looked forward to the return of the colonists all my life—I wanted to be one of you."

"Unless something happened to change that, and your disappointment turned to bitterness." A dark shadow crossed her face and she looked at the ground. "The way you embarrassed me that day in Borealis was quite effective in spoiling our first impression."

A ragged sigh of frustration escaped from his throat and his eyes stung. He got to his feet.

"If that's how little you really think of me after all this time, there's not much I can say." He stooped and made his way toward the entrance. "I'm still heading north. You go wherever you want to go. Signal Hind, if that's what you want."

"Your mother . . . ."

Killian turned. "He has no *intention* of curing my mother! That man is the real liar. Maybe one day you'll see that." He strode away and climbed over some rocks to regain the course they'd been following.

A few minutes later he heard her call his name. He waited for her to catch up and said, "I thought you wanted to spend time trying to access the 'stolen information', or did you change your mind?"

"No, but if you leave me here, I'll have no choice but to call them. I could never find my way back without you."

"You underestimate yourself. You've learned more than you realize."

"Let me come with you to the secret base."

"So you can hand me over?"

This time it was her turn to try to hide tears.

Finally, he said, "Come if you want," and resumed walking. He heard her follow, but neither spoke again.

Their earlier accord of silence returned. Killian yearned to break it, to take her in his arms and show her that he was innocent of Hind's accusations; but he had no proof. How do you prove a negative? She'd believe what she wanted to believe. And everything she'd ever known would compel her to return to a life she loved, not pursue a meagre existence with a man so much her inferior.

They travelled through more rugged country now. High ridges and deep valleys lay across their path: a ragged succession of tumbled boulders, sharp gravel, and dense growth. The valley floors were filled with lakes and marshes, the slopes with waterfalls—and three substantial rivers had to be crossed, or possibly the same one that wound like a snake.

Making rafts would have taken too long. And Natira's lift vest didn't work over water. Killian recklessly dived into the strong current, trailing the long rope he'd salvaged with his fire-damaged pack. The water was cold, but tolerable. Once safely across, he anchored the rope to a tree and pulled Natira more quickly than she could have swum on her own. One of the crossings was too wide for the rope, but the current was slower. He tied her a few meters behind him, and they crossed without incident.

He began to tie them together on some of the increasingly steep slopes, too, because it seemed to give her more confidence. She did all of the climbing on her own, only using her lift vest on the most difficult stretches, her newly adapted muscles rarely letting her down. In fact, he felt proud watching her, when he was sure she wouldn't catch him looking.

Whether because of fatigue or the monotony of the terrain, his attention sometimes wandered, and it was a shock when he became aware that more light came through the trees ahead than behind. They were coming to the middle of a large plateau slightly higher than the surrounding ridges. A breath of wind carried a faint smell of chemicals. Cursing under his breath, he waved for Natira to stop and tried hard to remember the last quarter mile of forest. Had there been anything unusual? Had they already given themselves away? He assumed that Confederacy detection technology was easily hidden. But there was no point obsessing over it—he probably couldn't avoid such devices even if he knew where they were.

Even so, he used extra caution as they approached the edge of the trees and surveyed a cleared space beyond. The facility before them was easily as large as the base near Borealis, but with fewer buildings, none taller than one story. The central construction looked as big as the Depot, flanked by two much smaller buildings with rounded tops. There might be more structures on the far side, hidden by the main one. One end of the clearing looked like the landing pads of the base he'd visited, but there were no spacecraft to be seen. In fact, there was no sign of any vehicles or activity of any kind. That didn't mean the place was empty—he couldn't know that without a lot more observation—but his spirits rose. Since the Confederacy had openly returned to Earth and involved itself in the planet's governance, maybe they had no further need of a clandestine base.

He settled into a comfortable position, well-hidden, and prepared to spend an hour or two watching and waiting. Natira seemed to understand and quietly passed him some pemmican from her pack. She sat with her arm and shoulder pressed lightly against his, watching with him; but as the day wore on, her head tipped forward.

He awoke her when the sun was two-thirds of the way past its zenith. The only movement he'd seen was a small flight of birds that alighted on the flat roof of the main building for a time. It crossed his mind that they could be artificial birds keeping the area under secret surveillance, but their wheeling, intertwining paths seemed much too random.

"If there's anyone here, they're staying inside," he said. "And they might not come outside for days. I think it's worth the risk to look around."

"Should we sneak over to that corner where the trees are closest to the building?"

"You tell me. If they're concerned about intruders, wouldn't they have technology to sense us coming without having to see us?"

"Then why did you hide in these trees for hours?"

"Because the place might be abandoned. Or someone might come back at any time, especially if their search for us is based here. I thought it was worth the wait. But I'm tired of waiting." He got up and strode out into the open. She followed quickly.

He wasn't nearly as confident as he'd tried to sound. He kept thoroughly alert, eyes straight ahead paying attention to his peripheral vision, the better to detect motion. There was nothing.

Natira suggested that the smaller buildings were probably support facilities or even residences; so, they went directly to the nearest entrance of the central complex. It didn't open automatically, and there were no visible door handles. That was a problem.

"Buildings that require security usually have hand or face scanners like this glass plate over here," Natira said. "But this one looks really old. It might only have been intended to keep animals out. Try passing your hand over this spot."

"Why me?"

"Because if it is a more complex scanner, it could measure the pattern of blood vessels in the skin, or even DNA. Then they'd know I'm here. Yours won't be on file."

At first, nothing happened. Then the door split in two, each half sliding away into the wall.

"It just let me in? An Earth man?"

"There might be a reason." She hesitated, looking uncomfortable. "The virus you caught from me may have stopped harming you, but it wasn't killed—it's still in your body. The Tellurian medicine had to . . . make some changes to your DNA to cure you and keep you from being contagious. Otherwise, you could spread the virus to others of your people. The scanner might be mistaking you for a Tellurian." The flicker of a glance she gave him looked as if she was braced for an explosion.

Words of outrage rose in his throat, but he swallowed them.

What was done was done.

"You probably won't have access to any sensitive places," she added, "but at least we'll be inside."

They soon found that she was right. They were allowed into three not-very-large rooms nearby, but no others. Waiting rooms or meeting spaces, perhaps. Maybe they were even meant for Earth people. And that opened up a whole new set of questions.

In the meantime, they were at an impasse. Access to the rest of the building required a face scan. Natira said the equipment was primitive compared to what was used in the high security buildings of Capita, but it wouldn't approve Killian's features; and when she finally decided to risk being scanned herself, she was no more welcome than he. The system played dead.

"Let's just hope it doesn't bring a troop of guards down on us," Killian said, then began to make a closer inspection of the rooms that they could get into. Maybe there were some subtly camouflaged controls or compartments that contained food or tools.

Natira sat cross-legged on the floor and switched on her Synappt. When she gave a tiny cry of surprise, he knelt by her side.

"Another message."

The head of Basu Hind resolved itself in mid-air. As before, it looked real enough to make Killian shudder.

"I wish we did have his head here," he muttered. "His face might get us through the doors."

Natira paused the message and looked at him in amazement. Without a word, she did something on the Synappt that made the holographic image even sharper. Then she carried it toward the stubbornly locked door. It took a few tries to place the hologram at just the right spot and the right angle to keep Hind's missing body out of view of the scanner; but finally, there was a click, and the doorway split open.

"Old tech, meet new tech," Natira said with a smile. They hurried through before the hapless door mechanism could change its mind. Inside was a series of barely separated rooms that included places meant for eating, desktops for work, and lounge areas for relaxation. She sat on a couch and placed the Synappt on a low table before restarting Hind's message.

Hind's face showed a convincing expression of regret.

"My dear Natira. Since you've chosen not to respond to my message, I must take that as a refusal of my offer of clemency. That's a tragic shame. You were my favorite protégée, so promising; and to watch you throw it all away is heartbreaking. The more so because you've clearly suffered some sort of breakdown to be so thoroughly misled by a savage son of a rejected planet.

"I tried to intervene on your behalf with your Patriarch, but he would not be persuaded and has officially disowned you. Your foolish . . . rebellion . . . has cost you the right to call yourself a Celestia. As Natira Tellurian once again, you will remain a fugitive sought by Confederacy security forces wherever you go."

Natira's chest spasmed and tears sprang to her eyes. She looked as if she might vomit.

"For now," Hind continued, "you're being sought as a lawbreaker. But if you ignore my warning again and continue to investigate information for which you have no official clearance, you'll be regarded as a traitor—and then no one will be able to help you." The holographic Hind cleared his throat. "I assume that the Earthman is still with you.

"Mr. Morningcloud, I hope you're satisfied with having ruined this woman's life. I must wonder what it is you think you're accomplishing that you would willingly sacrifice your mother's life as well. A son who would choose his own foolhardy pursuits over the well-being of his mother isn't much of a son, is he? I wonder if you're also so heartless as a nephew?" The corners of Hind's mouth again turned down in a simulation of regret but there was pleasure in his eyes.

"Your uncle, Lewis Partridge, has been detained and charged with aiding fugitives. It's very possible that when his case is heard in one week's time, he will be sent to Mars to serve the punishment that you so selfishly avoided. A great pity. He seems to care about you very much. I would hope that you're not contemplating some kind of hostile action against the Confederacy. Should you commit such action, the charge against him would be upgraded to seditious conspiracy. And the penalty for sedition is death."

The man's blank features concealed an inner smile that burned Killian like a brand. He longed for a way to reach through the hologram and twist the man's neck. The end of the message left Hind's mocking head floating frozen in space.

Sobs shook Natira's body.

"We have to give ourselves up," she choked.

"No!"

"What do you mean? How can you ignore your mother, and let your uncle be exiled, or even die because of you?"

"It's not because of me. Or you. It's because of that man." He pointed a trembling finger at Hind's head. "What we have to do is find out what they're so afraid of in that information archive and figure some way to use it against them! That's what my uncle would want."

Her face showed only astonishment.

Seething with bitterness, he turned away and tried to concentrate on investigating the room. When it revealed nothing useful, he went into another room, then a third. The one after that seemed to be a dormitory with beds arranged in rows, but they were beds like none he'd ever seen. Each was surrounded by a thin metallic stripe in the flooring, and the mattress was no more than a layer of fabric embedded with a mesh of some kind on top of a metal plate. The floor would probably be more comfortable!

There was a hum so soft he might have imagined it, and the air held a hint of that storm-just-passed smell.

In disgust, he returned to the room with tables and opened his pack to find something to eat. Natira appeared holding out a packaged meal like the ones in the glider cave, but with an even more appetizing smell.

It tasted better, too. Killian's hunger surged at the first bite, and he'd eaten half of his portion before he remembered to thank her. She couldn't manage a smile, but she passed him a flask of a liquid with the flavor of some unidentifiable fruit. It was refreshing and a welcome change. They'd drunk nothing but water and various kinds of wild tea for weeks.

"This facility is newer than the cave," she said. "Or, at least, this part of it is. More like the buildings in Capita. Most supplies and amenities are in the walls and floor." She demonstrated with a gesture of her hand. A wall nearby opened to reveal a huge number of flat packages of food, stacked perfectly. There was probably some kind of order to it—arranged by flavor or food type, perhaps—but it wasn't obvious to Killian.

"Well, that will save us some long hikes. The forest around this clearing has almost no undergrowth. We'd have to go a long way to find anything we could eat."

"Certain frequencies of sound encourage some types of plants to grow and discourage others. That method's used on all of Telluria's crop-asteroids to improve yield and prevent weeds."

All his life Killian had been fascinated to learn about such things; but, more important to him now, talk about technology distracted Natira from the terrible blow her self-esteem had just been given. He told her about the dormitory with the useless metal beds.

She actually laughed. "The beds use repulsion to make the mesh and anything above it float on air. It's wonderfully comfortable. You'll see."

"Well not for a couple of hours yet, but it must be past sunset by now. Can we count on these lights, or will we have to do something to keep them on?"

310

"They'll stay on as long as we move around from time to time."

"Then I'm going to explore some more. Do you want to come?"

She shook her head but clearly had something to say.

"I've been able to get access to the main computer network for the base, and I saw some symbols that look similar to the coding used to lock the archive on my Synappt. If I'm right, my friend wasn't able to decode it because it's an ancient encryption in some sort of data format we don't use anymore. But the computer here might have the key."

"Then you agree with me that the best way to protect ourselves and my family is to find something to use against Hind?"

Her face clouded over.

"I didn't say that. But I admit that whatever's in the archive must be a very powerful or very dangerous secret. I . . . at least want to know whether that option is open to us." She turned away toward the lounge room. He realized that she hadn't brought one of the meals for herself.

When he'd finished eating, he returned to his own search. Now that he knew how to activate the wall panels, he discovered hidden spaces full of uniforms, unidentifiable tools and equipment, small vehicles with three wheels, building materials with odd textures, and many projections of moving images in bright colors accompanied by strange music. Some walls did not open, but only flashed symbols in bright red. Even he could figure out that those were warnings, probably signifying a storehouse of weapons for which special permission was required.

In the bush, his nose gave him as much information as his eyes. Here, it was of little help. There were many scents, but they were almost entirely unfamiliar. A few he had come to associate with machinery since his experience at the glider cave. Others reminded him of the materials Natira called *plastic*, but with slight variations. Unlike the cave, this place still held odors of men and women. It probably hadn't been unoccupied for more than a few weeks. Did that mean that the Confederacy presence on Earth had entered a new phase?

They wouldn't simply abandon so much equipment and food. Then again, it would be strategically wise not to reveal that they had brought equipment, weaponry, and food enough to supply large numbers of soldiers.

In contrast to the chill that gripped him, there was a pleasant odor that vied for his attention.

It was a trace of Natira in the air: a clean, sweet scent that had become as familiar as his own and far more welcome. He looked up in anticipation, but she wasn't there.

He found her just outside the entrance of the room, slumped on the floor with her back against a wall and her legs splayed. He dropped to his knees, afraid that she must have injured herself. But when she lifted her face, it was clear that the hurt came from a deeper wound.

"I was right," she said. "The encryption isn't especially complex, it's just in a form that our current digital devices don't use. The base's central processor has opened the locks on the files so I can read them on my Synappt."

"And...?"

She started to reply but had to stop. When she tried again, her voice was reedy, barely under control.

"I haven't read anything yet. I'm not ready—not yet, not right now. Maybe in the morning." She didn't sound very sure.

"Yes. That makes sense. Tackle it when you're fresh—you don't want to misunderstand something because you're tired."

"It's not that." She pulled her knees to her chest and wrapped her arms around them. "If ... if I take this final step, I'll be a traitor to my people." She looked into his face as if willing him to understand. "I can never live in Telluria again. I'll be sent into exile." Tears threatened to spill. "The most despised of criminals, with nowhere to call home."

He took her hands in his.

"Hind says you'll be a traitor, but can you trust anything he says anymore? We don't know that what's in the archive is dangerous to your people, only that Hind and the Patriarch don't want it to become known. For all we know, you might uncover something criminal, or discover willful government incompetence—things your people do need to know." He gave her fingers a squeeze. "Whatever you find, there's nothing that says you have to *tell* anyone. If it would harm Telluria, keep it a secret. In fact, maybe once Hind knows you've read the archive it'll give you some leverage. You're a famous communicator—he might be willing to buy your silence."

She slowly shook her head, far from convinced. He couldn't really blame her. But her doubts didn't explain why she had chosen to sit outside the room he was in. She must have come to find him but changed her mind.

Her mouth quivered with uncertainty, but her eyes were full of need.

"Hold me," she said.

As he wrapped her in his arms a torrent of heartache found its release, her body racked with sobs. To witness such devastation in this amazing woman brought tears to his own eyes. He pressed her against him as if he could make them one body, and draw her pain into him instead.

Though Hind had cast Killian as a villain, and he was sick at the thought of Lewis coming to harm, his own sorrow was nothing compared to Natira's. She'd lost everything. Everyone she'd considered family, and probably all her friends, too, now that her leaders had branded her a criminal. Her hopes for the future had been swept away—an entire life built over nearly thirty years utterly destroyed. How could anyone recover from that?

If Hind and his people had any decency, they would have been content to punish Killian and give Natira an honorable way to redeem herself instead of dangling it in front of her as a reward to betray him. His contempt for them was a white-hot cinder in his brain.

Even now she might be able to plead for mercy and save herself at his expense.

That was what she should do—he should do his best to convince her of that.

But even as he had the thought, he knew that she could have betrayed him at any time, yet she hadn't. She wouldn't do so now.

Like a flash of lightning, two truths became clear:

He would gladly sacrifice himself for her sake.

And she felt the same about him.

He raised her face and kissed her with all the fire inside him, and she returned its heat in full measure.

"It's nothing compared to what you've lost," he whispered huskily, feeling tears spill from his eyes. "But you have me as long as you want me."

Her answer was another kiss that left them panting.

She pulled upward on his tunic. He raised his arms to let it slide over his head, and she pressed her face against the skin of his chest as if to listen to the voice of his heart.

With a laugh, he swept her up in his arms and carried her to the dormitory room to experience the magic of its beds.

39

Natira lay in the dark and listened to Killian breathe. He'd fallen into a light sleep. And it was a sleep well-deserved!

The thought made her smile, her eyes still wide with wonder.

As the heat from his back warmed her own skin, she gave a slow shake of her head. Even the knowledge that she could reach out and caress his arm, his hip, his thigh—the full extent of his nakedness—the nerve endings of her fingertips lightly gliding over the soft hairs and invisible pores . . . even that couldn't fully crystallize the past hour into reality.

It was a fevered blur, though she yearned to remember every tiny detail: each tentative stroke, each gasp of fresh delight, each shuddering release. He had touched her in places she'd never been touched by another in all her life; and the molten heat of Earth itself had erupted within her, awakening a hunger so fierce it became a kind of madness. Banishing fear, she had held him deep inside her, and their ecstasy had been a fusion of two beings such as she'd never believed possible.

She thought of Valenti. No doubt he had cancelled their Intention agreement; and she should feel regret, or loss, or even shame for giving herself to another—but she didn't. Giving up a life with Valenti brought only relief. She was able to admit his flaws now, and they were many, not least that he was a terrible lover. Self-centered. Egotistical. Pompous. And for all that he'd subtly bragged about the many women with whom he'd shared simu-sex, he'd never learned anything about how to please a woman. Killian had either made a point of learning such skills, or was so attuned to her that he instinctively knew how to take her to heights she'd never imagined. The memory of her times with Valenti would have made her laugh, but for the realization of how close she had come to spending her life without knowing how good sex could be.

But she owed her newfound happiness and contentment to much more than skillful sex.

This man who lay at her side had overturned a lifetime of restraint and carefully constructed order, and with his gift of chaos had brought a bliss she could scarcely comprehend. While her body burned to be touched again and again, more strange and wonderful was the fire that had awakened at her core and asked for nothing more than to be with him.

It was sweet sadness, that feeling. An acknowledgement that she had taken a step too far, could never go back, and could never again be the person she'd once been.

She didn't even know what to call the feeling within her. There was a word that the ancients had used, but she had never understood it, since they used it for so many things from relationships to favorite foods. Better not to confine such a wondrous state of being to a mere word. Whatever it was, it wasn't something you chose, or decided, or defined. It was undefinable. Unmistakable. And irresistible.

With a delicious feeling of wantonness, she rolled onto her side, pressed her breasts lightly against his back and nuzzled into his long hair. Sleep came quickly.

# # #

When she awoke, she felt Killian's nearness right away, and a fresh warmth spread through her. But even without touching him she sensed the rigidity of his muscles. When she moved her arm, he quickly rose from the bed and dressed. He looked toward her, and she gave him a smile, but it wasn't returned. If anything, he looked uncomfortable, and

316

muttered something about breakfast as he left in the direction of the lunchroom.

She followed him there a few minutes later. He was already finishing his meal and stood as she entered.

"I want to have a look at some of the tools I found last night. See if there's anything we can use." His tone was businesslike—not angry but not warm either. She just nodded and watched him walk away.

What was wrong? Had she done something to upset him? She couldn't imagine what it might be.

Had she snored? Accidentally hit him in her sleep? Drooled in his hair?

No, that was ridiculous. Maybe people of Earth just didn't like to talk about it after having sex—it wouldn't be their strangest custom.

Or could it be that she hadn't pleased him nearly as much as he'd pleased her? Had the encounter she'd thought so passionate been a disappointment to him, a sign that they weren't meant to be together?

A chill gripped her chest and turned her stomach.

Maybe she was just imagining things. There were tasks she should be doing. She still wasn't quite ready to read the archive, but she could use the central computer to get an inventory of supplies at the base. That would be useful. If there was something wrong, Killian would tell her. Sooner or later.

Her forced tranquility was impossible to maintain. She fretted over every little thing. The few times she saw him, her cheery questions were met with responses that were curt to the point of being rude. Again, she wondered what she'd done wrong. Her blissful mood of the night before had given way to an anxiety that left a sour taste in her throat.

When they found themselves in the same room for a midday meal, she couldn't keep silent anymore.

"Have I done something to make you angry?" she asked.

"No, why?"

"Because you've been avoiding me. You barely talk to me." Her voice became softer. "Is it because of last night? Was it . . . was it a mistake?"

The look on his face made her stomach sink. That was it—he regretted what they'd done. He didn't feel the same way she did. She took a ragged breath.

"I took advantage of you," he said quietly.

"You *what?*"

"You were suffering. Your heart was broken and I . . . I used the opportunity to do something you wouldn't have done otherwise. I didn't plan for it to happen, but it was still wrong. I've wronged you again—I keep doing it, and I never learn."

"Is *that* what's gotten into you? You feel guilty because we had sex?"

He didn't say anything, but he couldn't look her in the eye.

"Listen," she continued, "you didn't make me do anything I didn't want to do. Yes, I was heartbroken. I needed to feel that someone somewhere cared about me. That I hadn't lost everything. And that's just what you showed me. At least I thought it was. I'd never known that sex could mean so much." She shook her head in wonder at the memory. "Unless now you're saying that it didn't mean anything—that it was just for pleasure. That I'm not special to you."

"*No!* Of course, you're special. I can't imagine . . ." He sighed and dropped his voice. "I can't imagine my life without you in it. I don't want to."

She suddenly knew what people mean when they say that their heart leapt into their throat.

"Then don't be stupid. I asked you to hold me. I was the one who started undressing you. And what we did . . . was wonderful. Beautiful. Exactly what I needed, and more than I knew I needed. Until this morning when you suddenly acted like I'd borrowed something from you and didn't give it back."

He had the good grace to look ashamed.

"It was still reckless of me. You could get pregnant."

She gasped. "Are you serious? It could happen that quickly—by accident?"

318

"Of course. Most pregnancies are unexpected. There are ways to increase the odds, but it's mostly by chance. And it's most likely to happen in the middle of your cycle, between bleeding times."

She slumped in the chair. She'd been taught all the facts about pregnancy, but in such a clinical way that the true haphazardness of it all had never sunk in. Making the calculations in her mind, she realized that it had been almost two weeks since she'd bled.

"How would I know . . . if I was pregnant?" Her voice was little more than a whisper.

"We have no way to know right away. If your next bleed doesn't come, it could mean that you're pregnant; although sometimes women miss it for no reason that we understand, especially if they're very young or sick in certain ways." He shrugged apologetically. "You see? I had no right."

She thought about his words.

"It's not a sure thing."

"No, not at all."

"And until two weeks ago I hadn't had my . . . cycle since the very first one, in my teens. So, we have no way to know that my body even works that way anymore." Tellurian medics would know. Even how to end a pregnancy, she imagined.

"What matters in all this," she said, "is how you feel about sex. In Telluria sex is solely for pleasure—it has no other purpose. Is that what it is for you?"

He'd obviously never considered the question before.

"It . . . was, I guess. Until now."

"Is that what it was for you last night?" She swallowed, and hoped he didn't see.

"No." The sincerity was plain in his face and his voice. "Last night . . . I don't know how to say it. First, I just wanted to comfort you and take your pain away. To take it into me. But that feeling got away on us, and I realized that I . . . ." He cleared his throat. "That I wanted you more than anything I've ever wanted. I wanted us to join our lives together. To commit ourselves to each other. It was . . . the most wonderful thing I've ever experienced." He stopped and shook his head. "I'm saying it badly."

Tears spilled down her cheeks. She threw her arms around him.

"You're saying it just right." And she kissed him and held him; and he wiped the tears away. As she buried her face in his hair she whispered, "Just don't ever be so dumb again, OK?"

He laughed and said, "I promise."

40

Their moment of happiness was short-lived.

It had given Natira the strength to finally face the archive; but as she shared what she read with Killian, their joyful mood collapsed under the weight of the past.

Their guess had been right—it was a fiercely guarded secret record of the Confederacy's actions over the past half-millennium, and Natira had never suspected the appalling extent of it.

The beginning was a repeat of what she and her tech friend Reece had already learned about the time before the Divide: the gap between the 'haves' and the 'have-nots' was the widest it had ever been in human history. A fortunate few commanded resources beyond those of most countries, while the rest of the population had almost nothing. The wealthy had created miniature paradises for themselves in isolated and heavily secured places on Earth, and then had done the same on the planets and asteroids. With no way to right the imbalance, the most impoverished and hopeless took revenge by *hunting* their oppressors, even though it usually meant sacrificing themselves. They had nothing to lose.

Then had come the treachery of pretended colony ships; and the suffering citizens of Earth understood that they had been cheated once again, left with a ravaged planet—and, in an even greater betrayal, robbed of both knowledge and technology that might have helped make their lives tolerable. Instead, they were forcibly thrown back into dark, primitive times, and left to endure lives of stagnation and misery.

That much Natira already knew. But even worse was to come.

The Allocations with their Depots were no act of altruism. They were a means to force the abandoned multitudes to leave the cities where the strong-willed might have retained enough self-worth to try to rebuild their lives, into pockets of isolation where they could never combine with enough strength to threaten the departed overlords.

And Depot food all but sterilized those who consumed it. Depot-supplied medicine included genetic analysis and manipulation to suppress certain traits in order to stall evolutionary improvements to the species. Humans of Earth were to remain disadvantaged and inferior, though kept from undergoing any actual *regression* of type. The reason for that last fact took some time for Natira to uncover.

The emerging Confederacy spread news about the Allocations throughout Earth's remaining population, but very few went to them voluntarily. Then came the plagues.

When she'd first learned about those, she'd been heartsick to think that her people could watch fellow humans ravaged by disease and do nothing to help.

The truth was worse.

The colonists had created the plagues.

Their intent was twofold: first, to drastically reduce global population and its continuing strain on the resources of the planet—the overlords eventually wanted Earth back, after all—and second, to force holdouts in the cities to abandon their homes in favor of the Allocations in the hope of receiving life-saving medicine.

Some were saved. Most were not. As with everything else, the Depots' distribution of medicines was methodically programmed. Selected individuals were given real medicine, the rest placebos. And when the population of an Allocation grew larger than the builders intended, its Depot would alert the inhabitants that it could no longer produce enough medicine and food. The desperate villagers would drive away newcomers, and the resulting bloodshed reduced the population still more.

At least the settlements hadn't been induced to go to war with each other—they were deliberately placed too far apart. Then Natira realized the reason for that.

War was a driver of technological progress. And progress was exactly what the colonists did not want for their abandoned cousins on Earth.

The Confederacy maintained a system of satellites in Earth orbit and a secret presence on the planet itself. Under the guise of protecting the ravaged ecosystem, all attempts by the people to feed themselves independently were thwarted ruthlessly, reinforcing dependence on the Depots. Independence was a disease to be wiped out. And so, traits that drove humanity to understand the forces of the universe and reach beyond its planetary cradle were systematically eliminated.

So were its people. Within fifty years, the human population of Earth had been reduced to one hundredth of its pre-Divide level; and all but an untrackable few had surrendered to Allocation life.

The whole series of events was an intricate plan, meticulously calculated and carried out with ruthless efficiency: genetic engineering at its most vile, and on the largest of scales.

The loss of human life was utterly appalling. The destruction of human initiative was even worse.

As the truth unfolded for her, Natira had to rush to the hygienic facility several times to vomit, her face streaming tears. Killian sat staring into the depths of his imagination, almost catatonic.

The concluding entries in the archive confirmed what Killian had overheard: a conspiracy to pillage Earth once again, though the reasons for the measure surprised them both.

While plans for the Earth unfolded slowly, a much more urgent crisis had arisen elsewhere. Despite subtle and not-so-subtle repression, the citizens of the Confederacy's outer colonies had developed feelings of territorial identity. They began to see themselves as *Martians* or *Europans* or *Cereans* first, and Confederacy citizens second. With that had come a desire for independence, both collectively and individually. The outer colonies were becoming less subservient to their central government. Unions and other aggregate organs of resistance grew, and spread, and became more powerful. In Telluria, the outer colonists began to be seen as 'difficult.'

Such a development was unwelcome, but not unforeseen. After all, the architects of the Divide had been the rulers of industry and the holders of wealth for centuries. They'd known all about the sociological traits of the worker class. Even before the Exodus, they'd put the most rigorously researched social engineering to work to slow the inevitable slide of their colonies toward autonomy, while knowing that those efforts would ultimately fail. When it did, the cheap resources they coveted would become harder to get, along with the supply of compliant labor.

So, there was a long-term plan. It involved a partially healed Earth and its debased populace.

Five hundred years would be enough to make them ready.

## 41

Natira picked at her food. She didn't even know what she was eating, and her stomach still threatened to reject what little she had managed to swallow.

Killian had eaten more, chewing mechanically as he stared into space.

After a long time, he caught her watching him. At any other time, he would have assumed that she was judging his eating manners, or gruffly questioned her interest, or maybe even given her a smile. Now the muscles of his face hung listlessly; and his eyes, usually so full of life, were glassy and dull.

Even his voice was flat as he asked, "How could Hind have known that I overheard talk of a conspiracy?"

"That part's easy. Thanks to your visitor's tattoo, anyone could find out where you'd been, and when. You said you were in a storage closet next to the room where the conversation took place, right? Not hard to guess that you might have heard it, and nothing to lose by saying so, trying to draw you out. If you hadn't heard anything, you'd assume they were just concocting a story to make your crimes look even worse."

"He's clever, I'll give him that."

"Yes, he is. But apparently not clever enough to see that *he's* being manipulated. Probably by the Prime Councilor, or maybe by the heads of all five houses."

"You still don't believe he's involved of his own will?"

"No, I don't. Oh, he might turn a blind eye to some things out of self-interest, but he's not an evil man. Not like those who carried out the Divide, or the campaign against Earth since then. You just don't like him."

Killian frowned. "I never liked him. I wanted to. I wanted to like all your people—but something about him didn't feel right. And that was long before I fell in love with you."

Love. That was the word.

Natira thought about love, knowing that it was completely new to her understanding, and wondered if it was strong enough to withstand the horrible truths they'd just learned.

How could it? How could *anything*?

Killian was staring into emptiness again.

"What are you thinking?" she asked.

"I'm wondering if this is the price of exploring the universe."

"What do you mean?"

"This . . . division of the race. Does most of humankind have to live poorly so that a few have enough wealth to reach out to the stars?"

Natira gave a bitter laugh.

"No one's reached out to the stars. Is that what you think we do with our wealth?"

"But what about your Telluria Quinta? I was told it was being transformed into a great colony ship for an interstellar voyage."

"That's what our people are told, and an organization called SHE—the Society for Human Expansion—crows about it from time to time. But now I don't know what to believe. It might just be a distraction to keep our people from thinking too much about our declining population. I know for sure that it's years behind schedule because of funding cutbacks, and I've heard rumors that it's actually being outfitted for another purpose entirely.

"The only space exploration we've done for generations has been to find new resources. And that's not urgent because none of the colonies has room to store anything that no longer holds our interest. When we get tired of the latest toy or clothing in a month or two, we get rid of it, and everything discarded is remade as new toys and clothes."

His mouth hung slack.

"You sound like you don't care whether humans travel to the stars."

When put like that, the question annoyed her. "It wouldn't make our lives better. And we haven't outgrown the solar system. Why risk lives and resources to go somewhere we don't need to go? To build colonies there? It wouldn't be productive."

Killian gave a soft snort and turned away. Almost to himself, he muttered, "Guess it isn't only Earth people whose growth was stunted."

Natira felt heat rise into her face, but she shook her head and let her indignation subside.

He was right. Her people's leaders had wronged every single member of the human species. Maybe even stolen their birthright, not just by despoiling the Earth but also by renouncing the stars.

"I don't know what to think of any of this," she sighed, closing her eyes and rubbing her neck. "I don't want to think. I wish I could just turn off my brain. I wonder if this stupid base has any dream-chips, or Marsweed, or even just some alcohol?"

"Dream what?"

"Small wafers you stick to the roof of your mouth. They dissolve in a couple of hours, but in the meantime, they electronically stimulate your brain to give you amazing experiences. You never know what will happen. Usually it's good." She gave a sheepish shrug. "I think I smelled some Marsweed in Borealis. And you must have alcohol."

"Way too much for our own good. Most people make beer—even Lewis and my father. And wine from berries or dandelions. I like the taste, when they get it right, but I don't like getting stupid. That puts me in a minority, though. Most nights, half of Borealis gets drunk."

"Somehow, I'm not surprised that you don't. But let's see if we can help you relax."

A thorough search of the cupboards finally produced a large cylindrical carafe with a series of slider controls along one side. Natira found a container of mango juice, filled the carafe, then set the controls and activated it. In a few minutes she poured the result into two tall drinking glasses. The orange liquid fizzed slightly and had a froth on top.

"I gave it the consistency of beer," she said, "except it'll be sweeter and fruitier." She held a glass out to Killian, but he waited for her to drink first.

It was refreshing and flavorful, but with a significant kick. Just what she needed. After another large swallow, she could already feel her neck muscles loosening.

Killian didn't look impressed. She raised an eyebrow.

"Too sweet," he said, "but it does warm my stomach. And I like the color it puts in your cheeks."

She laughed and drew him to her for a kiss that tasted of mango.

Part of her felt guilty to want even a few moments of forgetfulness after the horrific things they'd just learned. Or was that a natural reaction? Despite what Killian had once said, she was human. Very, very human. And she felt such a strong need to embrace that side of her right then.

To embrace him, too. And the more she drank, the stronger that need became.

She pressed harder against him and shivered as she felt the evidence of his arousal. Then his hands began to wander over her body and the very core of her caught fire. In an instant the room dissolved into a maelstrom of moist lips, probing tongues, tangled limbs, skin rubbed deliciously against warm skin.

Much later, they lay sprawled in blissful exhaustion, thoroughly spent. Natira ran her hand across her abdomen, reveling in the mix of her sweat and his, and the way it cooled her skin.

It was stunning, how much things had changed. How much *she* had changed, in ways she never could have foreseen—would have fiercely denied with her every breath. But maybe it had to be that way. What she felt for Killian could only have been forged by their shared ordeal, both on Telluria and on Earth. Even now, the terrible knowledge that was such a threat to both of them . . . even that was a bond between them.

As devastating as the Divide and its impact had been, she had to accept that it was history. There was nothing she or Killian could do to change it. They could only try to defuse the current crisis, and she knew they would try. But they must not let the crimes of the past destroy the future that had revealed itself to the two of them.

Did that mean that he would go to live in Telluria, or that she would stay on Earth? She didn't know—couldn't even think that far ahead yet. She only knew what she saw in the deep blue eyes that looked into hers.

With a touch too gentle to be believed in such a physical man, he cupped her breast and brought his mouth to hers . . .

. . . just as a wailing whoop vibrated the walls of the room and brought them scrambling to their feet.

Natira leapt to a section of wall that pulsed red. She swept her hand through the air.

The view that appeared showed the sky above the base. Two giant birdlike shapes were spiralling down toward the roof. Within seconds, three more appeared from nowhere. Then another pair.

It had to be Tellurian security.

They'd been found!

42

It was a ridiculous quandary: whether or not to get dressed when every precious second might be needed to find a hiding place. But if Killian was about to be dragged away in restraints as a criminal, he refused to do it naked.

A band of bright red flashed urgently in the air. It displayed two long words—it was infuriating that he couldn't read them.

"What does that say?" he asked Natira.

"What? Oh! It says, 'Intruder Alert'. But that doesn't make sense. The base would recognize its own personnel. Their craft would send an automatic identification signal. How many of those landers did you see?"

"Seven. They looked like the glider we used. I guess they don't think we'll put up much of a fight."

"In a base that's probably full of weapons? I wouldn't take that chance, would you? And seven guards could never be sure of covering our escape from a big complex like this."

"Then who are they? Hind wouldn't send negotiators when he's already got the upper hand."

"They're already through the front entrance. If we're going to hide, we've got about five minutes to do it." Natira looked into his eyes. "I say we go to meet them."

Only days earlier he would have assumed that she'd decided to turn him in. Not anymore. He nodded.

The six men and one woman hadn't made it past the first set of rooms, perhaps stymied by the face scanner. They looked bemused when Natira opened the door.

A man with white hair said, "We weren't expecting one of those. I'm surprised you could get past it."

Killian gasped in recognition.

It was his grandfather.

Stunned, he couldn't even decide if he was grateful to see Jackson Ash instead of a troop of colonists.

Jackson gave a nod, showing no warmth but no surprise either. He had clearly known he would find his grandson in this remote outpost. That would be a story worth hearing.

All the newcomers wore dark clothing, though not uniforms. More like Depot clothes dyed in patches of forest green, grey, and brown. The men were of various ages and skin tones. The woman was small and dark, and Killian couldn't guess how old she was.

His grandfather spoke again. "Sorry. You were probably expecting Tellurians. I hope you haven't got weapons trained on us. We come in peace."

Natira crossed her arms. "If you're not Tellurians, who are you?"

Killian cleared his throat.

"Natira, this is my grandfather—my father's father—Jackson Ash."

The shock on her face would have made him laugh at any other time.

"I only hope you haven't led the Tellurians here," Killian said. "So many flyers together were probably detectable, even in stealth mode."

"Nice to see you, too," Jackson muttered. "You might have noticed that there's a storm about to break. We rode just beneath the clouds along the advancing front. I doubt if their satellites spotted us." His eyes narrowed. "You don't sound quite so adoring of the Confederacy as the last time we spoke."

Killian's jaw clenched and he bit back an angry retort. Like it or not, the man was right. That it made Killian feel like a fool didn't change anything.

Jackson Ash had been one of the most respected elders in Borealis, and the leader of the elder council for a dozen years. More important, he'd been one of Killian's favorite people— always a source of ready knowledge, rough wisdom, and a sturdy emotional shelter against the skinned knees and scalded hearts of childhood. While Lewis had taught Killian about wilderness survival, Jackson had taught him about life. But there was one subject on which they could never see eye to eye, and it eventually tore them apart.

Jackson had no wish for the departed colonists to return, and belittled his grandson's dreams. As the promised time of the return drew closer, their differences of opinion grew more heated. A lifetime of closeness only made the final schism more painful, with cruel words exchanged that had left each man feeling betrayed by the other.

That rift with his grandfather had left a hole in Killian's life. He'd done his best to forget it, but now that was no longer an option.

"All right," he said, "I did expect too much of the colonists. It wasn't realistic. But you were too negative. Natira is a Tellurian and she's . . . everything they ought to be." He caught her reaction in the corner of his eye but didn't want to look as if he were seeking approval.

Jackson smiled, and there was no smugness in it.

"I'm glad to hear it. People are people. Each has personal potential for goodness. It's when wealth and power are involved that things usually go wrong." Compared to his habitual rants on the subject, this was a surprising concession—an evident attempt at conciliation that Killian could accept.

There was much more to be said between them, but it would have to wait.

"I think you might know some of these others." Jackson gestured. One in particular looked very familiar, a man with white hair that sprang in tufts from behind his ears.

"Ud Littlebear!" Killian cried.

"So, you do remember me. My hair was still mostly brown the last time I saw you, and you weren't a teenager yet." He gave a belly laugh. "You're certainly not a kid anymore, and you've already stirred up a lifetime's worth of trouble, from the sound of it. Do you remember this guy, too?"

Yes, the tall man on his left with almond-shaped eyes had a strange name. "Yoan . . . I've forgotten your last name."

"MacIntosh." The man said. "Good to see you again, Killian." He held out a hand and Killian shook it. That triggered a round of introductions, while Natira still stood dumbfounded.

"Ud and Yoan are trappers," Killian explained. "That's what Uncle Lewis told me. They gather animal furs. Though I never knew that trappers made their rounds with stealth gliders."

Littlebear laughed again. "We'll explain all that."

The stocky man in the back with a bush of brown hair that completely encircled his face was named Baird Grum. Beside him was a wiry man probably only a few years older than Killian who fidgeted restlessly. His name was Leeyum Frost, a strange name for someone with hair the color of fire. The sixth man, Ret Habbard, had deep brown skin over a solid frame that was twice Frost's bulk and an extra head taller. The lone woman, Win Chung, also had darker skin and more prominent lips than most people Killian had known. She kept her silence for now, only acknowledging him with a sharp nod from a head that barely reached the height of Killian's shoulder.

"I don't suppose we could do our explaining over some food?" MacIntosh asked. "Tea would be good, too. Brandy would be even better." He looked at Killian. "Don't worry, Jackson's right. The Tellurians won't have followed us."

"But the base identified you as intruders," Natira said. "It's probably sent out an alert."

The men all looked at Chung, who exhaled in a long whistle.

"In that case, we'd better take Win to the control center, if you know where it is," Jackson urged. "She might be able to make it look like a malfunction or spoof the signal to send security forces to the wrong place. As long as it didn't send visuals. The rest of us better get hunting for weapons."

"I think I know where some are kept," Killian said as they began to move. "But they're locked up."

"Just a minute!" Natira held up a hand. "I may not be on great terms with my people right now, but what makes you think I'm going to let you use weapons against them?" She shot a look of reproof at Killian.

He caught his grandfather's frown and felt annoyed to be caught in the middle of such conflicting loyalties.

"They've already tried to kill us," he said to Natira. "So, I don't think they'll throw us a party for getting into their secret base. You know I don't want to hurt anyone. But if they give us no choice but to defend ourselves, I'd like to be ready." He reached out to grasp her hand. "I'm not about to let them take you or hurt you."

She must have sensed total conviction in his words. She just gave a sharp nod and led the way to the base control station. Win Chung immediately set to work on the computers, while Killian showed the others to the wall sections that featured red warning-indicators. Littlebear agreed that they were certainly weapons caches, but there was no way to open them without a security code. They'd have to hope Chung could work some magic in the control room once she finished masking their arrival.

When the group returned, Grum gave a chuckle.

"Can we do our waiting in the mess hall? Either the Confederacy security forces will be fooled by Win's trick, or they'll swoop in with guns at the ready. If so, there's no place we can escape to in time that they won't find us."

"Not even with gliders?"

Littlebear nodded. "So, you did use one? We thought so. But it won't fool the Confeds once they're expecting you. They'll have mass detectors. You two are very badly wanted."

"What about the rest of you?" Killian asked as he took them to the mess.

"Us? They don't look for us. They still think we're just a persistent myth." Littlebear looked amused, in spite of the danger. In fact, none of the newcomers looked particularly anxious. Even Frost's restlessness just looked habitual.

"What's going on anyway?" Killian persisted. "What are you doing here, and how did you know you'd find us?"

Jackson looked at the others and took their silence as agreement for him to answer. But first he accepted a carafe of brandy from Natira, shared it around, and raised his glass in a silent toast. He sipped, sighed in appreciation, and then replied.

"You must have wondered how Lewis knew about the cave, and what the stealth suits would do for you. It's because he's one of us. We call ourselves the Keepers. You can think of us as custodians."

Killian and Natira shared a sharp look. It was the name Hind had used.

"Custodians of what?"

"Of knowledge," Littlebear answered. "Of the old ways. Of Earth. Whatever needs to be preserved. Many of us are what our Tellurian friend here would call scientists—that was the prevailing term before the Divide; but afterward the word became a pejorative because people felt that the Exodus was the scientists' fault. The obscenely rich ordered it, but it was the scientists who sold their souls to make it happen."

"Did they have a choice?" Natira sounded irritated.

"Of course they did! Throughout history, people have made discoveries that were used to cause unthinkable carnage and suffering, but it's almost never the pure discovery of a scientific fact or principle that causes the harm. It's what someone chooses to make of it. And that someone always has a choice."

"Uncle Lewis isn't a scientist."

"Not in the formal sense, no. And not by education. He's more a natural *savant*, incredibly knowledgeable and intuitive about the workings of nature, and has learned almost all of it from direct experience. Others can tell you about genes and organelles and cells, but Lewis can tell you what it all means in the *real* world. That's critically valuable knowledge. And he claims you take after him, Killian. I'm not surprised."

"He's been captured by the Confederacy because of me. He could be sentenced to hard labor on Mars, or worse."

"We know." Jackson softened his voice. "He managed to get word to us just before he was caught, and told us where you were headed. We've been on our way here ever since, but each of us lives a great distance away, and travel is much slower when you have to stay hidden. We're trying very hard to come up with some way to rescue him."

The words were surprisingly calm from a man talking about the plight of his own son.

Chung's shout echoed down the hall. "Good news! I was able to make the alert look like a malfunction. Bur there's bad news, too."

They returned to her side.

"What is it?" Jackson asked, staring around a room lit by pulses of brilliant crimson.

"I tampered with the controls but then couldn't provide correct identification." She looked up with a face of stone. "It might have triggered a self-destruct mechanism."

"What!" Killian cried. "Why would they want to destroy their own base?"

"To keep its secrets." Jackson's expression was grim. "Is there any chance we can get somewhere safe in time?"

"No idea. Don't know for sure that I triggered it, how long we've got, or how serious they are about destroying this place. Down to the walls, or down to its atoms?"

No one spoke for long seconds. Then Jackson spoke, his voice full of gravel and gravity, "Do what you can to shut it off. We'll use the time to find whatever we can." He gestured for Killian to lead them to the weapons.

"Are you serious? This place might be about to blow up and you don't want to at least try to save ourselves?"

"Win's right. This base isn't supposed to be here. If it's been rigged to detonate when infiltrated, they wouldn't want a speck of dust left behind that could be identified as Confederacy-made. And they wouldn't give invaders time to escape. All we can do is hope Win can stop it."

Killian hesitated, then left the room, noting the location of the nearest hygiene station in case he needed to throw up. The calmness of his voice surprised him.

"Is Uncle Lewis's capture why you came here first? To get Confederacy weapons?"

"We have weapons of our own," Frost said, "but they go unused." His frown and crossed arms reflected thwarted desire.

"And for the sake of the Earth Mother they'll remain that way," MacIntosh replied, taking a large swallow of the brandy he still carried. Grum merely glared at Frost.

"I still don't understand who you are," Natira interrupted. "Or what you do."

"We're guardians of knowledge." Grum's voice was a growl. "Knowledge is too valuable a thing to lose. Or to have stolen from you. Keepers are dedicated to preserving knowledge against *any* efforts to destroy it. To ensure it's widespread enough to survive regional catastrophes. And to make sure it will still be available when the people of Earth are ready to make use of it again."

"Knowledge could mean almost anything."

"Natira, you'll know terms like physics, chemistry, astronomy, biology . . . ." Littlebear explained, his eyes unconsciously darting back toward the flashing lights in the control room as they turned a corner. "No one in the Allocations uses those terms, Killian, and we rarely do, either. But we do make a distinction between useful knowledge and junk. And that includes a great deal of knowhow that those departing colonists were confident they'd eliminated, like Win Chung's abilities with computer technologies. And Habbard's facility with stealth systems."

"I've taken the basic principles used by their spacecraft and suits and adapted them to all of our refuges," the big man said with a smile that belied the sheen of sweat on his forehead. "If the Confederacy had done that, we would never have known about this base or any of the others."

They'd reached the secure lockup that Killian had found. Habbard and Littlebear began to examine the wall. The ceiling now pulsed red like the control room. The vivid light made Killian picture the room melting.

"You said 'others.' How many bases are there like this one?" he asked, brushing a finger through the bristly stubble of his upper lip.

"Hundreds around the planet. And many smaller depots like the cave you found. The Confederacy never really left Earth, although even the Keepers didn't discover that for almost a century after the Exodus. They almost wiped us out in one giant, coordinated, worldwide raid because we didn't know they were still around."

"*Worldwide?*"

"Yes, Killian. The Keepers are well-established and well-hidden in every corner of the globe, and have been here since the Divide, waiting for a time when people can be roused out of their lethargy and want to make something of themselves again."

"You must have created the secret schools." He gave his grandfather a suspicious look.

"No. That's something we didn't do and didn't even want. But then we realized that, while such places might be risky and bring down reprisals from the Confederacy, they might also be a good way to identify potential candidates to become Keepers. That was why Lewis and I arranged for you to meet Ud and some others all those years ago."

"I was being considered?"

"You were. But then you became entranced with colonist ways as you imagined them, and the time of their return was drawing close. We couldn't be sure which way your loyalties would turn, and so recruiting you was too great a risk. As you can imagine, our devotion to secrecy has had to be rigorous."

"Ridiculous is more like it," Frost snorted. His pacing had increased until he looked like a caricature of himself.

"Necessary!" Habbard snapped, surprising everyone. A drop of sweat fell from his eyebrow and splashed silently on the floor.

The weapons locker refused to open. Grum grunted with frustration as he slammed his massive forearms against the wall, but it had no effect and Littlebear only rolled his eyes.

"Yet now, here you are, explaining everything about yourself in front of a Tellurian." Natira gave Killian a meaningful look and cleared her throat. "Does that mean you don't intend for me to live?"

Killian gasped. Frost and Grum looked shocked too, but not the others.

"You're very astute." Jackson gave a gentle smile. "But I promise you that you're in no danger from us. We didn't recruit Killian years ago, but there's no question that he's worthy Keeper material now. And he seems to have absolute trust in you. Because of that, and your own actions helping him, we're sufficiently convinced that, even if you don't choose to side with us, you won't betray us. In spite of that camera recorder you wear on your head. From what we've seen, you're a very exceptional representative of your people, Natira Celestia. An exceptional representative of humankind."

Killian felt a swell of pride for her, but she could only cough and say, "It's Natira Tellurian now."

Littlebear huffed. "If your Patriarch is as clever as I think he is, he's made no such announcement and never will. You're much too admired throughout the colonies. He won't risk the wrath of such a devoted following unless there's no other choice."

For the first time in hours, the lines in Natira's face relaxed a little. Killian could tell she was afraid to give in to such a powerful hope. He didn't know whether to be happy for her, or fearful about what her obvious relief said about her ultimate loyalty. In a choice between Killian and the land of her upbringing, which would win?

No, that wasn't fair. But then, nothing about the situation was fair.

Natira stepped toward the wall and swept her hand through the air in a pattern of swooping curves. A panel slid open to reveal racks upon racks of tubelike objects slightly larger than a man's arm. Jackson gave her a look of respect while Littlebear lightly clapped his hands and said, "We've seen pictures of these. They're arm-guns. Point and shoot."

"It's a symbol I found in the commander's quarters," she told them in a voice that said no further explanation would be forthcoming. Habbard pulled out one of the tubes, slid it over his arm, then pointed his fist at the wall. It showed a bright dot but nothing else happened.

A loud braying laugh froze them like statues.

A breathless Chung appeared in the doorway and leaned on the wall in another fit of laughter just as Killian noticed that the pulsing red lights had stopped.

"It wasn't a self-destruct after all." She gasped. "It just shut down the control network, probably on a timer. I'll do what I can to get it up and running again. Sorry about the scare!" She brayed again and left for the control room.

"The woman is mad!" Frost muttered. But everyone slumped in unashamed relief.

"I was about ready to shit my pants," MacIntosh said.

Grum's laugh was like an explosion.

Jackson passed around two of the arm-guns for the others to examine.

Littlebear rocked his head to ease the muscles of his neck and said, "Weapons are all very well, but we need a better look at the layout of this place if we're going to make a plan of defense."

"Wait," Killian said. "How do you know about Natira's job and her 'devoted following' in the colonies? Do you mean you have ways of seeing what happens on the colony worlds?"

"We do, although we've never been able to devise a way to communicate with them directly that wouldn't immediately be discovered by Confederacy security. It's hard enough to communicate among ourselves without giving away our existence."

"How do you?" Natira asked. "You might encrypt messages well enough to defy decoding, but any electromagnetic radiation would be detectable. And the source located."

"Very true. The answer was conceived early on, but it took nearly two centuries to perfect the method. Before that, believe it or not, we used homing pigeons—specially trained birds who carried written messages."

Habbard chuckled and looked into Killian's puzzled face. "Seismic waves. A kind of very broad, very powerful vibration that's caused naturally by earthquakes and can travel through the entire planet from one side to the other. Except we make ours with enormous pistons in the Earth. Many of our refuges are in abandoned mines or deep cave systems anyway, so it was natural to think of messages that could travel through ground. Seismic sensing equipment was around for hundreds of years before the Divide, but for some reason the Confederacy has never felt a need to know what was happening *under* the earth." He gave a loud laugh. "Always try to know the heart of your enemy."

With some hand gestures Natira called up a projection of the base's architecture in three-dimensional diagrams, but just then Chung shouted again from the control room.

"Maybe they didn't buy my trick with the alert signal. There's a drone on the way to look us over. Somebody better make sure those goddamn gliders are under cover!"

43

Chung spoke through gritted teeth. "The drone will be here in less than fifteen minutes. The good news is, I'm back into the control system. For now."

"Well, Yoan's double-checking that the gliders are well hidden, and there shouldn't be any other traces of our landing," Jackson said. "Think they'll know we're here?"

"We don't know the current communication codes—the drone will, so the base is guaranteed to report our presence. Might even share video from the entrance area."

They exchanged looks, faces grim. Frost began to pace again, and his unusual gait made Natira think his left leg might be shorter than his right. Grum ran fingers through his thick growth of beard as if searching for a solution there.

Frost asked, "Will the drone be armed?"

"I think we have to assume it will be," Littlebear replied. "But the base must have defenses."

"Who would they have to defend against?" asked Killian. "None of our people have anything more dangerous than a shovel."

"But they don't really know that." Littlebear folded his arms and leaned against the wall. "We couldn't prevent all word of the existence of the Keepers from getting out, so we decided to spread some inventive rumors of our own. To make them think we're more widespread and better armed. It was really our only defense except secrecy."

"Some brave souls in a Minnsoda Allocation actually damaged a colonist base with a makeshift bomb," Jackson rumbled. "Though they blew themselves up, too."

"That was an offensive without direct provocation, and I didn't agree with it." Littlebear frowned.

Natira drew a sharp breath. She hadn't heard about the incident, but then she hadn't been told that the Confederacy had maintained a presence on Earth either. And even though there had been attempts on her life and Killian's, it had never really struck home to her that this conflict might spill blood on a large scale.

She hesitated before speaking but decided that she had a duty to both sides. As bizarre as it seemed, the more the antagonists respected each other's strength, the more likely they'd be to settle their differences without weapons.

"The base almost certainly has a defense screen and maybe other weapons too," she said. "Most Tellurians don't know it, but there are some renegades from the outer colonies that cause trouble for us when they can. They don't like being part of a central government and think that harassment of our outposts will help them gain independence. The outer colonies have a stronger attachment to Earth too, for some reason. I've always thought it was just sentimental, but it might be that stories of old Earth are even more appealing to people who live in such harsh environments."

"People who struggle just to survive usually don't appreciate a bunch of pampered princes telling them what to do." Leeyum Frost had stopped his pacing to deliver his pronouncement. His blue eyes sparked with a fire that seemed to kindle his red hair into greater brightness.

Killian looked about to defend Natira, but Jackson raised a hand. "Governments are never perfect. I should know. But this plan to enslave the Earth—it's the powerful and the wealthy once again feeling entitled to anything they can take. The leaders of Telluria. I very much doubt that they've announced this to their people as official policy, especially not to the outer colonies. The question is, how do we thwart their plan for the sake of all our people?"

Yoan MacIntosh returned from his task, leaned against a wall to catch his breath, and nodded to Jackson. The gliders were securely hidden.

"Hey!" Chung called out. "A small fusion generator should be more than enough to power a base this size, shouldn't it? So why does this one have a geo-conduit down to Earth's mantle?"

"Plain language please, Win," MacIntosh complained.

"It's a power conduit running through the Earth's crust to the mantle layer to draw energy from the heat of its molten rock. Enormous amounts of energy—much more than such a modest base should require."

"Unless for a defense shield." Littlebear wore a big grin. "Now we just have to find out how to turn it on." By 'we' he meant Chung, and she knew that, and immediately turned back to the control board to pore over it yet again.

"Am I the only one who doesn't understand any of this?" Killian perched on the edge of a desk, arms stiffly crossed.

"The Earth is made up of layers with the hard crust on top, then a semi-molten layer..."

"I was taught about that, Ud. And I assume the base can get energy from the heat or something. But what's this shield you're talking about? A hidden roof of some kind?"

"A good guess." Natira tried to sound encouraging but not condescending. "Except not a solid structure. The shields involve very powerful electromagnetic fields a certain distance apart from each other. You know magnetism, right?" He nodded. "And the space between those fields is filled with... tiny particles, too small to see, but billions of them. They're called nanoparticles. When the shield is up, its processor analyzes where incoming weapons will strike and magnetically aligns the nanoparticles in the zone under attack into an almost impenetrable barrier. Tellurian colonies have always needed those shields to protect us from micrometeoroids."

344

"Micro . . . like the rock that hit the shuttle when I was on my way there."

"Yes, the shuttle wasn't shielded. Only very large spacecraft can generate enough power to run shields."

"How do they defend against energy weapons?" Habbard asked.

"It's not general knowledge, but a guard once told me that the fields and nanoparticles combine to channel all excess energy to a heat sink. In this case, the ground itself."

Grum snorted. "They could melt a moat around us with enough firepower."

"*Found it!*" crowed Chung. "At least, I'm pretty sure I have it narrowed down to one of two controls. I think the shield is this one." She pointed.

"What's the other one?" Jackson asked.

"My best guess is *that's* the self-destruct device."

After a collective moan, there was a long silence. Chung finally broke it.

"Well? Do I activate this thing or not? The drone's about three minutes away."

"If we put up a shield, that's a dead giveaway that we're not Confederacy," Habbard advised.

"I think that ship has sailed." Jackson gave Chung a tight smile. She lifted a hand.

"No, wait," Killian said. Everyone looked at him. "You said the machines will talk to each other. Could the drone order the base to bring down the shield?"

Mouths fell open in dismay. Chung was already darting her hands through the air, searching the holographic representation of the controls. "Goddamn, I should have thought of that."

"In that case," Killian continued, "raising the shield won't help and will only show that the base has been infiltrated. There's a good chance they still think they're investigating a false alarm, and if we can just keep the base from revealing us to the drone . . . ."

For a very long couple of minutes Chung's fingers flew like hummingbirds and a sheen of sweat appeared on her face, but finally she sat back and released a loud breath.

"The best I could do was to initiate a code change. That means the system's waiting for authorization to accept a new set of codes, which we can't provide without the old ones. The Confeds will have those, but they'll have to enter them here, in person. In the meantime, it won't accept remote commands. I've tried to make it look like a system error that was also responsible for the false alarm. And, if we're lucky, they won't consider this base important enough to send someone right away. Unfortunately, we're stuck with only giving commands from this room, too, but it's better than letting the bad guys take over."

Natira bridled at the term 'bad guys' but didn't say anything. The citizens in the other base weren't her enemies, but for now they were a potential threat to her life.

"Good work. And good thinking, Killian," Jackson offered. "Maybe we would be able to defend ourselves, but it'll be much better if they don't know we're here. I think they'll come at us extra hard if they learn that you and Natira are in this base."

"How long could we hold out if they do?" Killian asked.

They all looked to Natira. She straightened and said, "I don't know that much about security matters, but I think only the largest of our Defender-class cruisers has plasma weapons that could breach a shield. Which would seriously damage this base for the sake of capturing nine people. Otherwise . . . I don't know—is there a way they could cut off the power from the geo-conduit? Beyond that, we seem to have food and water to last a very long time."

'But we'd just be sitting here doing nothing?"

She shrugged, knowing she was disappointing him, but she didn't have an answer.

"There's an impressive supply of portable weapons around this place," Grum said. "From our monitoring of Confederacy news sources, we suspected there was unrest in the outer colonies. But we never knew about those renegades you were

346

talking about. If they're a real threat, shouldn't this base be equipped with long-range weapons, too? Maybe all the way to orbital distance?"

"That makes sense," Natira agreed. "But haven't you found any before now on other bases?"

Grum looked at his companions. "We never thought to look for them. Couldn't imagine the need."

That led to more discussion. It kept their minds from thinking about the drone now circling overhead, perhaps only moments away from sending out an alarm that would bring the wrath of the Confederacy down on their heads.

Natira pointed out the antiquated security system at the entrance, evidence that a base of its age might not have upgraded weaponry either. She secretly hoped it didn't. It wouldn't matter if the Confederacy lost a drone or two, but she wasn't eager to have their outposts in near-Earth orbit come under attack. Once lives were lost, it would be harder to stop the conflict from escalating, and Frost, at least, seemed capable of doing something like that.

Chung suddenly crowed.

"It's all right. The drone is leaving! The base's core system was as disobliging as a virgin on the first date!" She brayed her loud laugh, and Natira hoped that the drone wasn't equipped with sensitive sonic detectors.

44

It was late in the evening before Killian finally had a chance to be alone with his grandfather.

Both men were tired, and they'd discovered a lounge area with chairs that were like floating on air, but they found it difficult to relax with each other. Along with the newly reawakened pain of the argument that had soured their relationship, there was also a feeling of being on the brink of something dire. The fate of many lives would be affected by what would be done in the coming days.

"I have to hand it to the Confeds—they do know how to make comfortable chairs," Jackson said with a smile.

Killian nodded, began to speak, stopped, then tried again.

"I regret a lot of things I said the last time we were together. I didn't mean them."

The older man gave a nod. "I know you didn't. And I hope, deep in your heart, you knew that I didn't mean the hurtful things I said, either. I wouldn't have been so angry if you hadn't meant so much to me." He looked away awkwardly, then forced himself to look back. "But I always wondered, why did you . . . worship the colonists so much?"

"Why did you hate them so much?"

"A fair question. But you first."

Killian looked at his hands. He'd always known the answer, but it wasn't easily put into words. "I spent my life watching my family—mother and father, you, Regina and

Lewis—and you were all smart, strong . . . you deserved *better* than just a life in Borealis. As a people, we all were meant for more. And then I learned about the Divide and the colonists, and I realized that there *was* more, and that at least some humans were pursuing the kind of challenges that make us reach higher. Learn more. Push back the darkness. And the colonists were out there doing it! I wanted to be with them, to be one of them."

His grandfather nodded solemnly. "Of course, you wouldn't be content in Borealis, living a life that never changed from day to day. But what about the challenges of living off the land, like Lewis and Regina? And the freedom of that life."

"That does make my blood sing. Even being on the run through the wilderness these past weeks, struggling just to survive and keep Natira safe, I've felt more alive than I can ever remember. But I also need to believe I'm accomplishing something--especially something important for my own people." He felt himself blush. "I know that sounds childish. And arrogant."

Jackson looked at him for a long time as if the words triggered some deep thought.

"Your turn," Killian said. "Why have you always hated the colonists? You never even met any."

"True. Although, unlike you, I did know that they were secretly still active on Earth, and what they were doing wasn't anything to benefit us." He shrugged. "Hate them? Yes, I suppose I do. Because when they left the Earth behind, they also left *me* behind. They trapped me in the same dull life that made you so restless. I wanted more. To *be* more! And it was their fault that I couldn't. Their fault that I could never aspire to be more than the so-called leader of a group of complainers making meaningless decisions."

"But they'd promised to return," Killian insisted. "There was a good chance that you'd live to see it; and as a leader, you might be given a chance to join their ranks in some way."

"Look at me. I'm an old man, and the world they made for me has taken my youth. What would they want me for? No, I knew there would never be a place for me among them.

"When the Keepers recruited me, I had a moment of joy, believing that there really might be a way to escape from the cage they put us in—only to find out that the colonists were still coming here to carry out their own selfish plans. Undermining any progress our own people might make. Keeping us all caged.

"And my cherished grandson was all but ready to worship at their feet."

"You could have told me the truth!"

"I tried, but as a Keeper, I couldn't give away what I knew. And you didn't want to hear the truth about these people who had become your gods."

"They're not *gods*. I never thought . . . ."

Except he had, more or less. He'd imagined superhuman beings with abilities that would be pure magic to his people. There was some truth to that. But he'd also expected godlike wisdom and goodness. In that belief, he couldn't have been more wrong.

His grandfather shook his head. "Now you've learned you can never be one of them, but you can't give up your dream entirely, so, what?—second best is having a Confederacy woman for your own."

Killian leapt to his feet.

"You take that back! You don't know Natira, or anything about our time together! At first, we were each other's worst enemy. We learned how wrong we were. Now we know better, and for the sake of us all, you'd better hope there are a lot more like her in the Confederacy!"

Jackson's eyes were wide. Killian would never strike him, but the force of the response had surprised him. He raised a hand.

"I apologize, Killian. I had no right to belittle your relationship. And I meant what I said to Natira—from what we've heard, she's someone very special. Maybe . . . maybe I've just forgotten what love is like. It's been a long time."

350

Slowly, Killian returned to his seat, but said nothing. He had never known his grandmother.

"She took her own life, your grandma." The words were so quiet Killian could barely hear them.

"No!"

"She went Starwalking. Young Lewis was in school most days and your father was less than a year old. Lanella had a difficult time fighting off sadness after giving birth. To keep her company, we were looking after her niece and nephew—twins, about twelve, whose parents had frozen in a fluke March storm when they were coming back from the artisans' village. Naturally, the twins were quiet and kept to themselves . . . had some trouble fitting in to our neighborhood. But we thought they'd get over it. Turned out they'd made friends with the wrong people—other youngsters who were just as disillusioned as they were—and they all made a pact to go . . . Starwalking."

His voice had become hoarse, and he cleared his throat.

Killian didn't speak. He'd known half a dozen young people who'd taken their lives that way, unable to find any meaning for their existence and unwilling to face an endless succession of days with nothing to look forward to. But such self-destruction was much less common among adults. He could never understand why the Depot, so smart in every other way, would provide a medicine supposed to relieve sadness and also offer a powerful sleep aid as well. Large doses of the combination were fatal, though apparently painless. In fact, a childhood friend of Killian's whose sister had survived a more timid dose had told of wonderful visions of travelling the cosmos, and a sense of utter peace. Such accounts had made Starwalking a tragic tradition that now was centuries old.

The sister had succeeded in her second try.

"The young people did what they did while on an outing to a beautiful clearing just outside the village, which Lanella had shown them because it had been a favorite childhood place of hers. When she heard the news, she never recovered, and a week later she took those same drugs herself."

The man's face was lined with pain as he raised his eyes to look into Killian's.

"I don't think I'd truly hated the colonists before that. But they took her from me, along with everything else." His voice sharpened. "And knowing about the wonders of their world makes ours seem so pathetic in comparison that our children can't face a life here. Especially our best and brightest. The Confederacy is a poison to our people even without their direct interference.

"Your generation has had fewer go Starwalking than most, because, like you, they dreamed the colonists would return and either welcome them with open arms as equals or remake our world with wondrous technology. Neither of those things is going to happen. So how long do you think it will be until we begin to lose all the most promising of *your* contemporaries? That's why I was always afraid for you. I knew you were setting yourself up for bitter disappointment, but I couldn't talk you out of it."

"I almost did go Starwalking once," Killian confirmed softly. "Summer was able to change my mind."

"I'd wondered about that."

Killian gave a snort. "If that's true, it didn't make you any more sympathetic. The hardline attitude you take, even with the ones you care about, I don't know how you ever made it onto the Elder Council let alone as Chief Elder for five terms."

"I see that I took the wrong approach with you. Maybe I cared too much."

Strangely, Killian could accept that. There'd never been any question that his grandfather had loved him. Only that one subject had been toxic to their relationship. Was it still?

That would probably depend on Killian himself.

# # #

Chung insisted on staying in the control room overnight, just in case Confederacy security hadn't been fooled and planned a surprise attack under cover of darkness. The others retired to the dormitory, but Natira gently led Killian to the base commander's quarters instead. No one made any comment.

352

After some tender lovemaking, Natira gently stroked his chest and said, "The arrival of the Keepers has changed your plans, hasn't it?"

"It's changed everything," he agreed. "Suddenly I find out that there are people of *my* world who understand technology, as well as the natural world, and are even trying to make us stand up for ourselves."

"You've stood taller since they got here. Talked more. *Thought* more. But what is it you're thinking?"

He sighed and pulled her close.

"We have to let all the people of the Earth know what's going on. The Confederacy's secret plans, but also the full extent of what they've done to us. And it can't wait—who knows how far their plans have progressed?"

"There's no way to find out, either."

"Yes, there may be a way. The Confederacy will probably work through the Elders—trick them first so they'll help persuade their own communities. If I can talk to Momoko Quarry and find out what Hind and others have been telling her . . ."

Natira sat up. "It'll take you weeks to get back to Borealis."

"Not by glider.

"Then I'll come with you."

"No. The Keepers need your help to figure out how to talk to all of the other Allocations. Not just leaders, but common people too. Maybe through the Depots. Pounding out secret underground messages won't work for this. You're an expert in telling large numbers of people what they need to know, and the Keepers can use that experience."

"I doubt if this base has any way to communicate with the Depots. The only thing I can think of would be a command ship, able to commandeer the near-Earth-orbit satellite network."

Killian jackknifed into a sitting position and stared off as if trying to read the answers he needed in the blanket of darkness. Then he suddenly took hold of her face and kissed her.

"I have an idea," he said, "and you're not going to like it at all."

"Huh. Then you'd better tell me every last detail. And be prepared to make it up to me with some very loving attention!"

45

The glider shot through the air at least three times faster than the one that had carried Killian and Natira from the cave. It was a newer design, but most of the difference in speed came from the half-hour of coaching that Yoan MacIntosh gave Killian before he took flight. He'd travelled faster on the shuttle to and from Telluria, but that offered nothing like this glider's incredible sensation of speed. Maneuvering the skeletal craft hundreds of meters above untamed forest was a constant challenge, but his responses to changes in wind direction and thermal updrafts were becoming more automatic, and his balance improved with each passing minute. The flight would take a few hours and the craft had a small degree of automated flight capability; but he knew that the more he could train his body to pilot the craft by reflex, the safer he'd be.

His plan had upset Natira even more than he'd expected.

"If they catch you, they will just kill you right away—save the trouble of a trial!" she'd declared, her beautiful face marred by blotches of heat.

"Not if they think they still need me to get to you."

"But even if they don't kill you, you'll have no chance of escape. No insider to help you."

"I'd like to think there are lots of people who'd want to help me."

"Borealans. As helpless before the Confederacy as you are." When he only shrugged, she blurted, "I have to come with you."

"Not a chance. For one thing, you'd stand out too much. But, more important, I need you here. Without you here, the plan fails."

They had made love afterward, but even that didn't relieve her agitation.

Now northern wilderness, prickly and inhospitable, stretched beneath him without a smooth place to land in sight. Fortunately, this time, the glider had an extra safety feature.

"We incorporated some of the little repulsion engines used in devices like Natira's lift belt," MacIntosh had told him. "They're not antigravity—they just repel most types of matter the way magnets repel other magnets' opposite poles, and the degree of repulsion is controllable. In an emergency you could lift the glider into the air when there's no convenient slope to launch it from. And it can soften your fall if something goes wrong. But the battery pack won't take that kind of drain more than a few times. Otherwise, Natira could use her belt to fly everywhere she wanted to go."

They'd launched from a steep grassy slope within half a kilometer of the base, but Killian had still needed some artificial lift to reach a rising air current above the trees. He'd been fortunate enough to catch a tailwind. Every little bit helped.

With the wind moving in the direction he wanted to go, it felt as if he was floating in still air with only an occasional breath of breeze to tug a wingtip upward or tease out his long hair. A few fluffy clouds seemed to keep pace, looking much closer than they really were, like guardian spirits watching over him. Once, he even saw an eagle *below* him, effortlessly riding invisible waves as the primary feathers of its mighty wings caressed the air like a musical instrument.

He would never forget his first sight of the Earth from space: a frosty blue globe aglitter with sun-sparks of incredible intensity. Barely real—certainly beyond touch. His view from the glider, on the other hand, left no doubt that he was part of the world he traversed. The river of air he rode was little different from the rivers of water he passed over, all overlaid elements of the same wondrous orb, like the layers of bone, organs, and skin of a living body.

Suspended between Earth and space in near-perfect silence, time almost stood still for him. His mind expanded to grasp past, present, and future as a true continuum; prior events in sharp focus led inexorably to his place right here, right now; and his course for the future began to resolve in his mind's eye....

A blare of sound nearly jolted him from his saddle as a triangular patch of the glider's nose flashed like fire.

Another new feature: proximity sensors. Killian hadn't expected them to trigger unless he was about to hit a cliff. But in this case, he wasn't approaching an obstacle.

Instead, two airborne objects were approaching him from the southeast.

A jittery holographic image appeared before his eyes.

There were two drones on a curved trajectory that would intersect his own just ahead. The image was grainy—obviously magnified many times—but he focused on some tubular shapes slung under the batlike craft.

Were those weapons?

A chill ran up his spine.

Could the drones' presence be a coincidence? His controls said that the glider's stealth mode was still active. The drones might just be following a circular search pattern for some reason unrelated to him.

Either way, it would be foolish to trust his invisibility too far. There might be other ways they could detect him, perhaps even by turbulence of the air disturbed by his passage.

When creatures of the wild were hunted, they knew better than to stay out in the open, and sought the nearest cover or a busy background where their natural camouflage would be effective.

Killian couldn't climb into the clouds. His only possible refuge was straight down, amid the forbidding terrain of the northland. Clenching his jaw, he shifted his weight forward and passed his hand over a control that reshaped the airfoil above his head, spoiling its lift. The craft quickly slid into a dive, a steep one. The instruments now showed the drones less than five minutes away. He grimaced as his stomach was left behind, and he rocked back to swing the nose up a little.

Nothing seemed changed at first, and then suddenly the trees charged toward him. Frantically, he re-curved the great wing; and as the glider levelled out, his feet jerked up in a reflex action. In fact, he was still ten meters or more above the treetops, but the nearness of those grasping branches made his speed seem doubled, and it was hard to breathe.

His neck itched fiercely, but he didn't dare look up to try to find the drones. The sensor readout told him that they were nearly overhead. Now would come the test. Would they be able to detect him amid the clutter of untamed forest? He desperately wanted to see what they were doing, but couldn't spare any attention from the task of keeping above the dark green spikes of spruce that rose before him like jagged javelins. Any loss of height and he'd be among those bristling spires before he could react.

Like that giant white pine straight ahead, ten meters taller than the spruce beside it!

He rolled to his right instinctively and the glider responded. The screech of a branch against the undercarriage brought his heart into his throat. But then he was clear and drawing great whooping breaths to feed his racing blood. However, the dodge had cost him height. Now there were more trees that just might be tall enough to reach him. He swayed and steered around them in near panic, helplessly aware that his erratic movements were much more likely to call attention to him if the drones could somehow penetrate his stealth screen.

Realization struck him like a fist: He'd gone too low. The layer of air just above the treetops was too still to give him lift.

In minutes, even less, he'd go down.

Was it time to use the emergency lift engines? They might just reduce the force of his collision enough to save him from broken bones or impalement on a branch, but the crash of the glider into the treetops at any speed was sure to be seen by the vigilant drones. Maybe they could even detect the energy expenditure of technology that resembled their own.

If he could only stay up long enough for them to pass him by.

Yes, they'd pulled ahead! They hadn't found him—might still be on nothing more than a routine patrol.

Breathing hard, he kept the glider aloft by pure force of will until finally he had no choice but to trigger the repulsion mechanism. The resiny tang of needle-covered spruce branches tugged at his nostrils and the sensor readout pulled at his eyes. The drones had moved well ahead, but he was still within visual range. He had to hold on.

A raven burst from a treetop and startled him badly, but he managed to keep his balance while the craft stabilized.

A branch scratched the underside. Another. Only seconds left.

And suddenly the power readout of the repulsion engines slid to zero.

Killian raised his arms to shield his face as the glider plunged downward.

Except he didn't hit.

In disbelief, he opened his eyes.

He was still airborne. In fact, the trees now looked to be fifty or sixty meters below him. How could that be?

As he felt the glider's airfoil twitch in a sudden updraft, he craned his neck to look behind.

And right behind him, a towering precipice blocked the sky. He'd just sailed off a gigantic cliff!

At its base was a high plateau—he and Natira had struggled over that same rising ground for what seemed like weeks. Here, the change in elevation was sudden, and it could not have come at a better time.

Had the drones caught his dramatic swoop from the clifftop? No, they were even farther away now, continuing a slowly curving path that made it look more and more as if they'd been on a routine flight.

He hadn't been seen. He was still free. He was still alive.

A painful shudder passed through his body. Then he shook the tension from his muscles, wiped sweaty palms on his pant legs, and resumed his grip on the controls, urging the glider to lift its nose and stretch out on the rising air.

Onward to Borealis.

46

MacIntosh had told him that at one time, satellites had ringed the Earth and enabled anyone to know exactly where he was on the globe, any time.

Those satellites were long gone, but Confederacy navigation systems were just as effective. Though Borealis wasn't programmed into the nav system of MacIntosh's glider, he'd been able to set a clear path for Killian, including a half dozen recognizable landmarks. As he sighted each one, Killian breathed a little easier.

His own memory supplied the location of a cleared field on the outskirts of the community where large outdoor events were held. Deepening dusk and mist from a nearby bog helped him land unseen, and he quickly folded and dragged the glider among the trees. There wasn't much hope that he could use the craft for a return journey from land that was mostly uphill, but he'd never really expected to leave that way anyway.

The walkways of Borealis were deserted—convenient for the sake of secrecy, but the emptiness and silence made him feel lonely. Part of him hoped for a familiar face.

Why were the paths so empty? Had Confederacy forces already begun to take people away? If so, he'd made a useless trip. The thought made him pick up his pace.

Momoko Quarry's hut was sparingly decorated. A finely crafted bronze casting of a many-pointed sun hung over the door. Impossible to mistake, especially since the last time he'd visited there had been the birth of a baby! He knocked lightly on the door before entering. A soft voice gave him permission.

The interior of the hut looked very different from his most recent memory of it. The bed had disappeared, presumably behind a pair of decorative sliding panels, which were closed. Elder Quarry herself sat just in front of the panels in a pool of light from a small Depot lamp that barely revealed the walls of the room. Enough to show that she was alone, though. Killian let out a tightly held breath. Saying nothing, he approached her and gave a respectful bow as she turned to him.

"Killian Morningcloud! A surprise guest. Or maybe not entirely a surprise. From what I hear, you've been a busy young man. Have you come to report on your adventures, plead for forgiveness, or perhaps . . . hold me hostage?" Her eyebrows rose with the final words.

"I would never do that!"

"So you say. But what about that Tellurian woman? The very one you embarrassed so badly on the day they returned. Don't tell me she forgave you so easily and came with you willingly."

Killian hadn't expected to be put on the defensive so quickly. But he did have a lot of explaining to do, and he accepted her gestured invitation to sit. He described his flight with Natira from Confederacy security forces as concisely as he could, leaving out any mention of the Keepers or his own family's involvement. Quarry didn't interrupt, not even to ask questions, until he was done. That surprised him too.

"A secret information archive, you say? How can you even know it's true—that it's not just someone's made-up story?"

"The place Natira found it convinced her of its authenticity. And Ambassador Hind has accused her of being a traitor just for looking into it. So, he *has* to know that it's genuine."

"An account claiming that the plagues were deliberately caused by the colonists. And there was a secret pact to keep the five families in power forever. And colonists have been coming to Earth all along, to ensure that our people never prospered or progressed. Yet now you say that the Confederacy needs us?"

"As slave labor!" Killian had never heard of slavery until Natira had explained it to him, but he was sure the elder would know what it meant. "And as soldiers in their fight to keep control of the outer colonies. They also want us out of the way so they can plunder Earth for metals and other resources again. Ruin it, just like before. They don't care about us or the planet, except as *things* they can use." He realized that he was sweating and tried to calm down. "I hoped that you could help me find out just how far they've been able to advance their plan, and maybe even come up with some ways to interfere with it. Or to at least warn the rest of the Allocations about what's being planned."

Quarry's eyes shone in the glow of the lamp, her face smooth and unconcerned.

Didn't she believe a word he'd said?

"You Killian, more than anyone, wanted the colonists to return to Earth. To end our isolation and make us part of their great, system-wide Confederacy. Isn't that what you've always dreamed of?"

"Yes! But that was before I knew what they'd really done to us. And before I overheard their plans."

"So, if you had the power to do so, would you just reject them now? Send them back where they came from? Doom the people of our Allocations to continue in lives without hope, without opportunity, real education . . . *medicine*?"

Killian swallowed. He couldn't deny the truth of her words. Was that really what he wanted?

He tried to change the subject.

"Please tell me . . . has the Confederacy been mobilizing? Have they brought more and more ships to Earth? Have they been talking to all of the Allocations together, filling people's heads with stories of work and wealth on the other colonies?"

"Assuredly." Quarry showed gleaming teeth in a beautiful smile. It was a smile that had made him fall a little in love with her, in spite of their difference in age. A smile that had made him trust her implicitly. "I've told people the same things for years as we waited for the colonists' return. You know I have. I told them to you. And you listened so very thoroughly. It's why I paid so much attention to you all these years. Because, when the time came, I knew that you would see that the colonists' return is the best thing that could happen to us. And you would be right in the forefront with me, ensuring that all these things came to pass."

He wanted so badly to deny what she was saying, but all he could think to reply was, "I know better now. The Confederacy will use us. Trick us. Betray you."

"Oh, I don't think so," she said lightly. "I've dealt with them for a long time." Her eyes shifted to something behind him just as he noticed a breath of cooler air on his neck.

In the doorway stood two Tellurian security people, taller than Killian with heavily muscled torsos and expressionless faces. He snapped his head back to Quarry in time to see the decorated panels behind her slide apart.

Between them stood Basu Hind.

Killian couldn't prevent an involuntary step backward.

"Our drones detected your glider with their mass sensors, but it suited our purposes to allow you to come here. There's no need to be afraid of me, Mr. Morningcloud. Or should I say *Citizen* Morningcloud? It could be that, you know. A full citizen of the Confederacy, including some special privileges that Elder Quarry can tell you about."

A wave of cold blood swept through Killian and nausea with it. His eyes sought Quarry's, expecting them to look away in shame or denial, but they met his gaze and held it. Her smile was without triumph or malice, only hopeful expectancy.

"You've known all along that the Confederacy has been coming to Earth," he breathed. "You've been helping them prepare for this."

364

She dipped her head in acknowledgment. "Preparing people like you. The smart ones. The ones who know better than to be satisfied with our pitiful lot in life. The ones who can be leaders of a new Earth." Her voice rose in pride with the last words. Hind gave a broad smile of his own.

"A new Earth indeed. With your people as full partners in the Confederacy. Benefitting from our technology. Eligible for a galaxy of opportunities."

Hind seemed to be trying just a little too hard with that speech, Killian thought; but the man showed no awareness of it. No doubt he felt he was speaking to a pair of simpletons. Did Quarry sense that? Yes, her eyes rolled a little at Killian, as if sharing a joke.

"Ambassador Hind isn't wrong," she said. "The change in our quality of life will be enormous. Most of all because our lives can have meaning again. Exciting new challenges to face. No more reason to feel hopeless. No more need to go *Starwalking*."

His eyes darted to hers again. Did she know about his grandmother? But that hardly mattered. Everyone in Borealis had lost friends and family to the endlessly tempting suicide.

Still, she certainly knew the words to tempt him. She'd known them for a long time.

"Elder Quarry has told me again and again that you were among her most promising protégés," Hind said. "Though you and I have had our . . . differences, she's convinced me. I'm willing to invite you to join our efforts and make your world the kind of paradise it should be."

"By spoiling the land again? The air? The water?"

Hind's face showed irritation, but he answered, "That doesn't have to happen anymore. We've lived for five hundred years in closed environments that have to be monitored and protected with extreme care. There's no need to ruin the Earth to get what we need."

Could it be true? That argument was logical, but how could anyone know that the vastness of a whole planet wouldn't make everyone forget the need for judicious stewardship? That was what had happened before. It was a rare person who could see an entire planet as an integral, indivisible whole, but that was exactly what was needed to avoid a repetition of the past. Killian was certain that Hind did not have that vision. Did Momoko Quarry? And were there more like her? Would they be enough?

Quarry had clearly been taken in, possibly for years, by Hind's charm and undeniable gift of persuasion. But so had Natira, and they were both incredibly smart. He still clung to the hope that Hind's 'spell' over them could be broken.

"Why so reluctant, Killian, if I may call you that?" Hind asked. "Is it the woman, Natira?" He obviously read an answer in Killian's face. "Of course, she's very desirable. Exceptionally beautiful and extraordinarily intelligent. One of my most promising protégés. It hurts me to see her so confused. I'd even blamed that on you—it's plain to see that you have a great deal of charisma yourself. But perhaps there was weakness in her that I never saw."

Killian bridled at the insult to the woman he loved, and Hind must have noticed.

"Maybe I've said it badly. Any of us can make mistakes when we don't know all the facts. Natira has always been highly motivated and sincere. But she's always had difficulty seeing what really does matter and what is less important. When sacrifices have to be made for the greater good, sometimes it may seem as if integrity has been compromised. Being a leader is not an easy task. Perhaps Elder Quarry is right, and you have the insight to see that hard choices must sometimes be made." He gave a smile that he probably meant to be companionable. "How long have you known Natira? A few weeks? Wouldn't you admit that she often appears . . . naive?"

Much as Killian wanted to deny it, he couldn't. He'd blamed it on a sheltered upbringing among a people who never knew real hardship. Yet it was one of the many things he loved about her. Maybe those feelings and his own inexperience had blinded him. He'd been unable to read the archive for himself. Was it possible that she'd jumped to the wrong conclusions? And if Natira could misconstrue the contents of the archive, then others easily could, too. That could explain Hind's eagerness to suppress it.

He cleared his throat. "Are you saying that there's no conspiracy to enslave Earth's people or draft them into military service?"

"What you overheard . . . let me just say that sometimes it's necessary to tell people what they want to hear." There was no indication that the man appreciated the irony of his words. "If the First Councilor of the Confederacy and some others want to believe that they're superior, sometimes it's best to let them believe that. But think about it. Recruiting *unwilling* soldiers and workers would only cause trouble for us. Will we need more workers? Of course we will, especially if we are to bring Earth fully into the Confederacy and raise your standard of living. But slaves? Certainly not!"

"You expect me to believe that you want nothing but the best for my people?"

"I don't expect you to believe that I do *everything* out of a pure selfless nobility! No one does! A fruitful and prosperous Earth will make my life better too, though my improvement will certainly not be as great as that for your family and friends. And especially for people like you and Elder Quarry who have the ability and the foresight to lead your people to a better way."

"You should remember, Killian," Quarry added, "the Confederacy will have to go to great expense and effort just to educate our people enough to make them productive workers. But they're willing to make that investment. And think of how much our people will benefit from those new skills alone!"

Uncertainty flowed through Killian's veins like fever. Was it possible that he and Natira had been so wrong? What about the Keepers? Had they misjudged the colonists for all these centuries?

And Mother Earth. Had Earth healed sufficiently to meet new demands upon her so her children could prosper? Or, at least, the two-legged ones.

"So, you're willing to forget my theft of medicine and escape from custody? What about Natira? You call her a traitor, a criminal. She's already been disavowed by her family, and lost her place in society, thanks to you."

"Thanks to her own actions," Hind said sternly, then his voice softened. "But it doesn't have to be that way. If she gives up the archive and keeps silent about it, everything can be as it was. She's been a highly respected and popular member of our Confederacy. Her Patriarch isn't eager to lose that. I'm sure that I'll be able to persuade him to forgive her and restore her status, if she cooperates."

As if Hind hadn't been the engineer of Natira's punishment himself. Killian suppressed a snort of disgust. Still, the ambassador's words confirmed what Ud Littlebear had said—Natira was too popular to be tried as a traitor without serious repercussions. It was all too likely that the Patriarch had made no public announcement about her and would be glad to let the whole series of events remain a secret. Just one of many.

There was so much to think about. He wished he had days to consider it all, free of the pressure he felt from Hind's and Quarry's presence. Not to mention the two guards who still stood behind him. But he wouldn't be given that time, he knew. Their offer was on the table, and he must give his answer: either to work with them, or to be taken away for punishment. Worse, Uncle Lewis would almost certainly be sent with him. What would happen to Aunt Regina? Or his mother?

"Are you thinking about your mother?" Quarry asked softly. Killian started, but she just smiled. "She'll be given the medicine she needs, of course. Not to ensure your cooperation, but because *everyone* who needs it will be *given* it. That's what citizenship means."

The words, spoken with such quiet conviction, struck him to the core. His mother healed. A world without the wasting disease, without Starwalking.

If he refused them, Natira would be kept safe for a time, but perhaps not for long. Grandfather and his fellow Keepers were badly outnumbered and outgunned, especially now that the Confederacy forces were operating openly on Earth and about to do so with the blessing of the planet's leaders, such as they were. For if Momoko Quarry had been enlisted to the cause, he had little doubt that there were many others who'd been similarly persuaded.

Hind seemed about to speak again but a gesture from Quarry made him stay silent. They let Killian think it over. At long last he raised his head.

"I want to be completely clear about this. Earth will become an equal member of the Confederacy, just like every other colony?"

"You have my word," said Hind.

Killian nodded.

"Then I'll take you to Natira."

SCOTT OVERTON

47

Natira felt terribly lonely once the Keepers had gone, but being without Killian was far worse. Helplessly wondering what had happened to him. Fearing for his life.

When she got her answer, it brought small comfort.

The huge ship appeared overhead with the first light of dawn, though not without warning. Win Chung had shown her how to read the control center's readouts, and she'd been alerted to the approach of the craft twenty minutes before it eased to a landing beside the base. Plenty of time to raise the defense shield. But she didn't.

Though it was many times larger than the shuttle that had first brought them to Borealis, she had no doubt whose ship it was. It was no surprise when Basu Hind followed two tall Tellurian guards out into the sunshine, but she gasped when he was joined by Momoko Quarry. And she felt both relieved and sick to her stomach when Quarry was closely followed by Killian.

She waited at the base entrance until Killian stepped to the door and said, "It's all right, Natira. We were wrong. You can let us in. No one's going to hurt us."

She did. There was never really any doubt that she would.

Killian could barely meet her eyes, but she knew that hurt showed in her own. After that she didn't want to look at him again. Instead, she turned to face Hind. It was so very strange to see her beloved mentor under those circumstances, to see

370

the handsome face that epitomized wisdom to her. The smile, the particular smile, that she'd thought he reserved for her alone.

"Hello, Natira. I first want to say that you're forgiven for what you've done. We all make mistakes. And I know that you only act with the best of intentions. You were misguided, that's all. Both you and *Citizen* Morningcloud."

At the title, her head snapped toward Killian, but he didn't look up. Instead, he cleared his throat and said, "Elder Quarry, this base has some amazing food supplies and other luxuries I'm sure you'll appreciate." And he led her out of the room. One of the two guards followed them while the other remained just outside the door. It occurred to Natira that Hind must feel fully confident to have so few protectors with him.

"So Killian isn't a prisoner?" It was obvious, but she needed to hear the words.

"No. Far from it. Killian has learned that you and he were mistaken. What's more, he understands that the Confederacy's interests are also in the best interests of his kind. He's going to join the Quarry woman and other Earth leaders in persuading their people to cooperate fully with us."

"*What!* To become willing slaves and laser fodder in a Tellurian conflict?"

"Of course not. I've given him my word that Earth is to become a full and equal partner in the Confederacy."

Her mouth fell open.

"I don't believe you!"

"But *he* does." Hind gave a slight shrug, then indicated a chair with his hand while he seated himself in another. Natira wanted to refuse, but it would be a hollow protest. She sat, and he continued. "Are any of the other colonies truly equal to Telluria? There's even a natural hierarchy among the five Tellurian habitats themselves, but we must speak the language of equality because it's expected, and it keeps things running smoothly."

He reached out a hand, and for a revolting moment she thought he was going to pat her knee; but instead he sliced the air to show a flat surface.

"There is partnership, but partnership does not necessarily mean equal. Each party brings what they can offer. Would it be possible for the Earth to be equal partners with us? Of course not. It would take a generation and more for us to even provide most Earth dwellers with enough education to use the simplest of our technologies. You mustn't judge these people by your experience with Killian Morningcloud. He's an exception with a sharp mind and a thirst for knowledge—not that it does him any good." He gave a sad smile, as if he felt pity.

"You see, intelligence has actually been bred out of them. For centuries. Natural selection, truly. The brightest and most promising commit suicide rather than be trapped in such a dull life." The tone of his voice reflected none of the horror of his words. To him, it was a simple fact. Natira thought about the Keepers she'd met, all clearly intelligent and perceptive people. She could only hope they'd been wise enough to get well clear of the base before Hind's ship had arrived.

Her lips thinned. "You can hardly call it natural when Tellurian forces have been coming here all this time to make sure they didn't progress. Stayed trapped in lives without hope. What did you do? Poison the Depot food?"

"There's no need to provoke me, my dear. All that was required was to discourage the ones who tried to be independent. Destroy a few boats. Spread rumors about people getting sick from eating wild fish and game. Shut down some Depots for a few days to punish settlements where hunters of wild animals were tolerated. Peer pressure took care of the rest." He leaned forward. "What you fail to understand is that most people aren't interested in such things as *progress* for their people. Not even Tellurians. They want security above all—a Depot that may suddenly refuse to provide sustenance is a very powerful incentive to keep their neighbors in line—and they want comfort when they can get it, all with as little effort as possible."

Natira thought about Lewis and Regina living off the land. Either they were especially cautious or Confederacy enforcers had become slack. Maybe just preoccupied with other tasks, like stockpiling weapons.

As if reading her thoughts, Hind added, "As the years passed, less and less intervention was required. The humans of Earth became docile and stupid—like sheep. I often wonder if they haven't devolved into a lesser species by now. Even their best, like the Quarry woman, are easily deceived by a few simple half-truths."

Natira wanted to ask if Hind was proud of lying to such people, but the answer was readily apparent. Instead, she said, "You deceive our people, too. There are things in the data archive that our citizens have a right to know."

"Such as?"

"That our ancestors didn't create the Allocations and Depots to help Earth people, but to cripple them. And then actually sent the *plagues* to drive the ones we left behind from their homes in the cities to the Allocations in order to make them dependent!"

Hind's eyelids were half closed. "Has it made your life better to know these things? No? Then why do you imagine that any of our citizens would want to know them? It's ancient history—*we* didn't do it."

"But you still support the secret pact that keeps the five families in power. A mockery of what democratic government is supposed to be. No better than the hereditary dictatorships of primitive times!" She felt the heat in her face and was embarrassed by her inability to stay calm.

"They called them monarchies, and they often worked quite well, because the kings and emperors had to rule through chosen representatives. Bureaucrats. Besides," he smiled and raised his arms in an expressive shrug, "you know better than most that our five families are scarcely 'families' at all, in the sense of genetic connections. It's more accurate to think of them as *organizations* that compete for the very best of each new generation, guaranteeing that government *governs* through the most capable people of our society. As it should be. And the occasional transfer of power from one family to another ensures that established ways of doing things don't become too rigid—changes of style and approach keep our society vibrant and progressive."

"*Progressive?* The only progress we've made in centuries has been to make our lives more comfortable, with ever-fancier toys." As she said the words, she was aware that her own eyes had been closed to that as much as anyone's until her experiences on Earth.

"There's nothing wrong with comfort and security."

A sudden understanding brought a sour taste to her mouth. "Telluria Quinta isn't really being made into an interstellar colony ship, is it?"

He shook his head. "Do you think humankind is better off suffering hardship for the sake of nebulous goals that offer no benefits? Like exploring star systems too far away to matter to anyone? Of course not. But we do have need for a very large ship to transport great numbers of Earth . . . recruits to the outer reaches of the solar system." He smiled, but it was met with a disgusted scowl, and his own eyes narrowed. "You surprise me, Natira. I'd always thought of you as practical, at least."

His words stung. And it irritated her that he had an answer for everything.

"So, if the archive is only ancient history, as you say, why are you so determined to keep it a secret?"

"It would benefit no one to spread that information, but it would make some citizens unhappy. Maybe a few would even be loudly disruptive, an impediment to smooth government, that's all."

"But you still want me to surrender my Synappt with the copy of the archive. What new threats are you offering?"

"No threats at all. At first, I was very upset that you'd fallen in with one of those 'noble savages' you romanticized so much, and I'll admit that I overreacted. But now that I see the two of you, and how obviously mismatched you are, I feel sure that reasoned persuasion will be enough to convince you. You're still a Tellurian. You can never be like him. I know you still want what's best for your people."

She swallowed hard.

"Tricking the Earth people into serving us and fighting—dying—for us is what's best for my people?"

Hind sat back and folded his hands in his lap as if pondering how much to say. Then his lips pursed, and he spoke in a quieter voice.

"The general population hasn't been told the true state of affairs with the outer colonies. You know that there's some disaffection among them. There have always been a few who agitated for independence from the Confederacy. But now there's a powerful wave of discontent. There were disease outbreaks on some colony worlds and the central government was accused of not responding quickly enough. Food shortages also occurred, and malcontents stirred up bitter feelings with exaggerated stories of Tellurian excess. And, unfortunately, there's been an unusually high number of fatal accidents at outer world mining and processing facilities, triggering accusations that the government is stingy and letting equipment fall into disrepair."

"How much truth is there to these accusations?"

For the first time, weariness showed in his eyes. "Who can say? It's not my field. But I do know that some colonies have begun to reduce their exports to Telluria, including material and manufactured parts critical to our security forces. We are becoming vulnerable at a time when we can least afford to be vulnerable." He turned his palms up. "You must understand. We need those resources; and though we still have firm control on the Moon, its range of ores is very limited. The only other place to get the ores we need is from Earth. And to do so, we need workers. Manual labor. Tellurians aren't suited to be miners and smelters."

"What about robotic equipment?"

"You've lived in Telluria all your life. How much automated machinery have you ever seen, except service robots of one kind or another? It's all confined to the processing facilities that refresh our air, water, and soil—

highly specialized, and there is none to spare. It's the outer colonies that have all the machinery."

"I never noticed any shortages."

"You wouldn't. Yet. But it's coming. Things will get very much worse; and by the time they do, we *must* have Earth facilities up and running with Earth labor. If not, we'll have to move against the outer worlds in force, and that will be bloody. No matter what, their cries for independence have grown too strong. Some of the colonies will try to break away, and that will mean *war*. Civil war. Can you picture it? Without new battalions of soldiers, the central government will have to redirect existing security forces to the battles, leaving other colonies unsecured. Our orderly Confederacy will dissolve into chaos—every colony for itself. Bloodshed and destruction throughout the solar system!"

Hind was more agitated than she'd ever seen him. For once, his carefully calculated demeanor had given way to real emotion. He was genuinely afraid. It shocked her.

He reached his hands out, almost grasping hers.

"You have the power to reduce that bloodshed. Perhaps save thousands of lives. Millions."

"By helping you suppress the archive and keeping my mouth shut?"

"Yes! By helping to keep the Earth on our side. You know that the contents of that archive won't make any difference to the citizens of Telluria, but they might inspire resistance among the primitive people here who just aren't capable of comprehending the reasons for what happened."

She flinched at his callous assessment, picturing not only Killian but the members of his family, Jackson Ash and the other Keepers, even Momoko Quarry, none of whom matched Hind's dismissive description. But she couldn't refute his assessment of the danger to the Confederacy.

If she threw in her lot with Hind, it would be a betrayal of Killian and all his people; and, sooner or later, he would know the choice she'd made. Yet, if she thwarted Hind's plans for the Earth, she'd cause great suffering among Tellurians. Was she capable of betraying her own kind?

"Will you throw away everything you've ever known? Every friend, every family member . . . our very way of life?" Hind's voice was barely above a whisper.

Just then Killian and Momoko Quarry stepped back into the room.

Killian looked at her. His face was cold.

Natira turned back to Hind.

"I'll give you the archive."

# # #

Natira had hidden her Synappt in a food container among hundreds of identical containers in the storage lockers.

Hind nodded at his guards and immediately walked toward the exit, holding the processor like a tray of jewels. Natira, Killian, and Quarry followed him. In silence, they boarded the Tellurian spacecraft, Hind unmistakably satisfied with himself, and Quarry wearing a gentle smile.

If you only knew . . . Natira thought. She didn't speak to Killian, and he made no effort to meet her gaze.

Once they were in the ship's main control room, Hind signaled to the pilot and seated himself in the center chair, which was slightly raised, reserved for the captain. There didn't appear to be one. Hind passed the Synappt from hand to hand, while the spacecraft rose slowly and quietly into the air. External sensors projected a complete sphere of the exterior throughout the control center, and a quick glance at Killian showed that the view made him uncomfortable. It didn't bother Natira, but she was puzzled that the craft lifted about three hundred meters straight into the air and stayed there, suspended above the base.

"I don't know if you've been told everything that's in the archive," Natira said to Hind. "I suspect not, because some of it clearly shows you've been betrayed."

"The Confederacy?"

"No, you, personally."

He looked startled, but then smiled and wagged a finger at her.

"Well, I suppose we'll find out soon enough, won't we? First, I'd like to know what happened to your Keeper friends?"

As she tried desperately to keep any reaction from her face, Hind laughed.

"While we were inside the base some of my people ran a scan of the surroundings. They found the gliders. Six of them. Counting the one Killian took to Borealis, I'd guess you've had seven visitors very recently. You see, the gliders transmit a short-range ID code, not only making it easy to find them but also to match them with gliders we've suspected were stolen by the Keepers. So where have your friends gone? Did they scatter into the forest when you found out we were coming?"

"I . . . I don't know where they went. They left two days ago."

"Without their gliders? Just hiked off into the wild? I don't think so." He smirked. "Last chance."

She attempted a convincing shrug but said nothing. Hind shook his head in mock sadness then flicked a hand signal to the pilot.

The room lit with a blinding flash of white light, but the amorphous afterimages came in nearly every color. Before they'd completely faded from her eyes, Natira could already see what the searing light had done.

The base was gone, and so was at least a square kilometer of forest, replaced by a blackened crust partly obscured by the rising smoke of a new forest fire.

She collapsed into a chair, choking back a sob.

Killian slumped heavily on a railing as if his knees couldn't support him. Natira was afraid his shock would betray him into saying something about the cold-blooded murder of his grandfather. Revealing a family connection to the Keepers would doom his uncle Lewis and possibly the rest too. But he seemed to understand the danger. His eyes blazed with hatred for Hind, who was looking toward Natira and didn't notice. Quarry did, but revulsion battled with shame on her own face.

"People like that do not make good friends, my dear." Hind seemed to find the event amusing. "They are altogether too good at making a nuisance of themselves. And they know too much, though I daresay they didn't know the capabilities of this new ship design.

No one else in the room could speak. Even the guards standing behind them looked pale.

"Now, Natira," Hind continued. "Let's see if you're telling the truth. The ship's brain can easily connect with such a basic processor and search for any mention of me." He touched the slim case in several places as he spoke and made gestures in the air. "As I thought. No mention of my name."

"No, not in the original entries. It's the coded addendum that mentions you, and my Synappt is programmed with the code-breaking algorithm. The command word to activate it is . . . *Killian*." She flicked an embarrassed glance toward him, but it wasn't returned. Hind gave a sour chuckle and entered the command.

No one was prepared when the ship dropped from the sky like a stone

SCOTT OVERTON

48

The air vibrated with noise: the wails of five different sirens, shouting voices, groans of pain.

It was a miracle that none of them were dead. Emergency lift engines had fired, triggered by the sudden descent, but the craft had been too low to the ground for them to provide full cushioning.

Sparks snapped loudly in several directions but smoke and vapor hid them. Dimly, Natira could make out the silhouette of their pilot trying to access a wall panel marked *Emergency*, but the ship itself had automatically sprayed a dense gas to suppress fire, then activated a powerful venting system. The air was already beginning to clear.

Natira's eyes searched for Killian first. He'd just regained his feet and was trying to help Momoko Quarry stand up, but she collapsed again in obvious pain.

Hind was still down. His face was pale with disbelief, his eyes transfixed by Natira's Synappt.

Both guards were down, one flat on his back moaning, the other having trouble staying on his knees. Natira began to move, but Killian was quicker, snatching the arm-guns from both guards and handing one of them to her.

"She's crippled," the pilot cried, and at first Natira thought he was talking about Quarry. "The ship is crippled! None of the controls respond and the drive system is completely

380

dead." He turned an accusing glare on Natira. "What did you do?"

"It was the archive. Wasn't it?" Hind muttered. "Somehow, she provided it with a trojan command to infiltrate the ship's systems and shut them down. Although killing the drive of a ship in mid-air isn't a smart thing to do."

Natira thought about denying it. Instead, she said, "The drive . . . that wasn't supposed to happen." She and Killian looked at each other and she shrugged in annoyance. Killian lifted Quarry and put her in a chair. She probably needed medical attention for her leg, but she wasn't bleeding and it would have to wait.

"I should have wondered why you were provoking me to look into the archive right away." Hind said sourly. "It appears I underestimated you a little."

"You underestimated the people you just killed," Killian snarled. "Now they have some revenge."

Momoko Quarry looked at Killian in astonishment.

"This was your plan all along?" she rasped. "To lure us here and cripple the ship? You knew what Hind and I would offer you?"

"Not at all. I never suspected that you would turn your back on your own people. This was the plan for if I got caught. I was going to make a bargain: I'd lead Hind to Natira in return for some leniency in my punishment."

Quarry snorted. "You're not the kind of man who betrays a woman to save himself."

"That was the weak link in the plan."

"But why, Natira?" Hind groaned. "Have you really become a traitor to your own people?"

"You talk a lot, *Ambassador*, but your words are entirely self-serving. Maybe you even fool yourself.

"You aren't interested in saving lives. All you want to save is the *Tellurian way of life*. And that way of life failed any ethical test long ago. Long before our ancestors left a ravaged Earth to a dying population. It's been a failure ever since some men and women convinced themselves they were better than others, and so, entitled to more."

Hind looked stunned. He seemed unable to believe that his adoring protégé could speak to him that way. His silver words had lost their power.

"Sorry I couldn't warn you about the way things went," Killian said to Natira.

"You must have been very convincing."

"Not really. He just thinks he can persuade anyone of anything. All I had to do was to let him think he's right."

Killian looked at Quarry, then back to Natira. "What did he tell you—did he claim that Earth was going to be an equal partner in the Confederacy?"

She shook her head and directed her answer to Quarry. "He said Elder Quarry was easily deceived, but your people aren't capable of being equal partners because you've become a subspecies of humanity."

Quarry turned her face away, visibly deflated.

"What now?" Natira asked. "Are you still going to follow through with the plan? If Elder Quarry was fooled . . . ."

"Most of the planet's other leaders probably have been too. But we should at least try to reach them. Maybe we'll even get some help from some of them." He looked down at the disconsolate woman beside him. "Except first we need to know what hasn't been broken on this ship."

While Natira kept her weapon raised and her eyes focused on Hind and the guards, Killian pointed his arm-gun at the pilot.

"You! Tell me what works and what doesn't. And it better be the truth. The people this madman just killed down there were friends of mine. Do you think I'd hesitate to kill any one of you?"

Killian's face was so utterly devoid of expression, it made Natira shudder. The pilot shook his head, plainly terrified, and answered in detail.

According to the ship's central computer, the drive system, damaged by the impact, could not be repaired without new parts and specialized lifting equipment—it had borne the brunt of the craft's fall. Yet the fusion power plant appeared to be functioning perfectly. It was a new design, the pilot babbled, with tremendous power for attack and defense, as they'd seen from the use of the craft's main weapon.

Air, water, heating, and cooling systems were all functional, but the integrity of the hull had been badly compromised. A death sentence if they'd been in space.

Ship security had failed. In fact, the doors were inoperative, otherwise four more crew would have stormed the control room by then—they were probably just outside it, examining their options.

"Only four?" Killian asked. "I'd have thought a ship this size would need a lot more. And carry armed troops."

"Uh . . . Ambassador Hind left those in Borealis to link up with the forces already there. A large crew isn't needed because the ship is almost fully automated." The pilot darted a guilty look at Hind, but the ambassador only sat on the floor with arms around his knees and eyes closed, as if he could shut out the reality of what was happening.

The communications equipment didn't indicate any malfunctions, to Killian's obvious relief. He reminded everyone that any attempt to signal other Tellurians would be punished instantly. He didn't bother to spell out the punishment.

Suddenly there were loud noises from beyond the door: shouts, and what sounded like weapons-fire followed by three hard thumps. In the stillness that followed, Natira thought she could hear her own heart.

Everyone instantly turned toward the door, and she gasped as it began to open. Not smoothly—it wasn't the work of machinery. With a jerk, it opened a final few centimeters, stuck, and then a voice called through.

"Don't shoot! We're the good guys!"

Natira gasped.

"*MacIntosh?* Is that you?" Killian motioned the guards well clear of the door and, taking a grip on the door edge, with a grunt helped slide it two-thirds of the way open.

Six Keepers squeezed into the room while Leeyum Frost remained outside with a weapon pointed at several still figures on the floor. All the newcomers carried weapons, which they aimed threateningly at Hind and his people. Killian embraced each in turn, with an extra-long hug for his grandfather. Natira slumped against a console.

"We thought you were dead," she said.

"Not yet," Ud Littlebear answered. "Win had the idea that we should hide in the shaft of the geo-conduit a few hundred meters beneath the base. None of us wanted to because it was cramped and cold, but it seems she was right."

Chung just grinned.

Jackson Ash gave a sigh of disappointment as he recognized a familiar face. "Elder Quarry, I'm very sad to find you here. It appears that you're a prisoner, and I'd have preferred that it wasn't my side that had to do it."

"She was tricked by Hind," Killian said. "Repeatedly, over many years. It's very easy to accept a lie you really want to be true."

She surprised them with a sad smile. "You give me too much credit, Killian. I'm sorry to disappoint you. My heart told me I shouldn't trust Hind. But . . . I was envious of their power and wealth, and I knew that's what he was offering. You think I'm strong and wise, but I can be as weak and blind as anyone."

Her head slumped and she said no more.

It pained Killian to hear the woman he'd idolized confess to such contemptible motives. Yet hadn't he hoped for much the same from the return of the colonists? A means to lift himself from the squalor and shame of his Allocation life? He had no right to judge her.

He cleared his throat and reported on the spacecraft's condition. Ret Habbard was especially disappointed that it wouldn't be flying anywhere, but the undamaged communications system was what mattered the most.

"So we should be able to link up with the NEO satellites and transmit to the Depots all over the planet?" Habbard turned to the pilot for confirmation. Some of the man's fear must have eased and his reply was surly.

"No. Multiple attempts to use the satellite network by an unauthorized source trigger a shutdown for twenty-four Earth hours. You can't use it."

"How will it know that we're unauthorized?"

"Because you don't have current codes—they change every twelve hours."

"But I'm betting you have them," Killian said." He lowered the aim of his arm-gun. "I'm also willing to bet that you'd rather not go through the rest of your life with only one foot."

The man blanched. He told them the codes.

After that, they moved Hind, his guards, and the ship's crew to a small room at the rear of the craft and confined them there. The locks didn't work, but the venomous looks on the faces of Frost and Grum as they stationed themselves at the door were more effective than any lock.

Out of habitual respect and in deference to her injury, the others allowed Momoko Quarry to remain in the control room where they began to prepare a counteroffensive.

"Once we do this, Confederacy security will come down on us hard," Littlebear said.

"How much warning will we get?" Killian asked. "Could we improve it by sending out drones? I was told the ship has some."

Win Chung rubbed her hands together and went off to find, program, and launch a pair of drones to patrol north and south.

The rest of them decided that the first step in the plan should be to use the Depots to announce an alert about a forthcoming transmission of great importance to the people of Earth. A third of the planet's population would be asleep at any given time, but a scheduled repetition ought to reach them.

Reassured that the Depots' sole use of the NorthAm language had made it a universally accepted trade-language, Natira began the transmission by introducing herself as a video presenter from the Confederacy. The hope was that Confederacy troops would know her by reputation, and her presence would lull them into letting the program proceed without interference. Most likely, only local forces had been informed about her involvement in Killian's escape. Her professional delivery would also help to convince viewers that the words they were about to hear were, indeed, official.

After stressing the critical importance of the message, she gave a brief summary of history from the time of the Divide and the Exodus. Then she introduced Killian, and the two of them began to reveal the elements of the story that the people of Earth had never heard. Killian was stiff at first, but as his anger grew, it made him more forceful and convincing. Finally, Jackson Ash joined in, representing the planet's elders, and the three of them explained about the new conspiracy: the plan to force the people of Earth into indentured labor for the Confederacy, and mandatory service as soldiers. Footage from Natira's camera of the secret Earth bases with their stores of weapons provided evidence to support his words.

By then Habbard had worked out how to access views from cameras at the Depots, so they were able to watch a scrolling display of the reactions of people all over the world.

The broadcast caused confusion, of course; but there was also widespread disbelief. After spending the past weeks celebrating the return of the colonists and dreaming about wonders to come, the scattered populations of the Allocations couldn't accept that their greatest hopes had suddenly been replaced by their worst fears.

Clusters of people began chanting denials. "Not true!" "Stop the lies!" "Confeds are our friends!" And in some places, they drowned out the transmission entirely as Natira, Killian, and Jackson calmly repeated their declarations.

Then they were taken by surprise when Momoko Quarry asked if she could speak. After a moment's hesitation, Killian nodded.

"My name is Momoko Quarry. I am chief Elder of the Allocation of Borealis and I am one of your enemies because I have cooperated with the Confederacy for several years. You will find that many of your leaders have done the same. I know, because I've conspired with them. Ask them—you'll see. Most aren't very good liars.

"Everything you've been told today is the truth, and I am deeply ashamed of my part in it. Please believe me, the Confederacy has told you only lies since their arrival. They do have the means to provide a better life for you and your families. However, they have no intention of doing so. They are not your friends."

With her words, support for the deniers began to falter; and after some jostling and outright fights, their voices were heard less and less.

Unfortunately, audiences in most settlements stood listlessly, some weeping dejectedly. Where Natira and the others had hoped to stir up righteous anger, they saw only bitter disappointment and pervasive hopelessness.

Killian stepped forward again.

"My brothers and sisters of Earth. We have been betrayed, but *not by the citizens of the Confederacy*. It is only their leaders who have betrayed us—the wealthy and the powerful. This horrific plan for the Earth is a conspiracy of a few. Telluria's everyday citizens will soon learn of this conspiracy, and we know that they will not tolerate it.

"*Do not give up hope.* The ones who have deceived you do not speak for all. You must resist their attempts to recruit you! And simply by refusing to cooperate, we can stop their depraved plans. But you must not give yourself to hate or to violence. That is not our way. Their plan was to conquer us by trickery, but now that we know the truth we will not *be* conquered! Their conspiracy will fail. The good people of the Confederacy—who are still our brothers and sisters—will prevail. Those of us who have told you these truths will continue to shine a light on the wrongs of the selfish few.

"We will speak to you again. Until then, take heart, and know that we are all children of Mother Earth, and *we are strong!*" He raised his muscular arms into the air and Habbard ended the transmission.

Natira stared at her man in amazement.

He looked at her and his expression turned sheepish.

"I got carried away."

"You were great. Just what was needed. We couldn't expect people to absorb all of this right away. Remember, we didn't want to believe it either, and we went looking for it."

"But you saw how most people reacted," Jackson said. "The seed has been planted. In fact, I think almost everyone has secretly feared all along that the return of the colonists wouldn't bring a new golden age. Gradually the truth will sink in." He sighed. "Even so, I don't think we should expect people to do anything forceful about it. We've become too complacent, and too dependent. From dreams of new lives of abundance, they'll begin to fear that the little they have now will be taken away. That if they don't cooperate with the Confederacy, the Depots will shut down. It's happened before."

"And that shutdown created strong peer pressure against anyone who broke the colonists' rules," Natira said. "Hind told me."

"I'm sure that's what the conspirators planned to do to get their way," Killian agreed. "So, what can we do about that?"

"Well, first we do what we promised—let the everyday citizens of Telluria and the colonies know what really happened centuries ago, and the criminal actions being taken now. That phase is up to me." Natira leaned close to Habbard and they went over what she needed. Time was pressing. By now, the Confederacy leadership had to know about their transmission and be developing measures to counteract it.

Habbard helped Natira reach her lifelong friend Serena Kelvin, assistant to the head of SolSys Control, the center coordinating space traffic throughout the colonies. Then they tapped into a secure and private back channel CCC journalists used to communicate directly with their boss, Roja Manno. Although Serena could reach a vast network of influential people, only Confederacy Central Communications could reach everyone. Manno couldn't get involved with Natira overtly without sacrificing his own career, but advance notice would prepare him to run with the full story once the news from Earth achieved momentum.

388

Seeing her boss's familiar face in the viewer gave Natira comfort, but it was clear that he felt far from comfortable himself. Consternation deepened the lines in his face, and he ran his hands through his scruff of hair.

"Natira, do you . . . do you know what you're saying? I mean . . . I'm sure you've been through a horrible ordeal, stranded on Earth and on the run."

"I would give almost anything to be wrong, but I'm not. I've collected compelling evidence, including footage from my camera and the location of the archive in the Central Network." She signalled to Habbard. "You should be receiving my data capsule now. Honestly, Roja, it'll make you sick to watch it; but we can't let the lies go on any longer."

"A conspiracy. Patriarch Celestia and Basu Hind, you say?"

"Probably others, too, but we don't have proof of that. Yet."

He gave a grunt of disgust. "Never trust somebody with a practised smile and perfect hair."

Natira gave her own smile of affection and said goodbye.

Habbard had fidgeted nervously as the conversations stretched on and was visibly relieved when Natira finished. As quickly as he could, he closed the connection to the satellite network, then attempted to reopen the link using random ID numbers. After three tries, the network shut him out—along with everyone else. The Tellurian government would be able to reactivate it, but that would take time. Until then, they'd be unable to use the Allocation Depots to announce any messages of their own. It was a ridiculous vulnerability in such a network, but the Confederacy had never expected technological mischief from Earth.

So far there was no sign of any Confederacy reaction to the first transmission, but it couldn't be much longer in coming. Chung had returned to report that her drones were on a high patrol and could spot any activity between surface and sky over much of the continent.

"Will Confederacy security forces already here be able to contact their government without the satellites?" asked Killian.

"Most likely," Chung answered. "They'll be able to use laser comms when Telluria's above the horizon, but their radio signals would probably get through the rest of the time, too. Weak, but workable."

"What about us?"

"Now that you mention it, I'll bet this ship could get a laser signal to Mars or even the outer colonies when we have line of sight." Her face lit with excitement.

After some discussion, they recorded a new message directed at the leaderships of the colonies beyond Earth's orbit. They couldn't predict what the reaction would be— probably no more than verbal support, if that— but it didn't hurt to keep any potential allies informed when you declared war.

Was that what they'd done? Natira wondered. Certainly, they'd attacked whoever was behind the conspiracy to enslave Earth, presumably the Tellurian leadership. But they hadn't attacked the Confederacy itself, and they'd taken no destructive action except to cripple Hind's ship. That could result in punishment for the perpetrators, but surely no retaliation against anyone else. And it remained to be seen whether the inhabitants of Earth would follow their lead to resist any Confederacy overtures.

That night they transmitted the recorded messages to Mars, as well as to the inhabited moons of Jupiter and Saturn, and requested that those transmissions be forwarded to the remaining colonies, especially colonies in the asteroid belt. Then they tried to rest, curled in chairs or on the floor of the control room, though without much success.

It was just before dawn when the ship's attack warnings sounded.

"The drones are detecting incoming ships headed right for us!" Chung shouted.

"How many?"

"Four! Two from orbit and two from the southwest."

"I told you they'd come down hard," Littlebear muttered. "And it might mean that the satellite network is back up. If it is, the ships will use it to coordinate their attack with the Confederacy's security command."

"Can we lock up the network again?" asked Killian.

Habbard shook his head. "If they haven't blocked that loophole by now, they'd have to be idiots."

"I hadn't expected them to attack so soon," Jackson admitted. "I figured they'd threaten us first, but I suppose they hoped to surprise us." He massaged his chin. "Are we helpless?"

"Oh, we can fire back!" Frost growled, MacIntosh having relieved him on guard duty. "In fact, we have to fire first if we're to have any chance."

"No," Killian barked. "We are not going to be the first to kill. We're not helpless. The pilot boasted to me about the mammoth power plant this ship can put to use, including for defense." He looked at Natira.

"A defense shield!"

She and Chung hurried to the controls.

"They might not attack at all," Jackson offered. He began to pace, rubbing his hands together as if washing them. "Or at least not right away, if they expect their presence alone will convince us to surrender first. After all, we have their Earth ambassador and his crew. Would they be willing to sacrifice the famous Basu Hind?"

The first bolt of energy struck the tail of the craft and the shock wave knocked them all off their feet. Alarms clamored.

"I guess that's your answer!" Littlebear shouted over the noise. "They attacked the stern to keep us from going anywhere, not knowing the drive was already wrecked. But I wouldn't count on that being their last shot."

"The defense shield is up!" Chung crowed, just before piercing light almost blinded them.

"Ouch! I'll dial down the outside view!" she said. "Looks like the fireworks have just begun."

Loud voices came from the doorway. Yoan MacIntosh held a struggling Basu Hind.

"It's a mistake!" Hind cried. "They must not know I'm here!"

There was another flash of lightning and the floor bounced but no new alarms sounded.

"He insists he can call them off," MacIntosh said. "Do we risk it?"

Killian gave a dark laugh. "How could he make it worse? Order them to kill us?" He nodded to Habbard to set up the signal.

"This is Basu Hind, Confederacy Ambassador to Earth. Whoever is in command of this attack, I order you to stop! This is my ship! You are attacking my ship with myself and my crew aboard. I am Ambassador to Earth. Cease your attack at once!" His voice was pitched higher than usual, but he'd still managed to infuse it with authority.

A double blast of searing white shook the spacecraft. Grass and scrub surrounding the vessel was burning from the diversion of deadly energy along the shield. In Killian's mind he could smell the smoke.

Hind was apoplectic. "Stop firing! I command you to stop this unauthorized attack!"

Habbard wearily pulled the man toward the door, ignoring his shouts and struggles.

"It appears that the Prime Councilor has cut you loose, *Citizen* Hind," Natira said. Her face was full of righteous anger, but tempered with regret.

"Wait!" Hind said. "I'm not going to let that bastard do this to me! Let me try again. I promise you won't regret it."

They all looked at Killian, though he didn't know why these decisions should be up to him. He scrutinized Hind's face and then nodded.

"This is Basu Hind. It may be that those of you in the attacking force are following orders that say that I am an impostor, not the real ambassador. In that case, I will have no choice but to reveal secret information about certain members of the government to prove my identity. I hope the threat of this disclosure alone will prove I am who I say, and end this attack. Stop your attack and verify what I say, because if you continue your fire, I will release the information on the broadest possible range of communication. I will give you twenty minutes." He closed his mouth with a fierce glint in his eyes.

"Clever," Frost sneered. "But couldn't you have made it five minutes?"

Hind shot him a killing look. Whether or not the message had reached whoever it was intended for, the firing stopped. At the very least, Killian thought, the captains of the attacking ships would pause long enough to give their commanders a chance to respond. It would not do to destroy a target only to be given the order to stand down, too late. Captains who did that would be the next scapegoats.

Chung sang out, "This lull gives us an opportunity. If we're willing to risk it, I can drop the shield for a second and send a microburst transmission in broad beam, telling whoever picks it up just what's happening to us and what we're up against. It's impossible to get a signal out while the shield is taking fire."

"Could you reach the other colonies?"

"Some of them, maybe. They're still above the horizon."

Natira spoke up, "Can you also order the drones in closer and have them record what's going on? Send out the images on multiple bands? They might be shot down, but . . . this ought to be seen."

"Witnesses to our last stand, you mean," Jackson said. "What do you think, Killian?"

"Let's risk it. If we have any friends out there, they need to know that we're under attack."

Natira immediately nodded assent, and the others agreed.

"Give me a minute to prepare the transmissions," Chung said. They waited, nervously glancing up from time to time, as if expecting the ceiling to fall in on them. Finally, Chung raised her head.

"Here goes nothing."

There was nothing to indicate when the shield came down or when it went back up again but a nod from Chung confirmed that the task was done. They could breathe again.

Only seconds later, a huge blast rocked them. It was followed by another, and a third. From then on, the barrage was nearly uninterrupted and endless. It was unthinkable that shield and ship could take so much punishment; but still, raging energy bolts rained down.

"I think your bosses heard your threat, Mr. Hind," Frost yelled. "And their solution was to make sure you couldn't get a transmission out."

Hind said nothing. The next shock knocked him to his knees, and he slumped to the floor.

Momoko Quarry was having trouble staying upright in her chair, wincing with each jerk. Natira hurriedly found the control that released emergency straps to support the older woman securely.

Like a battle of gods gone mad, energies of destruction strobed the air and shook the ground with continuous thunder.

Killian realized that Chung was watching a staticky holo-display. It was a view from one of the drones: a view of their ship trapped on the ground. In the scant seconds between flashes of white-hot intensity, he could see that the distortion of the image wasn't only because of the weakness of the signal through the shield. Vast sheets of rising smoke and steam nearly obscured the craft, and would have, if the ship itself hadn't been glowing a radiant blue. In contrast, the surrounding earth looked like the caldera of a volcano, bubbling and frothing bright crimson. The outpouring of energies had melted the very rock around them for a hundred meters or more.

That explained the howling whine he now heard between crashes—the ship must be reaching the limits of its ability to dissipate the heat. Frost asked Habbard to check the readings from the fusion power plant. The man's grim head shake said enough. Not even a shield generated by such colossal power could withstand that much deadly force forever.

Killian locked eyes with Natira. She came to him, and he put an arm around her, both sensing that the end was near.

But an hour later, they were still alive, although the power plant was reaching its limit. Then the shield would fail. The attackers had downed one of the drones, and the view from the remaining drone showed a gigantic column of steam, smoke, and ash rising thousands of meters into the sky. Invisible at its base lay their tortured ship, its own molecules about to join that roiling cloud.

Killian sent his thoughts into the ether. *Please let someone see this and know why we made this stand.*

"Power plant's been critically overheating for five minutes," Habbard called out. "I don't think it'll blow, but it can't be long before it goes into emergency shutdown."

There came the most violent shock yet, as if all four attacking ships had fired at once. No one remained upright, and a crack appeared in the ceiling.

"There it goes!" Habbard yelled to confirm the shield was down.

Killian held Natira tightly and waited for the shot that would blast them into oblivion.

It didn't come.

He heard gasping breaths, sleeves drawn over faces sheened with sweat, the dying howl of the air processing system. But he heard no thunder.

"Look! I don't believe it!" Chung whooped. She pointed at the now-sharp holo-view from the remaining drone, her whole body vibrating with excitement. They could clearly see two spacecraft streak past, with the smoke column in the background. "The other two already left," Chung said. "They stopped the attack! They're gone!"

She began to dance up and down. Others yelled or cried.

Killian looked into Natira's eyes and saw tears that mirrored his own. He kissed her hard, and never wanted to stop.

When they came up for breath, he asked, "Is there any way for us to get out of here? It would be pretty stupid to wait, in case they come back."

"Well, I'm afraid we have no choice for a while," Littlebear mused, "at least until the ground becomes solid again so we can walk on it."

"The ship has sunk halfway into the molten rock." Habbard stared at the readout, awestruck. "It's not going anywhere ever again."

"Lifeboat," mumbled Hind. They'd forgotten he was even there.

"Did he say, 'lifeboat'?"

"Yes! There is one!" Habbard cried. "A shuttle-size craft stored near the upper hull of the ship. If it's survived all that pounding."

And it had. The ship's crew, released from confinement, willingly gave the lifeboat a thorough inspection, knowing that their own lives depended on it. Some circuits were dead at first, but within an hour they'd restored all systems.

Despite its name, the vehicle was more like a personal luxury shuttle than an emergency escape vehicle. There was plenty of room and comfortable seating—even a couple of bunks aft. Like its mothership, it was a new, powerful design, and would carry them a good distance.

There was still the question of where to go. Wherever they flew, they might blunder right into hostile Confederacy forces.

Killian found himself looking to Quarry for a decision, but she shook her head and gave him a smile of encouragement. He nodded and straightened his back.

"Think about it," Killian said. "Those ships didn't just give up, or lose their weapons power at the same time. In fact, they must have seen the shield collapse. They were *ordered* to leave. Someone told them to stand down, and that ought to mean we've got a bit of a breather, at least. So, I say we head for Borealis."

He didn't need to add that he was thinking about his imprisoned uncle Lewis, but his grandfather gave a grateful smile.

Ret Habbard itched to try his hand at flying, but he was outvoted, and the ship's own pilot took them into the air.

50

At Killian's request, the lifeboat approached Borealis from the west, flying over the Confederacy base first. They flew slowly, not only so they wouldn't appear threatening, but also hoping to see some sign of where the security forces might be holding Lewis Partridge. A rescue attempt wasn't realistic, but to negotiate for his release they at least needed to know where he was.

As the base came into view, there were gasps of astonishment.

The site was surrounded by thousands of people—most of the population of Borealis. Killian told the pilot to use the landing pad farthest from the buildings; and as soon as the craft touched down, he hurried toward the ring of bystanders, while the Keepers and Natira stayed inside to keep watch on the Tellurian crew.

He immediately spotted two members of the Elder Council, Ledrin Beech and Alana Driftwood, and turned toward them; but the moment they recognized him there was a flurry of shouts followed by a huge cheer that swept around the vast circle.

"By the Earth Mother's breath, you're alive!" Driftwood shouted and threw her arms around him. Stunned, he couldn't think of a response. Beech clasped his forearm in greeting and shook it, then Killian was swarmed as dozens of others tried to get close enough to see him, touch him, talk to him. It was overwhelming, but not alarming because almost every face was familiar, and he was overcome with a feeling of belonging such as he'd never known.

"You saw us under attack?" he managed to choke out.

"On the Depot screen," Driftwood replied. "We couldn't believe it. That Confederacy ship a ball of blue fire, and somehow we knew you must be in it. Why else would they attack one of their own?"

"That was how you sent that message, wasn't it? From the ship?" Beech asked, and when Killian nodded, he said, "We all saw that, and we were sad, and angry too; but nobody could think of what to do about those things you said. Then when they attacked you, we knew it must all be true, and then people got *real* angry. Wasn't no way we could see to help you except to come here and tell them to stop."

"You told them to stop?" Killian couldn't help but smile at the mental image.

"People been waving their fists and yelling for hours now. Never seen Borealis people so upset. Us elders had a hard time stopping some of the young ones from trying to set fire to the place—we figured that would just give the Confederacy an excuse to use soldiers against all of us."

"You did the right thing. I don't want there to be violence. We have to have justice and honor on our side, to show Confederacy citizens what a disgrace their leaders have become."

He could barely get breath to say the words, buffeted by all the body contact. A few of the men tried to lift him onto their shoulders; but when he protested, they set him back down.

"Why did you come to the base?" Driftwood asked.

"We thought my uncle Lewis was probably being held here. Does anyone know?"

"In that big black building with the bulges on it," a voice said. Killian turned to see Barton Creek. The youth smiled. "I been watching the base most days this week. Seen them put Lewis in there and bring him out for some sunshine once a day. I think the bulges are either for spying or for shooting."

"I'll be careful." Killian tried to think of words to thank them all, but could only nod and wave, which produced another cheer. Then he turned and walked a little unsteadily back toward the lifeboat where Jackson was helping to support Momoko Quarry along with Natira, Ud Littlebear, and Leeyum Frost. Frost wore an arm gun, but when Killian pointed at it and shook his head, the man reluctantly removed the weapon and took it back inside the craft.

"Do you think you brought enough backup?" Natira asked, grinning.

Killian looked behind and found that the crowd was following him in a column, with more joining all the time. Their faces looked concerned, but eager. He couldn't help but laugh and squeeze Natira's hand.

As they turned toward the black building, they were surprised to see the heavy door slide open and three men walk out. The first and last were in the uniform of Confederacy security forces, but the man in the middle was a rumpled-looking Lewis Partridge.

Killian and Jackson quickened their pace and pulled the man into a crushing embrace. There was no reaction from the Tellurians. Finally, Killian turned toward the one on the left, who had more decorations on his shoulders.

"I've been ordered to release Lewis Partridge from custody without charge or penalty," the man said. "May I ask who is the leader of this . . . gathering?"

The officer's eyes turned questioningly to Quarry but fingers pointed to Killian. "He is," said Jackson Ash.

Killian had no time to deny it before the officer said, "May I assume that I'm speaking to Citizen Killian Morningcloud then?"

"The citizen part is questionable, but I'm Killian."

"The Prime Councilor has asked me to express his regret at the unfortunate misunderstanding that . . . caused some risk to your life. The situation has been rectified, and he assures you that you're no longer in any danger from Confederacy forces."

400

"Patriarch Celestia expects us to take his word for that?" Natira snapped.

The man turned to her with a strange expression and a nod of recognition.

"Citizen Celestia."

"Call me *Citizen Tellurian* now, please."

Killian's head snapped toward her in surprise, but Natira's face showed only grim resolve. The officer's words seemed to prove that her Patriarch had never announced her ejection from the First Family, yet now she was apparently renouncing that status herself.

"No, uh . . . Citizen. I'm referring to the new Prime Councilor, Garret Helios. Your Patriarch was . . . asked to step down . . . and apparently will face some charges of misconduct and breach of trust."

A clamor of voices from the surrounding crowd suddenly filled the air with questions, but the officer only held up his hand for quiet.

"It's not my place to explain or interpret the actions of the Confederacy government," he said. "I have merely been instructed to set Citizen Partridge free, extend our apologies to him and to you, and to ask that this large following of yours recognize that there is no further need for them to remain. As I understand it, our government is undergoing some transition and will be more than pleased to resume friendly relations with the leaders and people of Earth in the coming days."

"Very well said, Colonel." Natira gave him a nod. "One more thing, though. We have a lifeboat of yours, some crew members, and your ambassador. Which of them do you want back?"

The officer colored slightly, cleared his throat, and said, "We'd request that you release the crew to enter the base and resume their duties. I've been told to place the craft and its pilot at your service until such time as the new government asks for it back, or other arrangements are made. The ambassador . . ." His expression showed even more discomfort. "Well, we understand that Earth may wish to deal with Ambassador Hind through your own system of justice, and the government of the Confederacy will not stand in your way."

Killian turned toward Quarry who was still clearly in pain. "You should have your leg looked at, Elder Quarry. These people can obviously provide the best medical treatment."

She shook her head. "It's nothing life-threatening. And I would rather be among my people, please."

Her mouth fell open in surprise as another cheer erupted from the crowd.

With that, the colonel gave a small bow and turned back toward the black building. His subordinate beckoned to the relieved spacecraft crew.

An astonished Basu Hind slumped in the entrance of the lifeboat.

# # #

As the group turned back toward the shuttle, Killian was stunned to see Natira put her arms around Lewis and give him a firm hug. He and his uncle shared a look of surprise, the older man seeming to sense what a rare gift he'd been given. It brought a lump to Killian's throat.

Back aboard the shuttle, Killian went to the pilot and said, "I'm sorry that you're still stuck with us. This time it's not my doing."

"Not a problem, sir," the man replied. After a moment's hesitation, he extended his hand for Killian to shake. "My name is Lared Corona. A very junior member of that family," he said with a shy smile for Natira's benefit. "And I suppose we were on opposite sides for a time, but I don't feel that way now. After what we all went through . . . well I have to admit that I was impressed with your courage and tenacity—even if you nearly got me killed too!"

The others joined him in a laugh that broke the tension.

"Anyway, I'm glad to be of service," Corona continued in a lower voice. "And I have to admit that I've become a greater admirer of Citizen Natira Celestia than I am of Ambassador Hind. But one favor, please. I don't know what you plan to do now, and I'd rather not know, in case it puts me in an awkward position. So, if you don't mind, I'll use a sound suppression field around my pilot's chair. If you need to get my attention, just step into my peripheral vision."

Killian readily agreed and asked the man to take them to the open plaza near Borealis's Depot. He would rather have walked—he desperately needed to work off his nervous energy—but a Confederacy craft overflying the Allocation with Earth people in charge of it would be a potent symbol.

He was also eager to see his mother, and Lewis was in a hurry to be reunited with Regina, who was staying with Summer.

As the craft settled into a gentle landing, Momoko Quarry offered to have them stay in a large empty building near her hut.

Killian promised to return quickly after seeing his mother. But first, he made his way to Hind, sitting dejectedly at the back of the passenger cabin, and exchanged quiet words. The former ambassador gave a rueful frown then a sharp nod of agreement.

As Killian left with Lewis and Jackson, Natira surprised him by catching up and taking his arm. "Summer's the closest thing I have to a mother, you know," she said, and her words filled him with a strange sense of elation.

As they walked, Lewis impulsively put his arm around Killian's shoulder and gave him a fierce squeeze.

"You've become quite a man, my nephew. A survivor. Most of all, you came face to face with shattered dreams and came out stronger. I'm proud of you."

"Is that just another way of saying I was wrong to want to go out into space?"

"No, not wrong." His uncle held out a hand. "People have always looked at the bright lights in the sky and felt them calling to us. Humankind is *made* of stardust. Who can say that it's wrong to heed the call of like to like? Both views are equally valid: to follow the path of the stars and planets, or to remain in the bosom of Mother Earth and look after her children. What is *wrong* is to feel that we are masters of either the stars or the Earth. We are humble creatures of no more worth than a fox or a rabbit, but we're given an ability to help both, and an obligation to do so instead of only helping ourselves. For too long, human beings did nothing but take, and ignored the wiser course.

"When the Earth smiles, we all draw sweeter breath." He gave a smile of his own, though it was touched with melancholy as if harm done in the past would always be a thorn in his heart.

"You were right. The people of the Confederacy are no better people than we are," Killian said. "No more fit to be caretakers of the Earth or seekers of the stars."

"It would be astonishing if they were. You were brainwashed by their schooling—you are not to blame for that. Our people were badly wronged, but it was not the first time that people have suffered at the hands of brothers, and it will not be the last. Of all the things that science teaches us, the lesson we find hardest to learn is that no human being is of greater value than any other. And no less. You are beginning to see the qualities of your own people, I think—but in doing so, don't think that diminishes the worth of people in the colonies. They make mistakes, as is the lot of us all. Their mistakes are large because they seek large things."

He smiled at Natira, still holding on to Killian's arm and listening to every word.

"Our lovely friend here believes that our people have a special connection to the Earth."

"We don't."

"No, we don't. All of humankind is made of the same atoms—the dust of creation. We're all the same fragile cage of bones and muscles, needs and desires. What makes us different is how we choose to make use of what we are."

Killian looked downcast. "I've had to learn that our people are not any worse or better than the colonists. That I'm not anyone special either. But I still feel the pull of the stars. I still don't know if I can stay here for the rest of my life."

"That's honest. All I ask is that you be certain that it is your own calling, and not someone else's melody stitched onto the song of your life. Take the time to be sure of your heart." He gave a small shrug and looked again toward Natira. "Then follow it."

When they arrived at Summer's home, tears flowed. The women had been certain that Killian was dead and Jackson likely so. Regina's every moment since Lewis's arrest had been filled with fear. Since it was impossible to hear every detail of everyone's story, the rapid summaries riddled with interruptions left them laughing with confusion. More important than words were hugs, clutched hands, gentle caresses. Killian's eyes filled when he caught sight of Natira sitting blissfully between Summer and Regina with both women's arms around her.

After they'd all listened to most of the important events, Killian knelt in front of Summer and took her hands in his. They were still frail, but he thought they had more strength thanks to the Tellurian medicine.

"We should have started with the best news of all," he said, looking into her warm eyes. "On Basu Hind's ship there is a full medical treatment unit, better than some cities of the colonies. I spoke to him just before I left the ship, and he told me." He took a deep breath. "He also told me it can cure you. Completely."

Summer gasped and her hands flew to her face. A hesitant smile rose to her lips, but with it came tears.

"Do you mean the ship that was destroyed?"

"It was damaged, but not destroyed, otherwise we wouldn't be here."

"Oh, but the Confederacy will be sure to come for it."

Jackson laughed. "No. That's one ship that won't be going anywhere."

Killian pictured the burned and scarred wreck as they'd last seen it, half-buried in solidifying rock. It would never move again, but they could get into it through hatches in the upper hull. Even if the fusion plant was beyond repair, emergency batteries would be enough for Summer's treatment. Hind had confirmed to him that although the Confederacy would certainly want whatever equipment could be salvaged, they wouldn't be in any hurry. The ship was too much of an embarrassment.

Lewis stayed behind at Summer's when Killian decided it was time to leave. The excitement had left his mother exhausted; and as he kissed her goodnight, he promised to take her the next day for her cure. Her eyes overflowed again, and Natira had to brush wetness from her own cheeks too.

Though the pathways of Borealis were empty again, Killian could sense the energy of life from each of the huts they passed.

Jackson put a hand on Killian's shoulder. "This really is the beginning of a new age," he said. "And you're the right man to lead the changes."

"I don't want to be a leader, Grandfather. I never have."

"That's what makes you perfect for the job." Jackson laughed. "You'll hate every minute, so you'll do everything efficiently without wasting time. Best kind of leader." At Killian's scowl he added, "Just wait. See what the people have to say."

Killian kicked a clump of dirt. "I can't even begin to think that far ahead until I know how things really stand with the Confederacy. What happened to make them turn against the Prime Councilor, or even stop shooting at us? I need to know that."

"Don't worry," Natira said with a smile. "I know just the people who can tell us."

"Titan threatened to use its giant mass-drivers to lob boulders at Telluria Prime."

"They *didn't!*"

"Of course, the threat was nearly meaningless because it would have taken the projectiles years to reach their target, but I'm sure a few people in Capita soiled their leggings."

Roja Manno had a laugh loud enough that it almost seemed able to reach Earth, even without the vid transmission. When Natira had been put through to her boss's office, she half expected an angry reprimand for putting herself in danger and threatening the CCC's relationship with the government; but Manno seemed to find endless amusement in the series of events he described.

Thanks to Manno's willingness to turn a blind eye, Serena Kelvin had been able to access Natira's transmissions from Earth and relay them through the SolSys network to the outer colonies. Manno had even vidcast a lot of the footage over the CCC network, claiming that it was legitimate news coverage from a CCC presenter. That move could have ended his career, but he sensed that, especially with the revelations about the secret conspiracy, the Benjamin Celestia regime would topple before it could fire him.

He was right.

"But if everyone knew the mass-driver threat was hollow, why did Confederacy security call off the attack on us?"

SCOTT OVERTON

"Somebody realized that, while boulders would take a long time to get from Titan to Telluria, there was a huge Titan Colony ore transport on final approach to Telluria Quinta that would only have to change course a little, roll its cargo containers and fling millions of small rocks toward the Tellurian radiation shield."

Natira gasped at the image of the enormous bubble of water around her five home-colonies suddenly punctured like a sieve. Chaos would reign, and the potential damage was unimaginable. Manno chuckled that a brand-new law had just been quietly enacted so that all future ore shipments would be routed into orbit around the Moon, instead.

She had been right in her assessment of the outer colonies' devotion to Earth. Outraged to learn of a conspiracy to undermine their hopes for greater autonomy, they were livid about plans to plunder Earth a second time for the sake of Tellurian comfort. Serena had made sure that they saw plenty of images not only of the helpless spacecraft being attacked by four armed cruisers, but also of the angry mobs all over the Earth protesting future enslavement and attempts to murder those who'd exposed the plan.

As hoped, most of Earth's population had seen Natira's transmission, and since the Depots and learning centers had forced all the planet's inhabitants to at least learn the basics of the NorthAm language, her message was heard and understood.

Most of the protests on Earth had not been violent, but some Depots had come under attack. That people would be willing to destroy their chief source of food and goods to show their rejection of the Confederacy's intentions sent a strong message.

Unable to do much on Earth with only a limited armed presence there, the infuriated Prime Councilor Celestia himself ordered Confederacy security to use military force to suppress the uprisings in the outer colonies.

"What he didn't count on," Manno observed, "was that most of the troops in the outer system had been stationed there for so long that they had made lives for themselves.

408

They weren't about to attack friends and neighbors at the whim of a Prime Councilor who looked to be attempting murder and slavery. Squadron after squadron of security warships refused to acknowledge the order, pretending to have reception difficulties. General Callaghan, head of Confederacy security, was called back from leave, but when he learned about the order and the unwarranted attack on a helpless spacecraft by his own forces, he nearly burst a blood vessel. Word is, he ordered all security resources under his command in the vicinity of Telluria to mobilize immediately for an 'exercise' with a scenario involving 'the takeover of the Confederacy government by hostile aggressors.'" Manno shook his head at the memory. "The other ruling families quickly claimed that Celestia's actions were not authorized by Council and demanded his resignation."

"It wasn't just Earth people and the outer colonists who were enraged," Serena added. "I've never seen Tellurian citizens get so upset over anything. To think that their own government, who'd made such a huge public relations event out of the return to our home planet, planned to pervert it into a repeat of the atrocities our ancestors had carried out . . . well you know that the history of the Divide is like a cancer our people try to forget, but can't. A second betrayal of Earth was too appalling to contemplate. There were actual mobs around Capita Palace—Heroes Square was packed solid—and other protestors blocked the gates of the Celestia estate."

Natira couldn't even imagine such things. Her home had always seemed the very image of boring complacency. To get such a population to gather in protest was unthinkable.

"I have to admit that we played up the fact that you were aboard that ship, risking your life for your investigative duty to reveal the contents of that archive," Manno said. "And we may have neglected to mention that you'd helped a prisoner escape."

It was Natira's turn to laugh. "Thank you for that. Thank you both for . . . so much. For saving our lives. If the attack had lasted one more minute, we would have been vaporized."

Manno turned serious. "We did it for you, yes, and for Earth. But we also did it for ourselves. We don't want to think that the Confederacy we love is capable of such things. It had to be stopped. And, Cosmos willing, it *has* been stopped."

As Killian expressed his own heartfelt thanks, Natira felt glad to have him see Tellurians of such courage and integrity, after his experiences at the hands of others.

"There's one more thing you might appreciate," Manno added. "There was another huge outcry when citizens found out they'd been duped about the real purpose for Telluria Quinta's supposed refitting as a starship. So, inspired by venomous protests from the Society for Human Expansion, the Helios administration has vowed that it really will turn Quinta into the interstellar ship it was supposed to be. Apparently, it's not too late."

Natira saw a spark in Killian's eyes and wondered what would come of it.

"You look after our superstar correspondent," Manno told Killian, "and try really hard to keep her out of trouble for a while." With his well-known laugh, he added, "And the best of luck with that!"

Killian promised that he would. Natira put her arm around him, kissed his cheek, then broke the vid connection, feeling guilty pleasure at Manno and Kelvin's scandalized faces.

"You shocked them on purpose," Killian said.

"Uh huh. And now they'll imagine all kinds of things while trying not to believe them of me. There *are* Tellurians who take physical pleasure from each other, but they're considered deviants. One of the most vile of Tellurian expressions is a two-word name that means 'someone who has sex with a carcass'."

"That doesn't bother you now?"

"It bothers me that all the people I've ever known are so misguided that they miss out on the amazing pleasure of touch. I did too, and might have for my whole life if it hadn't been for you." She hugged him so hard it took his breath away.

410

"Glad to help. Maybe this calls for a refresher lesson." He laughed and pulled her toward the curtained off bedroom section of the building that afforded them some privacy.

Later, as they lay spent and naked, Killian ran a finger along her body in admiration.

"You see why we call the Earth a mother? She has magnificent mountains with pointed peaks. And smooth, flat plains. And deep valleys with canyons in them, and sometimes even caves...."

She slapped his hand.

"You call the Earth your mother because she gave birth to you."

"It's a horribly messy business, giving birth." He gave a mock shudder. "I've seen it. Lots of blood and lots of pain."

She could tell from his face that despite his light tone, he felt reverence for natural birth. But was he trying to tell her that he didn't want children? Or simply giving her lots of warning so that she could make a thoroughly informed decision, if it ever came to that?

"I have to wonder if our Mother Earth is tired of her birth pangs and despairing that her children will ever grow up." Killian looked at her for a response and they both laughed.

52

No one in Borealis had ever seen inside the Depot, except for a small alcove to receive food or goods. The interior was vast, mostly taken up by enormous pipes, tanks, and blocks of dull grey; but to everyone's surprise, there was a large room that contained almost nothing, set aside for the use of the Confederacy when they would return. It was also uniformly grey until its communication system was activated. The technician assigned to help the Borealans looked a little embarrassed as he showed them what the room could do.

Within a half-hour, an astonished Killian was looking at holographic images of council elders from all around the world. He and his Keeper friends had sent notifications from the shuttle at Borealis to the other Allocations to schedule introductory contacts, and to urge each community to have both elders and Keepers present. Including Keepers turned out to be easy because they had become part of almost every council. Alana Driftwood and Roscoe Lamp attended for Borealis. To keep things manageable, Killian and his group spoke to only twenty other Allocations at a time.

The process took three days.

At times rewarding, puzzling, frustrating, invigorating, galling, and yet productive, the meetings made Killian's head spin. The range of experiences, attitudes, and cultural differences that he encountered was mind boggling; and the only opinion that came through consistently was that Killian should be interim leader of an effort to organize some kind of collective governing structure. His initial amusement at the idea turned to irritation, resentment, and finally resignation.

After the last discussion came to an end, his grandfather gave him a hard slap on the back.

"What did I tell you? You're the natural choice."

"Only because they've all seen the video and have a ridiculous notion that I'm some kind of hero statesman." He snorted in disgust.

During the five days of Summer's course of treatment in Hind's immobile ship, he'd used the ship's computer archives to research forms of governance and skills related to each. The difficult task was made more irksome by the fact that because he couldn't read it himself: he had to have the computer read every entry aloud—and it felt like he had to ask the meaning of every third word. This mind-numbing exercise in arcane terminology, absurd compromises, and startling acts of faith, hadn't left him feeling any more prepared to wade into the deep waters of trans-global cooperation. If anything, coming face to face with how little he really knew was humbling in the extreme.

Worse, he'd had to use almost none of that new knowledge in this first round of holographic encounters with men and women from the far reaches of the Earth.

Natira gave him an encouraging squeeze and massaged his knotted neck.

"What did you expect?" asked Ud Littlebear.

"To be honest, I expected resistance to the whole idea of any worldwide cooperation. Like the old days I've been reading about, with everyone fiercely looking out for their own local interests. They used to call themselves nations, and each thought it was better than the rest."

"But, you see," said Littlebear, "the colonists crushed all sense of nationality when they decimated Earth's population and then forced us to live in Allocations that almost never have contact with any other. Even settlements in the same area of Earth don't feel any kinship or even shared regional interests. Every Allocation is virtually identical to every other. Everywhere."

"And all of them understand that with the colonists nearly succeeding in making slaves out of us, we have to unite in some way to stand up for ourselves," Jackson said. "We've got to shake off our dependence on the Depots and do things on our own for a change!"

"Naturally they all think you're the best choice for the job, Killian," Natira said gently. "You've already shown that you'll stand up to the Confederacy at the risk of your life."

Her hand was on his arm, and he grasped it. "I'd need you with me."

She shook her head. "That would send the wrong message—it might seem to some that you're taking orders through me."

He felt a weight on his chest. Was she trying to tell him that she'd be leaving?

Before he could ask, they arrived back at their quarters to find the entire Borealis Council of Elders waiting for them.

"Well, did they crown you Emperor of Earth?" Momoko Quarry asked with a look of cynicism Killian had never seen on her face before. He struggled to think of a reply.

Alana Driftwood beat him to it. "As a matter of fact, each and every Allocation wanted Killian to lead while we figure out a more permanent selection process. We're still trying to talk him into it. He doesn't want the job!"

Despite her betrayal, it hurt him to see Quarry's eyes still full of doubt. What had he done to deserve that? He thought he'd been more than fair in urging the council not to punish her for her secret dealings with the Confederacy, or even to dismiss her from their ranks. If she now saw him as her enemy, maybe he *should* use his new influence to make an example of her and remove her as a threat.

No. He would not sit in judgment or use power for revenge. He would carry through with his original impulse.

He stood straight and tall before them.

"All right. I'll take the position of *interim* leader, on the condition that Momoko Quarry will be my second-in-command, and if the people wish it, my successor."

There was a collective gasp and Quarry's eyes widened.

"You have great wisdom and a natural ability to bring people together," he told her quietly. "I don't know if it's even possible to get an entire planet to agree on how to govern itself, but if I'm to lead the attempt, then I want every important decision to be made by consensus. And that means I'm going to have to know when to tell people what they want to hear and when to keep my mouth shut—I'm not very good at those things." His audience laughed. "So, I'm going to need the best help I can get. That includes you."

He stepped toward her and took her hands. She gave a moment's resistance, then looked into his face and her eyes filled.

"I accept."

As the others nodded and smiled, he gave her a hug and turned to face them together. He was pleased to see approval in his grandfather's eyes.

#   #   #

Video link technology was an incredible tool for Killian and his team, but they knew that the kind of discussions needed would require face-to-face meetings. A firm foundation of trust, cooperation, and optimism would be absolutely critical from the very start, and that couldn't be built at a distance.

There was no transportation available to bring delegates together from so many places for in-person meetings. The new government of the Confederacy generously offered to ferry one hundred delegates from all over the planet to a chosen site. After lengthy discussion, it was agreed that those who would attend in person would be selected by random draw, and others could participate through video link, using NorthAM as their common language.

The inaugural meeting was held beneath a monolithic red-rock formation known as Uluru in the Australian continent on the far side of the world from Borealis. The people of that continent considered the site of great significance in the relationship between the Earth and her children. A huge temporary village of strong tents had been erected at the foot of the solitary mountain, grey-green lumps dotting the rusted landscape.

Still using the borrowed shuttle, Killian, Momoko, Natira, and Jackson were able to make the trip in a little more than an hour. Their arc up to the edge of space and back down gave Killian a brilliant inspiration. Before any discussions were held, he arranged for all one hundred delegates to be carried aboard their shuttles into an orbit high enough to see their cherished world as a precious jewel amid a sea of darkness.

If that view didn't put them in the right frame of mind to act as one in the interest of all, he didn't know what could.

The official meetings quickly confirmed Killian's position as interim leader, and they gradually fleshed out a structure of working groups, each assigned to explore the various services and their delivery that global government demands. It was grueling work. Killian's head reeled, his attention pulled in too many directions; and he had little appetite for food, which was just as well since he had little time to eat. He managed to be nearly everywhere, encouraging, guiding, and conciliating. He found Quarry's advice and assistance indispensable.

Though Natira stayed nearly invisible, her emotional support at the end of each day kept Killian sane. They made time each night for a walk and a view of the night sky. The Moon was waxing; and now that he knew where to look, he could see the spattering of dewdrops that was Tellurian habitats, including Telluria Quinta being prepared for its epic voyage to the stars.

Doomed to many more Earthbound meetings still to come, he became more exhausted, mentally and physically, than he could have imagined. What kept him going was the belief that the delegates were making progress, although painfully slowly, and in ways sometimes hard to see.

416

By the end of the week, a framework had been created to carry out elections for representatives to a new fifty-member United Earth Council scheduled to meet in six months. Committees had drafted documents describing the basic tenets of how the new government would work, to be shared with the people of every Allocation for their input. The first meeting of the newly elected council would begin to refine and expand these founding documents (by which time Killian vowed that he would have learned to read words longer than two syllables!)

On the final day, the Interim Prime Councilor of the Confederacy of Colonies, Garret Helios, had been invited to address the gathering, and a giant hologram of his head and upper torso floated against the stars in the clear night sky over the delegates' massed tents.

His words were impressive, declaring that the recent plans and illegal actions against Earth had been carried out by a misguided few, including his predecessor, but they in no way represented the attitude of Confederacy citizens toward their birth planet and its people. The perpetrators were being punished.

He went on to say that the crisis was unquestionably over. Earth would *not* be plundered, its citizens would *not* be subjugated, and that order had been restored within the Confederacy itself, pointing the way to a more prosperous future than ever.

With a holographic smile fully twenty meters wide, he assured them that the new government on Telluria Prime was fully committed to welcoming the Earth into the interplanetary fold and treating it as a full and equal member of the Confederacy of Colonies.

The applause he waited for was polite without being enthusiastic. It grew louder as a spotlight revealed Killian mounting the main podium, and his image joined that of Helios in the sky.

"Your Excellency, Prime Councilor Helios," his voice boomed, "it is with great pleasure that we hear your assurances that the Confederacy has no plans to impress its

417

values or its desires upon the Earth. Your invitation to join the Confederacy is a generous one

..." he paused, "and we hope you will accept our choice in the spirit of friendship when we *decline* your offer."

The crowd roared its approval.

"The Earth has a long road ahead of it as her people rediscover themselves and learn again to stand on our own feet. *But that is something we must learn*, and we cannot do so under the government of others, no matter how benign. Please let us assure you of our sincere intention to enter into friendly relationships with all human settlements throughout our solar system, and of our hope that a partnership can be formed with the Confederacy that will benefit us all.

"So say the voices of a *United Earth!*"

Pandemonium followed his words, the vocal thunder much too loud for any response from the Prime Councilor to be heard. The floating head gave a stiff nod, a forced smile, and vanished. In its place came a fountain of shooting sparks and loud explosions that someone told Killian were just fireworks, and he gazed at them in astonishment, his spirits as high as the highest flare.

"You talk a good game." Jackson appeared at his shoulder and laughed.

"Sometimes these days I don't recognize myself."

"You do what needs to be done. Don't worry, the behind-the-scenes talk will be a lot tougher, without all the bombast."

He was right, but with the help of Quarry and some gifted negotiators from other Allocations, Earth's leaders were able to claim reparations from the Confederacy. Nothing could make up for the horrors that were part of the Exodus, but the deliberate campaign to keep the people of Earth disenfranchised through the Confederacy's clandestine presence afterward was a different matter. Killian and his people insisted on a satellite communication system of their own to link the planet's Allocations. They also negotiated a commitment for a fleet of twenty-two short-range shuttles and six longer-range spacecraft for use by the United Earth government, as well as pilot and maintenance training for their terrestrial support crews.

And, because the leaders were determined from the beginning to hold the Confederacy to the most minimal of footprints on their planet, they demanded upgraded Depots, run by Earth crews, capable of producing a greater variety of foods and goods that reflected the technological gains of the past half-millennium. Though Depots seemed contrary to their goal of greater self-sufficiency, Killian insisted that independence wasn't about having to forage for food. It was about being able to find a purpose in life, and having the freedom to pursue it.

There was a new world to build, with plenty of challenges for everyone. Even the ancients had understood that a full stomach freed the mind for higher thoughts.

The most contentious point was Earth's demand to be able to communicate independently with all of the Confederacy's colonies, bypassing the Tellurian government in Capita. That concession was only reached after one-on-one private discussions with the Interim Prime Councilor in which Killian pointed out that the most militant period in the development of the secret Earth bases had come when the Helios family had held the reins of government.

Though Natira's archive had been made public, the volume of information was so large and the task of sifting through the dirty laundry so distasteful to most Tellurians, that there were still plenty of undiscovered nuggets of truth to provide valuable bargaining chips.

As Killian's reading skills improved, the archive was one of his favorite sources on which to practice.

53

It was one to thing to be told that the season called autumn changed the leaves of the temperate-zone forests, but another to actually witness its gleaming golds, its oranges like storm-warning sunrises, and its reds brighter than flame. Set against a crisp blue sky unique to the season, it was breathtaking; and Natira used whatever time she could spare to get outdoors to gather the fresh breezes into her lungs. She reveled in the strength and health of her body, and the sharpness of mind that seemed to come with it.

It finally occurred to her that she was saying goodbye.

Leading up to the elections, Killian's life was a whirlwind; so she couldn't bring herself to raise such a painful subject in the few precious hours they were able to share. But early one morning, she discovered his bed empty and eventually found him standing at the edge of Borealis looking toward the dawn.

Without turning his head, he said, "You're leaving."

She swallowed and said, "Yes. I have to."

"Have to? Why? You like it here now—I know you do."

"I love . . . so many things about it, but I still have a duty to my work and an obligation to my people. Roja and I agree that the short reports I've being doing aren't enough. Citizens of the Confederacy need to see in-depth how the conspiracy against Earth was born and grew to consume its government. History demands a full and thorough documentation of the evils at the time of the Exodus, so such things can never happen again. Both of our peoples need that, Killian. There's just no one else who can bring what I can to those projects."

"Unquestionably true." He gave a sad smile. "How long have you been working on that speech?"

Her eyes dropped. "I've known what I have to do for a while now. I just haven't been able to tell you."

"I haven't been around for you to tell me, either. Maybe my subconscious was trying to avoid this moment." He gently lifted her chin with his hand. "I love you."

"I know." She moved into his arms; and with cheeks pressed together, they faced the climbing sun. "And I love you. So much. I never imagined it was possible to feel like this."

"But you still have to leave."

"The thought of it hurts so terribly." She put her hand to his face and looked deep into his eyes. Her voice broke. "I'm not saying we'll be apart forever—I couldn't bear that. But to not do what I must do would leave a . . . hole in my being. It's an obligation I can't escape, and part of me hungers for it. You're helping your people, and this is how I need to help mine."

He only nodded and pressed her more tightly against him. He'd become incredibly skilled with words, yet still struggled to express his heart.

"Are you certain you won't run for the Presidency? You are the best choice, and the people's choice too. I'm sure the job would be yours."

"But I still don't want it. To govern a people, you should be able to put yourself in their place—see things as they see them. I've never been good at that. I'm kind of a loner. Ask me to look at a circling hawk and tell you what it's thinking, and I can probably answer that. The troubles and needs of the woman next door? Not so much. I'll lead everyone into the elections but then I'm out."

"What will you do?"

"I was thinking I'd . . . take a tour of Telluria Quinta."

She drew a sharp breath and pulled back.

"You don't mean you're thinking of going *with* them?" The warmth of their embrace was replaced by a paralyzing chill.

"*Thinking* of going on a voyage like that is something I've done since I was a little child. I need to find out what I feel about it as an adult."

Natira struggled to find words. She couldn't. She let her arms fall and stumbled a few steps away, her gorge rising. Maybe his hurt at her decision to leave had given him a need to strike back. If so, his aim was flawless.

She tried to speak but her voice wouldn't obey her. When it finally did, she could barely hear the words herself.

"When you do decide, will you let me be the first to know?"

"I promise."

# # #

Being back in Capita was like one of those disquieting dreams of an utterly familiar place where things are subtly wrong. She wasn't the same person she had been.

At first, the lighter Tellurian gravity not only gave a lift to her Earth-adapted muscles but her mood too. She amused her colleagues by practically leaping up steps, only to find herself just slightly off-balance as she bumped into things and sometimes other people. Their shocked faces curbed her exuberance a little.

It was wonderful to be back among friends and co-workers; but, without exception, they pestered her for every detail of her time with "her Earth man" in a tone of judgment they probably weren't even aware of, but she could not mistake.

Most of her month's hot water allotment was spent within the first week in luxuriously long baths, and she shamelessly indulged herself with every automatic service and feature her home could provide. Yet, when she decided that her wardrobe had fallen seriously behind the fashion during her time away, she didn't enjoy the shopping excursion nearly as much as she'd expected, and bought almost nothing.

The soaring vistas of the Planitia continent and Sagan Archipelago overhead were familiar and comforting, yet she found she missed the softly textured clouds of Earth painted in roseate highlights and mauve shadows, and the swooping birds that frisked on the wind. And she spent far too much time gazing at Earth's glowing blue orb as if her intense focus could somehow magnify her vision and show her the one inhabitant that she missed most.

It wasn't easy to see anything through the clear sections of Telluria Prime's cylinder walls, the *sunspans*. Occasionally at night, though, Natira could see the striped bars of light and shadow that belonged to Telluria Quinta. The sight that had once thrilled her now chilled her instead.

Whenever her feelings became too overpowering, work was her refuge. She spent long days immersed in every detail of her documentary productions, with a ruthless commitment to raw truth. She felt it as a sacred duty, and Roja Manno gave her unprecedented leeway. When her projects were finally vidcast across the entire Confederacy, acclaim was universal and nearly overwhelming. She was suddenly in demand for every special cause, prestige assignment, even political office. Turning down all such offers, she made herself available for a grueling schedule of personal appearances as far as Mars to bring the message of the programs directly to the people, to help them to face feelings of guilt and shame, and to answer every question she could.

She'd already been a celebrity. Now, for a time, she'd become the most famous person in the Confederacy. The treachery and tragedy behind her fame was never far from her mind, and hard to cope with; but she was determined that her campaign of truth would have a profound effect on the society she still loved.

Somehow amid the chaos, she was also able to produce her own personal account, seen through the lens she'd worn on her forehead for all those unforgettable weeks. There was spectacular scenery that made her ache, friendly faces that made her laugh, and heart-stopping footage of the glider escape, the forest fire, and the devastating attack on Hind's ship. Of necessity, though, the dominant presence of the piece was Killian. The force of his personality took control of the whole, and there wasn't anything Natira could do about it. So many times, the sight of his strong features, a playful glint in his eyes, or a twitch of the muscles of his mouth brought her heart into her throat. Very often she got no work done, getting lost in the images and her own memories.

What had been intended as a portrait of, and tribute to, the people of the Earth became a story of the struggle of one man and one woman from different worlds, and ultimately— she couldn't help herself—the revelation of their love for one another.

When it was finally done, she knew it was too personal—it could never be shown to the public. Yet it had to be seen by the man who'd lived it.

Though obviously uncomfortable at the thought of such an account, he promised to view it as soon as he could.

Natira spent the next twenty-four hours idly rearranging everything in her compartment and staring at blank walls.

When he finally called her back, his expression was still inscrutable, though there was a wistfulness in his eyes. She could feel that he wanted to give her an objective appraisal, but in the end, he could only say, "You made me too heroic. Too noble. Like your image of Earth people before you met any. I have a lot more flaws than that, and I made your life miserable."

Was it true? Had she turned him into something of her imagination?

Disappointed, she promised to look at it again, but assured him that he didn't have to worry anyway because it would never be shown. He raised an eyebrow at that and said, "Ask Manno what he thinks." But he wouldn't elaborate and had no more time to spare with elections only a day away.

In a funk, Natira stayed home and watched the program again as objectively as she could. He was wrong. She had portrayed him as he was—no more and no less— she was sure of it.

She agreed to let Roja Manno be the judge.

424

In all the years she'd worked for the man, she'd never seen him shed a tear. Long before the video was over, he was openly wiping his cheeks with the palm of his hand. At the end, he shocked her to her core by pulling her into a crushing hug.

"You have to let me show this!" he cried. "It is such powerful truth. I thought I had some idea of what you went through, but I was so wrong. Everyone must see it!"

She told him Killian's comments.

"Ridiculous! The man is a hero. And a villain, I suppose. But so utterly human. If you want Telluria to truly embrace the people of Earth as brothers and sisters again, you could never do better than this." He nearly tripped in his rush to play the holo again.

Natira's story received a special presentation across the entire CCC network a week later. On the heels of her earlier documentaries, which nearly every citizen had seen, this new account offered direct personification of the reconciliation between Confederacy and Earth they all so desperately hoped for. It was a sensation, and viewers downloaded it millions of times in subsequent weeks.

Natira was mobbed everywhere she went. She'd never before been so grateful for her people's aversion to physical touch—it was all that saved her from serious bruises. And while such adulation was flattering, it had a darker side. Her obvious physical relationship with Killian was scandalous to many, and spurred a seemingly insatiable hunger for more salacious details of their time together.

She lost all semblance of privacy.

Though the CCC was the only official communication and entertainment source that spanned the Confederacy, any citizen with desire and time could use their allocated bandwidth to distribute programming of their own throughout Telluria. Fierce competition for content meant that efforts to gain exclusive information about Natira were relentless.

In desperation, Manno asked the government for access to its top-level anti-surveillance technology and was given it.

Several times every day, Natira's home and the CCC offices were swept clean of nearly invisible drone bots and other eavesdropping devices, but there were always more to find. Manno gave Natira a fluff assignment on the Moon just to provide her a getaway for a while; but even there, unrelenting curiosity followed her.

A junior administrator of a gravity research center was helping her to seal her environment suit for a brief outside tour on the lunar surface when the woman said, "I hear your Earth man is going to be third-in-command of Telluria Quinta when it sets out for the stars. How do you feel about that? Are you planning to go too?"

The suit must have malfunctioned. Natira suddenly couldn't breathe, and they had to take her back to the nearest medical station to be checked over.

The first person to be elected President of the United Communities of Earth was Anru Chan from Viet on the southeast fringe of the Asian continent. Momoko Quarry was elected Vice-President.

Right until the vote, people urged Killian to put his name forward, especially Aylenn from Kaybekwest, who had joined his team early and had been like a bull whenever anyone put obstacles in his path. Killian felt bad about disappointing such fervent supporters, but he would have felt worse if he'd accepted the job when his heart wasn't in it.

The elections were not the end of his official responsibilities. He had agreed to be a presenter at the judgment of Basu Hind.

Others detailed Hind's treachery: his pivotal role in the conspiracy, his coordination of the Confederacy's clandestine military presence, and even his manipulation of Killian, painting a virtuous man as a criminal to provide an excuse to intervene on Earth.

Killian himself was now sure that Hind was one of the two voices he'd overheard in Capita, and assumed that the other was the disgraced First Councilor Benjamin Tempest Celestia. But he kept that information to himself. In fact, when he was asked to speak, he declared that Hind's offences were the result of social prejudices dating back to the Exodus and earlier. That Hind was a creature of his heritage. That the things he'd done had been done for power and gain, yes, but were acceptable to him because of a societal inability to see Earth people as fully human. That was an evil of which many Confederacy citizens were guilty through no fault of their own, and the only way to overcome it was through intensive education.

Hind was a consummate educator and orator. So, Killian proposed sentencing him to service to the community he had wronged: specifically, he would be required to take a lead role in a new effort to create and carry out a program of the very education Earth needed. An ambassador still, though now an ambassador of enlightenment.

Hind sat stunned, eyes wet as he heard the angry voices raised against such a lenient punishment. And when Killian's opinion won the day, Hind gave a sincerely humble nod of acceptance.

His duties accomplished, Killian had promised himself that he would disappear into the bush for at least a week to rest and clear his mind. His solitude only lasted for three days before restlessness won out. Within another forty-eight hours he was on his way to Telluria Quinta.

It was an indicator of his new fame and status that he was able to ask for a place on a Telluria-bound shuttle and receive it without delay. Almost all such shuttles went directly to Telluria Prime, but orbital dynamics had placed Quinta near the shuttle's flight path, and Killian's request gave the shuttle pilot an excuse to indulge his own curiosity with only a small detour.

The approach, the transit through the Halo shield's gargantuan protective water bubble, the views of floating farms, and the eventual docking with Quinta were all very much like Killian's first trip to the space colonies; but his attitude had utterly changed. Instead of feeling a wide-eyed wonder, he experienced a deeper appreciation of the immense scope of the endeavor—the creation of such vast living spaces surrounded by unforgiving vacuum, and the godlike technology that made such habitats nearly self-sufficient. And it was all even more impressive to him now because its creators weren't gods but simply men and women with a vision, and an implacable will.

Each small detail was also one more piece in the puzzle that was Natira. He still only knew her under a very special set of circumstances—he had almost no understanding of her upbringing or the day-to-day life that had made her the person she was. Learning more about the Confederacy made him feel closer to her, yet he hadn't decided if he would visit her on Telluria Prime after his Quinta tour. He still felt hurt by her choice to return there, and the unreasonableness of that feeling shamed him.

As he debarked at Quinta, it was clear that he was expected. Everyone called him Citizen Morningcloud, as if they hadn't heard that Earth had declined to join the Confederacy. He didn't correct them. Their welcome was warm, and his passage through the requisite screening and scanning was swift. Within a half-hour one of the top administrators on the Quinta refit, a woman named Lissa Montgomery, led him toward the north entrance of the giant cylinder's main enclosure. Killian remembered that "north" was always the leading end of a habitat in its path through Tellurian space, and what he thought of as East and West were spinward and anti-spinward here.

With a wide smile Montgomery ushered him through the final doorway into open air.

He gasped.

He'd forgotten how enormous the cylinder worlds were. The door he'd just come through was only a hundred meters above surface level, so as he raised his eyes to look across the entire diameter, he was looking straight up a wall that seemed to have no top, blending into the bluish haze of great distance. It was a wall to reach the far side of the sky. Quinta was like Telluria Prime in that respect—the opposite side of the cylinder was fully visible—but there were some startling differences.

"You've covered the windows," Killian said.

"The sunspans. Yes. Because Quinta will travel through interstellar space without the protection of Telluria's water bubble, cosmic radiation is a critical challenge, as is the possibility of micro-collisions at incredible speeds. We don't know how to make a transparent material that's as strong or as dense as we need. But then, until we get to our destination, there won't be enough sunlight to benefit us anyway. Specially-shielded cameras will show us views of the outside."

"Collisions? I thought space that far out was completely empty."

"Even dust is a danger at the speeds we'll be travelling. But don't worry, an enormously powerful electromagnetic shield well out in front will divert every scrap of matter around the ship. I understand you've had some experience with that kind of shielding." She raised an eyebrow.

"I owe my life to it."

"So you know you'll be perfectly safe with us, too."

Killian was puzzled by her phrasing but decided not to call attention to it.

Though it was an effort to pull his eyes away from the vista above him, the view straight ahead was equally stunning. Instead of the vast cityscape he'd expected, the surface was textured in irregular shapes almost like a cliff face lying on its back, except in subtle shades of white. More surprising, it looked as if the cylinder came to an end only a kilometer away. As he became able to orient the scene in his mind, he realized that he was looking at a colony layout of some kind from above, with depressions that looked like empty lake bottoms, irregular forms like machinery, and more regular shapes that he guessed were housing.

He looked at Montgomery for an explanation.

"A different perspective, isn't it?" She smiled with obvious pride. "Not your natural one, or mine, but a necessary configuration for a ship that will spend the first half of its journey accelerating and the last half slowing down. As you probably know, the thrust at the south end of the cylinder would make everything slide in that direction if we kept Quinta's landscape as it was. So once the engines start, *south* is *down*.

"The biggest problem comes at the halfway point of the journey when we must begin to slow down. Decelerate. And that means that we have to turn the ship around so the thrust of the engines is pointing toward where we're going. The deceleration will still mimic gravity, so south will still *feel* like down for the rest of the journey. It's the turnaround that's the problematic part, and we'll have to use some ingenious solutions to deal with it."

Perhaps Killian's eyes began to glaze over, because she added, "If you're interested, I can have one of our engineering team explain it to you later.

"The point is that, like in a tall building, we had to make dozens of floors, to divide the original cylinder into multiple habitats. And that's perfect because we want to be able to transport flora and fauna representative of the main ecosystems of Earth, from deserts to rainforests to tundra. That's what this northernmost zone will be—an arctic climate just like Earth's own north."

Seeing astonishment in Killian's face, she laughed and launched into great detail about each of the climate and vegetation zones they were trying to replicate and how they would be arranged in a tall stack. He'd been right about the surface's resemblance to a cliff. For this arctic ecology they wanted the cylinder walls to provide the impression of surrounding mountains of ice and snow.

Because they couldn't know precisely what conditions they would face on their new home in the Alpha Centauri system, and also to preserve as many species from Earth as possible, Quinta would be a modern Noah's Ark, Montgomery told him—but then had to explain just who Noah was. The target planet was definitely Earth-like though, if slightly larger and closer to its sun, Alpha Centauri-B. So, there was a good chance that most of the species would be able to adapt somewhere.

While the ship was underway, travel among habitats would use very large and swift elevators along the perimeter walls, although there were contingency measures to permit flying craft to drop through the floor of one level into the sky of the one below in emergencies.

For the next four hours, Killian and Montgomery rode a maglev car through a temporary vacuum tunnel that would eventually become an elevator shaft, racing from zone to zone and occasionally stopping to look around. Many of the other zones were further along in their development than the arctic because their natural temperatures were closer to the mean temperature chosen for construction purposes— about twenty degrees Celsius. The extremes of climate required by deserts and rainforests weren't worth maintaining until the plant and animal species were about to be brought aboard. And it was only in the final weeks before departure that the final touches could be completed, with soil, water, and plant life delivered to their proper places. In order to do so, the mammoth habitat would be launched into an expanding Figure-8 trajectory through the Earth-Moon system under constant, though low, acceleration. That acceleration would provide just enough force to replicate partial gravity in the same manner used during the ship's long voyage.

Killian's mind was staggered at the thought of being able to move such an enormous artefact, and then to recreate a planet within it.

"Irresistible, isn't it?" Montgomery grinned. "It would be worth going on the voyage just to see everything in place and functioning, even if we weren't undertaking humankind's greatest adventure ever!"

As she spoke, the car stopped at yet another habitat and the doors opened.

"This one's still got quite a lot of work left to be done, but when it's finished you ought to feel right at home. It's the boreal forest zone, just like your own community. And though the command center of the ship and related offices are in the north, near where you first entered, you're welcome to live here and commute by elevator to work every day—it will only take twenty minutes or so by the high-speed tube."

"Live here . . . ? Excuse me, but you talk as if you assume I'm coming with you."

It was Montgomery's turn to be nonplussed.

"Do you mean . . . you're not? But I was told . . . I mean, you're not going to be the Earth representative of the Triumvirate?"

"What's the Triumvirate?"

"The ship—well, the entire mission, really—will be commanded by a leadership of three: one representative each from the Confederacy and from Earth, and a Prime Commander who will be the tiebreaker when needed."

"Another Confederacy citizen."

"Well, yes, but required to be utterly neutral in that regard."

Killian didn't comment on that but instead asked, "Who told you that I was going to be the Earth representative?"

"My superiors in government. To be honest, I'm hoping to be chosen as one of the other two leaders, but that decision hasn't been made yet. Do you mean you *weren't* chosen by your people for this mission?"

Killian couldn't help but laugh, to the chagrin of his companion.

"I've just finished fending off endless efforts to make me President of Earth. I'm not equipped to lead a planet. And I'm certainly not capable of sharing command of a ship that's almost a small planet itself. I haven't even decided whether I would want to come along for the ride. That's why I'm here—to try to make up my mind."

He couldn't tell whether Montgomery was relieved or disappointed. Maybe both. Killian felt that he owed her more.

"Listen, I'm very sorry if there's been a misunderstanding," he said. "Your people couldn't be more welcoming, and I truly hope I haven't inconvenienced you too much. I do seem to have a lot of influence on my planet right now, though; so, whether I choose to come or not, you can count on me to be your most effective recruiter down there. This is a monumental mission—the embodiment of human drive to be

SCOTT OVERTON

all that we can be. I've dreamed of such a journey since I was a child, so part of me will fly with you, one way or the other."

"Then come along! I still have a few days to convince you anyway, because even you can't call up a shuttle to Earth before that."

They both laughed and Killian willingly continued the tour.

When Montgomery finally conducted him to a small sleeping compartment, he fell asleep quickly and dreamed he was a wolf loping through an endless world that changed with his every few steps from wet to dry, summer to winter— clinging mud to shifting sand to clutching undergrowth; yet he could never discover where he belonged.

The pace of subsequent days was less hectic, much of it spent in the company of various specialty teams charged with replicating his home planet within this colossal construct. With an enthusiasm as enormous as their project, they bombarded him with endless questions about Earth's original ecologies, and Killian was forced to admit to them that it had only been in the previous half-year that he'd seen any part of Earth beyond his northern woods, and his duties hadn't allowed time for sightseeing. Still, he had a strong sense of how species responded to seasonal variations and climate anomalies, and how they interacted with each other in the predator and prey cycle. Such knowledge was so deeply ingrained that it felt intuitive, and his new companions insisted that his authentic, life-forged expertise was exactly what they desperately needed.

Their assessment gave Killian a strange feeling. For the first time he saw that the knowledge he'd always taken for granted could be of value to others. It wasn't technology, it wasn't engineering, it was neither exotic nor progressive—it's importance could only be measured in the service of Life itself.

The epiphany was an eye-opener; and when he finally boarded his homebound shuttle, he owed his hosts heartfelt gratitude for showing him his life's path.

434

55

The rising sun spilled flame-red across the clouds and painted the inside of Killian's eyelids. Keeping his eyes closed, he let the wind describe his surroundings to him: needle-pointed pines dividing the sky, a distant shower rinsing new leaves of yesterday's dust, a flock of gulls rising from a pothole lake in a squabble over trout fingerlings, a shambling porcupine rooting for grubs under a mildewed log. Eyes, nose, ears—each kept him linked with his world in all its unimaginable variety. And more: he could taste pollen on the air, and lingering smoke from a faraway fire. Through the muscles of his legs came minute vibrations of a family of weasels scurrying over the hillside on which he sat, while newly warmed air from the small gulley just below his perch lifted up-slope to trail through the hairs of his arms.

But senses were only tools of the brain. Could he go beyond them and connect at an even more profound level with the Earth Mother?

He breathed deeply, slowed his heart, and stretched out his mind.

And found that he could.

Bracing air flowed over his wings and riffled his feathers as he rode the currents above a cliff edge, eyes darting downward to focus crisply on a scurrying grey mouse whose glossy fur was lightly raked by stiff blades of grass as it crossed a meadow that washed its back with dewdrops that

SCOTT OVERTON

slid and fell onto a questing earthworm that poked its loam-filmed tip into the new day's light for only a moment, then pushed below the surface again where dew and an earlier rain seeped through rich soil into an underground stream trickling beneath a hundred living things until the water reached a small escarpment and tumbled into a brook that was the home of one young trout finning its way over a pebbled bed while it scented the current to learn if it carried any breakfast, when its eye caught a glint of rising sun refracted by a ripple on the surface and, illuminated by that roseate light, a man sitting on a hillside.

Killian smiled, and felt the sun warm the creases in his face.

Now he sensed another presence behind him, not of this world, climbing the hill with slow strides; a presence more welcome than any other.

"You've come back!" he said, without turning around.

Laughter trilled in the air. "Am I so clumsy that you not only hear me coming but can even tell that it's me?"

Natira was struck by his posture: cross-legged with straight back, his hands resting on his knees. A meditative pose she'd seen others use, but never Killian.

Now he turned. The vision of her illuminated by the dawn was like a second sunrise.

"I sensed your coming with all my being, not just my ears. You're what I most wanted to see and hear. And feel."

The look on his face removed the last of her trepidation, and he'd barely risen to his feet before they were in each other's arms in a bruising kiss.

They settled gently onto the grass, eyes and hands caressing each other.

"Who told you where to find me?"

"Summer. She says you've been spending a lot of time on this hilltop since you came back. She looks fantastic!"

He nodded with a bright smile. "It could be argued that too much Confederacy brainpower is spent on trivial things, but their medical advances are a true miracle. They gave me back my mother." He squeezed her hand in thanks. "I saw your

436

documentaries, or most of them. I couldn't follow everything, but they were an eye opener. How did your people take them?"

"The reaction has been everything I could have hoped for. People are pushing governments to take action to prevent such horrors from ever being repeated. It looks as if the monopoly of power by the five leading families will be eliminated too." She laughed. "Roja keeps saying that the programs have made me the best-known personality in all the colonies. But you're the second most-famous."

"What! Oh, no! Do you know how hard it was for me to escape being pressed into some role in the Earth government? You should have told the truth about me—about what a clumsy, boorish jerk I was. I am."

She shook her head. "They had a pre-conception of an uncouth, primitive man, and it was important that I show them the truth, so I did." She leaned forward and pressed her head to his, suddenly not wanting him to see the emotion in her eyes.

"How was it, being back home in Telluria?"

"A relief. At first, anyway. Having all the conveniences available at my merest whim was wonderful—I bathed until my skin was red." She laughed. "But once that novelty wore off, it was . . . a bit sterile. Cold. I told myself I'd adjust and focused on my work, but then people wouldn't leave me alone. I had no privacy at all."

He took her hands. "So, this is your getaway? For how long?"

Her smile faltered. "That really . . . depends. With the way things are now, Confederacy Central Communications needs good reporting from Earth, including a chief Earth correspondent."

"They do?"

"I told them they do, and who's going to argue with the most famous personality in the Confederacy?" She laughed again. "But if that isn't enough, the new government in Capita has decided that, along with a state ambassador to handle diplomatic duties, they want to have a *good will* ambassador to Earth—someone to travel around presenting the best face of the Confederacy to the people here."

"You? Well, of course. Who could do it better? So you've accepted both jobs?"

She gave a small shake of her head, her mouth puckered. "Not yet." A half-smile flickered on and off her face so quickly he wasn't sure he'd seen it. She put his hands between hers and softly rubbed them. It was strange to realize how much she'd missed the sensation of touching another human being during her time in Telluria.

"What about you? I . . . heard you're going to be one of the three commanders of Telluria Quinta when it leaves for Alpha Centauri."

His eyebrows shot up.

"I still don't know where that rumor ever came from. That's what the Quinta team thought, too, but I'd never said so. It's true that it was a dream of mine from the time I could look up and see the stars. But . . . I've made my decision. I'm staying on Earth."

"You are? But I know they wouldn't have picked you as one of the three commanders if they didn't need you."

"The Tellurians are experts with self-sufficient enclosed environments for humans, but to add whole ecologies from Earth into the mix as they want to do, they desperately need terrestrial expertise in biology, zoology, and ecology . . . and probably a whole lot of 'ologies' I've never heard of. But they don't need me, they need experienced Keepers. Fortunately, there are a lot of those who want to go on the voyage."

"Keepers? But they're committed to the Earth!"

"They're committed to protect and preserve Earth *life*, and many of them believe that the best way to do that is to spread it elsewhere in the galaxy because Earth is too vulnerable to cosmic catastrophe. They also have much more scientific knowledge about plant and animal life than I do."

"That still doesn't mean they have what it takes to be on the command team of a colony ship. And would you just give up your lifelong dream?" Natira held her breath, though she was only saying what he must be thinking himself.

"I wanted to explore the stars, yes, but . . . how many years do most Tellurians live?"

"The average is about one-hundred and fifty."

"I've never known anyone older than a hundred. The ship will take more than eighty years just to reach its destination. If I'm still alive, I'd be a very old man. Too old to explore. Too old for a new planet to ever feel like home. I'd still die leaving far too many questions unanswered."

She hurriedly asked, "What will you do if you stay here?"

He gave a lopsided grin.

"The woman the Keepers consider to be their global leader has decided to go on the ship. So, they need a new one."

"You? But you just turned down the job of president of the whole planet!"

"Totally different. The head of the Keepers is what used to be called a *spiritual leader*, although it doesn't have anything to do with religion. It means leading by setting an example for the rest—being the most dedicated and devoted to the cause. Oh, there are sometimes gatherings and meetings, but all important decisions are made by consensus. It's not political. It's a philosophy—a way of life.

"Now they've come out of hiding and—with luck—can give up worrying quite so much about the Confederacy. So, they need to reinvent themselves—return to their original purpose and find new ways to carry it through. That's why they want fresh blood."

He pulled her closer. "I want to learn everything I can possibly learn about how the things and creatures and forces of our world work together as a whole. I want humanity on Earth to make Earth its first priority. To truly be the people of our Earth Mother. There is a place for technological progress, but the pursuit of a more complete understanding of *living* forces is just as valid. *That's* what I want to dedicate my life to."

He turned his head to take in the spreading greenery before him, a miracle of biochemistry soaking up the radiance of the sun and transforming it into fertility and growth in stunning diversity.

"I . . . don't think I could tell this to anyone else, but in these past weeks I've begun to have a sense of true connection with the life of the planet like nothing I've ever felt before. It really is as if every single living organism is a tiny, but essential, part of a whole. I seem to *feel* the Earth itself breathing, growing, and . . . reaching out." He looked into her face half expecting her to laugh, but the gleam in her eyes prompted him to continue. "If the whole Earth is like one living body, I'm beginning to wonder if the entire galaxy might be too. With a circulatory system, musculature, organs of perception." He chuckled. "It may be that my path will forge a link of communication with Alpha Centauri before the ship gets there."

"I remember reading about an old religion that had beliefs much like that," Natira said. "Their most accomplished practitioners spent a lifetime learning to commune with a universal oneness."

"You don't think it's silly?"

She shook her head. "Not at all. It sounds wonderful. Though I know that the colony ship project will be the weaker for not having you."

"I was able to leave a small mark," he said, with a glint in his eye. "I suggested—and it's been accepted—that the ship be called 'Starwalker'."

"But isn't that . . . ?"

He nodded. "What the lost young people of Earth call their method of killing themselves."

"Won't it seem like they're labelling it a suicide mission?"

"No one beyond Earth knows that definition of the term, only that it sounds dramatic and noble. And I want it to be noble. I want to completely change the meaning of that word to our youth by showing them new hope. New reasons to stay alive. The stifling Allocation life that had them trapped is over—a whole universe is opening up for the taking. I want our young to grasp that fact, and never again think that ending a life is the only way out."

The sharp cry of a gliding eagle drew their eyes skyward. They could see the Moon in the morning sky, and that meant that the cylinder worlds of Telluria and the gigantic *Starwalker* were there too, invisible in the vault of blue.

"So now that you know I won't be rocketing out of your life forever, will you take the positions on Earth?"

Natira nodded with a dazzling smile. "You know I will. But it would have been too painful to stay without you here." She grasped his hands. "As the new leader of the Keepers, won't you have to travel all over?"

He shrugged. "Now that Earth has flying craft of its own, I think I'll manage."

"Or you could travel as the consort of the Confederacy's Good Will Ambassador."

"Consort. Or husband?"

"What a quaint idea." She laughed as tears sprang to her eyes. She wrapped him in an embrace that took his breath away. "If that's a proposal, I accept!"

He squeezed her just as hard, and his own eyes spilled over.

She put her forehead to his. "I don't think you and I can ever be parted now, no matter how far we travel."

Killian turned them to face the sun in all its splendor. Then he took her hand and turned away from the hilltop, recalling the events of the past year distilled into a few salient moments, and understood that his world had been forever changed by them.

Many were saying that a new day had dawned for the Earth, but Killian knew that it was all one long day to the Earth Mother, stretching billions of years into both past and future while She watched, endlessly patient.

Like a body attacked by some of its own cells, her life had hung in the balance.

Now those malignant cells had been rooted out, and healing could truly begin.

THE END

SCOTT OVERTON

Acknowledgments

If you're not a writer yourself, you probably have only a vague idea about the process of creating a book. Coming up with an idea; engineering the plot; fleshing out the characters; and putting the words to the story, are certainly the essentials. But from there follows a whole lot of revising and rewriting. If you're lucky, you have a network of fellow writers and willing readers who will offer their valuable time and opinions to help you spot the gaffs, plug the holes, and push on when your energy is flagging.

For helping me in that way with *Indigent Earth*, I want to especially thank and applaud Dave Wickenden, Matthew Del Papa, Ken Wilson, Lindsay Bayes, and Kae Bagg. But I'm also grateful for all the members of the Sudbury Writers Guild. I remember a time when we were all newbies with dreams, and now I'm so proud of the quality creative work flowing from my friends. It inspires me.

My longtime editor, Robin Carson, helps me turn promising manuscripts into polished gems so that, when we're through, I'm eager to release these creations into the world.

I often sell copies of my books in person and get to meet my readers, and it means so much to me when you tell me how much you've enjoyed one of my books.

I would like to acknowledge funding support from the Ontario Arts Council and the Government of Ontario

And most of all, I thank my wife Terry-Lynne, because without your faith and encouragement I might have given this up long ago, and stories like *Indigent Earth* would never have been told.

AUGMENT NATION

This is your brain on silicon.
Since the age of fourteen Damon Leiter has had a brain-computer interface implanted beneath his skull to correct a neurological disorder. As a teenager, it branded him as an outcast—as an adult it endows him with extraordinary abilities. He may represent the next step in human evolution. When computerized brain augments replace smartphones as the must-have status item, mega-corporations and governments conspire together and marketing becomes mind control. Damon is uniquely equipped to lead a worldwide resistance, but the fight may cost him everything.

"Scott Overton is a terrific writer and his vision of tomorrow is both realistic and frightening. Read this book!"
-- Robert J. Sawyer, Hugo Award-winning author

Buy yours: https://books2read.com/Augment-Nation

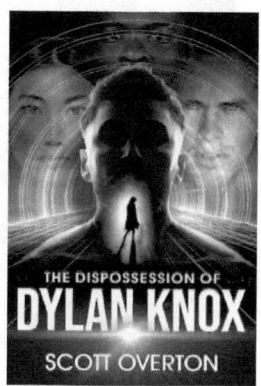

THE DISPOSSESSION OF DYLAN KNOX

Dylan Knox is not the man he was. He may be like no man who ever existed.

How do you *feel* if an old lover doesn't remember you? What do you *say* if they act like a different person each time you meet?

What should you *do* if they might be an impostor? Mentally unstable. A threat to the very security of your country.

Dylan's tale of a bold space mission, and a tragic accident is utter fantasy. Unless it's too crazy *not* to be true.

Brooke Chappelle has two choices: trust, or betrayal. And falling in love is the last thing she needs.

"The futuristic and technological elements combine seamlessly with political issues to create a plot that is timely and thought-provoking...will appeal to any reader who values the enduring human story of love and trust."
Renny deGroot—author of *Torn Asunder*

Buy yours: https://books2read.com/Dispossession

NAÏDA

The glowing structure at the bottom of a lonely northern lake is clearly not of this Earth, but scuba diver Michael Hart can't stay away. What it offers will change him forever, leaving him with astonishing abilities and a destiny he would never have imagined. Except it might be a destiny he no longer controls.

The actions Michael takes will make him a hero, or the greatest traitor the world has ever known.

Because he is no longer alone, not even in his own body.

There is another.

Naïda.

Readers say:

"A deep dive into the best parts of science fiction—thrilling and thought-provoking! *Naïda* is Overton's best book yet. I buy him on sight and never regret the choice."

"I COULD NOT PUT IT DOWN. ... Extraordinary. Enjoy."

Buy your copy: https://books2read.com/Naida

THE PRIMUS LABYRINTH

A woman's bloodstream has been seeded with destruction.

Curran Hunter almost died at the bottom of the ocean. Now an innocent victim will die unless Hunter can purge her body of deadly devices by piloting the *Primus*, a prototype submersible the size of a virus. Its control system uses *Virtual Reality*—its creators assure Hunter there can be no danger.

They are utterly wrong.

"Loved it! I give this book an enthusiastic four stars for its political intrigue, discussion of moral dilemmas, exciting action scenes, and fully fleshed characters..." Charlotte Graham—Reedsy Discovery reviewer

Buy yours: https://books2read.com/PrimusLabyrinth

BEYOND: Stories Beyond Time, Technology, and the Stars

Ride a bright flame of imagination across time and space with fifteen mind-stretching stories beyond time, beyond technology, and even beyond the stars.

A man who can walk through walls.

Agents who repair the mistakes of the past.

An invasion from beneath our feet.

A man who learns his replacement body was previously owned and died mysteriously.

A disastrous experiment to harness the awesome power of a hurricane.

Don't be afraid to go BEYOND.

"Scott Overton is a storyteller of boundless skill...a writer to watch." —Mark Leslie, author of *Haunted Hamilton* and *I, Death*

Buy yours: https://books2read.com/rl/scottovertonSFF

DEAD AIR

It's a hard thing to accept that someone wants you dead. It forces you to decide if you have anything worth living for.

When radio morning man Lee Garrett finds a death threat on his control console, he shrugs it off as a sick prank—until minor harassment turns into undeniable attempts on his life. When the deadliest assault yet claims an innocent victim, Garrett knows he has to force a confrontation.

"A gripping, insightful debut from a veteran radio personality and gifted wordsmith." —Sean Costello, author of *Here After*

Find out how to add these compelling reads to your own collection at www.scottoverton.ca .

Or https://books2read.com/DeadAir

ABOUT THE AUTHOR

A radio broadcaster for more than thirty years, Scott Overton described that world in his first novel, the mystery/thriller *Dead Air*, published by Scrivener Press. *Dead Air* was shortlisted for a Northern Lit Award in Ontario, Canada. But the rest of his writing is science fiction and fantasy, including his 2020 science fiction/thriller *The Primus Labyrinth*, the 2021 SF adventure *Naïda*, 2022's SF/psychological thriller *The Dispossession of Dylan Knox* and the chilling SF cautionary tale *Augment Nation*. His short fiction has been published in numerous magazines and anthologies, many of those stories brought together in his *BEYOND* collections.

Now a freelance author and voice talent, Scott works from his home on a lake in Northern Ontario. His favorite diversions include scuba diving and a vintage sports car.

You can learn more and read free stories at Scott's website www.scottoverton.ca .

A Word to the Reader.

Authors cherish our readers and readers can become devoted to their favorite authors. We always hope so!

If you enjoyed this book please consider leaving an honest *review* wherever you bought it, or with any reading communities you participate in. After buying our books, reviews are the absolute best way you can help us continue doing what we do and bringing you the stories you want to read. Just a few lines will do, and I'd truly appreciate it.

Thanks, and I hope you'll look for my other books too.

SCOTT OVERTON